THE KINGDOM OF ALMONDS

Also by Ariel Kaplan

The Pomegranate Gate
The Republic of Salt

THE KINGDOM OF ALMONDS

ARIEL KAPLAN

SOLARIS

Paperback edition published 2026 by Solaris
an imprint of Rebellion Publishing Ltd,
Riverside House, Osney Mead,
Oxford, OX2 0ES, UK

www.solarisbooks.com

First published 2026 by Solaris

ISBN: 978-1-83786-637-3

Copyright © 2026 Ariel Kaplan

Poems by Solomon ibn Gabirol from *Vulture in a Cage,* translated by Raymond Scheindlin © 2016, used with permission from Archipelago Books.

The right of the author to be identified as the author of this work has been asserted in accordance with the Copyright, Designs and Patents Act 1988.

All rights reserved. No part of this publication may be reproduced, stored in a retrieval system, or transmitted, in any form or by any means, electronic, mechanical, photocopying, recording or otherwise, without the prior permission of the copyright owners.

This book is a work of fiction. Names, characters, places and incidents are products of the author's imagination or are used fictitiously.

10 9 8 7 6 5 4 3 2 1

A CIP catalogue record for this book is available from the British Library.

Designed & typeset by Rebellion Publishing
Cover art by Micaela Alcaino
Map designs by Gemma Sheldrake

Printed in the UK

*For my father,
Jonathan Daniel Kaplan*

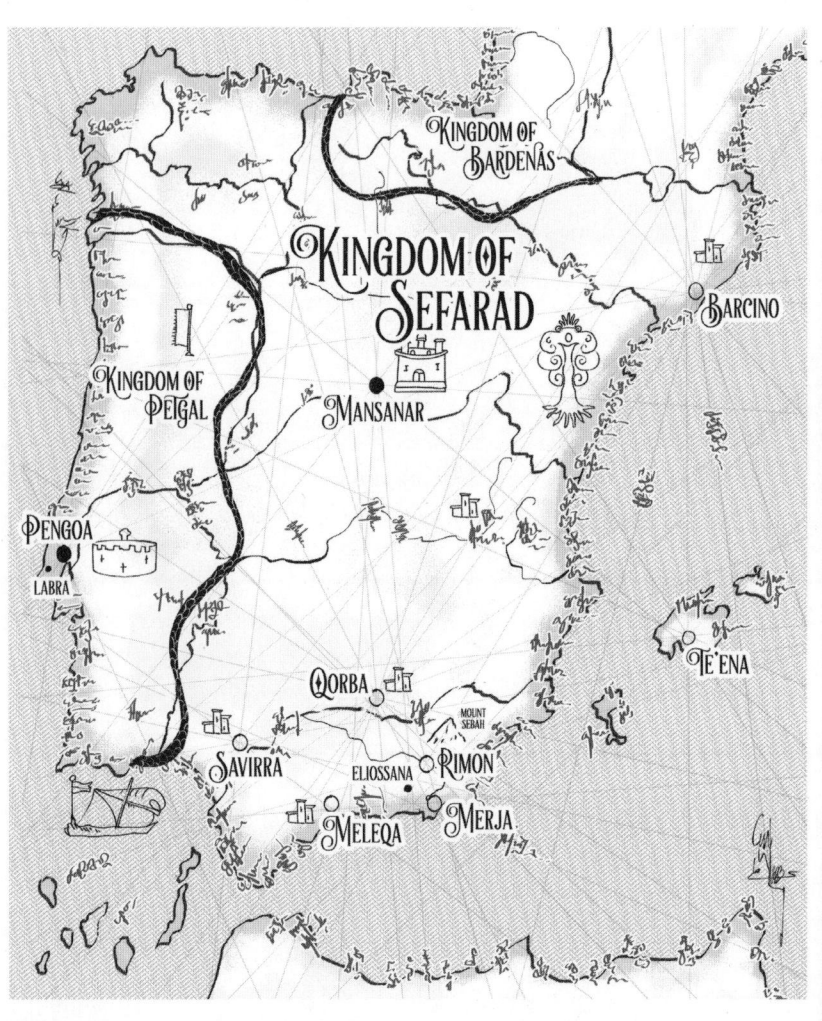

Dramatis Personae

From the Mortal World

Toba Peres: A half-Mazik from Rimon, daughter of Tarses and sister of the Courser. Toba is the buchuk of the original Toba, who was killed by her sister while rescuing Barsilay from La Cacería. Toba's Mazik name is Tsifra N'Dar; literally, the Splendid Bird.

Naftaly Cresques: A young man from Rimon, the latest in a long line of tailors. He has enough Mazik heritage to enter the dream-world, cast illusions, and have visions of the future. For untold generations, his family have been the guardians of the book containing the gate of Luz.

Elena Peres/Elena bat Beladen: The original Toba's grandmother. She speaks several languages and uses her own brand of mortal magic, despite being of very distant Mazik heritage.

Alasar Peres: Toba's grandfather, who relocated to Petgal after the exile. A former translator for the Emir of Rimon.

Penina Peres: Toba's mother, who died in childbirth.

The Old Woman: A former beggar from Rimon. Her real name is unknown. She considers Naftaly her only family, though they have no blood relationship. She suffered damage to her lungs when she inhaled decayed salt in Zayit and only survived thanks to the help of Asmel and Barsilay.

Dawid ben Aron: A half-Mazik from Luz before the Fall. He and the other mortals in Luz were convinced by Tarses to pull out their gate and hide it in a book, after which Dawid was held some fifty years in the prison of P'ri Hadar before escaping with the book and the Ziz. He attempted to take both to his friend Marah in Rimon, but after Tarses's betrayal Dawid left the book with a mortal prostitute with instructions to burn it. Instead, she gave it to the child conceived that night, who became Naftaly's ancestor.

From the Mazik World

Asmel b'Asmoda (known in the Dreamworld as Adon Sof'rim, the Lord of Books): An astronomer and minor Rimoni adon. Formerly Marah's husband and the head of Rimon's university. Asmel was forced to become mortal by pulling his magic into a safira but regained his magic thanks to Toba.

Barsilay b'Droer: The Heir of Luz. A former member of ha-Moh'to, and at one point a medical student. He is also Asmel's nephew, through Asmel's marriage to Marah. He lost his left arm to the Courser in La Cacería's prison.

Nehama: A half-Mazik astronomer from Luz, lost in Aravoth since the Second Age after leading an expedition there. Omer of Te'ena was her mentor.

Marah Ystehar: Former envoy to mortal Luz. Asmel's wife, Barsilay's aunt, and Elena and Toba's ancestor. She was the founder of ha-Moh'to and the guardian of its killstone. She was forced to pull her magic into a safira after being trapped in the mortal realm by Tarses; the safira was later absorbed by Atalef the demon and destroyed with his death.

Rafeq of Katlav: An expert on demons and member of ha-Mah'to. He spent the greater part of the current age imprisoned under Mount Sebah and was killed by Atalef the demon after his escape. He helped Elena develop a machine that renders safiras into small enough particles to be inhaled.

Tarses b'Shemhazai: The Caçador of Rimon and King Consort. A former member of ha-Moh'to and at one time a close confidant of Marah. He is the father of both Toba and the

Courser, and is famous for his prescience, though he is only able to see the distant future.

Tsidon b'Noem: The Lymer of Rimon, one of Tarses's top lieutenants in La Cacería, and commander of the Hounds and Alaunts. At Tarses's siege castle in Zayit, Tsidon captured and tortured Toba, finally throwing his sword into an open gate to prevent her escape. This had the unfortunate effect of impaling Tarses, who barely survived.

Relam b'Gidon: The deceased King of Rimon, who died after riding his horse into the sea.

Queen Oneca: The Queen of Rimon.

The Courser/Tsifra: Tarses's personal aide-de-camp. A half-Mazik and Tarses's daughter. Because she has no use-name, she thinks of herself with her true name, Tsifra N'Dar, which she shares with her half-sister, Toba. She recently became the Queen of mortal Rimon after murdering the former Queen and taking her place in disguise.

The Peregrine: The Caçador's most trusted lieutenant, originally from the city of Baobab. She commands the Falcons—responsible for work abroad consisting mainly of espionage—and is widely considered the most deadly assassin in Mazikdom. She has been working as a double agent with Barsilay, who she hopes can break her contract with Tarses by changing her name.

Atalef: A demon with Mazik magic created by Rafeq of Katlav, who was enslaved for some time by the Caçador until he turned on Tarses and was killed by him.

Saba b'Mazlia: A prominent doctor and teacher at Zayit's university, he was captured by Tarses at the battle for the grove of Zayit. Efra, the Savia della Mura of Zayit is his sister.

Efra b'Vashti: The Savia della Mura of Zayit, she was responsible for the defense of the city before it was burned by Tarses. She is the leader of the Zayiti refugees in P'ri Hadar. Saba is her brother.

Queen Kasfia: The Queen of P'ri Hadar, who has held her throne since the Fall of Luz. She is generally considered the oldest living Mazik.

Ayleth: The Princess of P'ri Hadar. Kasfia's daughter.

KING ABISHAI: The new King of Habush. He overthrew the previous King in a coup some fifty years ago.

OMER OF TE'ENA: Asmel's mentor at the university of Te'ena and one of the greatest astronomers in history. Before the Fall, he was a member of ha-Moh'to; Tsifra was ordered to kill him and failed, though she doesn't know this.

KING YEFET: The King of Anab, who was recently killed by the Peregrine.

GEOGRAPHICAL LOCATIONS

IN SEFARAD

RIMON: City-state in southern Sefarad.

MOUNT SEBAH: The highest peak in Rimon, very near the Rimon gate.

BARCINO: Northern port city in Sefarad, on the Dimah Sea.

SAVIRRA: The former residence of the old woman, home to a massive pogrom some years prior to the events of *The Pomegranate Gate*.

MANSANAR: The capital of the newly united Sefarad.

THE GAL'IN: The mountains between Sefarad and the land of the Franks. In the Mazik world, they are inhabited by large numbers of demons, who were promised permanent ownership of the land once Barsilay becomes King of Luz.

OTHER LOCATIONS

PETGAL: Country that shares the peninsula with Sefarad and destination of many of the Jews who were expelled from Sefarad by the Queen. Elena's husband Alasar is in the capital, Pengoa, along with her brother.

DASSOS: A large island to the east of Anab.

THE DIMAH SEA (THE SEA OF TEARS): The sea that rose after the Fall of Luz between Sefarad in the west and P'ri Hadar in the east.

THE ULIMAN EMPIRE: A great multi-ethnic empire in the east. Its capital is the gate city of Habush.

THE SAHARON BRIDGE: Considered the greatest feat of Mazik engineering, the Saharon Bridge connects both sides of the city of Habush, which was split in half by the rise of the Dimah Sea. The trade route that connects the western cities to those in the south and the east depends on this crossing.

THE ROSH HA-TANNIN: The Mazik name for the Hellespont, the narrow strait between Europe and Asia south of Habush.

The Gate Cities

LUZ: Legendary lost city, known as the location in which Jacob saw angels climbing a ladder to and from heaven, as well as the mythical source of tekhelet dye. The former seat of the Mazik Empire. Barsilay b'Droer is the heir to the throne.

P'RI HADAR: The great city of the east. Its queen is the oldest living Mazik.

BAOBAB: The most southern gate city, notable, like Tappuah, because of its great distance to the sea. On the mortal side, it is an important trade hub.

KATLAV: On the south-east side of the Dimah Sea, an important center for education.

EREZ: A city to the south of the Dimah Sea. Famous for its natural beauty and for being surrounded on three sides by a steep gorge, making it a natural fortress. The Mazik city is suffering from a blight on its lentil crop.

TAMAR: A city to the south of the Dimah Sea. An important producer of lentils, the Mazik city is suffering from a blight on their crop.

RIMON: The great city of the west. After the Fall of Luz, it suffered a series of bloody coups d'état that led to the rise of King Relam and La Cacería. After the assassination of Relam and his sons, the throne was taken by Queen Oneca, who made Tarses her King Consort.

TE'ENA: Made an island in the Fall. Located roughly midway between Rimon and Zayit. Once home to a university second in importance only to the school in Luz.

ZAYIT: An important port city north of the Dimah Sea. In the mortal world, it is known in particular for its prominence in the salt trade. The Mazik city was burned by Tarses; its gate is now shielded by three orbits of mines, rendering it unusable.

TAPPUAH: The city of the north. Because of its distance from the other gate cities, its Mazik residents are relatively isolated.

ANAB: An important trade city in the Uliman Empire in the mortal world. Until recently, Mazik Anab was ruled by King Yefet, widely regarded as the most benevolent of the Mazik monarchs.

HABUSH: The capital of the Uliman Empire in the east. Several hundred years ago, both the mortal and Mazik cities were sacked by the Zayitis. Since then, the Uliman Empire claimed the mortal city; the Mazik city was taken by King Abishai in a coup. Habush's main source of income is the toll levied on the crossing of the Saharon Bridge, the only easy passage between the western and southern cities.

A wind set sails of cloud against the moon and spread its veil against its face
  as if it wished just then to get a stream of rain
  and leaned against the clouds to make it flow.
The heavens dressed in black, the moon seemed dead, buried by the clouds,
  While over it, thick clouds of heaven wept
  as Arem once lamented Beor's son.
The night put on black chain mail — Thunder pierced it with a lightning lance,
  and then the lightning fluttered through the sky
  as if to mock its fate,
for like a bat the darkness spread its wings,
  and when they saw its flash, the crows of darkness fled.

                    — Solomon ibn Gabirol
                    (trans. Raymond P. Scheindlin)

Chapter One

Toba Peres was born a half-Mazik in the city of Rimon, under the reign of the Emir, before he sailed away in exile. She died a half-Mazik in the city of Rimon, under the reign of King Relam, before he rode his horse into the sea. For most of her life, she was bound by an amulet that left her small and weak. She could walk, but she could not run. She could talk, but she could not sing. She was sickly and she was often housebound, 'til the day her amulet was broken and she reclaimed her magic.

She made mud creatures that came alive, she made parts of herself into birds and knew what it felt like to fly, she became fish and knew what it felt like to breathe water. She'd learned to run and to sing, all in the space of a single season, the autumn of the year the Jews were sent away from Rimon.

Then she'd died, violently and quickly.

Nevertheless, during her abbreviated life, bookended by the amulet at one end and her murder at the other, Toba performed two feats never before carried out in all the history of Mazikdom. The first of these was to save the life of the heir of Luz. The second was to create a buchuk who became independent enough to survive Toba's own death.

No one (save possibly the Peregrine of Rimon) knew precisely how many of the heirs of Luz had been murdered since the death of the Queen, but it had been many. Until Toba saved Barsilay b'Droer in La Cacería's prison, none had survived more than a few months. This was significant in ways that Toba herself did not understand, because a surviving heir set things in motion that had been stalled since the day that Luz had fallen beneath the sea.

As for the buchuk, Toba did not know how or why she'd made her, if not to die in Toba's stead. It seemed to be the natural order, for the creation to die before the creator, or at least that was what had been decided when Toba Bet was sent to marry Tsidon the Lymer, while Toba herself went to rescue Barsilay. Toba the Elder had believed she was taking the safer path; Toba the Younger had believed she was on her way to her own end. Instead, Toba Bet had survived, and Toba had perished at the hand of the Courser of Rimon, a gruesome death that had sent her spirit hurtling into the void.

She and Toba Bet had both felt it, the initial pain, followed by the slow extinguishment of her consciousness, leaving nothing but the original Toba's awareness that she was very much alone in the void—and even this awareness was slowly winking out.

It was a screaming sort of horror, slipping into nonexistence, and Toba fought as it crept up through her mind, thinking, as all Maziks did in those final moments, that if she only willed herself to remain, she could not cease to exist. The edge of the void was terrible, they all told themselves, but it must be better than the void itself. Nothing could be worse than that.

Toba held fast for so long she began to think she had beaten it. Perhaps if she let her will drift from fighting, for one moment, and let her mind shift to more pleasant thoughts, she might know something other than nothingness.

This, of course, was how all Maziks died.

Only what happened to Toba was something different.

As what remained of her began to fade away, she heard the sounds of wings in her ears and thought, *There are no birds in the void, I don't think.* And then there were voices, melodious voices, whispering to her, "Little bird, you do not belong here."

Are you demons? Toba thought, because demons had whispered to her, and the demons she had known had called her not *Little bird*, but *Birdling*, which was very close.

The voices said, "No, we are not demons."

Then Toba felt herself return, and only then realized she had been returning for some time—first her hearing, then her sight, and then her physical body (or at least some reasonable approximation). She felt hands on her arms and there were so many sets of eyes she felt faint from them. She covered her face and cowered, and then the voices, no longer so melodious but now rather ordinary, said, "Open your eyes, Tsifra N'Dar."

Toba complied, because apparently her name was still her name, even in death. She looked down at herself and saw that she was rather insubstantial, much as the dead were in the dream-world, and knew that she had not returned to life. Instead, she was inside what looked to be a shul, an old stone building with horseshoe-topped arches, much like the shul she'd visited in Rimon. The walls were ornately carved with Hebrew poems, some of which she recognized and others not. Before her were three bearded men, dressed in the manner of rabbis, sitting behind a grand wooden table on a raised dais, while she stood on the floor beneath them.

"Where is this place?" she asked the men, and one said, "You have been brought here, to Aravoth."

"Aravoth," she whispered, then added, "Are you not a beit din?"

"We are," said the rabbi in the middle, who was the tallest and the one who had spoken. His eyes were not like a Mazik's, nor were they like a human's; they were simply black all the way across, which was deeply unsettling. Toba thought that these rabbis probably did not truly look like this. This was some trick of perception. If she were indeed in Aravoth—and she had no reason to suspect the rabbis were lying—then these were angels, and she was being called to account. She said, "Am I to be judged?"

"Not by us," the rabbi-angel said. "The matter at hand is what is to be done with you. You are too much a Mazik to die as a mortal, and too much a mortal to die as a Mazik. So we have discussed, and we leave the choice to you, to tell us where your heart lies. What is your spirit, truly?"

Choose an afterlife, what a decision.

She said, "I can hardly be the first half-Mazik ever to die."

The angel-rabbi looked quite consternated, a strange expression which did not suit his face. He said, "You are not the first half-Mazik to die. But you are the first to die both violently and awake. The others before you all chose a dreaming death. So we were not made to be involved."

She said, "I was told the dreaming death was given only to Maziks who died in their sleep, and the rest go to the void."

The rabbi-angel smiled and said, "They do go someplace different, however—"

"Well, where? Where is it Maziks go?"

"You are speaking quite out of turn, Tsifra N'Dar."

Toba prickled at this. "Seeing what's at stake, I believe I am entitled to ask questions."

The rabbi-angel looked quite affronted and said, "Entitled! To what are you entitled? You are a mortal creature—even Maziks are so. You have lived and you have died, and now all that remains is to decide where your spirit will go. Choose."

"I would be happy to choose," Toba said. "But as I have said, you have not told me what I am choosing between."

The rabbi to the left, who looked somewhat less happy to be having this conversation (that is to say, very unhappy indeed) said, "Perhaps you would prefer us to return you whence we found you?"

"I don't believe you can," Toba said. "Isn't that why I'm here?"

"Your impertinence is astounding," the first angel said (Toba had, by this point, stopped thinking of them as rabbis because a rabbi would have appreciated her argument). "You will recall that your unwavering belief in your own cleverness is what got you killed in the first place."

"My sister removing my head is what got me killed," Toba said. "Don't make that out to be my fault. And anyway, if you know what I was doing when I was killed—which is to say, saving someone's life—does that not also tend to sway things in my favor?"

"Your actions on that day had merit," he said. "They do not entitle you to additional consideration here. You must choose what happens to your soul based on how you feel it within you."

Refusing to give her the information she needed to make a reasonable decision irked Toba and struck her as terribly unfair.

What if Maziks really did go to the void? The mortal choice seemed the more sensible. On the other hand…

"I submit to you that it is unjust for me to be dead in the first place."

The angel made an expression that was not unlike the one Asmel had made when she'd argued with him back in the alcalá, when she'd rejected his hospitality in favor of a bargain with better terms. He'd been very angry that day. The angels were no less angry with her now. Before the angel could call her absurd and render her unable to speak (which she felt was the logical next step for him), she said, "In the Birchot HaShachar each day we say, 'Adonai, the soul You have placed within me is pure. You guard it while it is within me; someday it will return to You, and You will restore it to me in a time beyond time. As long as my soul is within me, I will thank You.' Listen. My soul is either within me, for which I thank Hashem, or else it is with Hashem. But half my soul is on earth with Toba Bet, because she is still alive! How can it be in both places? If I am split this way, does it not violate the sanctity of my soul?"

The angels thought this over, then the second among them—the one Toba thought of as preternaturally crabby—said, "Is it not also said that husband and wife share the same soul, and that when the younger is born, part of the elder's soul is given to them? Then, is not part of the soul on earth and part with God after one of them dies?"

Toba said, "Did I marry myself? How is that analogous, unless you are claiming that I am my own husband and Toba Bet is my wife?"

The chief angel said, "We reject your argument."

"You cannot simply reject my argument! You must refute it, which you have not done. This is the law."

"And who are you to lecture us about the law?"

"And who are you?" she shot back. "You are a being created by Hashem to serve whatever purpose you have been given. I am no different, nor am I inferior in reason. So you must either refute my argument, or else you must accept it, in which case I cannot remain dead."

A long silence stretched between them. She did think, at that time, that the angels meant to cast her back into the void. But she would not be sorry for making the argument. It was, she believed, her obligation to her very soul.

Finally, the chief angel said, "What would you have us do, then? Bring the other Toba here?"

"That would be murder," Toba said. "Would it not?" Before the angel could form an answer, she said, "I would be revived. Elijah and Elisha both revived the dead, and as they were only prophets, that must be in your power, as angels."

The angel said, "If we do as you ask, your soul and the other's are still part of the same whole, and the problem is unsolved. When one of you dies, we begin this argument again. You ask us to create a paradox. You cannot live forever." The third angel, the smallest of the three, and with the least quantity of beard, said something in his ear and he nodded. "We will confer among ourselves, Tsifra N'Dar."

The angels vanished, leaving Toba sitting alone in the shul, and she reached into her mind, looking for her other self. Until the moment of her death, they'd seen through one another's eyes, and she wondered that she hadn't had a sense of her counterpart since she'd been brought out of the void. She would have asked the angels how the connection had been severed, but since it did not seem to bolster her argument she decided she had better stay quiet on the matter.

The angels returned only a few moments later, reappearing in their original spots, and again the tallest spoke. "We have a solution," he said. "We cannot return you to life as you were. But we can give you a new body, a new name, and you will be born as someone else. In this way, your soul will be separated from the soul of your buchuk. You will live another life, and you will die, and at that time you will not speak before us again."

Toba said, "What will I remember of myself?"

"That we cannot say," the angel said. "You may remember, or you may not. But because you died protecting another, we will give you this choice, Tsifra N'Dar: Would you go to where you will be safest and no harm will ever come to you, or would you go to where you can do the most good?"

"What does that mean?" Toba insisted. "Where I will do the most good for whom?"

The angel slammed his hand down on the table, making a sound so loud that Toba, for the first time, felt afraid. "Your choice has been laid out for you," he said. "Make your decision."

Toba said, "Then I will choose to go where I can do the most good."

The angels nodded to one another. Then the smallest among them, who had not yet spoken aloud, came forward from behind the table and said, "Your name, from now on, shall be Dagah N'Dar. And there is one more thing, Dagah N'Dar: In payment for this new life, you must never take another."

And Toba opened her eyes on the day of her birth, and on her tongue was her new name. "Dagah N'Dar," she said, and felt her new name settle on her like a mantle—the Splendid Fish.

Chapter Two

Elena Peres's greatest desire in all the worlds was for a pocketful of salt, or a spoonful, or even a thimble's worth. She'd even have settled for a few grains, enough to give a Mazik a good long stomachache.

Alas, she'd used up what little salt she'd had rescuing Barsilay from disaster back in Zayit, and now here he was again, in a Mazik prison. The man seemed to have the worst luck imaginable; she only hoped they could get him out this time before he found himself short of any more limbs.

Elena did not give voice to any of these ruminations because she knew her desire for salt would cast her as murderous, and her feelings about Barsilay as glib, but she was neither, really. She was only a woman who had succeeded in staying alive a very long time under some very trying circumstances. One tended not to grow overemotional about impending doom the tenth or twelfth time around. She'd have thought that Maziks, with all their immortality, would be more understanding of the sentiment. But it seemed the Zayiti Maziks she'd thrown in with were unused to having their lives threatened.

Their current predicament—Elena's and the Maziks'—went something like this: She, Barsilay, Asmel, and the old woman had come to P'ri Hadar together with some hundreds of Zayiti refugees, who had been forced to flee when Tarses had used some sort of demonic fire to burn their city to ash.

While they had been sent to the great city of the east in the hope of safety, Toba and Naftaly had passed into the mystical third realm of Aravoth in order to find the Ziz, that she might help them restore the gate of Luz to the firmament.

This was a great deal of information, even for Elena.

Unfortunately for them, Queen Kasfia of P'ri Hadar had some foreknowledge that Barsilay was the heir of Luz, information they'd believed would not have reached so far, and at the first sight of him she had thrown him in her dungeon. In the aftermath, Elena had been left before Queen Kasfia with Efra b'Vashti, the Savia della Mura of Zayit, who seemed to be the highest-ranking official to have survived the razing of the city. Efra had spoken very fast to Kasfia about the inhospitality of arresting a man who had come seeking aid, and which unwritten Mazik code this violated. She'd listed several. The Queen had been unmoved.

"Get them out of here," she'd told her guards, referencing Efra and Elena both, as Barsilay was already being dragged away, his real and phantom wrists both chained. Elena had managed to get close enough to him to say, "I have a plan" (untrue, she had none), but he'd replied, "Don't make her our enemy," and then he'd been pulled one way down the main corridor and Efra and Elena the other.

And now, the two women were left somewhat dumbfounded, standing outside the palace gates. Elena said, "Did you expect her to do that?"

Efra said, "I did not expect she'd know him as the heir of Luz, no. Disaster upon disaster; we didn't so much as get a sack of lentils for all our people."

The only thing that had gone well was that the Queen hadn't recognized Elena as a mortal, which itself surprised her. She was veiled, but it wasn't such a good disguise. She wondered if Kasfia in fact had recognized her, but chosen not to call attention to it. "What will she do with him?" she asked.

"Will she execute him?" Efra asked. "I don't know. It was already a violation of the code of hosts for her to arrest him only for being the heir to a throne she'd like forgotten; I don't know what she'll do with him now. What did he say to you?"

"Not to make her our enemy."

"Too late for that," Efra said.

"My guess is he's hoping we'll find a solution that encourages the Queen to help us restore the gate." Elena huffed a little. She was exhausted and she'd breathed too much smoke back in Zayit. "I need to think."

"We need to find a way to feed and house all the Zayitis," Efra said. "We never even got to put that request in."

"Isn't there someone else we could ask? I don't suppose Maziks have leagues for widows and orphans?"

Efra said, "No, we certainly don't." She set her jaw and began to walk down the palace steps. The sun was rising over the city, a vast place carved—or magicked—from beige sandstone. The buildings lacked the color of Zayit, but the contrast between the vivid blue of the sky and the yellow of the buildings was dazzling nevertheless. Flanking the steps were two statues of what Elena knew must be Leviathans, great fish leaping into the air from massive bowls of quicksilver. The statues themselves were either made entirely of silver or plated in the stuff. Floating in the bowls of quicksilver were lotus flowers carved from alabaster. As they passed, Elena could have sworn the blossoms smelled real. From the front of the palace one could look all the way down to the sea, bluer even than the sky.

She decided she would ask Asmel about the statues later—the matter at hand was feeding the Zayitis. There were three avenues to persuade a woman like Kasfia: pity (only she appeared to be without any), threats from someone even more powerful (only she had imprisoned Barsilay, making him her enemy), and of course, the universal lubricant: money (only they had none). The Zayitis were the wealthiest Maziks in existence, but they'd escaped with little more than the clothes on their backs. Perhaps, if they were very lucky, one of them had run away with a purse in their pocket.

"What is your plan?" Elena asked as she followed Efra back through the stone city, past the gated courtyards of the Maziks wealthy enough to live near the palace, all filled with orange trees that were covered with blooms and left the streets smelling like perfume. It was early enough in the day that there were few Maziks about, only a few shades sweeping doorways and the occasional cat watching them from the top of a wall.

"Barsilay will have to wait," Efra said. "If history is any indication, she'll try to ransom him to us for some ungodly amount we'll never be able to pay." At that, Efra turned off the main street, down a side street, then another. The city was not altogether different from Rimon—the streets, once you got far enough from the palace, were all curved in such a way that you had to navigate by keeping one eye on the palace and the other on the wall, otherwise you'd be lost in five minutes.

"Are we not returning to the grove?" Elena asked, to which Efra replied, "Every luxury in P'ri Hadar came through the gate of Zayit and was sold by a Zayiti merchant. The trade guilds have a significant presence here."

"Wasn't it your salt guild that betrayed you to Tarses? You think the guildsmen here won't know you executed all their friends?"

Efra pursed her lips and said, "I doubt word will have traveled so fast. Anyway, the guilds are not so entirely enmeshed. We'll begin with the spice guild."

Only when they arrived in the Zayiti quarter, they discovered the door to the spice guild had been broken and the building was empty. Elena followed Efra inside, watching quietly as she walked the perimeter of the main room, taking in the scuffs on the floor and the dust on the windowsills. "They've been arrested," she said.

"Are you sure they didn't just flee? Perhaps they got wind of what happened to the salt guild in Zayit and were frightened."

"And they broke their own door in? No, they were taken, and someone knows why." She removed her earring and set it into the doorway. "The guilds aren't the only presence Zayit has in this city. The Queen may have taken the merchants. But she won't have captured the spies." She tapped the earring three times.

Barsilay had told Elena that Zayit ran on money and secrets, and their spy network was even more adept than Tarses's. "Do we wait here?" Elena asked her.

"No," Efra said, straightening. "They'll find us."

* * *

While Elena wished most for a handful of salt, what Toba wanted most of all was Elena.

This was the Toba formerly known as Toba Bet, the surviving buchuk of the Toba that had died in Rimon and been returned to life as Dagah N'Dar, and she felt herself as much Elena's grandchild as the original had been. And as Elena turned her path from the palace of P'ri Hadar, Toba felt herself slipping into memories that had belonged to her other self, of the childhood in which Elena loomed mythically large, as mothers and grandmothers often do.

In the house of Elena Peres, there had been one rule above all others: Toba was never to be left alone. When Elena was at home, Toba was nearby, mimicking her at her chores. And when Elena had to venture out—which was fairly often—she was left with Alasar, to follow along with his students or scratch some lines on a spare piece of paper.

But occasionally, when Toba was very small, Alasar would have his own errands to attend to. On those days, Toba was bundled up and taken with Elena as she went about her day.

She was not to speak on those occasions—Toba had not understood 'til later that this was to conceal the maturity of her mind. She was to wait quietly beside Elena until it was time to go home, and then she was allowed to ask all the questions she wanted.

When she was about seven years old, Alasar had been out visiting some academic friend or other, and Elena had received a message from the rabbi's wife, asking her to come to the house.

Toba recalled that Elena had very much not wanted to take Toba on this particular errand, and had asked the maid who had delivered the message if the rabbi's wife could wait 'til after lunch. But the maid had insisted the matter was urgent, so Elena reminded Toba of the rule, covered her with a shawl, and off they went. It was cold that day, Toba remembered, and her eyes had stung in the wind as she'd walked behind her grandmother. Her legs were short and it had seemed like a very long way to the rabbi's house.

The rabbi's wife had wanted Elena to write a letter on her behalf. Toba did not know who the letter was for or what it was about, but the rabbi's wife had insisted the two women have privacy for the transcription. Elena had balked. The rabbi's wife had insisted again and then offered her some extra payment.

And so Toba had been left in the kitchen with the maid and some treat to keep her quiet. But Toba had not liked the treat and she was not used to being without her grandparents and the maid had been busy with the making of lunch, so Toba set the uneaten sweet down on the table and slipped out of the kitchen.

She was looking for Elena when she found the rabbi's empty study. The room had a low table like the one her grandfather used, and the walls were lined with bookshelves, and here Toba paused, because these were different books than those she'd seen at home. Alasar translated science and poetry, in the main; these were holy books. Toba wondered if she could read them as easily as the books she was used to, and if they might tell her something interesting she could share with her grandfather later.

Standing on her toes, she reached for a book with an ornate spine set with gilt along the binding, but then hesitated because the book beside it was so old and worn. It looked like lots of people had read that one, so she slipped it off the shelf instead.

She set the book on the low table and opened it.

Inside, on the page to which it opened, there was a chart: seven spheres interlocking. And they had been labeled in a neat penmanship: the first sphere, Vilon, the second, Raqia. Her eyes scanned to the end of the list.

The seventh sphere: Aravoth.

She turned the page, which began with descriptions of each sphere, then flipped ahead because Aravoth had caught a thread in her mind. Had she heard it at home? From Alasar, maybe, or one of his students, the young men who came and murmured over ancient texts, with hands covered in ink and faces pale from hours spent indoors.

She turned to the page about Aravoth and began to read.

There is a dark place there, where one must not ever look, because it is there that Hashem resides, and no one shall ever look upon Him.

Toba began to tremble as her young mind whirled, and she began to imagine what such a place might look like: bright and then dark, filled with terrifying angels with eyes too numerous to count, their wings beating the air like ten million birds, in a din so loud that Toba, in the rabbi's study, had to put her hands over her ears just from imagining it. She wept a little and then loudly, with great heaving sobs, 'til Elena heard and came running into the room, the rabbi's wife behind her.

"She ought not to be in here!" the rabbi's wife said testily, as Elena took the book from Toba and shut it.

"I asked to keep her with me."

"If she can't mind you, she should be left at home—" Her eyes widened. "She can't have been reading that?"

"Of course not," Elena covered, though not too smoothly. "Why aren't you in the kitchen, Toba?"

"The wings," Toba wept.

Elena returned the book to the shelf without a word. "She's overtired. I'll take my leave now."

"But you haven't finished writing the letter," the rabbi's wife complained.

"Another time," Elena said, taking Toba by the wrist and pulling her through the door and all the way home.

"You shouldn't read books in other people's houses," Elena said. "You know better."

But Toba was too upset to reply or to complain or to ask about what she'd read, because in her mind she could still see all those eyes, all those wings, and it seemed to her to be the most frightening thing she could imagine.

She'd forgotten that book long before the day when Toba put her foot through the gate of Luz and stepped into Aravoth. In her hands was the book that held the gate, Naftaly had already passed through ahead of her, and she expected him to be the first thing she saw.

Instead, there was nothing in her vision but eyes, and nothing in her hearing but the sound of wings loud as thunder, or cannon fire, and she dropped to her knees and wept.

Tsifra N'Dar, the Courser of Mazik Rimon and Toba's sister, wished most of all for some clarity of purpose. She had been the left hand of the new age, a tool to manipulate the Mirror, and a vengeful angel. But now she would have to become an entirely different creature: a queen.

She'd killed the former Queen Of Sefarad, and now Tsifra wore her face. She'd spent days among her advisors in the city of Mansanar, to which she'd traveled after the fall of Zayit. And she'd learned more about the woman whose place she'd had stolen: She was bellicose without dirtying her own hands with the stain of battle; she was holy without claiming herself an icon; she was an administrator, a maker of law, and a leader of soldiers and pious men and farmers alike.

Tsifra was uncertain how to carry on in this woman's vein. She would need to oversee battles—which the former queen would not have done—and find some way to explain the obvious shifts in her character.

She had no model for any sort of rule besides Tarses and his twisted promises, his unwavering belief in his own personal importance. She'd wondered, in her younger days, whether he believed his own rhetoric: He'd called monarchy abomination but then put Relam on the throne of Rimon; he'd executed men for contact with mortals while conceiving two half-mortal children. What she'd come to realize is that Tarses was a man of faith, and the central figure of this faith was himself. Whatever else he might have done, or wherever else he'd seemed to alter his course, he believed, truly, that he was the savior of the Maziks.

The only way forward Tsifra could see was by casting herself in a similar mold, a mirror of her father, but within the boundaries of the woman whose name she'd claimed. She settled into her persona, felt around the edges, and wondered what she might do if, like Tarses, she were a savior—no, not a savior. She was still too much herself, the Courser of Rimon. And the Courser of Rimon was a messenger.

On the night before she was to leave for Barcino she went to her advisors and said, "The Angel of Zayit has visited me this night and gifted me with a vision. She has shown me the heretics of Zayit turned to ash, and bade me continue on to Anab, where she set me a task. I am to take a ship with twelve men and land at the point she has shown me, some miles from the city. Then, together, we are to walk until we find a tree felled by lightning, and in that spot we are to lay the foundation of a church. Once we do that, we will be granted an easy victory over Anab."

Her advisors were amazed by the vision she'd been given, and when Tsifra went to sleep that night, she wondered at how easy it was to make mortals trust her as the Queen. As she retired to the Queen's bedchamber and stood at the window, combing out the Queen's red hair, she saw shapes in the stars she'd never seen before. And as she watched, the land became the sea and the stars became ships, all spread out to the horizon, and leading them was the Angel of Zayit.

Chapter Three

Barsilay b'Droer, the heir of Luz, had been imprisoned four times in his very long life.

The first of these imprisonments had been relatively brief and painless: He had followed his aunt to a meeting of ha-Moh'to and been caught in a spell that sent him to some oubliette-like room, where he'd been left with no food or water for several days before Marah realized what had happened to him.

The second was after Asmel had given a lecture about Aravoth and been imprisoned by La Cacería. His uncle had sent him word to flee, and Barsilay had made it all the way to Baobab and thought himself thoroughly escaped 'til he'd spent too much time in the wrong bed and found himself dragged back to Rimon, used as a pawn to force Asmel to accept the sigils of silence. That imprisonment had likewise been relatively short and painless, so far as those things went. No one had touched him.

The third was when he'd been captured by La Cacería while asking too many questions about half-mortal children, and that had resulted in weeks of torture and the loss of his left arm. It had also led him to Naftaly, who had managed to dream his way into Barsilay's cell. So far as trades went, Barsilay felt that an arm for a great love was not a bad one.

And now he was imprisoned again, in the dungeon of the

Queen of P'ri Hadar, who had known what she should not: that he was the heir of Luz.

No one yet had laid a hand on him. He'd been fed and watered like a horse and put in a stone stall with no window or light besides the light-stone he'd made himself from one of his buttons. The cell was so small that when he lay down with his head at one end, his feet reached the other side. The air was entirely still, and it felt horribly like a coffin. He was not sure how long he had been there; it could have been a day or it might have been three. Twice he'd been delivered two lentils and a bowl of water, both of which appeared by magic. But he saw no one: no guard, no shade, no other prisoner.

As in La Cacería's prison, his dreams were as confined to his cell as he was. But while Naftaly had once been able to dream past the wards meant to keep Barsilay as isolated sleeping as awake, now he was in Aravoth, far beyond the range of dreaming. So when Barsilay slept—fitfully and rarely—it was no different than waking: He sat alone in the dark cubby and wondered how long his sanity would hold out.

Unlike the prison in Rimon, this prison had rats. Barsilay could hear them, squeaking and skittering outside his cell and behind the walls, in the small spaces that had been left for the passage of sewage. Once he had seen one poke its head up from the grate in a corner of the floor, hoping for a stray crumb possibly, or a dead Mazik more likely. Barsilay had thrown his boot at it, which he later regretted because when he went to retrieve it, he found it covered in marks from gnawing teeth.

There was no comfort in sleep, but he found he slept anyway, exhausted from the bad air and lack of light. The sounds of the rats followed him into the dream-world, where he sat in his cell and tried to pass the time by remembering Naftaly's handsome face… at least 'til he woke from the sudden pain of a bite on his ankle.

He sat up with a start, kicking out at the silver-eyed rat that had grown bold, and made to summon a bit of flame or something else he might throw at the thing. But then through the wall came a cat the color of smoke, leaping out of the stone as if it were water or illusion. It fell on the rat, snapping its neck, and then sat back to savor the meal.

Barsilay carefully increased the light in the room, tapping his button light-stone with a finger, and then watched as the light passed through the cat, leaving no shadow.

It was no cat. It was a demon.

He watched it consume the rat, unsure how to proceed, but then through the wall came another cat, and another, 'til there were nine, all made of shadow, all staring at him intently—save the one that was still eating the rat. And then when the rat was nothing but bones, that cat-demon looked up and said, "Show us the mark."

Barsilay said, "I beg your pardon?"

The demons began to whisper, "Heir of Luz, show your mark."

Some of the demons began to lose their shape a bit, morphing into creatures with tentacles and extra hands and faces before shifting back into cats, and they hissed at him, "*The mark.*"

There did not seem to be much to lose. So Barsilay uncovered the mark of Luz beneath his left collarbone, and then the demons began to whisper among themselves, and some of them began flying around the room, abandoning the pretense of cat-ness. One of these flying demons came to rest on Barsilay's shoulder and whispered in his ear, "We were at the Gal'in, Barsilay of Luz, and we remember what you promised."

Whether he meant all of these demons had been in the Gal'in was unclear, because in Barsilay's admittedly limited experience demons did not think of themselves as singular. If only one demon had been present, that would have been the same as all. Or perhaps they had somehow followed him all the way from the mountains. Demons did not obey the same laws as other creatures and how they moved was something of a mystery, at least to Barsilay. What he had promised the demons was permanent residence in the Gal'in should he ever become the King of Luz, which at the moment seemed highly unlikely. He said, "I am not king yet."

"You are food for rats," the demon whispered.

"Rat food seldom keeps its promises," Barsilay said.

The demons—cat-shaped and demon-shaped alike—laughed.

"Then you must not be eaten, Heir of Luz. We shall assist you, as we are able."

"Can you get me out of this prison?"

"No, we can come and go, but you may not. None may escape."

Barsilay said, "Yet one did, if the stories are true." By this, he meant Dawid ben Aron, the half-Mazik who had escaped the Fall of Luz only to be imprisoned by Kasfia for some fifty years before he somehow managed to escape with the book and the Ziz both. How he'd done so was of no small interest to Barsilay.

"That was long ago," the demons said. "It is different now. Different walls, different spells."

"Yet you can come and go. You aren't bound by the prison?"

"No, Heir of Luz, and we can be your eyes and ears, 'til you are freed."

Barsilay had few enough allies; the mortals—Elena and the old woman—would be with Asmel and Efra trying to negotiate his release. Obviously Kasfia wanted something in exchange for him, otherwise he'd already be dead. Money, and a lot, most likely, which meant he was probably going to be there a very long time while they figured out how to raise it, since none of them had any. Asmel might know someone in P'ri Hadar—academics always seemed to have contacts in different cities. Sending word to his friends seemed to be a waste of favors, since they obviously knew where he was; *Come quick, there are rats*, seemed like a misuse of everyone's time indeed.

He was fairly sure the demons could not get into Aravoth, where he might have sent them to help Naftaly and Toba, and he was not sure what they could do there, in any case.

There was one person they might be able to help: Saba b'Mazlia, Efra's brother, the doctor, who had been lost to them back in Zayit, either killed or captured. If he were still alive, he was probably in a bad state; Tarses did not simply toss you in a room with food and water and forget about you.

Finally, he said, "I want you to find Saba b'Mazlia, and if he is still alive, I want you to help him."

They whispered "Saba b'Mazlia" several times, and then one of the demons went back out through the wall. Barsilay sat in the company of the remaining eight. "Are you to stay and watch over me?" he asked them, in a manner so childish he cringed at his own words—listen to him, begging demons not to leave him alone.

The demons said, "We must hunt, Heir of Luz. But do not fear the darkness of this prison." And then one of them said, in an uncanny version of Naftaly's voice, "We are here with you," and that same demon took on a shadowed version of Naftaly's face and kissed him on the cheek, leaving a cold place that did not warm again for several hours.

IT WAS ALL Naftaly could do to keep his feet, so overwhelmed were all his senses with color and light and the sounds of wings. Toba had collapsed and was weeping with her hands over her ears, the book containing the gate of Luz at her feet. He thought he might faint, and then it occurred to him that if he did he might not wake up again. Turning a circle, he could see the sky was neither light nor dark, but somewhere in between, like twilight but without sun or moon or stars. In one direction, the strange light faded to black; it was as if nothing existed there but darkness.

Deciding to pretend he was lost in one of his visions, Naftaly breathed in and out, feeling the air in his lungs and looking for one point he might focus on, perhaps something familiar he had brought with him. His pockets were sadly empty, but as he ran his fingers over his coat he caught at one of the buttons, and so he took it, still sewn firmly in place, and held it near his eye, blocking out everything else: the strange light, the darkness.

It was a mortal-made button. When he'd been in Zayit they'd given him new clothes, but the buttons on his new coat had been less fine than those on the one sewn by his father—brass buttons cast with starbursts. Naftaly even remembered the man who had made them, a man called Abu Rahman. He'd been an affable fellow who made all sorts of things from metal, and the buttons were some he'd made as a lark. His father had agreed to buy fifty of them when Naftaly had begged, even though they'd been far too expensive. "People will want coats with these buttons," he'd told his father, "even if my stitching isn't perfect."

So he'd sewn those buttons on his Mazik coat back in Zayit. Barsilay had teased him for his small vanity, and Naftaly had offered to put them on Barsilay's coat instead, but he'd refused them, saying, "It is no small thing, to have something touched by one's father. Keep them." Naftaly had not thought of that moment since it had happened, but he could hear Barsilay's voice as if he'd only just spoken, and then his mind went back farther still, to the day his father put those buttons on his coat. He felt himself back in his father's house, his mother making a cholent in the kitchen while his father quickly, silently, sewed on one after the other. So complete was his memory that he could even smell the onions in his mother's stew.

When he looked up from the button, the light seemed to bother him less, and he took in the details of his strange surroundings: trees, mainly, the likes of which Naftaly had never seen before. The nearest of these had neither leaves nor needles but something in between, almost like curved claws. At its base, long, thin cones littered the ground; he carefully picked one up and held it to his nose, finding that it smelled mostly like pine. He inhaled it for several seconds before offering it to Toba, saying, "Smell this."

She did, and the act seemed to relieve some of her panic. Without opening her eyes, she said, "We cannot stay here. I cannot even look."

The light still bothered Naftaly, too, but it was bearable. He said, "You have more magic than I do, and you're more than half Mazik." He tore the hem off his tunic and used it to make a strip of fabric he tied over Toba's eyes.

"I cannot do anything like this," she said.

"Just rest a minute," he said. "Your eyes may adjust. Mine have."

"Naftaly—"

The rustle of wings got much louder and then stopped. When Naftaly looked up, there was a woman on the other side of the tree, dressed in a gray robe, her dark hair pulled back from a face incongruous for bearing Mazik eyes and, around those eyes, the beginnings of wrinkles. She said, "The angels have gone. They were only curious."

Naftaly was so stunned by the appearance of another person

he could do little but stare for a moment before he blurted out, "Angels?" when really he wanted to ask who she was, or how she'd come there, or if they were really angels.

"You can't see them properly," she said. "All you can make out is the edges. At least that's all I can see of them." To Toba, she said, "You may try uncovering your eyes."

Toba cautiously lowered the blindfold made from Naftaly's shirt and then gasped and raised it again. "I can't," she said. "It's too painful."

"Ah," said the woman. "I think you are too much Mazik, maybe." Turning to Naftaly, she said, "What have you got in your pocket?"

"In my pocket?" Naftaly repeated—who was this woman?—but she strode over and thrust her hand into Naftaly's coat, while he moved to push her away, saying, "Who are you?"

The woman seemed satisfied with her quarry and came out with the small box of al'qot that Naftaly still carried. He hadn't used one since the olive grove, but since he couldn't return them to Saba he'd just kept the box in his jacket. "You can't want those," Naftaly said.

"They aren't for me," the woman said, opening the box and stirring the leeches around with her finger. "Let's start with two." And she put one on Toba's temple, and then another on the other side, before pulling off the blindfold.

Toba's eyes were still screwed shut, but she took a careful blink, and then another, and then looked up at Naftaly, who said, "Are you able to see now?"

"Not perfectly, but there's less pain now. How did you know to do that? Who are you?"

The woman wiped the al'qa residue from her fingers onto her tattered dress. Really, the woman was a mess—dark hair in tangles, a dress that looked like it had been put back together more than a dozen times in a hurry; the hem was ratty and uneven (even by Naftaly's standards). Her face and hands had not been washed recently, and she had what looked like dried blood on the back of one hand, as if she'd wiped away a nosebleed some time ago. The addition of a little leech-slime on her clothing hardly seemed to matter. She pushed her thatch of tangles out of her face, as if noticing for the first time that her hair was was a mess, and said, "When I had a spoken name, I was called Nehama. But I have been here so long, it's a wonder I even recall it." She pointed at the book. "Tell me what that is."

Toba was not quite all right yet, and she wiped at the tears that were still leaking from her squinting eyes and answered, "It's a book. How did you come to be here?"

"I came with two others and was separated from them. Long ago. How is there a gate in your book?"

Someone had told Naftaly a story like this once. Barsilay, he thought, or Asmel, had told him about an expedition into Aravoth. But that had been ages ago—before Barsilay had been born, Naftaly believed. He said, a little gently, "How *long* have you been here?"

"There's no way to tell such things," she said, and for the first time he noticed that her eyes were not only square, but golden.

"You came from Luz," Naftaly said, not wanting to tell her that gave him some idea that she had been there ages, because her home was beneath the sea. Toba, likewise, said nothing. Nehama said, "None of us is meant to be here."

"We don't intend to stay longer than necessary," Toba said. "We're only here—"

"For the Ziz? I assumed someone would come looking for her, but it's been a long time. She's no longer tame."

"I have her name," Toba said.

Nehama looked thoughtful and shrugged. "It's a start. It may not be enough."

THE OLD WOMAN was not sure she would ever completely recover from having inhaled decayed salt back in Zayit. Her lungs hurt when she inhaled and when she exhaled. They hurt when she held her breath. They hurt when she ate and drank and spoke. Barsilay had done his best to heal her before traipsing off to see the Queen—the idiot—but the damage had been so severe, and she herself so old and incapable of healing on her own, that the results had been only middling at best. And now he was in a prison cell, and they had no other doctor who might help her.

Asmel had done his best, but truth be told the man was better suited to staring at the sky than probing around in anyone's insides with his prickly magic. She presumed the Maziks would just leave her out on the hillside to die, but some handsome Mazik or other—one of Efra's soldiers, she thought—had explained they owed her something for having alerted them to the faulty deal the Prince and the Council of Ten had made with Tarses, exchanging the decayed salt for his departure from the city.

The fact that this information had done them absolutely no good seemed like something better left unmentioned.

She was very, very angry to learn that Naftaly had not come with them, having gone off on some fool's errand which would almost certainly be the end of him. The old woman was no scholar, but she'd paid enough attention in the synagogue to know that one did not risk coming face-to-face with Hashem. Unknowable things were unknowable for a reason.

The Maziks had set up a camp in the citron grove, making tents from fallen leaves. These did not do quite enough, in the old woman's opinion, to keep the cold out, and she wondered when they would move to a more permanent situation. Surely they could not remain there long; if nothing else, they were blocking the use of the gate. Or did the P'ri Hadaris not use their gate? She had no idea if the city was like Rimon, which had seeded the mortal side of their grove with wolves, or like Zayit, which seemed to take full advantage of theirs. Elena had set the old woman up on a cot in Efra's tent, Efra being of the opinion that mortals were best kept close and watched. Asmel had gifted her with some bit of magic that lived in her ear and whispered translations to her, and she sat with Elena and listened as best she could as Efra took stock of their few resources and waited for word from the local Zayiti expatriates.

This came late in the afternoon, by which time Efra had grown so strained she was snapping at anyone who came close enough to listen, not that the old woman blamed her. She'd lost her brother, the very fine doctor, and she'd lost nearly all her soldiers—those on the wall, who could not have escaped, and those who had fought in the grove, who were not near enough to the piazza to get out through Naftaly's gate. And now what was left of the city—some two hundred Maziks, by the latest count—were all under her care, and she had nothing with which to provide them.

The Zayiti who found their camp later that day was tall and olive-skinned and looked only slightly less tense than Efra. He was not, he told the guards at Efra's tent, the Zayiti spymaster, but the local Nagid; the spies were all in hiding and would not risk being seen in public.

He and Efra stared at each other for quite some time, sharing some unspoken understanding, before he said, "Yours was my second summons this morning, and so I am come late, Savia."

Efra said, "The first summons?"

"The Queen." He looked around the tent at the few Maziks gathered there, wondering, the old woman was sure, if any of his kin from Zayit had survived somehow, but unable to ask in the face of so much loss. "She had a message for the Zayiti trade guilds, and another for you."

"For me?"

"A reply, to your request to free your puppet, she said." Efra's face looked quite sour, and he said, "She has offered a ransom."

"I assumed as much. The amount?"

"Twenty thousand ksafim."

Here, Efra inhaled sharply, and the other Maziks present swore. The old woman knew nothing of the local currency, but Efra said, "She's refusing to free him, then, with such a sum. Could the trade guilds gather even half that amount?"

His face was very stony, and he said, "Why should the last men of Zayit pay even one kesef to ransom the heir of Luz?"

"Do you have it?" she snapped.

"No, we don't have it, Savia!"

"Lower your voice," she said. "You forget yourself."

"Do I? You sit among the ruins of our city and ask only what Kasfia wants in exchange for your heir of Luz, but you care so little for your own people you have not asked what message she had for the guilds."

"The guilds! It is because of the guilds that Zayit fell. The guilds look after themselves."

"Not anymore," he said. "Not here." He pulled back his hair, revealing the characteristic earring of the Zayiti tradesmen, only instead of an emerald, this was set with a topaz. "The Zayitis have been declared the property of the crown of P'ri Hadar. She has seized all our assets, save our unsold goods, and declared that we are to establish a new port of trade here, through the gate of P'ri Hadar. Zayit is no more." He dropped his hair back over his ear. "It was either this or the Queen's prison. So we have no money for ourselves, let alone to ransom your heir. If you want my suggestion, take the people you have left and leave straightaway for Habush, before Kasfia decides to claim them, too."

Efra exhaled loudly. The old woman thought she looked like a wife who had been told there was no money for flour, when she knew there had been coins in her purse yesterday, and suspected her husband had spent the grocery money on wine instead. She said, "Kasfia cannot have found all your assets."

The Nagid said, "Most of our assets were held in Zayit! The Queen has been raising tariffs on the guilds for years now. We felt it was better not to keep so much money on hand, lest she seize that, too."

"I was unaware that the guilds were having difficulties here."

"Surely you must have heard the intelligence coming out of P'ri Hadar the past years, Savia."

"I heard only rumors," she said. "That Kasfia had become erratic. But nothing verified."

"In that case, the Council was keeping things from you," he said. "Allow me to verify those rumors myself. Ever since the coup in Habush, Kasfia has been seeking out additional sources of revenue."

"Are you telling me Kasfia supported that coup?"

"She did more than support it. It was P'ri Hadari silver that paid Abishai's soldiers."

"For what purpose? P'ri Hadar and Habush have always been allied—since the Fall!"

"We don't know for what purpose," he told her. "And it grows stranger still… Not only did Kasfia fund the coup, she's been sending money to Habush ever since."

Efra scowled. "Why pay tribute to a king she put on the throne herself? Is this widely known?"

"It isn't. And as to why, we don't know. We assumed she was trying to press for better terms for using the Saharon Bridge, but nothing's come of it. All we know is that twice a year, she very quietly passes Abishai a chest of silver, for which she seems to receive nothing in return. Up until recently, a good deal of that silver came from tariffs she assigned to the trade guilds. What money we had is gone, Savia. Now, if I have your leave, I would like to look among your number for any of my kin."

"Go," she said, and he left.

Efra then looked to her man, the one who had assured the old woman she was not about to be turned out into the wilderness, and said, "Have they finished the inventory?"

He produced several pieces of paper, saying, "There's little, Savia. Some few hundred silver and the emeralds in the ears of the guild members."

Efra went through the list and frowned. "This won't serve. It's not even an eighth of what we need." She huffed. "Is it possible the guildsmen are holding out?"

"It's always possible," he said, and together the two of them left the tent to go and lean a little harder on the Zayitis who had lost everything but their pocket money and the clothes on their backs.

As a point of fact, one of their number was holding out, but it wasn't one of the guildsmen; it was the old woman herself, and she hadn't intended to. She'd just been too sick to recall that among the flotsam and jetsam in her pockets—a handful of coins she'd gotten from Elena, a silk handkerchief she'd found in the palace, a small knife with a curved blade—was an item she knew to be incalculably valuable.

Elena, who all this time had been standing to the side, uncharacteristically quiet, sat down heavily on the old woman's cot and cursed in two different languages, because sometimes just one set of oaths wasn't enough.

The old woman whispered, "Do you remember what Barsilay told us about spices?"

"You mean that Maziks can't make them? Yes, I presume we'll

be eating food that tastes like old beans for the foreseeable future. If we're very lucky."

"No," she said quietly. "About their value. Worth their weight in gold in the mortal world, and doubly so here." And from her pocket, she produced a glass jar, filled with red filaments and labeled in Mazik. "I took this from the kitchen in the palazzo in Zayit."

It was saffron. A great deal of it.

Even in the mortal realm, that one jar would have been worth a fortune. And if it had been worth double in the Mazik world, that was before Zayit and its trading stock had been burnt to ash. She'd picked it up on a whim, and having lived half her life as a beggar, she did what beggars always did—she kept it on her person, because one did not risk leaving one's treasure unguarded.

Elena held the jar in both hands and said, "Don't tell them how you got it."

The old woman looked at her blankly and then said, "What do you mean, how I got it? Do they think old mortals just traipse around with such things in their pockets?"

Elena pushed the jar back into the old woman's hands and said again, "*Don't tell them how you got it.* If they find out it's stolen, they might try to take it back, and they might decide they have a better use for it. If it's yours, you get to decide what to do with it."

The old woman nodded. Efra, she was fairly sure, would insist on using the saffron to ransom Barsilay, but Efra was only one person and she lacked any real authority outside of Zayit. The Zayitis from the trade guilds she trusted not at all. She said, "How do I tell them I got it, then?"

"It doesn't matter—say you brought it with you from mortal Rimon, or say nothing at all. All that matters is they believe it is yours by rights."

And so Elena went off to find Efra and tell her the old woman had an asset she was willing to use, and there began the negotiation between Elena and the master of the Zayiti spice guild.

Chapter Four

Asmel found himself lost in a miasma of his own dark thoughts as he ruminated on how to help those dearest to him. Toba was beyond his aid, and truly, with each passing hour, he wondered if he would see her again, or if she would be lost to Aravoth forever. He had no idea what was inside Aravoth, or how long it would take her to find the Ziz, or if she would be able to control it once she did.

The sum of Barsilay's ransom was truly beyond imagination. Leaving the raising of it to two mortals and Efra seemed like dereliction, but they'd reminded him—often—that he was a scholar and knew nothing about money or trade. Oughtn't he to occupy himself someplace he might actually do some good?

It rankled a bit to be dismissed, but they were correct, of course. He'd spent the better part of the current age in a mostly ruined castle, living off whatever money was left from his days running the university in Rimon, and spending it pretty much only on lentils. Maziks required very little to live, unless they were bent on profligacy. Most of their needs were met with magic. Clothes could be easily repaired or made over, lentils were cheap, and spices were unnecessary. A mortal and a Zayiti would know more about how to raise money than he did.

So he decided to think several steps ahead and make himself useful that way, and he set off to the University of P'ri Hadar.

As in Rimon, the university was outside of the city proper, in the hills where the stars were brighter, and it took Asmel 'til past midday to walk there. Given the temperate climate, the university featured several buildings linked by covered walkways. The buildings themselves featured large, lattice-edged windows designed to allow for as much light and air as possible in the classrooms, with two notable exceptions: at one end of the assembled buildings was the library of P'ri Hadar, an octagonal building with no windows at all, and on the other end was the observatory, topped with a glass dome where the roof would have been. It was here that Asmel set his steps.

He did not know the astronomers of P'ri Hadar; he'd been too long isolated and the distance too great. There were some he knew by reputation, and so he determined to ask after whomever might be available, among the blue-robed Maziks who were engaged in quiet conversations in the antechamber.

It struck him, suddenly, as unspeakably odd that among all the conversations he'd overheard that day—in the city, in the university—he'd heard no one mention the Zayiti refugees, nor had he heard a single person mention Tarses.

Plucking the sleeve of a student who had stopped to adjust the satchel over his shoulder, Asmel said, "I am searching for Lyor b'Sona. Do you know where I might find him?"

"He's likely upstairs in the orrery," the man said, indicating a hallway toward the back of the room, which Asmel followed to a curved staircase that led up to a massive circular observatory. The sight of it gave him a pang of homesickness, so much was it like his own: shelves along the walls with astrolabes and books and yellowing scrolls, the dome overhead revealing the impossibly blue P'ri Hadar sky, the stone floor set with a brass azimuth circle. A model of the heavens took up most of the room, rotating slowly as the planets went through their orbits. The moon had been magicked to show its phases along with its position, and if he watched it long enough he could see it glowing less and less as it waned away from full.

In the center of all this, tinkering over a sextant, was a black-haired man Asmel presumed to be Lyor, who glanced up at Asmel's approach and said, without malice, "I don't know you."

Not the politest of greetings, but astronomers were not generally known for their social graces, Asmel included. They spent too much time staring at the sky and too little making conversation. He said, "Forgive me, I am Asmel of Rimon."

"I believed you were dead?"

"Not just yet," Asmel said.

"Then you're very far from home." Lyor set the sextant on one of the nearby tables. "If you're looking for a position, though, there isn't one here. You should have stopped to ask in Zayit first."

Asmel did not know quite how to reply to this. None would know Zayit had burned; news could not have traveled so fast. But surely they knew about the siege? That had lasted weeks, and the Zayitis in P'ri Hadar would certainly have known about that. He said, "I'm sorry to bear the news, but Zayit has fallen."

Lyor stepped back, saying, "Why are you here?"

The man was being so deliberately cagey that Asmel wasn't sure continuing the conversation had any point to it. On the other hand, he'd come all that way, and he had little to lose besides more time. He said, "I am here to ask for aid in repairing the firmament."

Lyor laced his fingers together and asked, "What use has the firmament for mending?"

"Surely, you must know what is happening to the Dimah Sea," Asmel insisted. "You must have seen it rising with your own eyes."

Lyor's eyes cut away to the door. "I think you should go back to Rimon. The sea is not rising. You are mistaken."

Asmel took the man by the arm to the great window on the western side of the building. The university had enough elevation that they could see the ocean's edge on the horizon. Pointing at the double walls that stood between the city and the coast, he asked, "If the sea is not rising, why was a second wall constructed?"

Lyor then stepped so close to Asmel he could feel his breath on his cheek. "Listen to me now and then be silent. Of course we know about the firmament—do you know how many scholars went to prison for repeating what you have said?"

"The Queen does not want the gate replaced," Asmel surmised.

"Kasfia was in possession of the gate of Luz for nearly fifty years.

She could have replaced it; the scholars begged her to do so. She refused. She would do nothing that would return the rule of Luz. And she wanted to keep the book… You know of what I speak."

Of course Asmel knew the book, and Kasfia would have it still if Dawid ben Aron had not somehow stolen it back from her. How he had managed that was a question for another time.

"Now go," Lyor said, "before you and I both end up in prison or worse."

AFTER MUCH DELIBERATION and no small amount of shouting—which the old woman found so exhausting she actually fell asleep twice—Elena agreed to allow the trade guild to sell the saffron on the old woman's behalf and pay them a commission of fifteen percent. Elena had asked for ten, and the guild had asked twenty-five, and the discussion had gotten rather heated before Efra had intervened and asked what the devil the guild intended to do with the money if not to use it for the ransom or the good of the Zayiti refugees.

"You are the Savia della Mura," they had responded. "You have no authority over the guilds, and this is already a lower commission than we would ever accept."

"You would argue over money while your city lies in ash?" she demanded.

So they had agreed to fifteen percent.

The remaining problem was that the Zayitis were under obligation to the Queen. The only way to avoid her tariffs would be to sell the saffron in secret, and, further, to drive up the price before the saffron was sold. This, of course, would take time. The old woman had hoped they might be able to free Barsilay in a matter of days. Efra explained that it would, in fact, take weeks.

It was an interesting lesson for Elena, who by all accounts had known scholars and bankers but never traders, and had not understood 'til now the possibilities for manipulating a market. Over the course of the next few days, the Zayitis spread news of the city's destruction—and the inoperable status of Zayit's gate—while withholding the Queen's plan for creating her own market.

The next thing they did, at Elena's suggestion, was to begin making requests at local inns and bakeries and food stalls for foods from Zayit or Rimon that required the use of saffron. The Maziks who made those requests then helpfully supplied the recipes for these dishes: saffron-laden meatballs and saffron-coated eggplants and saffron-tinted rice, so yellow it might have been coated in gold dust (and cost nearly as much to produce). When the people of P'ri Hadar caught the scent of these new foods, they began to demand the same for themselves, creating a hunger for anything made with saffron.

The third thing the Zayitis did was to sell off all their remaining spices and luxury goods to the wealthiest in P'ri Hadar, who bought everything in a panic.

Then, they waited.

The old woman found herself unmoored by Naftaly's absence, even more than when they'd been separated in Zayit. There, at least, she'd known he was close, and she'd been busy trying to prevent Elena from falling into disaster with Rafeq and their various experiments. Now, though, there was little for her to do, besides wait for the Zayitis to sell her jar of saffron.

She did not care for the Zayitis. They were too much like an element she'd known in Rimon—the type of people who had never known suffering and felt greatly pained when it was pointed out in others. She was glad, actually, that Elena had exhorted her not to tell the Zayitis the saffron had been stolen. They probably would have found some other use for the money than ransoming Barsilay. It was useful, she thought, to have someone around who understood the darker impulses of other people.

The old woman's grandfather had been like that as well—he had found himself at the wrong end of so many situations it was a miracle he'd survived into his old age, but he'd never been in a position to use any of that understanding, and so instead, the fear and unhappiness had turned inward, leaving him broken from the strain of it. She'd spent much of her childhood at his knee, singing him all the songs she knew, because music seemed his only comfort. Singing had felt like her particular duty, and after he'd died—long before the burning of Savirra—she'd stopped, because singing had never felt particularly joyful to her, only like labor. She'd never had any grandchild to sing to *her*. The closest she'd come to comfort in her old age had been a blanket or an extra meatball from Naftaly, and now he was Hashem-knew-where—quite literally, as terrifying as that sounded.

She did not like to think about that too closely.

While the old woman waited for news from Efra and Elena, she allowed herself to wander, veiled, away from the grove toward the sea. There would be no Maziks there, she reasoned, and she might have a little time to clear her head. Sea air was said to be good for the lungs, at least for mortals.

The view was extraordinary, even to someone who had lived so long in picturesque Rimon. She walked between the buff stone wall of the city and the sea, the water so blue it might have been painted. She wondered what the Maziks thought of the view: a horizon full of beauty that would kill them if they touched it.

She was huffing then, probably she had overexerted herself, and she felt a little dizzy and decided to sit for a moment, lowering herself to the ground with a grunt. One did tire of old age. She resolved to sit for a quarter hour and then make her way back.

Only as the wind shifted, the smell of the air went from sweet ocean to something horrible—a stench she could only describe as rot—and she covered her face with her shawl.

A touch at her elbow took her attention from the sea. It was Asmel, who had come behind her, his silver hair blowing in the wind that rose with the tide. "What is that dreadful smell?" she asked him.

Asmel's face was very grim, and he said, "Something has washed up on the shore. Can you not see it?"

She couldn't see much, sitting on the sand, and Asmel helped her to her feet. Farther down, she could make out a large dark shape just out of range of the waves. "There are Maziks there," he said. "Can you return to the grove on your own? I would like to look closer."

The old woman had no wish to be left alone on the beach with whatever might be happening. "I'll go with you," she said, and she took his elbow and they walked closer to the dark shape. The smell was really quite horrible, and she pressed her face into Asmel's arm as they walked. "Do you hear it?" he asked her.

Strains of music, drifting on the wind. The Maziks were singing. It almost sounded like a psalm, one of the sadder ones. The shade in the old woman's ear seemed not to know the language they used, and though she strained to listen, she had no idea what they might be singing about. Why would Maziks come and sing by the sea? "It sounds like a lament," she told him.

Asmel stopped walking and let out a sound of dismay. "It is a lament," he told her. "Hashem help us."

"What? Whom do they lament?"

He said, "It is the Leviathan."

The old woman looked again at the dark shape. Now they'd come closer, she could see it was a great fish; its fin, turned skyward, was longer than Asmel was tall. It was covered in silver-blue scales that shined like the sea itself. "The Leviathan," she echoed, and trembled under Asmel's arm.

She was no scholar; she'd never studied. But she knew the stories from her grandfather, that the death of the Leviathan was meant to happen at the end of days. "How can it have died?" she asked.

"Look," he said, as the Maziks on the beach broke off singing. Some of them wept; she could hear them even from where she and Asmel stood. "It's been cut open."

She gasped a little. "Cut! Are you saying it was killed by a Mazik?"

"No Mazik could have done this," he said. "There is only one creature said to be able to kill the Leviathan."

"I've heard those stories," the old woman said. "The Shamir, you mean?" The Shamir was a creature with the power to cut through anything, given by Ashmodai to King Solomon in order to build the temple—according to her grandfather, anyway. "But it's a worm. How can it have done this on its own?" She began to cough again. The foul air was certainly not helping her lungs, and Asmel turned them both around and began walking back in the direction of the grove.

"The Shamir was rumored to be kept in a lead box by the Queen of Luz," he told her. "No one has seen it since the Fall." He cast a glance over his shoulder. "It seems someone found it. Or else has had it all this time."

"But what use could there be in killing the Leviathan?"

Asmel said, "I don't know."

The wind shifted again, and the air cleared, but the old woman was still too weak. She'd walked too far, fool of a thing, and she had to stop and catch her breath. "I will carry you," Asmel told her. "What were you thinking, coming all the way down here alone?"

"You go places alone," she grumped, as he settled her weight on his back. "Do you think I do not also wish for a bit of peace now and then?"

He straightened again. He really was tall and strong and rather handsome. If she'd been prone to that sort of thing, she'd probably be half in love with him now, carrying her on the beach and not even complaining about it. "Did you find the astronomers?" she asked. "Will they help you?"

"There wasn't much help to be had there," he said. "This city is not much better than Rimon." He looked out at the water. "I fear P'ri Hadar will suffer the same fate as Zayit. The men here are either too complacent or too cowed to plan for what is coming."

"Well," she replied, "Zayit planned, and it burned regardless. There is no way to fight those flame demons."

"No, there isn't. But I do wonder if there might be a way to unmake them." Asmel watched the sea for so long the old woman thought he'd retreated into his own mind, ending the conversation. But then he said, "We need a way to reach Rafeq."

Rafeq! "Isn't he quite dead?"

"He was killed by the killstone, so his was a dreaming death. He could still help us from the dream-world, if we could reach him."

"Can't *you* reach him?"

Asmel said, "Reaching the dead in the dream-world is not so simple; they must wish to be found, and Rafeq despised me. He might speak to Barsilay or Toba, for Marah's sake. But we don't know when Toba will return, or how long it will take us to get Barsilay out of prison. There is one person I'm sure he would speak to, if she could reach him."

"Elena, you mean? But she only dreams like a regular person."

Asmel was very quiet again, thinking the deep thoughts of an ancient Mazik, and then he said, "Do you happen to have any salt?"

Picking her way across the landscape of Aravoth, Toba found herself continually turning her face toward the dark place on the horizon.

"Stop looking that way," Nehama snapped. "You'll go blind or worse."

"How can one go blind from darkness?"

"Because it isn't darkness!" Toba had turned toward the offending space again, and Nehama put her hands on either side of Toba's face and turned her away. "It's not *nothing* that you see. It's so much that your eyes, your mind, can't take it all in, and it begins to burn away at you—that is the darkness you think you see. And it calls you, I know, but you must not look at it, not ever, even through your eyelids, even through a blindfold. You are more than half-Mazik, and so it is worse for you."

They walked again, only a few paces, and then Nehama said, "Stop. You tripped there."

Toba stopped, but said, "Who tripped there?"

"You did. You will."

"Which do you mean?"

"One. Both. Don't step there."

Toba felt Naftaly take her arm and lead her around… something. "Was there something there?" she whispered.

"Not that I saw," he said. "She's been here a long time."

At that, Nehama laughed. "A long time, indeed. And yet I know not how long, because there is no time here. No sun rises or sets, there are no dreams. I tried counting the seconds once, and after fifteen I counted three and I don't even know why."

"What are you saying?" Toba asked, a little crossly, because she was still feeling poorly and now she had a prickling feeling beneath her skin like she was being stuck with needles, and she rubbed at her forearms to try to will the sensation away.

"If time exists in this place, it isn't as we know it."

"That cannot be," Toba argued. "We arrived, and I was ill, and then you came, and now here we are. It's all perfectly linear."

"It seems so, doesn't it? And yet I've seen Naftaly lead you around that stone twice now."

"There was no stone," Naftaly said.

"Wasn't there?"

"No," he said. "Where are you taking us?"

"Where did you want to go?"

"To find the Ziz!" Toba said. "Only you haven't told us where she is. Or if you even know."

"Yes," Nehama said. "Yes, that's where we're going." She sighed and Naftaly pulled Toba to a halt. "I think we'd better sit down for a while. Eat something."

"I don't think—" Toba began, but Naftaly said, "Toba, I can see what's ahead."

Coming from Naftaly, she was not sure whether that meant he could see where they were going in the literal sense, or if he could envision it with his prescience. But she allowed herself to be sat down on the hard ground and then one of them—she was not sure who—handed her some sour-tasting bread and a flask of water and some fruit that tasted like nothing she'd ever eaten before. When they'd rested for what seemed like far too long, Naftaly asked, "Why have you remained here all these years? Do not all the gates open each month? Surely you could have found one of them."

"There is no sun here, nor moon," Nehama said. "The light is always the same. There is no way to count time, nor to navigate, and the gates move here as in the mortal world, but faster. And in this light when the gates do open, they aren't easily seen unless you are very close. I have been wandering all this time, hoping to be close enough to a gate to see one when it opened. But I have never been able to do it."

"You've been alone here, all this time? Could not the angels have helped you?"

"The angels are watching," Nehama told them, "but they don't speak to me."

"How do you know they are watching?"

"I hear them sometimes. And there's this." She opened the pouch at her hip, which was filled with lentils. "Fabric doesn't wear here, so I've never had to replace this. But the lentils never run out, nor does my water. I can only assume that's the angels."

"If they want to make sure you don't starve, why not help you find a gate and leave?"

"I don't know. Don't think I haven't asked. I shouted at them, in the beginning, but they don't answer me, not ever, and in case you are wondering you don't have proper dreams here, either. I have mortal dreams, about places I have been and people I used to know. Nothing more."

Toba had never had a mortal dream, and wondered what it might be like—an echo of some earlier day, perhaps, or of a wish or a fear. She felt herself tipping into it, the dream, and sleep, and then Nehama pushed against her shoulder and said, "Wake up."

"What is wrong with her?" Naftaly asked.

"Too much Mazik," Nehama said. "We should keep moving. I've positioned us so that the dark place is behind us, and we needn't walk in that direction again. But you must resist the urge to look."

"All right," Toba said, but still, the admonition irked her. Hadn't Naftaly looked? It seemed unfair that he should have seen while she should not. She, who was so much cleverer, and who might hope to understand what was there.

"Toba," Naftaly warned. "I see your thoughts. Don't."

"You have looked."

"I haven't," he said. "I don't wish to."

"That is a lie."

"It's the truth," he said. "Look what's before you instead."

In fact, now that her eyes worked more or less normally, she found she was able to focus on what was in front of them—off to their right was a forest, so vast she could not see beyond the mass of strange, stone trees. Some phantom wind blew through them, creating a sound like a rough sea. And looming in their midst, one tree rose higher than all the others—a spire of a great tree, ten times taller than the rest, and ten times as big around—a behemot of a tree. "What is that?" Toba whispered.

Nehama craned her own neck back, taking in the vast tree, and said, "When the Ziz arrived here, she came to this forest, and she watered the trees with her tears. That tree grew tallest. And that is where the Ziz resides."

Toba scanned up to the top of the tree, so high she could scarcely imagine it. The tree was smooth and branchless for most of its span. It was unclimbable by any normal means, and she could think of no magic that might help them. The prickling in her skin had grown worse, and Toba rubbed her arms again, feeling the sensation now in her neck and face.

She was consumed with a longing so great her eyes filled with tears, though for what she could not have said.

Chapter Five

Barsilay was well acquainted with the crushing weight of claustrophobia from his time in La Cacería's prison, and his mind slid back into the old horror of it almost immediately—he wanted air, badly, and the sky, and the voice of another person. The lack of dreams made the situation even more difficult to tolerate; there was nothing for him but the cold walls of his cell and stale air that had never tasted a breeze. He tried to visualize some other vista—his childhood home in Luz, Asmel's garden in Rimon, a hillside looking down to the sea, with grass blowing in a dreamworld wind and Naftaly beside him, his face reflecting the stars. It did little to ease his mounting anxiety. What he wanted most of all was not to be alone.

Well, he wasn't really alone. There were the demons.

He wished he'd made more of an effort to befriend Rafeq, back in Luz. He might have given him some useful advice for dealing with the demons, or befriending them, or not being lit on fire by them. But Rafeq had always made him uneasy, and he'd mostly avoided the man. He was too much motivated by puzzles and possibilities; a darker mirror of Asmel, he sometimes thought.

Barsilay was not sure what hell there would be to pay for making deals with the catlike creatures in the dungeons of P'ri Hadar, but that course had been set when he'd treated with the demons in the Gal'in, and there was no going back. He supposed he was short enough on allies not to be overly picky.

At least no one had been in to torture or question him. Food continued to arrive twice a day (or so he presumed, having no way to mark the time besides the hourglass of his stomach). It had been, he believed, seven days since he'd been taken, and that morning he'd been gifted with a pail of water to wash himself, a luxury he could not have imagined in the Cacería prison.

Stripping down to his skin, he heated the water and splashed himself with his hands—there was no soap and he had nothing to make into any besides his treasured lentils, so he wasn't precisely clean, but at least he could imagine he was. After rinsing out his clothes and leaving them to dry, he took two saved-up lentils and made one into a round of very bland cheese and another into a round of bread. Satisfied, he sat down naked on the cold stone floor to enjoy his feast before the rats showed up.

He'd eaten a third of his meal when one of the demon-cats slid through the wall and sat down across from him. It did not speak, but thrashed its tail, rather like a real cat would have done. Barsilay tore off a large chunk of the cheese and slid it over. The demon sniffed it and then ate it slowly as Barsilay finished his bread, and then it proceeded to clean its whiskers.

Barsilay was not sure how to approach this creature, and did not even know if it was one of the demons he'd spoken with earlier. Did it matter? That they were all the same being was their consistent point; what that really meant, Barsilay had no idea. Did they share knowledge? No, that could not be, or else they would not have left to seek answers to Barsilay's questions; they could have simply asked the demons near Zayit to look for Saba. How convenient that might have been.

Finally, the demon said, "You are dull, Heir of Luz, and your cheese is tasteless as the dust on your boots."

"Accept my pardon for the lack of conversation," Barsilay said. "I did not wish to trouble you while you were eating. As to the quality of the food—well, I will not argue. The cheese was mediocre."

"Your kingship will likewise be mediocre," the demon said.

"How optimistic you are," Barsilay replied, "given my current circumstances, naked and alone in this prison."

"But you are not alone," the demon said. "We are here."

"Yes," Barsilay said, "and I thank you for that—"

"And you do not even ask us about the task you set us! You do not even ask!"

"Forgive me, I wasn't certain you were the same—"

"We are all the same! There is no one or the other, there is only us, you fool of a Mazik!"

This was going poorly. Barsilay had little experience with demons and no idea how one avoided insulting one. Better, probably, to be blunt, since his attempts at politeness were all failing. "Give me your news," he said. "I presume you've found something, else you would not have come here."

The cat had lost its shape and turned into a shadow with waving claws. It was agitated, and it hissed inarticulately. Barsilay took the remains of his drinking water, turned it to milk, and pushed it toward the demon. "Drink, if you are weary," he said, and the demon turned back into a cat and drained the bowl. "Now, what have you found, friend?"

"Friend," the demon repeated. "Friend, we found your friend, but he doesn't trust us."

Barsilay could hardly believe it. Quelling his eagerness, he said, "Do you mean to tell me you found Saba?"

"We found him," they said. "We found him, the Caçador has him in a place like this, but we found him."

"In Zayit?"

"No," they said. "Not in Zayit, Tarses has gone on to Anab, and taken Saba with him. Saba the Great, who healed the Caçador when he would have bled out on the ground."

Saba would not have healed Tarses even to save his own life, and Barsilay asked, "Why?"

"Because," the demon said, "the Caçador knows his name. Foolish Maziks and their names. Why even have one, when it can be used so? What is their purpose, but to be ill-used?"

How Tarses learned Saba's name was irrelevant; he must have tricked him out of it, or else traded him for something, though nothing Barsilay could imagine. He'd forced Saba into his service—Saba, the greatest doctor in Zayit, and possibly in Mazikdom itself—and that was a disaster no matter how Tarses had done it. "Did Saba give you some message?"

"Saba does not trust us," the demon said again. "And Saba is being watched besides. There was no message. None but this—" And the demon stood up on its back legs, resting its shadowy claws against the stone wall, and from inside itself it pulled out a scroll, which it cast at Barsilay's feet.

Barsilay carefully unrolled it. The paper was thin as onion skin, and it crackled in his hands. It appeared blank at first glance, but he passed his hand over it, putting out a little magic, and a series of symbols appeared there, written in blue light.

"This is the message Saba would consent to give us, under the eyes of the Hounds that watch him."

"He wrote this for you?"

"Saba is doing more than healing," the demon said. "He is doing things, and he is writing, and he is always, always watched. This he wrote down and this we bring to you."

"How do you know it was intended for me?"

"Look closer, Heir of Luz."

Barsilay put his eyes very near the scroll. There were many lines of symbols he did not recognize; they were neither Mazik writing nor any human script he knew. But the very first, in the upper right corner, was a pictograph of an almond.

It was a cypher, and it was meant for Barsilay.

But he had no idea how to read it.

ELENA HAD SPENT the day sitting with Efra, hoping to hear news of the sale of the saffron (which had, in fact, not been sold just yet, as the Zayitis were hoping to sweat out the adons of P'ri Hadar and thereby drive the price up further). She was strained from having had no word from Toba, nor Naftaly, nor Barsilay. But she ruminated most of all on Alasar, her husband on the other side of the world in Petgal, who certainly thought she was dead.

She missed him more than she would have thought possible. His rough hands, gnarled by arthritis, and his gentle wit. What he would make of the person she had become was anyone's guess, but Elena had to admit he probably would have found her transformation rather amusing.

Later that evening, after Asmel had returned from visiting the university, he pulled her outside where they could speak privately. He was troubled, and there was a line between his eyebrows she did not recall having seen before, which disappeared when she pointed it out.

"I'm only thinking," he said as they walked out of the encampment, "I feel I'm trapped in a farce. How many died in Zayit, do you suppose?"

"I could not say," Elena admitted.

"Nor I," Asmel told her. "Thousands. All but the few in this camp. Tarses will come here, too, eventually. And the Queen isn't doing a thing to stop him."

"What do you think will happen, when he gets here?"

"Kasfia will never surrender to him," he told her.

"So you think he'll burn P'ri Hadar, too."

Asmel nodded grimly, then removed something from his pocket and presented it to Elena. It was the remaining shard of his safira, the bit of his own magic that Atalef had failed to process because he'd run out of salt to break it down. Elena turned it over in her palm. It was the same blue as the safira Toba had worn in her amulet most of her life, and it was warm and alive against her skin.

"I have been considering," Asmel said, "how best to use this."

"It's yours," Elena said. "Don't you want it back?"

"I do, of course," he said. "There are memories and power there I would rather not do without. But there is a greater purpose at stake than what I wish for myself." Here he met Elena's eyes. "We have few allies. Our strongest are in Aravoth. And we need someone who can dream to Rafeq, someone he might help."

"You want me to take this?" she asked.

"You were prepared to take all of Marah's magic," Asmel reminded her. "This is but a fraction of mine. Enough to dream, but perhaps not much else. Though with your mortal magic, you might be able to do more."

She considered this. For most of her life, she had longed for the dream-world, since her own mother had explained it to her and young Elena had realized that, sadly, she lacked the ability to dream there, too. She said, "My mother died in her sleep."

"Did she dream?" When Elena nodded, he said, "Then she is there, somewhere."

Elena turned the shard in her palm. "It is not only a matter of my accepting this. It will take a good deal of salt, and the machine Rafeq and I used to break down Marah's safira was no small task to construct. And I don't trust the Zayitis to help with either."

Asmel said, "How much salt?"

They'd had twenty pounds on hand to process Marah's safira, but they hadn't used it all and she hadn't had time to measure what they'd had leftover. Moreover, she could not be sure of the weight of what was in her hand. Less than a quarter of the full safira, surely. A tenth? A twelfth? "Without a balance, I can't be sure," she said. "My best guess would be one or two pounds, but you are forgetting something important… This will result in more of the decayed salt. I believe you objected rather strongly to my producing it before."

"I did," Asmel said. "I don't believe we have a choice."

"Then what do you propose we do with the decayed salt once we've made it?"

"Bury it," he said. "Far from the city. I won't risk Tarses getting any more of it, and I don't trust the Queen with it, either."

"As you say," she said, somewhat unconvinced. "What about the salt?"

There was no money to buy it, even if someone would be willing to sell it to them. And when Elena suggested distilling it from seawater, Asmel forbade it. "You'd be too visible from the city," he said. "If anyone were to see you, you'd be arrested at once."

"I could go at night," Elena suggested.

"It's too great a risk," Asmel said. "We can't afford to have another of us in prison, and the Zayitis wouldn't give two lentils to ransom you out. You'd be there 'til you die."

Wasn't that a pleasant thought. "What do you propose, then? We just find some salt lying around?"

"Not lying around," he said. "But there could be a deposit somewhere near the city, someplace you might go without being seen. I thought you could use that locator spell that's been so helpful."

"That only works on people."

"You used it on the gate of Luz," he reminded her.

"But that book has a name. What you want me to find is just salt. It would be like looking for dirt or… or… air."

"In the mortal world, maybe. But here?"

"The sea is still full of salt! Honestly, are you sure all your wits have returned?"

Asmel harrumphed a few times, and then said, "I'd have thought you more creative than this."

"You want me to make up a new spell? Why can't you do it?"

"Because I already tried it," he admitted. "It didn't work. Perhaps my magic is unable to find something capable of destroying it—the point is, I can't do it, and I'd like you to try, because the alternative is you risking death or imprisonment."

Elena said, "Your way does sound better," and then she thought about her spell for finding people and her spell for making a little of something go just a bit farther in the kitchen, and she said, "Like seeks like. If I had a little salt, I think I could use that to find more. But I haven't got any."

"Well," Asmel said, "you have your tears."

Elena was slightly peeved she hadn't thought of that, but then she asked, "Does that mean your tears have no salt?"

Asmel laughed a little. Crouching, he took a dried leaf and smoothed it on the ground between them. "Since our eyes aren't all shriveled and blackened, it does mean that."

"But—"

"Think of something very sad," he said, transforming the leaf into a map.

Of course, Elena had plenty to weep over. But she'd long ago trained herself away from the habit of crying, or else she'd have been unable to go on more than once. She thought of Toba, of Alasar. Of Penina.

None of it worked, and it frightened her a little how calloused her heart had become, that she could not even weep over the memory of her dead daughter.

Finally, she had to admit defeat. "I need more than sadness," she said. "Do you have any lentils?"

"Do you think you're more likely to weep on a full stomach?"

"Of course not," she said. "I want you to make me an onion. A strong one."

He did so. Elena sat on the ground and held the cut onion between her eyes for a few moments, 'til she was rewarded with a stream of tears from both eyes. She let them fall onto the table, wishing her eyes were not bleary from the onion because it was hard to see what was happening as she recited her little rhyme. "If my tears all go toward the sea, this was a waste of an onion," she told Asmel.

"I didn't include the sea on the map," he said as she scrubbed at her eyes. "I started with— Look."

The tears had begun to slide over the surface, one of them moving away from their current location, and then stopping on a point Elena knew from experience was the Queen's palace. "Stands to reason," she told him. "But it doesn't help us if that's all there is."

In fact, most of the other tears had slid toward the palace as well, adhering themselves into a single drop. But one tiny teardrop had moved first into the city, then slid though it and settled well beyond the wall.

"What's there?" Elena asked. "Your map shows nothing."

Asmel said, "I don't know what might be there. A natural deposit, perhaps? I don't see what else it could be. Whatever it is, it's a smaller amount than in the palace."

"Could someone have hidden some salt there? Is it safe for us to go looking about?"

"We'll be cautious," Asmel said. "We should set out soon, so we can return before it gets dark."

Elena and Asmel made their way past the city's eastern wall. There was little there but lentil farms, and so early in the year those were all barren. It was a cold evening and Elena's breath came out in little puffs; Asmel, who was naturally a warmer creature, looked a little like a dragon exhaling steam in comparison.

The map had shown the salt about an hour's walk outside the

city, and as they came to the top of a hill, they could see an edifice atop the crest of the next hill beyond them—a long-abandoned stone building with a domed roof and a bell tower. Maziks and their ruins. Though these particular ruins looked more modest than those she'd seen elsewhere, which is to say, nothing was tall. The building would not have been out of place in the mortal world.

"What is that?" Elena asked, as Asmel had taken to running his finger over his lip in the way he did when he was troubled—which is to say, rather often.

"You lived in Rimon all your life. What do you think it is?"

Maziks and their riddles, as if it would be too much trouble to say, "It's a bathhouse," or something along those lines. Elena pondered the bell tower, which seemed empty, though at their current distance she supposed it might not be. Or maybe the bell rang by magic. "It looks like a church," she said.

"Yes," Asmel said. "Doesn't it?"

"Are there Christian Maziks?"

"Not that I've ever been aware of," he said. "I'm not sure which is odder, that it was constructed in the first place or that it's abandoned now."

"Do you think it's perhaps something else? It could be anything, couldn't it? Just because it happens to look like a church to people living on the other side of the sea doesn't mean it is one."

"That is true," Asmel said.

"Do you think it's safe to go in?"

"I don't think it's occupied," he said. "I will have to be careful for any salt that might be there, but I don't think anyone will notice our coming or going. The lentil farmers aren't even here this time of year. They'll all have gone into the city to celebrate the end of the harvest."

So Elena followed him toward the church which, once they were closer, turned out to have another, lower building behind it, all surrounded by overgrown land that had once been a garden. Asmel made himself a walking stick out of a twig and picked at some of the overgrowth, coming to some ceramic oblongs sitting on stands. Stopping to ask Elena's opinion before continuing, he broke one open with his stick, only to find it full of dust. "What in the name…?" he muttered, and then went to break open the next before Elena stopped him.

"I know what these are," she said. "They're beehives."

"Bees do not make ceramic objects," Asmel told her flatly.

"The bees didn't make them! People make the hives and then introduce the bees. It's so they can farm their honey."

This explanation did little to satisfy Asmel, who said, "Maziks do not farm honey. We make it from water."

Elena took one of the broken shards and sniffed it, then carefully touched the tip of her tongue to it. "It's sweet," she said. "Maybe this was someone's hobby? Or else they were trying to pass the honey off as mortal-made in the market. There seemed to be a fetish for that sort of thing back in Zayit."

"That could be," Asmel said, and took his stick and went into the low building, which consisted of many rooms linked together in a series, surrounding a central courtyard which was as overgrown as the garden outside. The rooms were full of heavy furniture in various states of decay, and eventually they came to an especially long room filled with a row of narrow beds. The linens had fallen to rags and everything was covered in dust.

"This is a dormitory," Elena told Asmel, if he were having trouble working it out for himself. "This was a monastery at one time. I should have guessed from the bees."

"Maziks do not produce monastics," Asmel said. "Celibacy is no virtue among us. Who were these people? And why is this still here?"

"Maziks seem to do a number of things you insist they do not," Elena said. "But where do you suppose the salt is? And what would Mazik monks have been doing with poison?"

They did not wonder long. Through the next set of doors was what had been the monastery's great hall, where the monks—or nuns, possibly—would have taken their meals together. Wooden tables in two rows ran the length of the room.

At the front of the room were some dozen skeletons, their clothes disintegrated to scraps; the flesh had departed ages ago. Asmel used his cuff to cover his mouth and nose, but there was no smell Elena could detect.

"The salt," he said through his sleeve. "They were poisoned with salt."

"Go back out," she told him. "I'll see what I can do."

Asmel hurried back through the door, and Elena sighed as she approached the bones of the Maziks who had lived in this place, keeping bees and praying and doing other things that were decidedly unMazik-like. Was that why they'd been murdered, for practicing a religion apart from the rest of them?

But why let them build the monastery at all, then, in plain view of the city? It made no sense.

The salt was everywhere, on the bones, on the ground—what of it hadn't blown away in the intervening years. She wasn't sure it would be enough for their needs, and she certainly did not want to dust salt off the bones of murdered Maziks, but she recited her rhyme while she carefully—and apologetically—ran the little whisk broom Asmel had made her around the ground, and was able to sweep perhaps half a cupful into the glass jar Asmel had given her, which she sealed with a cork before going back out of the room.

She showed him the jar. "This is what was left."

"Will it be enough?"

"It might," she said. "There must be something we can do for these people. Can we bury them?"

"It would be dangerous for me and impossible for you," he said. "I'm sorry to say it. In any case, it will be dark soon, and we need to return."

But Elena could not just leave them all, so she went back out to the garden and gathered a pailful of small stones, which she brought back inside and scattered over the bones, saying a prayer these Maziks would not have recognized, but it was all she knew for burying the dead.

As they walked back to the city in the dwindling light, Asmel said, "The only person in P'ri Hadar with enough salt at hand to pour out over a dozen Maziks is the Queen herself."

"They must have run afoul of her somehow," Elena said.

Asmel was quiet as they walked up the next hill and down it again, and then he said, "There are rumors about Kasfia. I never put much stock in them, but now I wonder."

"What sorts of rumors?"

"That she's mad."

"And why did you discount them?"

"It seemed unlikely to me that a mad woman could rule a city as prosperous as P'ri Hadar for an entire age."

"I've wondered about that, too," Elena said. "If Mazik history follows the Mirror, how has P'ri Hadar had the same queen since the Fall? Do you know how often it's changed hands in the mortal world?"

"I do," Asmel said. "And that is one of the great mysteries of Mazikdom. The belief is that she's ruled so ruthlessly that none could oppose her, and none try."

"And the rumors of madness? It's entirely possible to be both ruthless and mad." Elena stepped around a rock in the road. "But ultimately does it matter? Once Barsilay is king of all the Maziks, all the current monarchs are out on their ears anyway."

"Barsilay cannot be King unless we raise Luz, and we can't raise Luz without the Queen. I'd hoped to appeal to her logically; the city is against the sea, and the Maziks here know it's rising. But they are forbidden to discuss it, so I can't even make the argument."

Elena shook her head. "If we can't appeal to her logically, we're going to have to offer her something she wants."

Asmel said, "You are probably correct. And whatever it is she wants, I have a feeling we aren't going to like it."

THE TREE LOOMED before Naftaly, dwarfing the rest of the forest, the landscape, himself. The wind sounded like it had in the Gal'in, like a running river mixed with the hiss of demons… He mentally shook himself. There were no demons here. There were no people here, nor Maziks. There were only angels, and his companions, and the Ziz. He felt like a thorn stuck in the side of some fantastical beast, like he'd come there by accident and in a moment someone would realize and pluck him out. He felt wholly unworthy of the task before him.

His vision turned inward, to a great bird with an eye the size of a wagon wheel, and a voice saying, "*Either you will succeed, or she will kill you.*" This time, he knew the voice: It was Nehama.

For the first time, he felt a terrible, terrifying urge to look into the darkness.

"Don't," Nehama said.

Naftaly stilled himself as best he could and asked again, "What is there in the dark place?"

"I don't know. I can't know," she said. "Stop asking. What we are meant to know, we know." She gestured ahead. "You can barely comprehend that tree! You have seen a thousand trees, and that one eludes you only because of its size. If your mind gawps at a tall tree, you think to know what is in that darkness? Stop looking. Stop asking."

Toba said, "I don't believe you. I won't believe you never looked."

"Why did you come here?" Nehama snapped. "I am trying to help you. The Ziz is at the top of the great tree. Not in the dark place."

"It's unclimbable," Toba whispered. "We will have to fly up."

"There's no way to do that," Naftaly said. "Can we lure the Ziz down?"

"Have you something she wants?"

Naftaly shook his head. Then he said, "Are you well?" because, once again, Toba was rubbing at her arms, and this time she was not stopping. Nehama said, "Show me."

Toba allowed Nehama to pull back her sleeve, which revealed black pinpricks all along her arm. Naftaly gasped, "What is that?"

Toba whispered, "Feathers," and as they watched, they continued to push through her skin 'til they were as long as fingernails. Naftaly said, "What is happening to her?"

Nehama said, "What is your name?"

"Toba Peres. I am Toba Peres."

Nehama looked startled, but then she shook Toba a little by the shoulders. "No," she demanded, "what is your *name*?"

Toba said, "I am Tsifra N'Dar."

Nehama whispered, "The Splendid Bird?" and turned her head slightly toward the dark place before correcting herself. Then she looked back to Naftaly and said, "Did you know this?"

"Did I know what? Her name? Of course not. I don't even know my own."

Nehama said, "You gave yourself this name? Why?"

"My ancestor gave it to me," Toba said strangely. "Marah. It was"—she gasped at the pain of the feathers—"part of a spell. It hurts. I've become birds before. It never hurt."

"You are becoming your name. Your nature is changing, and not as it did before, with some temporary magic. You are becoming a Ziz."

"How can I stop it?" Toba begged.

"You can't," Nehama told her. "Open a gate and go back through, leave Naftaly to find the Ziz. Save yourself."

Toba said, "This task is mine." She gasped, drawing a deep breath and shuddering.

"Toba!" Naftaly cried, taking out the book and beginning to read, as Nehama urged him to hurry.

Before he could read three lines, Toba screamed, and feathers sprouted forth all at once: blue-green and shining and terrible. Naftaly's voice cut off. He felt as if he were seeing the world from some strange new vantage. The book in his hands was hot as flame, the air became a glittering mist, and the ground beneath his feet began to swirl. He squeezed his eyes shut against it, and when he opened them again, the air was air, the ground was ground, and Toba, covered in feathers, met his eyes and whispered, "Naftaly."

Her face contorted, her body grew, and there was no Toba.

A great bird, a Ziz, remained. Her clothing torn, her eye the size of a wagon wheel, she looked at Naftaly and shrieked.

"Keep reading!" Nehama ordered him. "If we can put her through the gate, she may yet regain herself."

But then Toba flew away, toward the dark place. Naftaly cried out in dismay.

"Calm yourself," Nehama told him.

"But she's going exactly where you said she could not! We'll have to go after her!"

Nehama shouted, "How?"

Naftaly did not know how. Toba was already nearly out of sight. But he'd lost her before back in Rimon, when she'd gone through the gate leaving him behind. This seemed infinitely worse. He was not even sure there was a Toba left to save. "I cannot abandon my friend," he said.

Nehama's face took on a pained expression, and she turned away, before saying, "We can't go after her on foot. But if we had the Ziz, perhaps we could try."

Naftaly watched Toba's shape disappear into the trees. "Yes," he said. "Yes, all right. But— But how can we climb that tree?"

She said, "It's climbable if you know how. Hurry now."

So Naftaly hurried after her through the stone trees, aware that every moment Toba was getting farther away. He kept his eyes on the tallest tree—the Ziz's tree—and though his mind stretched backward, he kept moving toward it.

And then, very suddenly, what Naftaly saw before him was not the tree, nor Toba, but Barsilay, dressed in embroidered silk, his brow furrowed with worry. And beside him was a woman Naftaly did not know, wearing a diadem of golden stones. Naftaly felt himself reach for Barsilay, and stop, and ask, "Who is this?" And Barsilay did not answer, but in some part of his mind Naftaly knew who it must be, who stood at Barsilay's side while Barsilay stood silent and bereft, offering no word of comfort.

Nehama pulled him from the vision, his breath burning in his chest, and he was very angry because he wanted to see Barsilay, to hear his explanation, and to understand whether this was now or next year or a hundred years from now. Swallowing the dryness in his throat, he took a deep breath, and then another, and wondered helplessly if his vision had been a version of the future in which they had succeeded, or in which they had failed.

***

TSIFRA LEFT MANSANAR in the hands of the Queen's advisors and reunited with her fleet in Zayit. From there, they'd sailed to Anab, which had surrendered immediately rather than suffer the same fate as her earlier conquest. The taking of Anab had been so bloodless she hardly knew what to do with herself, but she offered the terms Tarses had given her: Sefarad would have ultimate power over the city, but the Anabis would carry out its day-to-day administration, handing off their taxes, and providing however many horses, ships, and men Tsifra requested.

It all seemed very contrived to her, a transfer of power without a proper battle. She was set to leave a small garrison and a troop of administrators in the city to sort everything out.

As she now resembled the Queen of Sefarad and not herself, her men did not recognize her as the angel who had helped them take Zayit, and Tsifra thought this might be for the best; let that character remain the stuff of legends. It also meant that as the Queen of Sefarad, she could not fight without causing considerable confusion, as it was well known the Queen was no warrior.

She felt somewhat limited by the constrictions of her new role, but at least it meant she would no longer be at risk of losing control of herself and her more violent impulses, as she had in Zayit.

Instead, she was the wise, devout Queen who would not be trifled with, but who showed mercy to those who deserved it. Zayit had resisted and had been punished. Anab had surrendered and been left whole. Tarses's hope was that Habush would witness this and elect to follow Anab into her empire if not happily, at least willingly. Mortal Habush had only recently changed hands. It stood to reason many in the city would not be loyal to their new Sultan and might be unwilling to fight for him.

Still, she did not trust the Anabis enough to sleep in their palace. Nor could she stay on her ship, because she would not be able to dream while on the sea. Instead, she snuck out of the city alone, dressed as if she were still only the Courser, and into the hills, near the spot where the Rimonis were building the church she had ordered. It was still only a foundation, but she'd needed so few soldiers to hold the city that she'd assigned extra men to its construction and, on the suggestion of her advisors, expanded its footprint. It would be a great site, they told her. And the relic of the patron saint of Anab, once housed in the city's greatest church, would be moved here.

Every night, she used magic to add a little to the construction—a few layers of stone, the beginnings of the bell tower. She could have completed it already, but dragging it out seemed more effective: instead of one miracle, there was one every night. Each morning, the workmen would arrive and marvel that more had been done the day prior than they could account for.

An hour's walk from this, Tsifra had made herself a small stone house, raised with magic from the rocky soil, left rustic enough that it might have been a hut for a goatherd. It had a single room with a low ceiling, a dirt floor, and a soft bed she'd made from a pile of leaves. It was upon this that she allowed herself to sleep.

Tsifra had been unable to dream of Tarses for more than a week. She did not know if this meant he might be too occupied to sleep, or if something might have happened to him. She had tried to dream of the Peregrine and failed that, too, and then Tsidon, and when even that failed, she had begun to worry.

Perhaps, she thought, someone had remained in Zayit who could tell her what had become of Tarses. But when she tried to dream of the city, it was as if it had been wiped clean from the dream-world entirely, and only marshland remained. Not a single Mazik was anywhere she could find.

The city had fallen, and there had been no survivors. But where was Tarses?

She dreamed back to Anab and walked the streets long enough to realize that it was full of Maziks, but they were all in hiding. She knocked on one door, and another, and then on the third the answer came, "You have killed our King and you have taken our city, but you shall not have our dreams."

Tsifra considered breaking the door down, which would have been within her power, but thought better of it. She had learned what she needed to know: La Cacería had come to Mazik Anab and it had fallen alongside its mortal counterpart, which meant that Tarses was decidedly alive. Why she could not find him was another matter. Why was he not looking for her?

She walked away from the center of the deserted city, toward the sea. The sky in dream-Anab was different than the sky she was used to—she'd never before been so far east, and the stars were unfamiliar as she watched them spin overhead. She considered staying atop the hill overlooking the sea for the rest of the night, watching those strange stars, when below her, near the shore, she saw a dark shape on the sand.

There was a Mazik lying there, and a sense of familiarity pricked her mind, so she went to them.

Tarses lay on the beach, the water licking at his bare feet, stretched out on his back. He was undressed above the waist, revealing an angry wound in his shoulder. White scar tissue spiraled around it—someone had healed this wound, and skillfully, too.

She knelt at Tarses's side, as his open eyes were only on the stars above.

"At last," he said.

"I have been trying to find you," she said. "For days."

"I have not dreamt in days," he said, without turning his head. He lifted his right hand and moved it over the wound on his shoulder. "I lost a great deal of blood."

"Who could have done such a thing?" she asked, and Tarses's face went very stony, and he gave no answer.

"Where are you?" he asked.

"Here," she said. "Anab. I have taken the city. It was bloodless."

He took his hand from his shoulder and encircled her wrist. "You are Queen?"

"Yes."

"Then nothing important has been lost." With his other hand, he made a map in the air above their heads, points of light illuminating all the cities. "We have Rimon, Zayit, and Anab. What happens next will require your trust."

She said, "Of course you have it."

Tarses gave no indication that he heard her answer. "I have had a vision, as I have lain unable to dream. A storm is coming. If we lure Habush to the open sea, their fleet will be destroyed."

Tsifra hesitated before she asked, "When?"

"As the moon wanes," he said. "The storm will come. I have seen it."

There were two issues with this proclamation. The first was that this ran counter to everything she had understood about Tarses's visions, which were highly accurate at a distance and did not—so far as Tsifra knew—exist at close range. That he was seeing something only weeks off indicated either something had changed, or else it was not a true vision. The second issue, of course, was that "the waning moon" indicated a period of two weeks.

"Father," she said, very, very carefully, "you were badly injured."

"You are questioning my vision?" Lying on the sand, Tarses laughed. "It is wise for you to do so. But I have a gift now I did not have before." He touched his wound again. "The man who healed this is skillful indeed, and he has opened pathways in my mind I did not know were there."

"This man," Tsifra said. "You trust him so much, even with your visions?"

"I trust him," Tarses said. "I have his name." He turned to face her then, the first time he'd done so. "I need one thing more from you, my Courser—at the next moon you must pass through the gate, for one night only, to carry out an errand I can entrust to no one else."

"What can I do in only one night?"

"I want you to find the Lymer," Tarses said, "and I want you to kill him. I do not think you will mind so much."

No, truthfully Tsifra would be altogether delighted to kill the Lymer. The man was certainly her greatest enemy in La Cacería; she'd killed his Alaunts to shore up her position and he'd never forgotten it. The man was an insufferable braggart and utterly two-faced besides. She'd have been pleased to make an end of him several times over, but to find and kill him in one night was something else. She said, "Why?"

"Because," he said, "he gave me this wound, and it cannot be known that he lived afterward. And because he stole from me."

She'd heard whispers in the dream-world about that wound, that Tsidon the Lymer had thrown his sword through an open gate, Toba his intended target, but his blade had found Tarses instead. It was an error so grievous and so foolish Tsifra had discounted the rumor 'til now, but perhaps there was truth in it after all. "What did he take?" she asked.

He looked like he did not want to admit to whatever it was, but then he said, "He has taken the Shamir."

Tsifra looked at him in shock. The Shamir was rumored to have been lost with Luz. Had Tarses kept it secret all this time? And for what?

"How can I possibly find him and kill him in a single night?"

Tarses said, "He is very near a gate; I have seen that, too. The Lymer is in P'ri Hadar."

Chapter Six

It was much easier for Elena to draw up the plans for her machine the second time around, though she did improve upon her earlier version. Most notably, she realized that using a bladder to hold the miasma was poorly thought out, since any leakage (or sabotage) could kill anyone in the room. Instead, she had Asmel create a very long, thin tube that would release the miasma a little at a time out the window of the small hut he'd made to house the entire apparatus, far away from the rest of the Maziks. Since there was not much safira left—and since the other safira had deteriorated so much more rapidly than she'd estimated—she also made the machine smaller, the handle shorter.

Unlike Rafeq, Asmel did not hide in the other room as she processed the safira with the salt they'd gathered a few days prior, and she wondered if he were less fearful or if he simply trusted her better not to accidentally kill him. Still, he stayed a few paces away by the door, keeping his eye on the setup with the window to make sure the tube remained whole and nothing leaked back into the room.

"When you planned this with Rafeq," he said, "did you discuss any potential downsides to your taking Marah's magic?"

Elena stopped turning the crank long enough to wipe her face with her apron. "You mean whether it was likely to alter my character? Yes, we did discuss that. He thought it was unlikely.

Why, do you think this is apt to turn me into another version of you?"

Asmel laughed a little. "I meant physical downsides. Effects to your health."

Elena turned toward him. "No. He didn't mention any. But Maziks have excellent health, so what can you mean?"

Asmel sighed. "The boy has some issues with his magic."

Naftaly, he meant. But Rafeq of course had not known that, and at the time Elena had not known it was because his Mazikness was not evenly expressed in his body, leaving the more mortal parts too fragile to handle his magic. Asmel said, "I want to be very honest, we don't really know what this will do to you."

"You might have mentioned this before we started," she said.

"I did not realize the source of Naftaly's issues until recently," he said. "When the old woman mentioned it to me. And I do have some idea of how to mitigate the risk."

"Do tell," she said, turning the crank again.

"If the goal is only for you to dream, you may not need all the magic contained in this shard. I think we should divide it into smaller doses and give them to you one at a time, then have you sleep, so that you are taking the minimum amount of magic possible."

"And then give you back the rest," she said. "That sounds like a reasonable course. My mother had the dreams, so I may not need much to have them myself."

"But even so, there is still some risk. To my knowledge, this has never been done before. The theories we are using are Rafeq's, and he was not particularly interested in the safety of his subjects."

Elena was a little irritated by the implication, because in her estimation she and Rafeq had been friends. Asmel was suggesting that he'd seen her as a vessel and had no care for her life. He'd offered to take her to Luz with him when it was restored, to rebuild the university there. At the time, it hadn't felt like a manipulation. Moreover, if she had died, the safira would have been irrevocably lost, and that would have been a disaster for Rafeq anyway. "Rafeq did not think I would die," she said. "And that was ingesting the entire safira."

Asmel said, "Yes, I know." And then he was very quiet.

"Are you trying to decide what to tell Toba if this kills me?"

Asmel said, "I am now."

Elena did not quite know how to respond, and she felt a little cross about Asmel pretending the decision was hers after he'd already told her what was at stake. "Well then," she said, "tell her I knew what I was doing." The resistance in the crank disappeared, and the rasp of metal on metal signaled the safira was gone. "I'm finished." She opened the machine, revealing what remained of the safira, a fine blue powder clinging to a sphere of Asmel's magic. Asmel approached and drew this upward, flicking his fingertips so that the powder swirled through the air into a glass phial he held in his other hand.

Asmel's suggestion was to divide the powder into tenths, which Elena thought overly conservative. She took the first dose, then Asmel set his hand on her head, willing her to sleep.

She woke a while later and said, "If I dreamed at all, I don't remember it."

So she took the second dose, and when that had no effect, the third.

When Elena opened her eyes next, she was not in the room with Asmel; she was outdoors, near the sea. The sky was dark and without sun or moon, but overhead, the stars spun madly, as if they were a cloud of fireflies caught in a whirlwind. The sea was near enough that she could hear it, but she seemed to be unable to turn her head to look. Beneath her the sand was cold and damp.

It was the cold, she decided, that was leaving her so numb, and she wondered that she wasn't shivering. But her body was not really there, was it?

But if her body was in the waking world, how was she so cold?

She willed herself to sit up and could not.

She lay on the cold, wet sand for what seemed like hours before Asmel found her, his face grimmer even than normal.

"I cannot wake you," he said. "Are you all right?"

Seeing that she could neither move nor speak, Asmel swore and took her hands in his. "You are ice," he said. "Disaster upon disasters." Getting up, he made another small building not unlike the one he'd made for the machine, then carried her inside and lay her carefully on a soft bed near a blazing fire in the hearth. He covered her with blankets and said, "I don't know if the dose was too large or not large enough. I'm afraid if I give you more, it might make things worse, but if I don't, you may not be able to wake." He huffed out a noisy breath. "We need Barsilay. Is there a chance you could dream your way to him? You should be able to bypass the salt and wards on the prison since you have only a little magic. If he sees you, he might know what to do."

But Elena could not think how to do that. She imagined Barsilay and thought, *I would like to be with him*, and nothing happened.

Asmel looked troubled and said, "I am sorry. This is beyond me, and I won't risk making you worse. I will need to consult with a doctor." He set his hand on Elena's cheek. "I will come back as soon as I can."

He vanished.

Elena thought a great number of unflattering things about Maziks, and then, when she'd just decided that at least she was warm and dry and not still on the cold beach, she found herself back on the beach again.

The stars were too bright in her eyes and her clothes were becoming wetter by the moment. Somewhere, Toba was in Aravoth, and Elena wondered vaguely what Asmel would tell her when he saw her (she would not let herself think *if* he saw her). She felt her mind sink into itself, into the sand. Toba had explained to her about the void, the nothingness that claimed Maziks when they died, if they had not died asleep. What she felt was not nothingness; she still had her mind, and her senses. But though Asmel had been gone only minutes, she felt the loneliness pressing in on her. She decided to do sums in her head to stave off the rising tide of anxiety, but even then her mind kept returning to the inescapable fact that there could not possibly be a doctor in P'ri Hadar who knew what to do with a mortal who had breathed magic.

BARSILAY HAD COPIED Saba's cypher on the wall, on the floor, and on a different wall, hoping that the act of recreating it might make something leap out. It did not.

Perhaps if he had an inkling of what Saba might be trying to tell him. His location? Tarses's plans?

He would not have written in a code Barsilay could not understand… but if he were using a Zayiti code, he might assume Barsilay still had access to Efra.

He set his hand on the wall and wiped the cypher away again. There was salt there, Barsilay could feel it, not in the surface but deeper beneath, as there had been salt in the prison in Rimon and in the palazzo in Zayit.

He wondered: How were the demons coming and going? He approached the other wall the demons always seemed to slide through and touched it with his fingertips. It, too, contained salt. Salt in the stone, salt in the mortar. He wished Toba were there. Salt would not hold her.

Or would it? Dawid ben Aron had been in this prison for half a century. What had held him, and how had he escaped?

He poured out the last of his water, turned it to milk, and waited for the demon to reappear.

"How long have you been in this prison?" Barsilay asked, when it arrived and crouched down to dip its shadow-tongue into the milk.

The demon gave no reply, and Barsilay thought it was possible demons did not mark time as Maziks did. He asked, "Did you know Dawid ben Aron?"

At that, the demon turned its head from the milk. "Our friend Dawid? We know our friend Dawid."

"You speak about him as if he were still alive," Barsilay said, because he knew definitively that he was not.

"He is not alive *here*," the demon said. "He is alive *elsewhere*. He is our friend."

It seemed the demons considered a dreaming death to be some sort of life. Toba had seen him once, in the dream-world, so some part of Dawid persisted. Whether that counted as living Barsilay doubted very much. "Your friend," Barsilay mused. Then, "Was it you who helped him escape this prison?"

"We helped," they said. "The Ziz, too, is our friend. We did not like to see her locked away from the sky and the sun."

"Is there a way out, then?"

"If you have the book of Luz, there are many ways out," the demon answered.

"It was you who brought Dawid the book!"

"No," the demon said. "We only helped."

"Then who—" Barsilay said, and then stopped himself, because it did not matter who had helped Dawid and the Ziz escape; the book of Luz was in Aravoth with Naftaly, and this line of thinking was a waste of time.

"The Queen was very angry," the demon said, taking on the shape of Kasfia's face, her mouth snarling. The face told him, "She sent many Maziks into the prison that day. And the outer walls were laid with more salt."

"Then how are you getting out?" Barsilay asked, because salt affected demons as much as Maziks.

"We can make ourselves much smaller than you. It is difficult to contain us, unless you are very clever. And the Queen cares not if we eat her rats."

"She probably doesn't know you helped Dawid, then. Hold on a moment, she reinforced the outer walls? What about the inner walls?"

The demon chuckled. "Some of them. But Maziks are lazy."

Barsilay nodded thoughtfully. "And salt is expensive, and what difference does it make if a prisoner goes from one cell to another, really?"

The demon finished the last of the milk and flicked the empty bowl across the room, where it collided with Barsilay's outstretched leg. "Ask your question, Heir of Luz."

Barsilay tapped at the mortar in the wall beside him and thought before asking, "How many prisoners are there?"

"Many prisoners," the demon said. "The Queen never executes anyone, she puts them here and forgets about them, and then they forget about themselves." And they would not want a dreaming death, because then they would forever be trapped in the prison, even in the dream-world. The demon said, "But they do not speak to us. It has not occurred to them even to try."

Perhaps they didn't realize the demons could speak. Barsilay said, "Are there any from Zayit?"

The demon seemed to turn itself inside out and said, "We don't know. Perhaps there are."

Barsilay knit his brow. Then he said to the demon, "Tell me all you can about this prison." And the demon told him, and Barsilay began to devise a plan.

BARSILAY HAD NOT seen a guard during the entirety of his imprisonment, nor had he seen so much as a shade—the dungeon was apparently guarded only from the outside, or else from some exterior corridors he could not hear from within his cell. So if the prisoners traveled only between their cells, they would have relative freedom of movement and association. The prison, according to the demons, went up two levels from Barsilay's cell and down another two, and each level was occupied by roughly ten Maziks.

So many prisoners… It was an unheard-of thing, and Barsilay had asked the demon twice if it was certain that was the correct number. What had they all done to cross the Queen? He'd heard the stories, of course, that the Queen of P'ri Hadar was subject to occasional bouts of madness, but he'd discounted them. Still, the overpopulation of the prison seemed to support the theory that there was something amiss, although that she was keeping them around without torture or execution put her at a higher caste of leader than Relam or Tarses.

The demon was not capable of writing or drawing a map (and he knew better, from past experience, than to teach it such things), and so it had dictated several pages of maps and corresponding notes to Barsilay, which he'd recorded using paper he'd made from the bottoms of his trousers (paper made from stone being too brittle to hold up to handling).

Not every cell could be accessed easily, but entering those on Barsilay's floor seemed to be reasonably straightforward, provided you were oriented correctly. The interior walls had less salt embedded than the exterior. The problem was that it was impossible to determine which walls were the interior ones, since there were no windows anywhere. Barsilay could not remember which wall he'd initially come through, and he could not tell from feeling the walls which ones were completely impassable and which ones were barely, painfully traversable. If the demon were lying to him, he would pass into the wrong wall and then be forced back—if he were lucky—or simply eviscerated if he became turned around inside the stone.

It did not seem to be in the demon's interest for him to be killed. Though he supposed the demon might be doing all this out of mischief, or boredom, or spite.

According to the demon—who had, by now, departed in pursuit of another rat—the wall against which his lentils appeared every morning led into a row of cells that went the entire length of the prison.

If only he could test it. Asmel would have some clever idea, using some bauble or other he could push through—

Ah, he was a fool. He had a perfectly serviceable, expendable item he could use to test the wall. He only hoped it wouldn't alarm the Mazik in the next cell too badly.

"Listen," he called to the next cell, "don't be frightened. I'm only going to try something. All right?"

When no answer came, he took one of his remaining lentils, made it into an apple, and plunged his false arm through the stone. Since that arm had no sensation, he would not know if the salt had destroyed it. If he dropped the apple on the other side, he could assume he'd lost it. If he pulled it back, then he could assume the wall was safe.

He waited the count of five and pulled it back. He was still holding the apple.

"Well done, you," he told himself, and then stepped through the wall himself.

On the other side, a Mazik cowered in the corner, his arms over his face, trembling and saying, "The walls have hands."

Barsilay put the apple into his pocket. The Mazik on the floor had dark hair falling in tangles to his hips and smelled like an unwashed mortal. "I'm sorry to have frightened you," he said, kneeling down while the other man cautiously peered through his hands. "That was my hand. It turns out the interior walls of this prison are passable, if you know which ones they are."

The Mazik said, "This is a trick."

"No trick," Barsilay said. "What is your name?"

"Either you've been sent to torture me or else I've gone mad."

Barsilay recalled having made a similar statement to Naftaly once upon a time. "I assure you neither is true. I am only a fellow prisoner, who happened to come into a useful piece of information."

"From where?"

Barsilay did not think telling him he was in cahoots with the demons in the prison was likely to get him very far, so he said, "I have my sources. My name is Barsilay. And you—"

"You are of Luz," the man said, getting a look at Barsilay's face. "So I know I must be mad. Kasfia wouldn't keep someone from Luz alive."

"I'm just very unlucky," Barsilay said.

"What did you do to land yourself in prison?"

"Nothing of note," Barsilay said. "What did you do?"

"Only what I was ordered," said the man. "My name is Tarek b'Ornan. And for ten days I was the King of P'ri Hadar."

THE ZAYITIS WERE in a state of panic, which the old woman found to be completely justified. Tarses was coming; he'd taken Anab, and still the Queen of P'ri Hadar had made no move to counter him. The Zayitis were stranded outside the wall, where they had even less protection than they'd had in Zayit, for all the little good their own city wall had done them.

A debate was had, between Efra and some of the other Maziks, about what to do next, and there were many who wanted to abandon the quest to rescue Barsilay and flee. Unfortunately, as Efra pointed out, there was no place left to flee. The lentil blight in the southern cities had left both Tamar and lately Erez in shambles; Katlav had held off with a quarantine, but who knew for how long? Baobab was far enough removed from the rest of the cities that it might hope to hold out longer, but as it had no standing army nor wall, it depended entirely on distance to keep itself safe. Barsilay, Efra told the men of Zayit, was their only hope for salvation. But it seemed to the old woman it was really Kasfia who needed to be moved to act.

The Zayitis were entirely exposed in their tents, and Efra concluded this was only adding to the strain on her people. The Queen had refused to allow them to settle inside the city itself, and so Efra moved them into a second encampment set between the city and the sea, a site that was nominally easier to defend with the barrier of the water at their backs. They constructed small stone houses and put up a perimeter with what salt they'd managed to bring with them (because of course the Zayitis traveled with a bit of salt, always).

The old woman was given a house which she shared with Elena, or would do once Elena awoke. Several days had passed since Elena had fallen into her enchanted sleep, and the old woman could have murdered her and Asmel both for their foolishness. She supposed that demon of Tarses's had saved Elena when it had stolen the original safira… If a good pinch of Asmel's magic had been enough to put her in a permanent slumber, the entirety of Marah's probably would have killed her.

The old woman's lungs continued to improve—not to the state of normality, but enough that she could sleep comfortably, at least until she breathed some dust or the air was too cold or there was too much smoke from the fire, and then she was coughing again. But she was able to walk, and so occasionally, when no one was paying her much mind, she put on her veil and walked through the city, amazed that she had come to the far side of the world, and wondering what the mortal city would look like on the other side of the gate. She could be in Jerusalem next month, if she wanted. What a thought.

Efra came to her after many days, as she was sitting in the sun outside her little house having a think about Naftaly and wondering what he was doing just then. Efra said, "You stole the saffron."

The old woman only stared straight ahead and then said, "Why ask about this now? You've already agreed that it's mine."

Efra sighed a little. The old woman understood two things immediately: the spice guild had managed to sell all the saffron, and they'd gotten more money for it than the Zayitis had expected. And a third thing: they were reluctant to part with it. "How much did you get?" she asked.

Efra took the satchel that was hanging over her shoulder and set it on the old woman's lap, making her squawk because it was damned heavy. Pulling back the flap, she saw that it was filled with silver coins. Before she could ask the value of what was across her knees, Efra said, "The rest is in your house."

The old woman looked up and said, "There's more?"

"Indeed," Efra said. "You are now among the wealthiest women in P'ri Hadar."

Inside, the old woman surveilled her riches with numb shock. There was, Efra told her, enough to ransom Barsilay with money left over. Efra clearly wanted her to give the extra to the Zayitis, but she reminded her she had already assigned fifteen percent to the Zayitis in exchange for them selling the saffron, which itself was no small sum.

How the saffron had sold for so much spoke to the cleverness of the guild masters in driving the price up, as well as in Elena's plan for creating a craze for the stuff through her introduction of foreign recipes to the market.

"Let's go," the old woman said, once she'd been informed of the exact sum of her fortune. "We can have Barsilay out of prison by tonight if we leave now."

"We must be more careful than that," Efra told her. "I don't trust the Queen as far as Zayit is concerned. I would feel better if she thought the money were coming from someone with better backing."

"Meaning if she tries to double-deal you, you have no government you can turn to… But who can we say the money is coming from? Who else would want to claim Barsilay? Rimon wouldn't pay for him."

"I have been considering this," Efra said. "If Kasfia feels somehow beholden to Habush, I think our best course is to pass you off as a minor Habushi princess. King Abishai has ten children. It's not out of the realm of possibility you could be some offspring she never heard of."

"You can't be serious! You won't be able to pass me off as a Habushi house-cleaner!"

"We'll disguise you and send someone else to negotiate on your behalf," Efra said. "You won't need to speak to the Queen yourself."

"And why are you saying this Habushi princess is spending her fortune ransoming Barsilay? Is he my long-lost lover?"

"It's better if you don't present a reason. Let her think you have some plans for him. But if it will help you play your part, you may bear in mind the truth: You are parting with a fortune to save the great love of your dearest grandson."

Among the survivors of the burning of Zayit were two women who had once been much sought after for their unique ability to cast glamours. The old woman was puzzled by this—could not any Mazik cast a glamour? But these women had made something of a sensation not so much because of their magic, but because of the art they displayed in their creations: beautiful faces that reflected whatever the viewer found most desirable, or eyes that changed color with the bearer's emotions. They were particularly noteworthy because their clarity of vision allowed their glamours to last on other people (on other Maziks, the old woman reminded herself) for many days before they wore off. It was these two that Efra brought in to work on the old woman. One of them had hair the color of a ginger cat—which could not have been naturally occurring—and the other had hair that was black as ink but shone blue when the light hit it, and both were very graceful and entirely too tall.

The old woman needn't be very beautiful, Efra told them. She only needed to look like a Mazik—which was to say, not old, and with the proper eyes.

These two had never seen an elderly mortal before and found her equal parts fascinating and revolting. They took turns touching her crepey cheeks and then exclaiming in wonder. One of them took her gnarled hand and touched her knuckles, then turned and asked Efra a question she couldn't quite hear.

"She wants to know if it hurts," Efra told her.

Does what hurt? the old woman wondered. *My skin? My joints?*

The knowledge that I have limited days left above the ground? She said, "Of course it does." The woman looked suitably chastened and exchanged words over the old woman's head with her companion. The two put their hands on each of hers, which felt briefly warm and not unpleasant. When they let go, her hands were smooth, the age spots gone, the veins concealed beneath a layer of fat that had worn away decades ago.

They felt as arthritic as ever.

"How long will this last?" she asked.

"They think they can guarantee about two days before they'll need to start over," Efra said. "With luck we won't need that long. Kasfia and her court only need to see you arrive and agree to the exchange."

"No one needed to see me to sell the saffron," she pointed out.

"Barsilay is a prisoner, not a fungible commodity. The stakes are a bit higher, and we don't want the Queen to come up with an excuse to seize more assets from the trade guild if she learns the money is tied to us."

All this time, the two women had been applying their palms to the old woman's face, which she did not like much, and now they were running their fingers through her hair in a way she did not like at all.

Barsilay had offered once to make her younger, though the implication was it might be more permanent than a glamour. One of his jokes, or an attempt to charm. She wondered now what he might have done if she'd taken him up on it. She hadn't much cared for her youth when she'd had it, though she missed her younger joints and her stamina and, these days, lungs that did not cough for no reason. But she preferred not thinking about men and husbands and housekeeping. She liked being only herself. She liked being invisible.

She did not like being poked repeatedly in the neck. "Do they have to be so touchy?" she asked.

"They're nearly done," Efra said.

"But they've only just started."

"Hold your eyes open."

"My— Goodness, not so close."

One of the women conjured a looking glass from nowhere. The old woman peered into it, and the face that looked back was entirely her own from fifty years before.

"Hashem's sake," she said. "My eyes…"

"That was the trickiest part," Efra said.

They were a Mazik's eyes, dark as her own had been before age had dulled their color, with square pupils. She still had as much trouble seeing close-up as she'd had for the past half of her life, so she pulled away from the mirror for a better look.

She had not been a beauty, exactly, in her youth, but she found she appreciated things now differently than she had then—the roundness of her cheeks; her lips, unthinned by age; her hair, which was now thick and brown instead of sparse and white. Still, a Mazik princess should be something more than this, she thought.

"I only look younger," she said.

"The rest is only clothes and jewels," Efra said. "You will pass as a princess. At least for the next two days."

Chapter Seven

Inside the dungeon of P'ri Hadar, Barsilay sat on the floor opposite an extremely disheveled man who claimed to be the former king.

Only this was nonsense, because Kasfia had been Queen since the Fall, and even before that she'd been the vizier of the Queen of Luz, ruling the city on behalf of the Empire. P'ri Hadar had never had another ruler.

On the other hand, the man was in prison for *something*.

The man's muscles were wasted from disuse and he'd long ago abandoned the will to bathe. Barsilay said, "How long have you been here?"

Tarek said, "I could not guess. A hundred years? Five hundred?"

Barsilay sat down against the wall. The demon had followed him through and paced the short width of the room; Tarek's eyes followed it wherever it moved. Barsilay said, "Let me make you something to eat. And then you can tell me what happened to you."

Barsilay made Tarek a stew laden with dried apricots, which he explained was quite a fashion in Rimon, and turned some water to very weak wine (since he did not think Tarek could handle anything more). Once he'd eaten and drunk, Barsilay made some shears from his boot and cut the man's hair, and heated the water in Tarek's pail so that he could wash. When Tarek looked again like a Mazik, he said, "Thank you for your kindness. I am in your service."

It was quite a statement and Barsilay hardly knew how to answer. Tarek went on, "At some time in the past, I was an official of the Queen. I helped collect the taxes, that sort of thing. Nothing particularly heroic nor controversial. And then one day, out of quite nowhere, she came to me and said she was tiring of the throne and would be stepping down, and I would be King."

Barsilay said, "I have never heard such news out of P'ri Hadar."

"No, you wouldn't, because I ruled for ten days, and then Kasfia came to me, put a knife to my throat, and ordered me to renounce the throne again to her. And then I found myself here. And now you think I'm mad."

Barsilay would have objected, but in truth he did suspect Tarek might be mad—if not before his imprisonment, then from the duration of it. He knew full well how a long confinement ruined a mind. "Why do you believe Kasfia did such a thing?"

"Her reasons eluded me," Tarek said, stuffing his mouth. "When a queen shows up with many armed guards and shoves a crown on your head, you don't ask questions."

"No, I'd imagine not," Barsilay said.

In the corner, the demon was turning a circle, looking a little amused by this entire exchange. "Do you know something?" Barsilay asked it.

"The Queen is the Queen," the demon answered, and Tarek gaped.

"It speaks," he said. "Or else I really am mad and am imagining both of you."

"You aren't and it does," Barsilay said. "It showed me the way through the wall."

"But it's a demon!"

"I'm aware."

"Why would it help you?"

"I asked nicely," Barsilay said. "Listen, I don't suppose you know—"

"You mean I could have gone through that wall all this time?"

"Not all the way to the outdoors, but look, I need some help with a puzzle." Barsilay copied Saba's message onto the wall with his finger. "Do these symbols mean anything to you?"

Tarek looked a moment and said, "No, not remotely. I'm sorry."

Barsilay stood up from the floor, and Tarek said, "Don't leave."

"You see, that message is important, and I need to find someone who might help me decipher it." He nodded at the demon. "Can you show me the way through one of the other walls?"

The demon got up from the floor, turned from cat to tentacled creature and back again, and said, "Of course we can, Heir of Luz."

Tarek said, "Mother of monsters. What did it call you?"

"I'm not the mother of anything," Barsilay said. "But I agree it's appalling. Did you want to come with me?"

Tarek looked stunned, but he said, "Yes," and followed as the demon led them through the opposite wall, into a cell with a disheveled woman who shrieked and tried to claw Barsilay's eyes out.

A mistake, coming through straightaway, he thought, as Tarek tried to calm the woman down. When he'd come through Tarek's wall, his arm had been a warning. This woman thought he was a guard or something worse, and that there were two men was not helping. While Tarek tried to explain they were not there to murder or ravish the poor woman, Barsilay took his last lentil and made it into another bowl of stew.

Food, it seemed, solved all problems in the prison of P'ri Hadar, and the woman held off trying to kill him and fell on his offering instead. "I'm sorry," she said when she was halfway finished. "I have not seen another Mazik in more than a hundred years. Two hundred years? I don't know."

"It's quite understandable," Barsilay said. "My name is Barsilay, and I've only just arrived here. This is Tarek."

"Oh," she said, setting down her spoon. "We're doing this then. All right, my name is Sarai b'Alona, and for six days I was Queen of P'ri Hadar."

THE DEMON HAD taken Barsilay into two dozen cells, and he'd met and fed two dozen prisoners with lentils others had stashed away or been too despondent to eat themselves. Among those two dozen were eleven former monarchs of P'ri Hadar, seven academics of various standing, and one actual criminal—a man who had been sentenced for stealing spices from the Queen's kitchen and selling them at a profit. The longest-reigning monarch was a man called Abam, who had been King for all of six months. That one troubled Barsilay the most, because if P'ri Hadar had a new king for six months, he ought to have heard about it. And what did it mean for Kasfia to be continuously abdicating and then retaking power?

All of them, thus far, were from the city itself. None could decode Saba's message.

He'd been alone with Tarek, washing with a little drinking water, when the other man had noticed the mark of Luz and gone very still.

"Is that why you are here?" he had asked, and Barsilay, too fatigued to lie, had said yes.

Tarek had thought long on that as he washed with a cake of soap they had made of a lentil, and then he'd said, "Don't tell the others."

"They see my eyes," Barsilay had said.

"Knowing you are of Luz is not knowing you are its heir. They are grateful to you. But some of them remember the Queen of Luz, and that gratitude will only extend so far."

The demon had found an empty storage room filled with extra bowls and fabric for the thin blankets they used, which was big enough for six or seven Maziks to gather comfortably. The rest were left in the cells in twos or threes, all of the passable walls marked with glowing sigils so they could come and go as they liked. Maziks unwashed for fifty years or more bathed as well as they could in bowls of leftover drinking water; clothes tattered from centuries of wear were made whole again. Most of the Maziks could do little more than whisper with their unused voices, but whisper they did, carefully at first, as if expecting they'd fallen into some new trap of the Queen's, and then more confidently when they realized they'd managed to find some small degree of freedom. Barsilay expected from past experience that none of these Maziks would ever voluntarily be alone again.

They were such a strange assortment of personalities that he wondered if that was what had led them to this place, if their oddness was what had allowed the Queen to force them into taking up the throne for weeks or months and then pluck them out of the palace and stash them away. They could be written off as mad, or possibly they lacked the sort of friends that might have made a fuss or come looking for them.

Or they could have been completely ordinary before their imprisonment. It was impossible to say how much the confinement might have changed them. The one thing they had in common was a keen desire for company and a powerful urge to help Barsilay, whom they saw as their savior. They gathered together and copied the cypher on walls and floors, again and again, looking for some hint, some pattern, only there was none any of them could find. They thought the symbols might correspond to letters or even numbers, but all attempts to produce a translation came up as nonsense. He'd asked the demon to try to take the scroll to Efra, but apparently the Zayitis had taken one look at the demon and cast salt at it, which had the unfortunate consequence of enraging the demon and disintegrating the scroll. The demon had exacted its revenge by causing a dust-devil in the camp, and had slunk back to Barsilay and refused to go anywhere near there again.

Barsilay sat cross-legged on the floor of the storage room they'd turned into a communal area, eating some pheasant brought to him by one of the others, most of which he was breaking off into shreds and feeding to the demon curled up in the dark corner. "Tell him you don't like it," the demon said, to which Barsilay answered, "That would be rude."

"Then turn it into something else."

"Then you'd have nothing to eat," Barsilay replied, and threw it the last of a drumstick, which it consumed in a single bite, bones and all.

TOBA FLEW ON toward the dark place, her eyes straining to see within it and finding nothing. If she were closer, there would be something. Something, anything that would begin to explain reality, and what this place was, and why, and why there were three worlds, and why she had been made to exist.

The feathers burned in her skin; her face was aflame with the down that had erupted there, as new pinfeathers had already sprouted from her legs. She had been birds before, flown before, but this was something else, as if she were becoming some other thing entirely—not Toba's consciousness as birds, but an entirely different creature. Not a bird, and not Toba, but some third entity, which was at the same time both and neither of the other two.

The magic she felt inside herself was not her own; it was the magic of the firmament, an infinite well that stretched her mind and her will. It was impossible to resist. It poured into her and she was subsumed by it. For Maziks, magic and memory were so entwined one could not exist without the other. But this magic—the magic of the firmament—was something older, beyond memory, or at least the memory of any creation.

Perhaps the creature she was becoming would be able to make out the darkness, to find its way there, and to understand. To ask questions. Her eyes focused ahead, and she willed herself not to blink. Her eyes burned so greatly it was nearly unendurable, but still, she did not look away.

So focused was she on the dark place that she ignored the terrain all around her, and did not think to adjust her altitude to the rising elevation. The tips of her wings brushed the forest canopy, and as she moved to compensate, her left wing caught on a branch, sending her tumbling into the ground. Her left wing—her left arm—was all bad angles, hopelessly broken, and she wept with the pain of it, and the pain in her eyes.

The dark place had grown to be not just a spot on the far horizon, but everywhere around her, and it grew larger still, and then everything went dark. She was left in a silence, a darkness so complete she might have been back in the void.

Then all around her were the sounds of wings, and wings brushing her skin, and her own wings, and the feathers that had grown from her face.

There was much whispering in a language Toba did not know, and she felt her shattered wing extended then pulled sharply back into place, and then one of the whispers said, "This will not do, Tsifra N'Dar. You must have a new name."

"How can I?" Toba said through her distended throat, amazed she could still speak at all. She could feel new feathers coming in all over, and her face still lengthening, her legs drawing up. "I cannot rename myself."

"We will offer you a new name," they said. "If you will have it. But it will change you. You will not be quite the same with it."

"Change me how? I have a task. My name *is* my task, and I cannot abandon it."

The whispers came again, inarticulate to Toba's ears. After a while they said, "Very well. You are very young, Tsifra N'Dar, and you are not entirely yourself. We can make you as you were, but you will only remain so for a little while."

"Please," she said. "Please help me."

"As you ask," they said, and Toba felt herself surrounded by feathered touch, and the feathers growing from her arms began to melt away like water, leaving behind small red scars where the quills had been. She let herself sink down to the ground, clutching handfuls of soil as the pain slowly ebbed out. Then came the touch of feathers on her eyelids, and the pain there lessened, too.

"I am still blind," she said.

"We dare not return your sight to you, because you cannot resist looking at what you should not."

"I will resist it," she said.

"Can you truly?"

"I promise," she said, and then there was a feathered touch against her eyes. Toba exhaled and the last of the pain began to fade, and as the angels removed their wings from her eyes, she dared to look at them. But like the dark place, she could not see them properly. She saw infinite eyes, and infinite wings, and no other limbs or faces at all. Yet their voices she understood, and that puzzled her. She closed her eyes again, and opened them, and then instead of eyes and wings, she was looking at Nehama. Only Toba was somehow very sure that this was not truly her, but some fiction her mind had concocted to keep itself comfortable.

"Thank you," Toba said, and the angel said, "This place is not for you."

"I know," she said. "But it isn't for the Ziz, either. We're here for her, and then we will go."

"The Ziz is not what you hoped to find here," they said. "You are too much like the other who came before, so many questions on your tongue that you can barely speak."

"Is that wrong?"

"It is foolish. Any answers you seek are in your world already. Anything more is beyond you. Claim the Ziz and go, Toba bat Toba. There is nothing more for you here."

"I will do as you say," Toba said, as this seemed to be the only way to respond to the command of an angel, but then some darker impulse took over. Why should she accept the angel's order? Why was she less entitled to wisdom?

There were answers that she needed, to the problem with the way the worlds themselves had been constructed. A problem that Tarses had taken upon himself to solve with a great deal of bloodshed. Even if they managed to defeat him, it would be only a matter of time before another man rose up with similar aims.

So instead of doing as she was told, Toba blurted out, "No."

The angel looked, then, toward the dark place, as if confirming that Toba was really hers to deal with. "No?" she repeated.

"There is something more. Everything that has happened, all of it is because of the Mirror. And whatever we do now—taking the Ziz, repairing the gate—it will all be for nothing so long as the Mirror exists. The Maziks will fear it and use it both."

"It is the Mirror you complain of?"

"Yes! The law is not in heaven," Toba insisted. "It is in the world, in the hands of men. And so our fates must also be so."

The angels laughed, and it was a sound Toba could not have imagined—like a chime or a bird or the wind, and somehow like none of these at all. "Must it be, because you say?"

"It is not I who say it," Toba insisted.

The air was filled with whispers and the sound of wings she could not see, and Toba wondered how many angels were there, though she could see only one. The angel stepped closer and put something into Toba's hands, and looking down, she could see that it was a small axe with a silver blade. The angel indicated a tree, smaller than all the others but still taller than Toba and twice as big around. It was covered in white blossoms, and the angel said, "Fell the tree."

Toba gasped and said, "No. How could I kill such a thing?"

"You cannot kill it," the angel said. "Fell the tree. Or else ask no more questions."

So Toba took the axe in her hands and approached the tree. The smell of almond blossoms was strong in the air, and Toba knew what she did was wrong on some universal level she would be called to account for. But the angel had told her to, so she took the axe and swung it into the enormous stone trunk.

It cut through easily, and she swung again, and then again, and on the fourth swing the tree was felled. Toba thought she might be sick at the sight of it.

The angel approached and beckoned Toba to the downed tree, running her hand along the cut edge of the trunk. "The first to bloom and the last to bear fruit. What do you see?"

Toba's voice shook, and she said, "A felled tree. Those are the rings within it."

"So you do know," she said. "You knew before you came here."

"Knew what?"

"The nature," said the angel, "of time."

Toba put her fingers on the edge, tracing the rings as they grew out at irregular intervals, and failed to understand. "Time... grows ever outward? From here?"

The angels made no response.

"But that explains nothing," she said. "The Mirror is real; I have seen it. Things that happen in the mortal world, they happen again in Mazikdom. People die, cities fall—I've seen it! But... if time is like this..."

"Then there can be no Mirror," the angel told her. "And there is not, as you describe it. The Mirror is a story invented by those who misperceive, as you do. What makes reality?"

"Hashem has made it," she said.

"Are you certain?"

"Yes."

"And what do you see here?" The angel pointed to the dark place.

"Nothing," she said. "But I know I misperceive that."

"You acknowledge your misperception here," the angel said. "But you cannot understand you do so in your own world?"

"Speak plainly," she begged.

"We do speak plainly, little child, only you see so little and understand so much less." The angel bent down and took a feather—one of Toba's, which somehow had not yet ceased to exist—and held it out to her. "What is magic?" the angel asked.

The feather brushed Toba's fingertip and disappeared. She said, "It is intention."

"And what is intention, if not the inverse of perception? Now do you understand, a little? Where perception fails, intention falters. What you see is not a Mirror, but apathy."

Toba felt as if the ground beneath her shifted, and knew this too was only perception. But there was a Mirror; the Maziks had been using it all this time! They'd seen the effects of it. "But then…" she began. Why had the Maziks been forced to accept a Queen they did not want? Still, she had seen things the Mirror could not explain… moments that had felt like the Mirror reversed, like when she had taken Atalef's arm. Or even further back—it was La Cacería that had existed first, before the Inquisition.

If what the angels said was true, they were all of them pushing against the same arc of time, and what she was seeing was not a Mirror but a link.

Intention, they were telling her. It was all intention—the root of magic and the spark of all action, even from one linked world to the next. The Maziks were victims of their own magic; how could an immortal creature have as much intention as one who feared death daily?

Perhaps it had not always been this way, but if there had once been a balance between active and reactive, between intention's pull and perception's push, there no longer was.

"Was it meant to be this way?" she asked, not a little sadly.

Instead of replying, the angel approached the crown of the tree and took one of the smaller branches, heavy with white blossoms, and broke it off, saying, "There is hope, for a tree."

She put the branch into Toba's hands. It was the length of her forearm.

Toba said, "Was this a test?" and the angel said, "You are needed elsewhere," and pointed toward the direction she'd come from and the tallest tree at the center of the wood. There was the sound of many wings, and Toba felt herself lifted and carried back to the tree, only now, at the base, was a great lake that had not been there before, with a surface that mirrored the half-lit sky. The water was so clear she could see all the way to the bottom, and in the center of the lake, his face turned upward so that he might have seen her flying over him, was Naftaly.

THE OLD WOMAN looked like an ageless Mazik, but she did not *feel* like an ageless Mazik. While the Zayiti miracle workers had succeeded in making her look like she was thirty years old again, her joints felt the same, her posture was the same, and she still had the shuffle a woman her age had earned. She looked, Efra told her, like she'd been injured and healed badly.

"There's nothing I can do, unless you Maziks are hiding the cure for arthritis."

"What is arthritis?" Efra asked.

"Never mind," the old woman grumbled. "I can't move otherwise. You'll have to find a way to distract from it, or else I'll just sit still when anyone's watching."

There was a lot more grumbling, and someone suggested that the old one didn't not be present for the negotiation at all. But then Efra said the Queen would likely refuse such an arrangement, as she was disinclined to trust anyone and might assume this was all some Zayiti trick—which of course it was.

It didn't help that she'd tripped earlier in the day and was limping a little worse even than normal. It had happened like this: She'd been out getting some fresh air into her sore lungs, and she'd stumbled over a stone and rolled her ankle. She'd cursed the thing, but then she'd seen what she would have stepped into otherwise—there was a hole in the ground just ahead, and out of it scuttled a small yellow scorpion with an octet of purple eyes. If she hadn't tripped over the rock, she'd have put her foot into the nest instead.

So she'd stopped cursing the rock and said, "I suppose you

were a bit of good luck after all." The stone in question had been unremarkable in color—a dull gray, but unusual because of its smoothness, like a stone that had come from a river, only there was none nearby. She'd had a powerful desire then to pick it up and carry it with her; she'd had so little good luck, and maybe this was some kind of Mazik charm, which she certainly could use. *Why not?* she'd thought. Better to take comfort where it was offered.

But what good would it do her to be weighed down by a rock?

It was ridiculous, and she was too old for this sort of thing, so she let it be.

She recalled this now, in Efra's house, because she'd put her hand in her pocket to look for her handkerchief, and what she found instead was the rock. She tried to recall whether she had picked it up after all, but was fairly sure she hadn't. Taking it out of her pocket, she held the thing in her palm, scowled at it and said, "How did you get here?"

Efra, who had been consulting with one of her underlings, said, "Why are you speaking to a stone?"

"Because," she said, "it was in my pocket, and I didn't put it there."

The other Maziks quickly drew blades, and the old woman made a garbled little shriek. Efra said, "It appeared in your pocket?"

The old woman stammered, "I tripped over it earlier today, but I'm sure I never picked it up. I only just now noticed I had it."

Efra said, "Put it down and step back."

The old woman set it down in the middle of the tent and took three steps back. One of the other Maziks took a pouch from her hip and reached inside with a gloved hand.

The rock was no longer a rock. It was a small woman, and she took form so quickly the old woman did not even see how she came out of the stone... One moment she was the size of a chicken breast, and then the next, a Mazik. And she said, "You can keep your salt. If I intended harm, you'd be dead already."

It was, the old woman realized, the Peregrine. She was dressed head-to-toe in dark gray, her hair covered with a hood, and her hands in gloves of what might have been silk. Efra and the other

Maziks visibly sagged a little, and Efra said, "Was it really necessary to be so theatrical?"

"I would like my presence to remain secret from Kasfia," the Peregrine replied. "Better if I'm seen as little as possible." She eyed the old woman. "I did save you from a scorpion sting. You might thank me."

"I'm fairly certain you put the scorpion in my path to begin with."

The Peregrine smiled. Efra said, "According to Toba, you were caught as a double agent by Tsidon in Tarses's siege castle. What happened?"

"If you'll recall, Tsidon disarmed himself," she said, "throwing his sword through the gate. He wasn't much of a threat after that. He fled rather than lose his head, and no one else there knew I was the one who helped Toba escape."

"So Tsidon gave you a convenient place to lay blame," said Efra. "You told Tarses it was he who helped Toba?"

"It was not so difficult after he nearly killed the Caçador with that gambit with the sword. So I am still very much in Tarses's good graces."

"I presume that also means you killed King Yefet."

"Of course." The old woman felt the tension in the room rise further. Barsilay had known she planned to kill Yefet, and had weighed the Peregrine's allegiance heavier than the King's life when he sent her on her way. Efra had not been a party to that decision. At the moment, it didn't seem that she would have agreed to it, had anyone asked her.

"In that case," Efra said coldly, "why are you here?"

"At the moment," she said, "I am waiting."

"For what?"

"Circumstances," the Peregrine said vaguely. "There are rumors that Tarses is fumbling and overestimating his abilities. I am only waiting to be proved correct."

"And if he isn't fumbling?"

"I have precautions in place," she said.

"I would have you elaborate."

"I'm not your underling."

"Then perhaps you should leave."

The Peregrine smiled. "You are in a camp, Adona, surrounded by the few people who managed to flee the city burning around your ears after your prince betrayed it. You are in no position to turn away aid, whichever direction it comes from, and you do not have the luxury of casting me out. Your only hope is to ransom Barsilay from the Queen—"

"Which we are doing, now, without you."

"Yes," she said, eyeing the old woman. "She looks presentable, at least holding still, but she speaks only Rimoni and she sounds like a mortal. Who will negotiate?"

"I will!" And here Efra must have cast some spell upon herself, because her face changed and she resembled a woman with lighter hair and darker eyes, and she spat a string of curses at the Peregrine in Habushi, to which the Peregrine laughed.

"That was a creative use of language," she said. "But if you think the court won't pick up on your accent, you are mistaken. You don't want the Queen to know Barsilay is being ransomed by Zayit, but hiding your face won't be enough."

"You are proposing to negotiate Barsilay's release yourself?"

"I am," the Peregrine said. "You have no one better suited to the task. I can look and sound like a Mazik from anywhere, and no one will question it. If you want the Queen to believe he's being ransomed by an adona from Habush, either send me or else accept she'll know she's being lied to."

"I am not inclined to hand Barsilay's ransom over to you."

"As you should not. Leave the mortal in possession of the ransom. I'll do the speaking, and when the time comes, she can hand it over directly. Does that satisfy you?"

Efra looked troubled by this arrangement, but the old woman supposed she knew the Peregrine was correct, and the Peregrine had proved herself more than loyal to Barsilay. Efra said, "Do you swear on your name your intent is only to arrange Barsilay's release?"

"On my name," the Peregrine said, "I do swear it."

* * *

Tsifra had developed the habit of sneaking into Anab before the sun and then back out at midnight, to sleep in the safety of her shepherd's hut. It was not quite enough rest, but she reasoned it was more sleep than she'd get inside the city, where the possibility of assassination would require her to sleep with one eye open, under the guard of mortals she could never completely trust. Still, she kept her suite in the palace, which she used to meet with her advisors, and to house her extensive wardrobe. Every morning she would sneak back into her rooms and lie in her bed 'til her servants roused her.

In these rooms she kept a map of the coast, which she studied from all angles. Habush was well protected by geography, situated on both sides of a disconnected isthmus. There were silver models on her map, tiny ships of various types and sizes, demarking what intelligence she had of the strength of their fleet.

It was large enough to defeat her own fleet in a fair fight. She'd lost too many men to the plague sailing from Barcino, and the remainder were fatigued from fighting. She could only motivate them so much with money or religious fervor, and the easy victory in Anab might not be replicated—unless, of course, Tarses were correct, and the Habushi fleet was about to sink in a storm.

Luring the fleet into the open ocean would be no easy task. The Uliman Sultan knew the Sefardi fleet was coming and would not readily leave the city undefended. Mortal Habush had only recently changed hands, and if the Sultan were smart—and by accounts, he was—he would be expecting a challenge to the new order. It would take a great deal of artifice to convince him to send his ships away from his hard-won prize.

There were two advisors she'd brought with her from Sefarad, veterans of the wars with Rimon, and she called them to her as she ate a small breakfast after giving an entirely made-up confession to the priest she'd also brought along, since it would have been noteworthy for her not to do so.

She encouraged the advisors to sit and then said, "I need a list of any of the Anabi officials we've left in charge whom you think might be communicating with Habush in secret."

The men said, "If we had knowledge of such men, we'd have executed them, my queen."

"Look harder," she said. "And don't execute them. I have a use for such men. In the meantime, prepare the fleet for departure."

"To Habush? But we haven't finished—"

"My instructions come from my angel," she said, rising to her full height—taller, she knew, than the real Queen had been. "When it is time for you to know them, you shall. Bring me those names, gentlemen."

Tsifra waited in her tower, observing the ships readying themselves down in the harbor. At night, she snuck out to perform her miracles and sleep in her hut. And in two days, her men returned bearing a list of sixteen names.

"Are you sure this is exhaustive?"

"Those are all the highest-ranking men of Anab who are known to have business interests or families in Habush," they told her.

"Then I want you to make sure that everyone on this list sees, with their own eyes, the departure of the fleet tomorrow. So that when they send word to Habush, they will have no doubt that we are coming."

AT THE CROWNING of Tsifra as the new Queen of Anab, the entirety of the nobility was present in her new church. The building was not yet completed, but she'd insisted on using it anyway—the walls were only mostly done, and the roof was still open, but the speed at which it had been built had created whispers throughout the city. She knelt by the pulpit as the bishop she'd brought from Mansanar set a crown of amethysts on her head and prayed, and when he ordered her to rise again, she fell instead into a faint.

Exclamations rose from her own people, and whispers from the Anabi lords, and when she'd decided all eyes must be on her, she sat up, pushing away her advisors who'd meant to carry her away. She allowed herself to tremble, and she fell against the bishop. Casting her eyes heavenward, she said, "The angel is come. There! Do you not see?" And she knelt and wept.

The others in the church hardly knew what to do, and she said, "The angel is come, do you not hear?"

The bishop said, "What do you hear, our queen?"

Still trembling, she said, "She tells me one Sefardi ship shall be as three, and they shall cut through the fleet of Habush as a sword through untried flesh." She exhaled a shaky breath, then said, "She bids me leave the greater part of the fleet here, that our sailors may marshal their faith."

"My queen," her advisor said, in an effort to quiet her before the masses of Anabi lords. They might have been willing to accept a vision as legitimate. But to share military strategy like this—she could only be mad. She was risking her hold on the city with this plan. What came next would need to be done quickly.

She was helped to her feet, and the bishop told all who were there to pray for her as she was led quietly outside.

Her advisors exchanged nervous glances, and she told them, "It will be well, if you do as I say. Do nothing to prevent the movement of men or horses from the city. In three days' time, I will sail with half our fleet for Habush."

Chapter Eight

Naftaly followed Nehama through the stone forest, the sound of the wind reminding him all the time of the sea. The terrain was so uneven he could barely risk looking up, and so when Nehama came to a stop he was surprised to see how much closer they'd come to the great tree. It didn't seem possible for them to have covered so much ground so quickly, and Naftaly felt a strange turning inside his mind as he tried to reconcile the distance he'd seen with their current location.

The tree itself seemed even taller as they drew near, and the low light filtered through the leaves and left strange shadows on the ground. Under the canopy, it was nearly dark.

"Nehama," he said, "Toba was the one who knew the Ziz's name—she never gave it to me. How am I to tame a wild Ziz without it?"

"Well," Nehama said, "either you will succeed, or she will kill you."

Naftaly craned his neck to take in the entirety of the tree. It was impossible, the entire enterprise, and it only made sense that Toba had gone mad and abandoned him. What an absurdity, to come to Aravoth believing that either of them had the right to be there or had any kind of power to do anything in a place that belonged only to Hashem and the angels. Inside his coat, the book was warm and he set his hand over it. He could go back. What was the use of killing himself over an impossible task?

"You could leave," Nehama said, and Naftaly wondered if she was reading his thoughts or only his face. She went on, "But you would never forgive yourself. You want too much to be the hero of the piece."

Naftaly did not understand how a woman he had known only hours (or days, he thought—he had no dea how much time had passed) could make such a statement, and he wondered again what sort of being Nehama really was. He had no reason to believe she'd lied about being a half-Mazik from Luz. But he had a needling sense that there was something more to her, and he still couldn't square her tale with why the angels had simply left her to wander the wilds of Aravoth all this time. Either she was telling the truth, in which case he had a sinking suspicion he might also have trouble leaving the place, or else there was something more she had not said.

Naftaly looked again toward Toba's vanished path. He said, "How do we get to the top of the tree?"

Nehama turned Naftaly back toward the tree and put her hand over his eyes. "Nothing here is as you perceive it," she told him. "Not the ground, nor the sky, nor even the tree."

Naftaly wanted to remove her hand but stayed the impulse. "Is this some sort of riddle?"

"Not a riddle," she said, "only a reminder. You believe there should be sky, and ground, and so there is."

"And the tree?"

"And the tree."

"So what is it really?"

"If either of us could understand the reality, you would not need to misperceive them. Distance, too, is not real."

"So the tree isn't actually two hundred feet tall? Does that imply it's smaller or larger?"

She laughed a little, which was no answer at all.

"Are you mocking me?" he asked. "Or do you not know?"

She took his face in her hands, and turned his entire head to an angle, such that his eyes were perpendicular to the ground. "What do you see now?"

"Everything's cockeyed," he said. "And all the while Toba is flying farther away, and the Ziz is still very much above our heads." He cursed a little, and then, as she held his face, the world seemed to shift, and it appeared that the tree was just as tall, but growing horizontally.

Sometimes, after a vision, Naftaly's eyes would remain distorted for several hours. Things would appear too large or too small—faces, especially, were disturbingly big and he often wanted to be alone 'til the discomfort of it passed. He recalled once, as a boy, lying prone on his bedroom floor, looking up and thinking that it seemed the ceiling was the floor and he was looking down at it.

It was a similar sensation. Truth be told, it made him rather nauseated.

"Are you implying that if I believe the tree is sideways, I can simply walk across the trunk?"

"You are Mazik enough to understand," she said. "What is the difference between belief and intent? Is one not a reflection of the other?"

Naftaly had never considered such a thing, but he suspected Nehama was correct; spending all that time alone had probably led to many such insights. But if belief could alter perception, he ought to be able to make Aravoth look like anything he wanted, and he assuredly could not. And moreover: "Why is Toba now a bird, if we have so much control over the world here?"

"There can be only one reason," she said. "Only you don't want to accept it."

The implication being that Toba wished to be a Ziz. That, of course, was possible, but it also tended to render them blameless if they could not get Toba back, and that alone made the reasoning uncomfortable.

Naftaly sighed. "If we get the Ziz," he said, "can we use her to find Toba?"

"If you can tame the Ziz," she said, "you may do as you like."

Naftaly put his face back at a normal angle, letting the world shift back to a more typical view. If he was going to climb the tree, he still had to get to it, and he did not know how to use his perception to alter distance as well as up from sideways. "Let's go," he said.

* * *

If the first part of their trek had seemed uncannily short, it took what felt like hours for Naftaly and Nehama to walk the rest of the way. Naftaly was tired and footsore, but he dared not stop to rest, knowing that every minute he delayed, Toba was closer to destroying herself. Finally, at the base of the tree, they stopped and took a little food and water. Naftaly looked again to the crown of the tree; he was taking a lot on faith—that he could walk upward with belief, and that the Ziz was even there, when he could not see her.

"Are you sure she's really up there?"

"She is," Nehama said. "She has made a nest." And she pointed to a dark shape atop the lowest branch. At least it wasn't farther up.

Naftaly closed his eyes, opened them, and tried to reorient himself. "If I go back to seeing the tree as vertical, what will happen?"

"You'll fall," she said, so matter-of-factly that it might have been Toba speaking.

Naftaly put the sole of his foot against the trunk, slipped back toward the earth, and turned away. "I can't," he said. "You'll have to blindfold me."

"Then you will certainly fall."

He needed something more. Trees did not grow sideways, and no matter how much he tried to imagine it so, he could not. He decided to reach deeper into his mind, which often saw things as they were not, and put together some other sort of path for his feet.

He had never been able to will himself to a vision, though he'd come close in seeing what he was curious about in the past, and he'd never been able to move his body during a vision at all. But perhaps here, he might be able to do both. He imagined a long, straight path, with trees on either side—a garden, carefully kept and easy to navigate—and there was something remarkable at the other end of it, only just out of his reach.

Ah, he thought, and just so, his mind made another vista: on both sides of him forest, and before him a path of smooth stones. Was this more or less real than the tree? Naftaly had no idea, but he set his foot on the stone, and then took one step after the other, 'til Nehama said, "I shall come behind you. Only I think you should not look back."

Naftaly did not want to answer, so focused was he on the path ahead. He could hear the wind in the trees on either side of him, and faintly, the sounds of wings—either the angels' or the Ziz's. He could not see what was at the end of the path, but he hoped it bore enough resemblance to reality that he would not simply walk all the way to the top of the tree and fall off.

He walked that way a long time, focusing on the sounds of his shoes on the stone, the air moving around him, and Nehama following quietly behind him.

Ahead of him was a pavilion, not unlike those he'd seen in the garden of the Mazik King. There were three steps leading into it, and he climbed them 'til he was directly in the middle. There were three doors topped with horseshoe arches: one behind him, one ahead, and one to the right. He turned right and looked out, and there, before him, was Barsilay. He was dressed in pale yellow and wore a crown of silver almonds across his brow. He turned to the side—toward Asmel, Naftaly then saw—and said, "Naftaly will never forgive me." Asmel, looking not a little grim, replied, "Naftaly is no fool."

Naftaly set his hand on the edge of the pergola doorway and was shocked to feel not the smooth wood he saw, but rough stone, and under his hand was the bark of the great stone tree. The pergola gave way to leaves blowing in the wind, and in front of him was not Barsilay, but the Ziz.

Her nest was the size of his father's house; her wings, closed against her body, were as long as four men laid end to end. She had not seen Naftaly yet, but was looking out at the horizon, and then she closed her great eye and settled her head under her wing.

Naftaly was trembling at the size of her. His hand lay against a smaller branch, beneath his feet was the tree, and beneath that was a great deal of empty air. Behind him, Nehama said, "Look in the nest."

From his vantage point, Naftaly could barely see over the side, and he had to step up onto an auxiliary branch to see what she meant. But there, peeking out from beneath the Ziz's glorious tail feathers, was something smooth and golden. "She has an egg?" Naftaly whispered.

Nehama said, "This makes your task harder. She won't want to leave it."

Naftaly backed up against the trunk, so that Nehama was beside him. The Ziz would not agree to leave her egg, and it was too big to pick up and carry with them. He thought some very uncharitable things about Nehama, who might have mentioned the egg *before* they'd climbed all the way up. He said, "I have no idea what to do now."

"We must smash it," she said, and Naftaly gasped a little, loudly enough that the Ziz's eye opened a moment. When it had closed again, he said, "Are you mad?"

"It can't be fertile—she has no mate here. It is only an empty egg, and she will sit on it forever, waiting for a chick that does not exist."

"That is too cruel," he said.

"How? Is it not crueler to leave her endlessly in that nest alone?"

"So, are you suggesting I just walk up to the nest and throw it to the ground? Even if I could, she would kill me after, and she would certainly never trust me!"

"No," she said. "I will be the one to do it."

"Stop a minute," he said. "She's been here however long, all alone, and that egg is all she has. You don't know what it might do to her, if you break it. She's not an ordinary bird. The Ziz is eternal—"

"It matters little," Nehama said. "The egg is nothing. She must be made to return to the world."

"Not this way!"

"There is no other way!"

At this, the Ziz's eye opened completely and she turned toward them, standing at the crook between the branch and the trunk. Opening her great beak, she let out a shriek so loud Naftaly was forced to cover his ears. Then the Ziz flapped her great wings and rose, her feet gripping the stone branch with talons like a lion's, and she stepped toward them, once, twice, the stone trembling all along the branch.

"Naftaly," Nehama warned, throwing her arm in front of him.

Naftaly could not think of a way to escape, aside from climbing back down, and he tried to reconjure his garden path. But the Ziz was close, he could hear her breathing, and the vision would not come. So he only closed his eyes and imagined the path opening before him, and he put his foot on the first step, and then felt himself tumbling through the air.

In that first moment, he knew only the terror of the fall. But then as the wind burned Naftaly's eyes, he tried again to remind himself of Nehama's advice… None of this was as he perceived it. Not the air, not the ground, not even the law of nature that was causing him to plummet. Aravoth was something else, and everything that was happening to him was a product of his own mind.

Still he fell, because he could not quite make himself believe anything else was possible.

The ground came up to meet him, and he closed his eyes. But what he struck a moment later was not land, but water, which was only marginally more forgiving after a fall from such a height. His eyes opened as he went under and descended into the depths, the dim light of Aravoth barely breaking the surface. He flailed, hoping to halt the descent into the darkness, but Naftaly had grown up in the mountains and could not swim. He kicked against the water, which only seemed to tire his legs, and then the thought came unbidden: *I will drown.*

It was a death sentence to think so and Naftaly knew it, but pushing the words away only seemed to convince him further. He could not seem to propel himself upward; the water was heavy and there was so little light he could not even tell how deep he'd gone.

He needed his garden path again, but that was what had led him to fall in the first place, and he no longer trusted it. Barsilay had said Naftaly would not forgive him. That meant that whatever Barsilay had done, Naftaly must still be alive for it. He could not die in these waters.

Still, he was nearly out of breath.

Then, the water began to warm, only a little, and there was something white approaching from the direction Naftaly hoped was the sky. He reached his fingertips toward the shape and felt scales that seemed hot in the cold water. The creature was as long as his arm and looked at him with bright-blue eyes with square pupils—a Mazik's eyes. He tried again to grasp the fish, and could not, and then it took Naftaly's arm in its teeth and began to swim upward.

By now Naftaly was very much out of air, and his chest burned with the instinct to breathe. He could not help but struggle against the fish in his panic, and it let go and turned back to him.

Then the fish did the oddest thing—it kissed him.

It was not quite a kiss. But the fish's great broad mouth met Naftaly's and he felt a bubble of air pass into his throat. Then the fish took hold of him again and swam 'til it broke the surface, and Naftaly floated there, with his arm in the fish's teeth, gasping again and again.

In the nether light of Aravoth, the fish's scales were pale as milk, and it pulled him to the shore of the lake that had not been there before he'd fallen. When it was shallow enough to stand in, the fish let go. Naftaly stumbled out of the water, falling to his knees and then going belly-down on the hard ground. He looked back to find the fish, only to see a woman approach it and put her hands on it, and then it disappeared.

He'd expected Nehama. But it was Toba.

She came and set a hand on his back without speaking.

Naftaly said, "Did you make the water?"

"No," she said. "You were there when I got here." Then, "Naftaly, where is the book?"

Frantically patting at the front of his jacket, Naftaly saw that it was still there—but it had gone into the lake with him, and he wasn't sure the cloth he'd wrapped it in would have been enough to protect it, submerged as long as he was. With cold fingers, he unwrapped the book and found it utterly dry. "The lake is not a lake," he murmured. Only he himself was wet.

"And that book is not a book," Toba said. Naftaly then realized she was without feathers anywhere. "What happened?" he asked.

Toba was very quiet for a long time and said, "I am not able to say yet."

He decided to let it be and pulled his sodden body up to sit beside her.

"Where is Nehama?" she asked.

"Still in the tree, so far as I know. We found the Ziz. But she has an egg, and Nehama wanted to break it so she'd be willing to leave Aravoth."

"Naturally you refused," she said. "And then you fell out of the tree for your trouble."

"Something like that," Naftaly said. "Look, if we destroy that egg, fertile or no, the Ziz will never go anyplace with us, but you have her name. You can just… order her to fly through the gate."

"If I do that, she'll hate us just as much," Toba said. "I'll use her name to convince her to let us take the egg."

"You didn't see the size of it," Naftaly said.

"We have enough magic to make it smaller," she said. "At least I think so. That's what Asmel would do, if he were here."

Naftaly recalled that he'd just seen Asmel. He'd told Barsilay Naftaly was not a fool, which was no insignificant compliment. He wondered if he'd meant it. He also wondered if he could manage to climb the tree again; he did not think his mind would conjure the path for him a second time.

"Do you really think she will let you lay hands on it, even with her name on your tongue? We don't know what effect her name will have. She's not a Mazik."

"I suppose we should test it," Toba said, getting to her feet. Casting her face up at the nest above, she called, "Leb Ha-Yareakh, fly down to us."

Naftaly's eyes scanned the nest for any sign of movement. Unfortunately, he found himself unsurprised when nothing happened.

TOBA, AT THE base of the great tree, considered the paths each of them had chosen: Nehama's abandoning false hope, Naftaly's indecisive kindness that led to nothing, and her intended trick of using the Ziz's name, which got them closest to a solution but felt manipulative nonetheless.

Well, no matter: the Ziz didn't seem to respond to her name in any case.

Dawid ben Aron had gone to no small amount of trouble to ensure she knew the Ziz's name, and there must have been some reason for it. He must have presumed she could use it to command the Ziz, or at least to gain her trust.

"I don't suppose you're thinking she didn't hear you?" Naftaly said.

It had occurred to her, briefly. A new plan developed: They would steal the egg and flee through the gate, leaving the Ziz to follow. But it was too absurd even to consider. She said, "I don't know what to do, Naftaly. And I don't think Nehama is coming back to us."

Naftaly wrung some more of the water out of his hair, and Toba recalled that she had enough magic to dry him, at least a little, but no sooner had she reached out to touch his clothes than the water within them evaporated, along with the lake itself.

"Did you do that?" Naftaly asked.

"I don't even know," she said. "But if it was your lake, perhaps you simply stopped imagining it."

"Does that mean we're having some kind of shared hallucination?"

"I think it does," she said. What a concept. It reminded her of moments in her childhood, when she'd been too sickly and too unsocial to go outside. Her grandmother had found her sitting alone in the garden, pondering a blooming flower, and she had said, "This looks orange to me. Does it look orange to you?" and Elena had said, "Of course," and little Toba had said, "But what if what I mean as orange is not the same as what you mean? What if to you, it looks blue, but we only decided to call it the same thing?" and Elena had said, "Ask your grandfather."

Her grandfather had thought her question was very funny, and had said, "Does it matter if we see it differently? The flower is the same."

Toba had said, "But what if it isn't?"

And then he'd told her to be quiet because he was working.

Her mind was hazy from knowing nothing around her was real in any quantifiable sense, and it made her feel as if she were continually falling. Anchoring her senses did not help, because she knew they were lying to her. No, not completely. There was Naftaly, and he was real. She reached out and took his hand, turning it over and counting the lines in his palm. If he found this strange, he said nothing.

It was warm, Naftaly's hand, and calloused, and there was dirt under his fingernails—probably soot from the fires in Zayit. It was bigger than hers and smaller than Asmel's, and a little damp. But not with water from the fantastic lake, she realized. He was sweaty. She brought it to her face and smelled it.

"The Ziz had chicks," she said. "In Rimon. I saw them in the dream-world. Asmel said the King kept them in a menagerie. It never occurred to me before that meant that the chicks have Mazik dreams."

"Can you tell her?" Naftaly asked.

His hand was a lifeline for her mind, an anchor to a reality in which orange was always orange, or so she'd decided at the age of seven. She said, "I think I might be able to show her."

Toba was confident enough in her magic to make a ladder that grew out of the stone bark of the tree. It was some five hundred rungs high at least, but it was climbable and less susceptible to changes in perspective than Naftaly's garden path—or so they hoped. They climbed with Toba in front and him behind, very slowly, counting the rungs aloud as they climbed to be anchored by one another's voices.

Toba had counted six hundred when she reached the lowest branch. As she stepped off the ladder, she took Naftaly's hand and steadied him, and then Nehama's voice came from above them, saying, "You managed to climb back up."

Naftaly looked very displeased and said, "I fell out of this tree. I fell, and you did nothing."

"You survived," she said, and Naftaly wondered if the lake had been hers. Nehama dropped down from the higher branch with such ease that he wondered what she was perceiving, whether she saw the tree as he did or was even concerned about the height. "The Ziz was very agitated, but she's calmed now." To Toba, she said, "You seem to have saved yourself."

Toba only said, "No, I didn't." In the satchel over her shoulders was the almond branch she'd taken from the angels. She could not stop wondering if that had been a test, cutting down the tree, and whether she'd passed it or not, and what she was meant to do with the branch. It would need water, and soon, or it would die. She ought to have collected some from Naftaly's lake before it vanished, and she mentally chastised herself for not having thought of it earlier. She had not seen so much as a cloud in all the time they'd been there—did it rain in Aravoth?

Out on the end of the limb, the Ziz lifted her head and looked toward them, deciding, probably, whether she ought to rouse herself from her egg again. Toba said, "I have a better idea than smashing the egg." When Nehama made to object, Toba held up a hand and said, "Stop."

She tried to remember the young Zizim she'd seen in the dreamworld, horse-sized versions of their mother. But she couldn't conjure illusions of them without the risk of alienating the Ziz when she learned they weren't real. She said, "I'm going to try speaking to her first."

"I don't think that's wise," Naftaly said. To Nehama, he said, "Tell her."

But Nehama only crouched in the space between the trunk and the branch, waiting to see how Toba's plan would play out and whether she, too, would be thrown from the tree, or else eaten. Toba began a slow approach, unsure how close she could safely get, and Naftaly crept quietly after her. He was breathing so hard the Ziz must have been able to hear him, too, and Toba gave him a warning glare over her shoulder and hissed, "You're too loud."

"I didn't say anything."

"Go back and wait with Nehama. You're too frightened."

"You're getting too close!" he said.

"I can't show her anything from this distance. Just go back."

Naftaly only shook his head. Toba turned back toward the nest and proceeded, coming to stop some hundred paces from the bird, who had risen onto her haunches and was looking at Toba curiously and speaking in some quiet birdsong. Toba whispered, "Leb Ha-Yareakh."

The Ziz cocked her head left and right, and extended her neck, as if scenting the air. Perhaps Toba smelled of bird. She extended her arm, palm up, and waited.

Naftaly, over her shoulder, let out a long, slow breath. The Ziz reared up and cried out at the sound and began to charge, her legs rising over Toba's head and her steps shaking the limb so hard Toba thought they would certainly fall again. She called, "Stop!" in what she hoped was a commanding voice, which had no effect on the charging creature.

The Ziz was of Luz, she reminded herself, and she did not know what language they had spoken there, before the Fall. So she called out in Hebrew, "Your children yet live, Leb Ha-Yareakh!"

At either the sound of her name or Toba's message, the Ziz hesitated. Naftaly's eyes were closed, and Toba put her hand on his arm to steady him. "I have seen them," she said. "In the City of Pomegranates, they live. I will show you." And she cast an illusion of what she'd seen, the chicks in the garden of the King.

The Ziz let out a cry that shook Toba's feet beneath her, and she let the illusion drop. "That egg is not alive, but your children are waiting in the other world. If you help us, we will take you to them."

The Ziz turned her head, regarding them with one eye and then the other, then opened her beak and closed it again, clicking. Toba carefully slid past Naftaly, saying, "I can show you the inside of the egg." She held up her hands. "I won't damage it."

The Ziz cried out again when she saw that Toba meant to approach the nest, but Toba said, "Leb Ha-Yareakh, I swear on my name I will not harm this egg."

The Ziz stilled. Toba carefully walked past the bird, shivering, and climbed into the nest, where the egg was as golden as saffron and the size of a small boulder. Making a light with the palm of her hand, she placed it behind the egg, then willed it brighter, 'til the egg glowed from inside, empty.

The Ziz stepped back toward the nest carefully and reached her long neck closer, putting her beak to the egg, chattering quietly, and inspected the glowing shell.

"There is no chick," Toba said. "I am sorry. But your other children live."

The Ziz raised her head again. Toba climbed back out of the nest, and called out, "We will return you to the world, and you will help us repair the gate, as you meant to help Dawid ben Aron, and then I will take you to Rimon."

The Ziz looked at Toba with her enormous golden eye. Then she reached into her nest with her great beak and pushed the egg out. Toba watched it fall to the ground, so far down there was no way to see it break.

From his spot farther down the branch, Naftaly called, "Open the gate."

Toba hesitated… She was not sure what that might do to the tree, to have a gate opened in the middle of its largest branch, and she'd already killed one of the trees of Aravoth that day. To the Ziz, she said, "I will descend and make our way. Will you carry the others down?"

The Ziz turned back to Naftaly, clicking her beak, and lowered her head. Naftaly approached cautiously and set his hand on the bird's azure feathers, saying, "Hello."

"Don't forget Nehama," Toba told him, conjuring wings of air, as Asmel had showed her once, long ago. She felt the prick of feathers in her arms as she leaped from the tree and glided to the ground, and a keen longing for her own wings again; her name, it seemed, had not been completely quelled by whatever the angels had done. She was still Tsifra N'Dar, more than she had been.

And wasn't that an odd thing, too? There had been three Tsifra N'Dars only months before: herself, the original Toba, and her sister the Courser. Was she more her name than they had been, now that she had come to Aravoth? Was it because she'd been a buchuk, made of magic and not from flesh?

She landed gently beside the tree, where only minutes before there had been a lake. Then she opened the book and began to read, opening a gate to Asmel and the city of P'ri Hadar.

BARSILAY'S GIDDINESS AT escaping his cell and freeing the other prisoners from isolation was starting to subside, and he was feeling again the strain of captivity. He could not translate Saba's message, even with the help of the other prisoners, he could not dream outside the walls, and he could not even contact his friends. Twice he'd tried to convince the demons to try again to reach Asmel or even Elena, but the demons had refused, unwilling to risk an encounter with more salt. He felt as if he might be going a little mad and had taken to pacing the hallway in a futile attempt to quiet his mind.

He was doing this when Tarek came through the wall, saying, "There you are."

"Sorry," Barsilay said. "Was I missing?"

"You're usually in the storage room after dinner, with the others and the message. Nomi found something, and we thought we should show you."

Nomi was the seventh prisoner Barsilay had met. He hadn't been sure exactly why she was in the prison, but she'd at one time been a scholar of some kind. When they'd entered her cell, every available surface had been covered in writing, her ink magicked from her own blood. He'd hoped she might be the one to translate the message, and she'd copied it on the floor twice.

"Did she find something in the message?"

"I'm afraid not," Tarek said. "Come, would you? And bring the cat." The "cat" was how the other prisoners referred to the demon. Barsilay got up and followed, and at the end of a series of cells was one Barsilay knew to have been empty. He wondered why they'd even bothered coming inside.

"She was exploring a bit," Tarek explained. "She's been here even longer than I have. So she was in here this morning, and... look." He knelt down in a corner where the floor met the wall, and in the mortar there was a hole about a knuckle's width across. Barsilay traced the edge with his finger, and to the demon he said, "What made this?"

"Rats," the demon said. "Not us. We did not even know it was here." The demon hissed. "They made a hiding place."

"Does it go all the way through?" Barsilay asked.

The demon breathed into the opening and said, "It does. It goes down. It smells of many rats." The demon shrieked, and several others came rushing in through the walls. All of them—Barsilay's "cat" included—vanished into the hole in the floor.

"Well," said Barsilay, sitting back. "At least they'll be well fed for a while. And perhaps we'll have fewer vermin about."

Tarek shuddered and said, "Of the two of them, I'm not sure

I don't prefer the rats, to be honest. At least I understand what they're about."

"Biting your toes, you mean?" He rose and made to leave. "Thank you for showing me the entrance to the rat nest. The cats will be in your debt, assuredly."

"Barsilay—" Tarek began. "It isn't only the hole I wanted to discuss." He hesitated before saying, "You've been distressed the past few days."

Barsilay stopped his pacing. "Of course I'm distressed. We're all trapped in this place, waiting for Tarses to show up and set fire to the city. I can't get word to my friends to make sure they're all right, or to give them this message, which is important enough that Saba risked his life to entrust it to a demon under Tarses's very nose. And I thought… I don't know. Forty-six Maziks in this prison, and not one of us can even begin to decipher it. I'd hoped—"

"Forty-seven," Tarek corrected him.

Barsilay said, "I haven't met forty-seven."

"No, you wouldn't have. The last one we got to three days ago, but he won't come out of his cell or speak to anyone, so we left him there."

"Why wasn't I told?"

Tarek blinked at Barsilay's irritation and said, "I thought someone had. Forgive me."

"No, no, I'm sorry. But can you show me where he is?"

"I doubt he'll give any help," Tarek said. "He just demanded to be left alone and refused to say anything else."

But at least this was something different, besides staring at the prison walls. Even if he couldn't decode the message, here was another puzzle to solve. Why would anyone want to stay in isolation in this place? "Take me there," Barsilay said. "Please."

Tarek led Barsilay through several other cells to an upper level he had not visited before, and then through a doorless wall and into a cell which was absolutely pitch dark. His first instinct was to panic, thinking he'd been led into a trap, but he kept his voice steady and said, "I'm sorry to sneak up on you while you're at your leisure, but would you mind a bit of illumination?"

The gravelly voice from the other end of the cell said, "I was sleeping, and I do mind. I already told the others to leave me be."

Barsilay turned his face toward the voice in the darkness. The man had been speaking in P'ri Hadari. But his accent was Zayiti. "You aren't from the city," he said.

"No," the man replied. "And by your accent, neither are you. You sound like a Rimoni to me."

"Do I?" Barsilay mused. "Hm. Well, I presume you are from Zayit."

"I am."

Barsilay did his best to conceal his eagerness, recalling that the man's city had lately been burned to ash... A fact the man certainly did not know. He said, "And how is it you came to be here?"

At that came the sound of the man sitting up from the stone floor and lighting a light-stone, which illuminated a face haggard with fatigue but surprisingly clean. More to the point, his hair was still shorn, which meant that he was either keeping himself up better than the other prisoners or—more likely—he hadn't been there long. The man said, "I was a member of the spice guild, until Kasfia sent her soldiers to confiscate our goods." He looked rather darkly at his own bare feet and said, "I made the mistake of objecting, and for that I was brought here. Now go, please, since you know who I am. I only wish to sleep."

"How satisfying can sleep be for you in here? It is the next thing to the void."

"Yes," the man said. "I find that rather the point. You are wondering if I know about Zayit, and you are being very careful not to mention it. I know what happened there. I know what happened to the Zayiti guildsmen here. You'll not have found any of the rest of us in this prison."

"No."

"Because of me. I objected, and they wanted to ensure no other objections. So they killed my wife, and they killed my son, all while I watched, and then when they were convinced they'd broken the rest of us, they took me away. I have no interest in dreaming... Whom would I dream with? My wife and son are in the void. My family in Zayit is in the void. What is there for me in the dream-world or anywhere else? So I dream alone, beside the void, because I am a coward. And I hope that tomorrow will be the day I have the courage to put myself there."

In the dim cell, there was no sound beside the breathing of the two men. Barsilay said, "I am sorry, friend."

"I care not if you are sorry," the man said, "only that you leave me alone. Unless you have some great plan for vengeance on Kasfia, or on Tarses b'Shemhazai, or better, both."

Barsilay went quiet but did not leave, and the demon curled itself around his leg. If the man had noticed it, he did not let on, and instead he lay back down and closed his eyes. Eventually Barsilay said, "I may have, actually. Only I cannot promise it."

The man said, "What can you mean?"

"I have a coded message from a prisoner of Tarses b'Shemhazai that I cannot read. Whether it contains some clue for defeating him, I don't know. But it could. Those of us outside have been trying to decode it, but none of us are Zayiti, and we can't find the proper cypher."

He sat up again. "Zayiti cyphers are unbreakable, unless you've been trained."

"And have you?"

"I'm a guildsman," he said. "Of course I have. Show me your message, and let's hope it says something useful that will burn Tarses's world down around him."

Barsilay said, "Brighten your light-stone," and then he cast the cypher on the wall beside him. "Can you read it?"

The man climbed his way up from the floor and squinted at the wall for several minutes before saying, "I can read it. But it doesn't make sense to me."

"What does it say?"

The man got to his feet. He was taller even than Barsilay, and had to stoop under the low ceiling, and he tapped one of the glyphs with his fingers. "It means... rotten? But the next word is salt, and salt does not rot."

Barsilay's eyes lit, because if the message was about the decayed salt, it was urgent. Had Saba been forced to work with the stuff? If so, it would be a wonder if he were still alive. But that he'd managed to survive this long was itself something of a miracle. He kept his voice steady as he said, "What does it seem to say to you?"

"It says, 'The antidote to rotten salt is in the bezoar of a Leviathan.'"

As A YOUNG girl in Savirra, the old woman had lived, together with her own parents, in the house of her grandparents. She had been too young, then, to understand if these were her mother's parents or her father's. To be honest, she'd been surprised to learn they had been related to one another at all, believing, in the egocentric way of children, that they were somehow related only to her.

Her grandfather had suffered from terrible nerves, from the time before she'd been born, tracing back to some horror he had lived through—a pogrom, she later surmised. She only knew that her grandfather often went through bouts of being unable to speak, so great was his distress, and when that happened her mother sat her on his knee, encouraging her to sing to him whatever little child songs she knew. He would sit with his hand on her head 'til she grew bored, and then sometimes, after a little, he would speak to her and ask her if she'd eaten, or if the sun was shining that day. On his best days he'd be well enough to tell her a fairy story, and he'd delight her with tales of witches and princesses and demons with legs like chickens.

She did not suspect she'd ever have enough strength in her voice to sing again after inhaling the decayed salt, and Elena was hardly suffering an attack of nerves. But before she went off to see the Queen of P'ri Hadar to ransom Barsilay, the old woman sat down at the foot of Elena's bed to speak to her, in case she somehow might be able to hear. The old woman was dressed in a golden gown, her glossy, glamoured hair was braided in some elaborate, ridiculous coiffure, and to Elena she said, "Look what they've done to me, you cow."

Elena, of course, remained deeply asleep, but the old woman felt it was her duty to tell her what was happening. How she was on her way to pretend to be some great lady Mazik with a fortune so large she did not even know how to count the coins. "Look at this!" she said, opening the carved chest Efra had entrusted to her. "We could buy half of Rimon with money leftover, if they hadn't tossed us out. You think they'd let us back in with this?"

No, she knew they would not. Whatever came next—and she hardly even dared to guess at that anymore—it would not be returning to Rimon. Not in her lifetime, not even in Naftaly's, which might be long indeed if his Mazik blood had any say in the matter.

Then it was time, and she gathered up her embroidered skirts and her carved chest and set out with the Peregrine, who had been making some arrangements together with Efra that the old woman had not been privy to. She took the old woman beneath her gray cloak, under cover of darkness, to the north of the city, where she set them both on a horse and rode farther north still.

"Are we riding to Habush and back?" the old woman asked.

"We are riding far enough out that it won't spark questions about why no one saw us approaching the city," the Peregrine told her. "We're here now. Do you see it?"

"See what? It's still dark."

But it was nearly dawn, and in the early morning light she could see ahead a great group of Maziks and horses and some great animal she could not see properly that was bigger than all the horses put together. "What the devil is all this?"

"A woman as wealthy as you claim to be would not ride from Habush to P'ri Hadar alone on a horse," she said. "She would ride with an entourage."

"If I were that important, wouldn't Kasfia have heard of me?"

"She can't be bothered to know the names of every adona in every city," the Peregrine said, waving her off. "Especially in Habush, where there are twenty princesses at least. Are you ready? Your glamour will only hold another day."

"I suppose so," the old woman said, and the Peregrine replied, "From now 'til we have Barsilay, do not speak a single word." She frowned. "But just in case—" And here, she placed her finger over the old woman's lips, and suddenly her tongue felt as if it might be lead. "To keep you accidentally spilling our secret to the Queen."

The old woman had not agreed to this and would have argued—what happened if they failed to get the dratted man? Would she be silent forever?—but of course she could not, so she contented herself with giving the Peregrine a good, hard smack.

"It's for your own protection," the Peregrine said, and then glamoured herself over, too, making herself taller and fairer, and then, thinking differently about the entire affair, a man. "Oh," she said. "The world looks different from up here, doesn't it? Maybe I should have made you a man, too. But I don't think I could have made you look young. They really did some nice work there, didn't they? Do you suppose—"

The old woman glared, and the Peregrine said, "Quite right. Let's go."

They took their gray stallion up to the edge of the stalled procession, and the Peregrine passed one of the men a purse. The old woman was a bit miffed that her money might be paying for all this unnecessary pomp.

At the heart of the parade was an apparatus midway between a cart and a chariot, crafted of wood that gleamed silver in the rising sun. It was large enough to seat five people: the old woman, the Peregrine, two Maziks she supposed were posing as her servants, and the driver, a blond Mazik so handsome she could hardly look at him straight on. The chariot—that was in fact what the Peregrine called it—had two wheels on each side, a pair of large ones in front and smaller ones behind, and it seemed to move of its own accord as it was not actually attached to anything. Before it ran two lions the color of sunset. How they kept them from eating the horses was anyone's guess, but perhaps Mazik lions only ate grass, just as Mazik horses ate anyone who happened to stand too close.

The old woman, of course, could not speak to anyone because of the Peregrine's spell. The others conversed with the Peregrine in what she presumed to be Habushi, though she did not know whether that implied the retinue had actually been brought in from Habush to look more authentic, or if they were all pretenders, too. She found that Asmel's shade in her ear translated this well enough and wondered if there were any languages the man did not know, and what the shade would do if she encountered one—if it would remain silent or simply start making things up.

They arrived at the city as the sun cleared the horizon. A rider had been sent ahead, and as they approached, the gate was flung open. They passed through—the horses and the lions and the silver chariot, with another six horses behind them besides—and the old woman ruminated that six months ago she'd been begging for bread and a spot at the cobbler's hearth away from the cold. She wasn't entirely sure how she'd arrived at this point in her life. She also wasn't sure how she felt about it. The carved chest lay at her feet—she would not let it out of her sight—and she wondered what in the world the Queen of this grand city needed with even more money.

Mazik children peeked at them through windows and the occasional adult came to the door to look out as they rode through the main avenue toward the golden sandstone palace. The rising sun hit flecks of some incandescent stone in the cobbles, making the street itself appear laden with gemstones. Before them, the palace loomed; the statues of the twin Zizim rising up out of their pools were so lifelike the old woman gasped a little. In her ear, the Peregrine said, "Try not to look too impressed."

They rode to the base of the palace steps, where a retinue of the Queen's own came to greet them—Maziks dressed in robes as golden as the saffron she'd stolen, and together with the Peregrine she was led inside, through a golden hallway and into a vast chamber where the Queen sat on a throne lined with cushions of crimson silk. Around her neck, on a golden chain, hung a pearl the size of an egg. As they entered, she said, "You are here to ransom Barsilay b'Droer?"

"We are," said the Peregrine, in a deep voice that matched her manly appearance.

The Queen looked pointedly at the old woman and said, "Why?"

"It is a personal matter," said the Peregrine.

The Queen pondered this and said, "Do you know who he is?"

"We know he is the heir of Luz."

"And do you not think all of Mazikdom would be better served keeping him locked away?"

The Peregrine said, "No." Then she took the chest from the old woman's hands and presented it, saying, "We have the entirety of your requested ransom, plus ten percent as a gift to your compassion."

Kasfia said, "Do you understand what you are doing?"

"You set the terms for the ransom."

"I am aware of that. I ask you again, do you understand the ramifications of freeing him? What do you imagine he will try to do?" She paused and added, "Why do you want him?"

"He is dear to my adona," the Peregrine said.

"And for that, you would put the world back under the yoke of Luz?"

"You cannot refuse!"

"You cannot be serious!" Kasfia approached the old woman, so close she was worried she might see through the glamour, and said, "If you are not old enough to remember, then your mother was, or her mother. She would have told you the tales of Luz and her terrible queen. There is no one in this world so dear you should be willing to unleash him on us all."

The Peregrine said again, "You cannot refuse." She opened the chest, revealing the vast quantity of silver within, and the Queen flinched and turned away.

"You cannot dissuade us," the Peregrine said.

"Count it," Kasfia told one of her men. "Three times, count it. And if it is even one coin short, cast them both from the city."

But the Zayitis would not have been so foolish as to cheat the Queen. The money was all there, her twenty thousand plus ten percent extra, and the Queen looked angry enough to murder when she said, "Release him."

TSIFRA SAILED WITH the fleet, not on the flagship but on the smallest, fastest vessel, a caravel called *La Estrellita*. But while they stayed their course as long as they were in sight of Anab, once the city was no longer in view she ordered the fleet to turn and make way for the isle of Dassos, where they would drop anchor on the leeward side.

There was no port on that side of the island, which was too rocky for a harbor, and Tsifra's advisors were perplexed enough that they might have questioned her, if she hadn't threatened them with drowning for speaking out of turn. She ordered everyone off the *Estrellita*, save the dozen men without whom she could not sail, and told her admirals to wait for her return.

"This is madness," one of them told her, and she said, "It is faith, which you sadly lack."

She took the ship and the dozen sailors and continued on toward Habush.

* * *

Tsifra spent the next several days engaged in prayer while her sailors, twelve very uneasy men, sailed toward the strait the Maziks called the Rosh ha-Tannin. She wondered if she truly had enough magic for what she would need to do, or if Tarses truly had the foresight to predict what he'd seen. If the storm did not manifest, it would be an unrecoverable disaster.

When they were close enough, she gathered her sailors and told them, "What you are about to see is a gift from the Angel of Zayit." And she held up her hands, and on the sea all around them she conjured ships, the precise size of the fleet she'd left behind on Dassos. The sailors fell to their knees, but Tsifra wondered that none of them noticed her newly manifested fleet was still far too small to stand against the armada of Habush.

She stationed the phantom fleet across the strait, at intervals too great to do more than annoy the Sultan, and waited for his spies to carry word to him that the Mad Queen of Sefarad was blocking egress from his city with a fleet too small to threaten him. She watched the moon each night, until finally, on the night Tarses had foretold, a cry went up from her sailors, as the fleet of Habush sailed toward them from the north. Tsifra ordered her ship to break formation and her phantom fleet followed, toward the open sea.

The armada of Habush, unable to resist the easy victory, pursued. But the wind held steady, and on the western horizon the stars were obscured by clouds from a coming storm.

Tsifra's sailors were focused on their work, but she knew they were wondering why the angel's ships sailed away and did not fight. What was the purpose of a divine fleet that only fled in the face of poor odds? Tsifra stood at the stern of her ship and directed the phantoms at their back.

They sailed like this for hours, as she watched the sky. She curled her fingers over the railing and wondered if she might be better off dispelling her fleet. Perhaps Habush would be too confused to successfully pursue the only real ship that remained. She'd waited too long to break for the open sea, hoping the proximity would deter the fleet from turning back in the face of the storm. But they were on her now. They had more momentum, and bigger sails, and her phantom ships could not sail faster than her own caravel. As things stood, she would have to engage them before the storm was overhead.

A cannon fired, and the sailors around her tensed. The Habushis had hit nothing, aiming for the phantom ships, and would believe they'd missed. But at some point, surely, they would wonder why the ships of Sefarad failed to return a shot. Another cannon, and another—the fleet was closing. And if they cut through the false ships in the rear and began firing on Tsifra's ship, there would be little she could do. At the battle for Zayit, she'd been able to get in close and take the fight to the decks, where she could not be stopped by mortals. But here, Habush controlled the distance, and she would not be able to leap across before her ship was in range of their cannons.

Her palms tingled as it began to rain, the sound of it on the sails drowning out the voices of her sailors. The storm was coming, but it was too late. The wind had picked up and caught the fine hairs around her face and whipped them into her eyes.

She'd commanded the wind once, a lesson learned from the demons she'd freed from under Mount Sebah. Could she call an entire storm?

It would take more magic, and she was already using a great deal to hold the illusion of the fleet. But she had no better plan. She walked back to the main mast, because she needed to get higher up if this had any hope of succeeding, but she dared not allow herself to float in the air—if she succeeded in calling the storm, she might not be able to get back to the ship.

"My Queen!" one of the sailors called, seeing she intended to climb the mast. "That is no place for you. It isn't safe."

Turning away, she called, "I shall be safe in the palm of my angel," and began to climb. Once she reached the crow's nest, she dismissed the incredulous boy who had been made to sit there, watching the approaching battle. When he objected, she presented him with one of the many amulets she wore—a gift from the bishop in Mansanar, a medallion of a saint—and he took it as some sign and left.

Alone, she reached her arms to either side and breathed, and realized she could not, in fact, hold the illusion and feel the winds at the same time. She allowed the fleet to vanish, and without the drain on her magic, began to feel the whirlpool of the storm in the west. And she encouraged it, little by little, to come closer, to storm away where she was, and to adjust its path not east but north.

The ship rocked beneath her, and the wind became a howl in her ears. From below, she could hear a sailor screaming at her to come down. She willed the storm closer, closer, and when she opened her eyes, she could see towering waves on either side. The deck rolled, and her men were already in the process of lowering the sails.

On their own ships, the Habushis would be doing the same, and trying to understand how a storm so far away could have been upon them in an instant; it was almost as if the Sefardi fleet itself had turned into a storm. If there were any survivors—and Tsifra very much doubted there would be—they would tell this tale for the rest of their lives, of the demon fleet of Sefarad.

She would lose her own ship in this storm. There would be no saving it, and they were in the open sea, too far from land for any of her sailors to hope to wash ashore. She climbed down the mast of the rolling ship, and made it to the railing, and then, when her men would have stopped her, turned to them and said, "You shall be blessed."

She leapt overboard, striking the cold water with more force than she'd anticipated, and thought for a moment that she would drown. There was no light, and she could not see where sea became sky. But she did not need to see, she reminded herself; she was a Mazik, and she would survive. She made part of herself a pale, white fish, made it larger and larger still, 'til it was big enough for her to cling to its fin. The sea pelted her in the face, but the fish could breathe, and she felt some of that air in her own lungs as she willed the fish to swim away from the ship, from the armada, and the storm, 'til she reached land and dragged herself out of the surf.

She lay on the sand for many hours as the remainder of the storm ebbed away and day began to dawn. And then she rose and catalogued her rings and her necklaces and the jeweled dagger she'd hidden in her boot. In the morning, she would make her way toward P'ri Hadar. But now, exhausted and soaked to the skin, she dragged herself to dryer ground and slept.

Chapter Nine

Tsifra dreamt her way to P'ri Hadar, hoping there might be some rumor of Tsidon in the dream-world there. A man like that might try to keep himself quiet, but Tsifra knew him better. She spent much of the night listening to whispered conversations through windows and in gardens, but everything was as it should have been.

It occurred to her that he might not even be there, that Tarses was wrong.

She made her way to the outer wall of the city and perched on its edge, looking down to the dream-sea. It would be dawn soon, and she would wake. Already it was difficult for her to dream so far from her body, and she considered allowing herself to slip back. But then she caught sight of a figure down by the sea, lying so still she thought at first it was driftwood, and then she realized it was a person.

Most Maziks paid little heed to the sea, even in dreams, so it was little surprise no one had noticed the Mazik on the beach. Tsifra's first thought was that it was Tarses again, in which case she had better move him in case someone did notice him lying out in the open. She hopped down from the wall and went out through the unguarded gate, past Maziks whispering in the shadows with their dream-companions, past strains of music, past a poet telling a story of the death of the Leviathan, and the bezoar cut from its belly—a pearl the size of a hen's egg. A crowd had gathered to listen, some of them weeping silently.

When she came to the beach, she realized it was not Tarses lying there. It was a woman. Stranger, it was an old woman, old in the way that Maziks were not. She drew closer and knew that she'd seen this particular old woman once before—she had been there when Atalef had killed Rafeq. Her eyes widened in wonder. This was Elena, Toba's grandmother.

But how was she here, in the dream-world? Elena was fully mortal, so far as Tsifra had been told. Her eyes were open, but she did not move, as if she were in a trance.

The logical thing would have been to leave her there on the beach. This was the woman who had tricked Tarses out of his heir, and he would certainly consider her his enemy if he knew she were still alive. But Tsifra had always been intrigued by Elena, ever since she'd been very small and Toba had told her about her grandmother who doled out sweets and laid her bed with extra blankets in the winter. Elena had been to her a kind of mythical figure, no different than the Ziz or the Leviathan.

So perhaps it was those childish memories that led Tsifra to approach more closely. Curiosity, she told herself. But though Elena stared only at the sky, there was an awareness in her eyes, and Tsifra could not help but ask, "Are you well?"

Elena did not answer but continued to stare ahead. Her chest rose and fell with breath, so wherever her body was, she was still alive. Tsifra touched her hand to the woman's forehead and found it hot, which should not have been possible. "Can you hear me?"

Elena blinked once, then twice, which Tsifra took to mean that she could.

Tsifra sat back on her heels, wondering what had happened to this woman. She had no knowledge of how to do more than heal her own injuries, but she took her hands and ran them over Elena's head and limbs, looking for some obvious trouble. There was none she could see. "You can't wake yourself," Tsifra surmised, and then she slapped Elena's cheek as hard as she dared without injuring her, but she remained there on the sand.

Examining her further was pointless, she told herself, because this was not Elena's body, which was in the waking world. There wasn't much she could do from here, even if she did want to help.

And why should she? This woman was nothing to her. But still, Elena was clever enough to have thwarted the Caçador of Rimon, and loyal enough to have kept Toba alive and comfortable all her life, and those were qualities Tsifra could not help but admire.

Lifting Elena in her arms, she took her to the cottage she saw nearby, where there was an unmade bed—an oddity in a Mazik dream. She laid the woman down and covered her, then sat down at the foot of the bed to think.

Whatever was wrong with Elena must be a new problem, because she'd been awake and lively not long ago in Zayit, and if she'd been Mazik enough to dream before, Tsifra expected Toba might have mentioned as much.

Then she recalled when she'd seen Elena last, she'd been working with a safira.

"Someone has given you a safira and it's gone badly," Tsifra said, and Elena rewarded the assumption with two very slow blinks.

Probably it had been one of Toba's companions; Toba would have valued her grandmother's life too highly to have played with it this way. She would need a doctor, a Mazik doctor, who might have some way to help resolve whatever damage had been done. Probably that was why Elena was alone in the dream-world… They were off searching for that doctor. And Tsifra really ought to be gone before that person arrived.

But a niggling voice in her head reminded her Tarses had captured a doctor, and a very good one at that—one so skilled he'd been allowed to work on Tarses's own mind. Tsifra had never heard of such skill. A doctor like that, he might have a suggestion.

If the doctor was a prisoner of La Cacería, his dreams would be warded, as Barsilay's had been when he'd been Tarses's prisoner back in Rimon. And what she'd learned—and Tarses did not know—was that someone had been able to dream past those wards to Barsilay. It hadn't been Toba (Barsilay had confirmed as much) but someone else with enough magic to dream and not enough to trigger the wards.

This meant that Tsifra probably had too much magic to dream her way to the doctor, even if she could manage to find him. But the wards might not keep Elena out, if Tsifra could somehow get her to him.

In her waking mind, Tsifra could feel the sun touching the horizon. She told Elena, "If you are still here tonight, I will find a way to help you."

Barsilay left the Zayiti prisoner to his dreamless sleep and returned to the longest corridor where he liked to pace, which was blessedly empty. If there were an antidote to decayed salt, he needed to tell Efra immediately, though he could not imagine how anyone could get hold of a bezoar from a Leviathan—it wasn't as if you could just swim into the ocean and slaughter the beast. Still, it was important enough that Saba had taken some risk in getting them the message, so he must suspect Efra could do something with the information. If nothing else, she might be able to trade on it somehow.

If only there was some way for him to get it to her. Perhaps he needed to lean a little more on the demon he'd come to think of as his aide, who was still off somewhere consuming rats. "Where are you?" he muttered, and then wondered if he ought to give the thing a name, and then decided that was probably a bad idea. It was not lost on him that Rafeq had befriended demons as well, and that had not ended so well for him.

The demon in question returned some hours later. "Are you very fat now?" Barsilay asked it. "I'm surprised you could still fit through that hole in the floor."

"Glorious," the demon said. "A glorious feast."

"How marvelous for you."

"Yes," the demon agreed. "The rats made themselves a paradise down there, where we could not go."

"Down there?" Barsilay said. "Do you mean in the lowest level, where they kept the Ziz?"

"Just so," the demon said. "We have been kept out all this time, the Queen laid so much salt it kept even us out."

"Why bother?" Barsilay wondered. "There's nothing down there, is there?"

The demon had laid itself in the middle of the floor, and it rolled its distended body over, saying, "Hm? Oh, it is a paradise for rats." Here, it opened a single smoky eye. "And a paradise for Maziks."

"For Maziks? Why?"

"Because, Heir of Luz, the dream-wards do not reach there."

Barsilay squatted before the demon, which opened its other eye and blinked at him. "Are you certain?" he asked it. "I could dream there?"

"We have said so," the demon said.

"Then take me there."

Barsilay followed the demon through to the lowest level of the prison and stopped short once he came through to a vast open space. Overhead was what appeared to be a twilight sky; surrounding him were what he believed at first glance to be trees, but were actually stone sculptures with leaves made from impossibly thin sheets of basalt. "I don't understand," he said. "Have we come outside?"

"We are still inside the prison," the demon said. "This is the lowest part. Below us is earth."

"Doesn't much resemble a prison," Barsilay said, scanning the trees. The air was completely still, and his steps made little noise on the stone ground. Ahead of them, rising above the trees, was a tower, narrow-based with a top shaped like an onion. The entire edifice might have been crafted of alabaster, it was so white. Barsilay estimated it was at least five times taller than the trees around it. "A tower cell?" he guessed. "But who is inside?"

"We did not look," the demon admitted.

"Unlike you not to be curious."

"It is very high up."

"And you ate too many rats," Barsilay concluded. "Whoever's inside must have done something truly extraordinary to have landed in a tower beneath the prison."

"They can dream," the demon suggested.

"But could they always? Didn't you imply the wards had broken down here? Not that they hadn't existed in the first place?"

"We cannot say," the demon said. "Perhaps you should see who is there and ask."

Barsilay harumphed a little and cast his eyes upward, to the top of the tower. The base had no door, and in fact was not large enough to have one. There was no way inside but through the top. Approaching, he attempted to create rungs he might climb on, only to find that the tower was impervious to his attempts.

"What is it made of?" he wondered. Then, "Can you fly up there carrying me, or is your belly still too filled with rat?"

The demon spun a little, as if thinking this over, and made itself into something vaguely bat-shaped—then, reconsidering, into two of these creatures. Each attempted to take hold of one of Barsilay's shoulders, which of course did not work because most of Barsilay's left shoulder was missing. So with one demon on his right shoulder, the other clutching the back of his shirt, and no small amount of flapping and hissing, he was lifted off the ground.

The top of the tower was surrounded on all sides by pointed windows just large enough for Barsilay to slip inside if he turned sideways. Once through, he had to let his eyes adjust to the near darkness before recalling the light-stone in his pocket, which he lit to view the inside of the circular room. The demon re-formed itself into a single entity and took the shape of a shadowy crow, landing on Barsilay's shoulder.

Within the room there was only a small bed. Atop the bed was a woman, sleeping. Her dark hair had spilled over her pillow and down onto the floor, surrounding the bed in a vast pile. Crossed over her breast, her fingernails were long as daggers.

"Who is she?" Barsilay asked the demon.

"You must wake her and ask," it suggested.

"You are too invested not to have some idea of the answer," Barsilay said.

"Do you not? Look closer."

Barsilay crept closer to the bier, raising his light-stone to look at the woman's face. Truly, he had no idea who she might be… But then the light caught at the stones in the diadem across her forehead—citrons, and citrons in her ears, and citrons around her throat; stones only worn by the Queen, or by her heir.

It was the Princess of P'ri Hadar.

Barsilay watched the Princess sleep, looking for some sign of external magic that might be holding her in this state, and finding none with either his eyes or the magic he pushed out through the palm of his hand. There was no amulet, no poison he could see, nothing other than the fact that she was simply asleep, and—by the state of her hair and fingernails—had been so for ages. He recalled some vague knowledge that P'ri Hadar had, at one time, had a princess, but that was so long ago he'd presumed she'd died. He could not for the life of him remember what her name had been.

He wondered what it might take to wake her, and whether he should. Waking after centuries of enchanted sleep might be traumatic to her body and mind both, and he had no medicines of any kind that might help. At least in her current state she was not likely to get any worse.

"Kiss her," the demon suggested, and Barsilay looked at him rather incredulously and said, "I will do no such thing."

"Pushing magic through her lips will wake her," the demon said.

This was actually not a bad suggestion. When he'd nearly died after the loss of his arm, Naftaly had woken him in such a manner. Still, he and Naftaly had been intimate friends, and this was the Princess of P'ri Hadar. Kissing her without her permission—or her mother's—was the sort of gambit that got men like him killed.

Acknowledging this, he also couldn't very well leave her asleep under the prison and walk away. Moreover, if the Princess were an enemy of the Queen, she might be enlisted to help him somehow. He leaned in close and, without touching her, blew a breath of magic between her lips.

Three things occurred in quick succession: her eyes opened, a bell—which must have been hidden somewhere in the tower—sounded a clap so loud Barsilay jumped, and then the Princess slapped him very hard across the face.

This last bit was particularly horrible because of the state of her fingernails, which caught his cheek and would have gone clean through it, had he not already been recoiling from the sound of the bell.

"How dare you?" she said, or rather snarled, sitting up in the bed while Barsilay dabbed at his sliced-open face with the cuff of his sleeve. "How dare you wake me, you… you…" She stared at him, trying to find something to insult. What she came up with was, "You Luzite bastard."

Both of those suppositions were correct, but Barsilay had little interest in adjudicating either. "I beg your pardon?"

"I am meant to be asleep," she said. "And you've disturbed me."

"Hang on a moment, do you even know where you are? Or when?"

"I know precisely where I am and when. What I don't know is who you are and why you are in my tower, sticking your magic in my mouth when I never asked for it." She moved to get out of the bed, preparing to round on him as he backed away, but found herself held back by the weight of her hair on the ground.

"Hashem's sake," she said, and then, noticing her hands for the first time, uttered a string of curses.

"You are quite encumbered," he said. "If you'd like, I can make you some shears?"

"Do not patronize me!" she spat. "I can make my own shears."

"I'm sure you could," Barsilay said hesitantly, "but could you use them?"

She stared at her hands and let out a disgusted huff. Barsilay made a set of small shears from one of the Princess's slippers and carefully trimmed her nails. Once this was complete, she snatched the scissors from him so quickly he thought she might stab him. Instead, she began hacking at her hair, cutting it to her shoulders, and then rubbing a kink out of her neck. Then she took the hair, turned it into a golden ball, and threw it out the window.

"Your mother has kept you prisoner a long time," Barsilay attempted. "Have you any notion how long you've slept?"

"I told you, I know precisely how long I've slept," she replied. "And if you don't mind, I'd like to return to it."

"As you like," Barsilay said. "If you don't mind, I'll join you."

"You shall not!" she said indignantly.

"I have no interest in sharing your bed," he said. "But this tower is the only spot in the prison immune to the wards, and I've been out of contact with my friends for some time. I'm sure you understand."

"This tower is not a public inn," she said.

"I won't tell the others," Barsilay said innocently.

"The others? The other prisoners?" She went to the window and looked out, setting her hands on the sill. "Do they know I'm here?"

"I didn't know myself until half an hour ago," he said. "My companion here informed me that there was a spot in this prison immune to the wards. He didn't mention there was anyone here."

She turned back from the window to look at the crow on Barsilay's shoulder. Either she hadn't seen it before, or else she'd taken it to be a normal bird. Now that she got a better look at it, she recoiled.

"Don't be rude," Barsilay said.

"You ask me to watch my manners with a demon?"

"Well," he said, "yes."

She snorted, then said, "What is your name?"

"I am Barsilay. Forgive me, I don't remember yours either."

"Barsilay," she said, testing the name. "Why are you here?"

"The Queen gave no specific reason for my imprisonment," he said. "I suppose she did not like my face. Why are you here?"

"I owe you no explanation. Get out."

"Get out? Are you so eager resume your sentence of solitude?"

"I am no prisoner," she spat.

Barsilay came up short. "You aren't a prisoner? Then why in all the worlds are you inside a prison?"

The Princess went rather red.

Barsilay said, "If we could have an honest conversation, I'm sure—"

But this highly reasonable thought was cut short, because the Princess threw a bolt of golden magic from her palm, knocking him backward. Barsilay staggered against the sill of the window he'd come through and said, "What are you doing?"

"I told you to get out!" she answered, and hit him with another bolt, which this time managed to knock him back out the window. And Barsilay was so shocked by the entire situation that it did not occur to him to give himself some wings to glide down 'til it was too late, and he landed flat on his back on the stone ground outside with a very unpleasant thud.

He lay there and calculated his many injuries, because he really was in a great deal of pain. Still, it was better than having his arm cut off, at least slightly. The demon gently wafted down and landed in the middle of his chest.

"Thank you for your assistance," he told it.

"Maziks are fools," the demon told him.

Some of his ribs seemed to be cracked, and he pressed a little magic into the area—enough to dull the worst of the pain—before he gingerly sat up, allowing the demon to move to his shoulder. "I suppose I could sleep down here," he told it.

"She might drop something on you," the demon suggested.

That did seem likely. The entire scenario was almost comically odd. The Zayiti refusing to leave his cell Barsilay understood a little. The imprisoned princess he understood not at all.

But in any case, he'd just managed to get painfully to his feet when a shade—the first he'd seen anywhere inside the prison—appeared before him. Taking hold of Barsilay's arm, it said, "Barsilay b'Droer, your ransom has been paid."

Chapter Ten

Tsifra eventually found her way to an inn not far from the coast, unhappy to be spending the night among mortals but relieved by a hot meal and a bath she did not have to heat herself. She was still exhausted from conjuring the phantom fleet and calling the storm to her, and hoped she would recover before the moon. To that end, she spent most of the next day in a daze, and fell asleep the moment the sun set.

In the dream-world, she opened her eyes again to the beach at P'ri Hadar, expecting to find Elena gone. She was pleased to find the cottage empty, assuming that Toba had managed to wake her up, but then she saw a prone figure on the sand down on the beach, alone again.

"Did someone move you out here?" she asked, which was a ridiculous question she followed with, "Where are your people? Have they been here at all?"

Ridiculous again, to expect any sort of answer. She sat down beside Elena on the wet sand and looked up at the sky, wondering how it seemed to Elena, who must have been watching it endlessly since she'd first begun dreaming.

It would require a certain level of care to choose her next words, because she could not risk Tarses learning she'd helped his enemies, and because Elena had no reason to trust her. And she wasn't even sure Elena was cognizant enough to find Tarses's doctor in this state. Her eyes gave hints of understanding, but no more.

Of course if she were not really conscious, it wouldn't matter what Tsifra did.

She said, "I have heard of a Mazik doctor that is very adept at treating the mind. He is beyond my reach. But I think he is not beyond yours."

Elena's eyes darted sideways. She'd understood at least some of what Tsifra had said. "I cannot give you his name or his face. But I do know he's a Zayiti."

There was a clicking sound from Elena… Leaning closer, Tsifra realized she was grinding her teeth. "You know who this is? You should be able to dream to him." When Elena remained as she was, Tsifra concluded, "Either you don't know how to find him, or you haven't got enough magic, I think."

Tsifra wracked her brain. She couldn't take Elena to the doctor in a warded cell; it was impossible. And giving Elena more magic—even in this dream—was probably dangerous. "I can take you as far as Anab," she told her, "but I'm not sure if that helps." Grasping Elena's hand, Tsifra closed her eyes and willed them to Anab—not to the city itself, but to a dream-world facsimile of her shepherd's hut. Elena lay on the ground outside, and Tsifra craned her neck to see what the dream-world palace might look like.

Tarses liked to build odd structures in dreams—towers without doors that opened into labyrinths, that sort of thing. So when she saw a silver palace looming on the city's highest hill, she knew that it must be his. The doctor would probably be very deep inside that.

Tsifra conjured paper and wrote as brief a note as she could manage. If Elena knew the doctor, then he would know she was a mortal. And there was no reason to give away that it was Tsifra writing the letter… Let him think it had been one of Elena's own companions. She wrote, *She ingested a safira and cannot wake. How can we treat her?*

That done, she asked, "Can you try to find him there, now that you've seen it?" Elena blinked a few times, and Tsifra began to lose hope. Really, she could not take her any closer; she was already precariously near the city.

Elena needed more magic, but giving it to her might be dangerous. On the other hand, Elena was not really there... and if Elena were not really there, then giving her a little extra magic probably would not hurt her. Or so she hoped. "Here," Tsifra said. "Try this."

She bent down and put her thumb to the space between Elena's eyes and pressed in a small amount of her own magic. Elena's eyebrows rose, and then she vanished.

Less than a minute later, she returned every bit as prone, but the note she held had been opened and refolded. Slipping it from Elena's hand, Tsifra saw that the doctor had written, *If you were to rescue me, I could be of more help. Try some al'qot; you must still have some.*

Tsifra crumpled the paper. To Elena, she said, "Surely your friends are clever enough to have tried using al'qot if they have them on hand."

Foolish. Of course Elena would not know what they'd already tried. She made another leaf of paper and wrote, *Did not work. Other suggestions? Is there anything that can be done in the dream-world?*

She gave the paper back to Elena and waited for her to leave and return again. This time, the note said, *Who is this?*

Now here was a problem. Proper names were not used in the dream-world, and she did not know the dream epithets of any of Toba's friends, nor Toba's own. No—she knew one. So she wrote, *The Lord of Books.*

The next time Elena left, she was gone for nearly the remainder of the night, and Tsifra had just made her mind up to wake when Elena returned with a note that said, *She's not really dreaming—she only appears to be halfway here. The magic from the safira is within her, but it is not of her and she is too mortal to use it. I believe salt might destroy it, if she ingests it soon.* Then, scrawled along the bottom of the page, as if in a great hurry, he'd written, *Did my sister get the message I sent by way of the heir of Luz?*

Tsifra paused. She had no interest in doing anything but helping Elena, and she was coming perilously close to moving beyond that. She did not want to help the heir of Luz or anyone from Zayit, nor could she risk Tarses learning she'd been communicating with his imprisoned doctor. Which begged the question: How had he sent a message via the heir of Luz, who Tsifra knew firsthand could not dream past any wards? There was a mystery there she could not solve, nor could she risk asking without indicating she was anyone apart from who she'd told him. So she wrote, *Yes*. And before Elena left again, she said, "You are at great risk, either here or back on the beach in P'ri Hadar. When you go now, stay with the doctor. You'll be safer there. And I will find your waking body when I can and do what he has told me."

Elena looked as if she would have disagreed with this, and Tsifra said, "I will do all I've said. I swear it on my name." And then, Elena was gone.

BARSILAY FOUND HIMSELF deposited before Queen Kasfia, three splendidly dressed advisors, and a woman who stood behind the rest with a golden flagon of ruby-colored wine. With them was the Peregrine of all people, who was disguised as a man.

That he saw through the disguise so easily implied she'd intended for him to recognize her... The height and coloring were different, but the eyes were the same, as was the posture, and—in case all this were not enough—she tugged her earlobe, revealing a very feminine ear, and held his gaze long enough to make sure he knew her.

A Mazik woman he'd never laid eyes on exclaimed at the sight of him, and the Peregrine looked like she might have murdered her on the spot. The Queen cut her eyes to the woman, who clamped her mouth shut.

"You said he hadn't been tortured," the Peregrine said.

"He has not been," Kasfia answered.

"Look at him!" the Peregrine shouted, loudly enough that the sound echoed in the stone room. Barsilay did not think he'd ever heard her raised voice before. Calming herself, she said, "The conditions of our agreement were for Barsilay unharmed. And he is quite harmed."

Kasfia had a hushed conversation with her advisor before she turned back to the Peregrine and said, "He was not harmed by any of my people." To Barsilay she added, "Do you claim otherwise?"

Barsilay was not sure it was wise to explain he'd been hurt when the Princess had thrown him out of her tower, where he ought not to have been in the first place, and held his tongue. Anyway, if the Peregrine was angling for better terms, he ought to allow it. On the other hand, there were terms that he himself wanted that the Peregrine would not know.

Wetting his lips, Barsilay said, "Because of the severity of my injuries, I would like to add to the terms of my release."

"I am not negotiating with you," Kasfia said. "I am negotiating with her."

The second woman, she meant. She was young and not precisely beautiful, but Barsilay suspected this was a high level of artifice, and there were only two people it might have been. But Elena would not have slipped and cried out.

Why would they have brought the old woman?

The Peregrine said, "Allow me to speak with him."

The Queen inclined her head, but her face was furious. The Peregrine approached, and in hushed tones, said, "What in hell's name happened to you down there?"

"That is a conversation for later."

"Then what is it you want?"

"The rest of the prisoners," he said. "I want them released."

"She'll never agree to that!"

"I have at least three broken ribs," he said.

"But were they given to you by one of the Queen's people?"

"Actually," Barsilay said, "yes."

The Peregrine glanced darkly at the Queen and said, "We can negotiate for more. But do you really think that's the best use of this leverage? You could ask for help with Luz."

Barsilay knew she was correct; he ought to be thinking of what was important. But those Maziks in the prison had no other chance for release… If they had anyone to ransom them, they'd have been out long before. He might be able to press for them later, once he'd taken up the throne of Luz.

Or there might be something else he needed more then, and

the priority of the prisoners would get pushed down yet again. Barsilay said, "I cannot leave them there, if I can help it."

Turning back, the Peregrine said, "In recompense for his injuries, we demand the release of all of the Maziks in your prison."

Kasfia rose abruptly enough that her advisors took a step back from her. "Absolutely not. To even ask—"

"They are no threat to you or anyone," Barsilay said. "Unless you're concerned people will find out they were imprisoned for actions they undertook on your orders."

One of Kasfia's advisors, who must have known about the pretenders to the throne in the prison, whispered to the Queen. Barsilay said, "Banish them, then. Send them to Habush."

"You do not dictate to me!"

"I bear these injuries," Barsilay said, "and there is nothing else I will agree to."

"You cannot have been injured by any of mine, because I have no men in that prison! So I ask you again, how did you sustain them?"

The great cedar doors flung open.

The guards drew blades and then stopped, unsure how to proceed, because the person who had entered was the Princess herself, still in the faded gown she'd been wearing in her tower, and she said, "I gave him the injuries."

Kasfia said, "You cannot be here."

"I have come to tell you my mission has ended. There is nothing more I can do. So you may as well release the prisoners; it won't make any difference."

"We should speak in private."

"It matters not," she said. "I have done my duty, all these long years. But now I am here to tell you that the entirety of the fleet of mortal Habush is at the bottom of the sea."

"Get out," the Queen said. "Return to your mission."

"My mission is done!" the Princess said.

"Your mission," Barsilay said, and then he understood. The Princess had been dreaming all this age. This was why the Queen had held power when the mortal city had changed hands a hundred times over. The Princess must have informants in the mortal city—half-Maziks, likely—who told her all that was happening there. And Kasfia took that information and found other ways to draw off the power of the Mirror, away from herself. She allowed herself to be overthrown, and then took her power back, again and again. She sent tribute to Habush, a city that did not own hers, to satisfy the conditions of the mortal city.

That it had worked, for all these long years, was shocking. Either the Queen or the Princess possessed a level of brilliance unmatched by any Mazik ruler in history. It was what Tarses might have done if he'd had half the imagination or skill to be more than a blunt instrument of conquest.

The Princess said, "The mortal city will surrender. There is nothing left between P'ri Hadar and the Queen of Sefarad—and you know what that will mean here. It is over. Whatever you do next, the Mirror cannot help you."

Barsilay said, "I can help you. I should explain to you who I am."

The Princess gave him a look of disgust and said, "There is very little that I do not know, Heir of Luz, and I cannot see how you can offer anything but trouble to this city."

"There is much that I can do for P'ri Hadar, but first let us settle the matter at hand: If you release the other prisoners, my people and I will consider the matter of my ransom settled and my torture paid for."

"Torture!" the Princess spat. "Hardly."

"Those prisoners are no use to anyone," said Kasfia. "And I would hear what you have to say, since my daughter has failed to protect my city."

The Princess said, "I have done nothing else but protect this city for an entire age. I have not eaten a morsel of food, or drunk a sip of wine, or felt the sun upon my face in all that time, and you would say this to me, before this usurper?"

"You have your prisoners," Kasfia said, and Barsilay nodded toward the Peregrine and the old woman (who was not, at the moment, old) and said, "Then we consider the matter resolved. What I can offer you is the return of Luz."

Kasfia and her advisors shouted in disbelief.

Kasfia said, "Can you imagine that any in this city would want such a thing? Do you think none here remember Luz? Do you think I do not remember?"

She strode down the steps from the throne, coming to stand before Barsilay. She was taller, even, than he, and she looked down on him when she said, "My entire life has been spent in ensuring the throne of Luz could never return to us. Your queen—your foremother—was the most terrible Mazik this world has ever known."

"I am aware," Barsilay said. "I was there, then, too."

"You were in Luz," she said. "You were not *here*. Whatever she might have done in her own city was a hundredfold worse outside it. Men enslaved to work her mines, women forced to prostitute themselves for her soldiers, children left hungry to feed the belly of Luz when the crops failed three years running! You do not know, Barsilay of Luz, because while we suffered beneath her yoke, you lay fat and took your ease. Do you know how we celebrated when Luz fell? How many wept in the streets for joy? We will not submit to you. Tarses himself could be no worse."

Barsilay had to take a moment to collect himself. He had not been raised as the Queen's heir; she could not have known he even existed, so far removed was he from the throne, some bastard descendant of many generations. He'd been the next thing to ordinary, in his city. And he'd fought the Queen more than most, in ha-Moh'to, bringing word to Marah and thwarting the Queen whenever opportunity presented. What Kasfia said was true: He also had not suffered beneath her in the way she'd described.

He said, "All you say of her is true. I argue nothing on that front. But even without Tarses, the sea is rising, and in a hundred years, or two, your city will be as far beneath the sea as Luz, whether you are right or not, and no matter how many scholars you use to fill your prison. Repairing the firmament is the only way your city can survive, and as it happens, that will also protect your city now."

Kasfia said, "I see not how."

"Do you not, as wise as you have been, all these long years? To repair the firmament, Luz must be raised from beneath the sea. This moves your coast miles to the west. It moves the mortal city's coast miles to the west as well. The Courser's fleet cannot make land outside P'ri Hadar's gate. They will be forced to march overland, all that way—if they are not so terrified by the sight of the seabed rising to give up fighting altogether."

"But still, they will come," she said. "The mortals of Sefarad believe they follow an angel."

"Do they?" Barsilay said drily. "I know this angel, and she lacks the ability to hold the love of men. She will reveal herself to them in time, and they will follow her no longer." He held up his hand and made an illusion of P'ri Hadar, showing where he knew the coast of Luz had once been. "All this shall be barren," he said. "There will be no cover. Tarses's angel comes with sailors. They have no horses. They will be easily picked off by the mortals of your sister city, and Tarses will know this. With Luz as buffer between the city and the sea, you are far safer."

"Only the mortal city is safer," the Queen said. "Tarses has a Mazik army, too. The presence or absence of the coast affects us through the Mirror only."

"But Tarses will not act without it," Barsilay said. "He's shown as much—his bastard Courser exists for that very reason! This will buy you time, time you now do not have. Without Luz, P'ri Hadar will fall in weeks."

Kasfia's advisors looked alarmed, and she said, "Better, then, for the city to fall to you?"

"I have no intention of remaking Luz as it was," Barsilay said. "I swear that on my name."

"There is no oath you can give me that would gain my trust where Luz is concerned. I will not help you."

Helplessly, Barsilay said, "I do not see what guarantee I can make you."

Kasfia approached Barsilay's illusion on the stone wall, and she regarded her city with its new coastline. She would remember, Barsilay knew, that all that open space had once been a second city, very near to her own and the source of much of her people's suffering. But now, there would be nothing there but salt-soaked earth; no buildings would remain, the grove itself would not have survived. It was miles of uninhabitable nothingness.

It would be very easy, Barsilay knew, for her to take hold of that land, if it were not for the salt that would have soaked into the earth. Barsilay himself had wondered, in the darkness of the prison, how it might be possible to remove it; if there might be a way for some Mazik who was immune to it—Toba, more than likely—to make the land safe and fertile once again. Now, as he considered it, that would probably mean handing the territory over to P'ri Hadar. He had nothing with which to defend it. He could agree to that, now—to give it to the Queen in exchange for raising the land. And it might be the best outcome: The firmament would be restored, and Barsilay would never truly serve as King.

He was about to make this very argument when Kasfia said, "I shall help you repair the firmament and raise Luz from the sea, but not without recompense."

She would ask for the city, and he would have offered it. But instead she said, "You shall wed my daughter, Barsilay of Luz, and Ayleth will be your queen, and you shall be the Prince of P'ri Hadar. And in that way, my people will be as your own, and your heir will be mine."

Chapter Eleven

After she had been returned to the world by the angels of Aravoth, the woman once known as Toba Peres, now Dagah N'Dar, the Splendid Fish, was swaddled and fed and cared for by her new parents, a Mazik mother and a mortal father. She did remember, as it turned out, the details of her former life, and her parents were puzzled that she spoke Rimoni as a child, along with several other languages they had not taught her. But as she matured, she began to speak mainly in the language of her parents, though she always maintained an affinity for the languages she'd known in her life as Toba.

Eventually, her memories began to fade as her new life grew roots into her mind, and her memory of her time in Aravoth—which, after all, had consisted of less than an hour—was among the first to leave her. She had hazy memories of wings and eyes that left her frightened in ways she could not articulate, but her parents chalked them up to childish nightmares, which were forgotten as she grew. And as she grew, she forgot she'd once lived in Rimon, raised by mortal grandparents, and she forgot her father had been a wicked Mazik, and she forgot she'd made a buchuk. And while the angels had called her Dagah N'Dar, her parents also gave her a name to be used in the world, and they called her Nehama.

She was a clever child, as she'd been in Rimon—at a time that was somehow both long ago and also not yet—and she was given many opportunities to learn and study, as was common with Mazik children in the city of Luz. When Nehama was old enough, she was sent to study with the great astronomer Omer of Te'ena, who became a second father to her after her own father succumbed to his mortality. With Omer, she learned to measure the stars, to compare those in the Mazik world with those in the mortal, to draw charts and configure astrolabes. When his observatory was damaged in a storm, she helped him rebuild it, making a better one based on some imaginings she had of a great glass dome and the movements of the heavens marked on the floor.

When the Queen of Luz first took her throne, putting aside the rule of the Judges. Nehama was displeased. But her work was in the observatory, and the Queen promised not to interfere with the scholars, so long as they stayed out of her way. Still, she grumbled to the other Maziks, who told her to keep quiet, lest she cost them their livelihoods. Her grumblings about the new monarchy did cost her the tutoring position she'd won with a local family once the children began repeating some of Nehama's feelings about the Queen to their parents. Determining her influence was likely to get them into trouble, they promptly removed her from their orbit.

"Fools," she told Omer afterward.

"They did you a favor," he told her. "If the children started publicly repeating the sorts of things you're prone to saying, you'd be executed next week."

"And what have I said?"

"All that business about monarchy being an abomination."

"Well, isn't it?" she demanded.

"It doesn't matter if it is or if it isn't," he said. "The mortals wanted a king and the universe is a mirror."

"How wonderful for the universe," she'd said. "And how excellent for the Maziks, who never have to do anything."

"You are half-mortal," he reminded her. "Go and convince the mortals to get rid of their king."

"Convince the mortals?" she'd said with a snort. "I can't even convince the neighbors."

Omer had been very worried then, and decided to go back home to Te'ena, taking most of his scholars with him. He'd built another observatory, out of the shadow of the Queen, and for many years Nehama had studied and written and measured the stars.

And then, one day, she listened as Omer and his colleagues discussed Aravoth, and how one might access it.

This was a hypothetical discussion, and an old one at that. The theories about how one might get there ranged from the dangerous (bisect the firmament) to the ridiculous (dig far enough down, and you'd get there eventually). It was she herself who posed a new theory: "We have gates between the worlds already. Make use of those."

The others nearly laughed her out of the room. Of course that would not work! Did they not all use those gates to go to and from the mortal world? And none of them had accidentally wandered into Aravoth, which surely would have happened if her hypothesis were correct. But she stood firm, and so Omer constructed an experiment: They would push objects through the gates at varying degrees of egress and see if any of them failed to go out the other side. It was Nehama herself who waited on the mortal side of the gate, making notes as from the Mazik side a series of numbered pebbles were passed through at intervals of five degrees (Nehama had argued for more stones but the others had insisted this would take too long, and since she did not want to be stuck on the wrong side of the gate for a month waiting to report her findings, she had eventually agreed). The first stone entered at ninety degrees and then went outward toward the edge of the gate, then this sequence was repeated on the other side. Eventually she collected sixteen pebbles. Then she waited nearly 'til dawn for the last two.

When the moon was nearly down, she stepped back through with the pebbles in her bag, holding it up in victory—only for the Maziks there to burst out laughing, because they had held back the last two stones.

Nehama had been livid. They would have to wait another month to repeat the experiment, and Omer had to send the others away before she murdered them all. "I am sorry," he told her. "I did not see what they were doing."

"Why do they treat me so?" she asked.

"Because you are wiser and they are jealous," he said.

"In that case, why do you let them?"

"Because you are wiser and can put them in their place."

"Is that it? I thought it was because you needed more than one apprentice, and the others were the best you could find."

"There is that," he said. "It's a shame there can't be two of you."

So when the time came the next month, Omer sent the others away from the gate and it was he himself who pushed the pebbles through. And once again, Nehama was left with sixteen. She came through with her sack and asked, "How many did you send?" And he said, "Eighteen."

Triumphantly, she held up her sack and said, "Sixteen."

From there, they moved to sending larger stones, and then it was time to test it on living creatures. Mice were suggested, and cats, but the issue was that they needed something guaranteed to go in a straight line, and no animal would serve. So it was Nehama herself that did the first of these tests, at her own insistence, and it was she who, most unfortunately, discovered the capacity for error of this method (and realized the five-degree intervals had been too large) when she lost the two smallest toes on her right foot to the edge of the gate.

But it was on this day she saw her first glimpse of Aravoth: a sky with no heavenly bodies, a landscape full of trees that appeared to be made of stone, and a great dark place that somehow burned her eyes when she looked at it. The gate itself was different, too. There was not one aperture, but two in parallel. This explained how Aravoth was accessed—when one stepped into a gate in the mortal world, he stepped into Aravoth for an almost imperceptible instant, then directly into the egress gate which was in its path. Bypassing this path required traversing the steep angle Nehama had discovered, and so it was between the two gates that she found her missing stones.

Omer had insisted she not move more than five paces from the gate, and reluctantly she'd returned home. She'd been so excited she'd not even noticed the loss of part of her foot 'til Omer had— rather hysterically, she thought—pointed out the blood.

They'd devised a final experiment after that. Three of them would go exploring, from moonrise 'til moonset: Nehama herself, and two of Omer's other students—a Mazik, and an unlikely mortal who would come through the gate and study with them during the time of the moon. On that night—which happened to be the night of the Rimon Moon—they stepped through the gate.

At first, the other two were as amazed as Nehama herself had been, but within seconds, the Mazik collapsed, magic evaporating through his skin as if it were perspiration. The mortal's eyes fixed on the dark place Nehama had figured out quickly not to look at, and then she began to weep so uncontrollably Nehama thought she might die from it. She put the Mazik, who then was still alive, but barely, into the arms of the mortal and pushed them back through the gate, intent on following.

But she felt fine. Whatever had affected the other two had caused no issue for Nehama, but she knew Omer, and he was unlikely to allow her another chance to explore—he'd been difficult enough to convince after the loss of her toes. The moon had only just risen, and she had all night. She made herself an hourglass and gave herself two hours, at which point she would turn around and walk back.

So amazed was she by the landscape, with its shifting colors and trees taller even than Omer's observatory, that it was not until the hourglass ran out that she turned back and realized the gate was not where she had left it.

So eager had Nehama been to explore that it had not occurred to her that the gates in Aravoth moved as they did in the mortal world—faster, even. And here, there were no stars with which to navigate. So while she told herself not to worry, and that she would simply go through the gate again at the next moon, weeks became months, and her supply of lentils was somehow replenished while she slept.

The dark place called her relentlessly, but she'd developed a resistance to it after burning a hole in her vision during her early days. Keeping her eyes away from it, she explored every inch of Aravoth. At first she made maps, until she realized the landscape was not consistent and they were wrong as soon as she finished drawing them. Then she made catalogs of the plants she found—trees, mainly, of species she had never seen before. She spoke to the angels, who she could hear fluttering around her occasionally, but they never did speak back. She found a sea, and the urge to swim in it had been so profound she could not resist, and she'd become something else entirely: a giant fish—a leviathan. And as the Leviathan, she felt the magic of the deep flow into her, an infinite well that stretched her mind and her will.

If she had been younger, she might not have changed back. But Nehama was old, then, and while her power was nearly limitless there was nothing in Aravoth for her to expend it on. Her mind missed its normal boundaries, and her fins itched to be feet again, and she found she missed the sound of the leaves in the great stone trees.

She turned back into herself and walked out of the sea, feeling cold sand under her toes again and recalling there was a difference between wet and dry, water and sky, Leviathan and Nehama. When she turned around, the sea she had swum in was gone, and she never saw water there again; nor did it ever rain, nor snow. The water the angels left for her nightly was the only water she'd seen anyplace, and she had to conclude that the only type of water that existed in Aravoth must be salt.

She was in Aravoth longer than she'd been in Luz, longer than she'd been in Rimon, and in all that time, she slept and dreamed alone, and she wept alone.

Then, one day, a great plume of water appeared, connecting the ground to the sky, so high up she could not see where it ended. "What is that?" she asked the angels, who were fluttering so madly they must have been upset by it.

She did not know how much time had passed, if it was a hundred years or five hundred (she would not let herself think a thousand, because a number with more than three digits made her physically ill). And then a second thing appeared: a gate, not far from where she'd been, so close she nearly made it, as close as she'd ever come. And through that gate came the Ziz.

She'd seen her before, at a distance; the Ziz lived wild in the lands around Luz. Nehama could not fathom how she'd come through by accident, by herself, nor how she'd fit through the required angle, and half-hoped she represented some effort by

Omer to find her and bring her back. But the Ziz was very much alone.

She had another idea: With the Ziz, she might be able to fly to one of the gates when it opened and in that way return to the world. Making fruits the size of small boulders from her lentils, she set out to befriend the creature. For some time, it worked. The Ziz, as lonely as Nehama herself, allowed Nehama to preen her feathers with a stick—a very long stick. She ate the food Nehama gave her. And once a month, they would pick an open gate and attempt to fly to it.

They were never able to make it in time. Nehama began to wonder if that was related to the shifting maps; if Aravoth itself were deliberately making it impossible to leave.

After some time had passed like this, Nehama awoke one morning from her lonely sleep and discovered the Ziz had left the nest she'd constructed for her at the base of one of the great trees. Panicking, she'd searched the entire area before realizing the Ziz had simply flown up into the tree, and built herself a new nest, and in this nest she'd laid an egg.

Nehama climbed the tree and spoke to the Ziz, who now ignored her. When the next month came and the gates opened, she refused to leave her nest.

"That egg can't be alive," she told the Ziz. "You have no mate."

The Ziz had screamed so loudly at that the entire tree had shaken.

"Would you spend eternity sitting on a stone? Because that's what you have there!"

The Ziz had raged and risen on her giant legs, and for the first time in weeks left her nest to run at Nehama. She'd had to flee, gliding down to the ground on wings made from air, and even then the Ziz had pursued her, 'til there had been the sound of wings and many pairs of eyes and then a great wind. And then the Ziz returned to her nest, and Nehama never approached her again. At least not for a very long time.

Time passed again, and Nehama forgot what little remained of her first life and much of her second—no longer Toba of Rimon or Nehama of Luz, but Nehama of Aravoth.

Chapter Twelve

Barsilay turned to his companions, hoping for a pause that might give him time to counter the Queen's proposal without committing fatal insult. Kasfia likely thought offering the hand of her only daughter an unearned honor for Barsilay, and in truth it was. But that did not change the fact that he would rather be cast into the sea than marry Ayleth or anyone else.

The Peregrine had gone very still, and the old woman had lifted her eyes heavenward, and might have been having a mental argument with the divine. He wished Asmel had been there—he'd managed to get out of marrying the Infanta of Rimon. Of course, that might have been a poor choice, given that she was now married to Tarses.

The implications of such a match were several. He would be permanently linked to Kasfia, a woman he did not trust and who was even now using him as a pawn in her plan to maintain power over her city. He would be committed to siring an heir and could no longer pretend to be a king when it suited him; he would be establishing a line of kings, extending infinitely into the future. And then there was Naftaly.

Princess Ayleth looked none too pleased with this turn, either, and it did not escape Barsilay that her own mother had kept her asleep beneath the prison for the entire past age; whatever maternal affection might have existed had long ago worn away in the face of Kasfia's ambition. Ayleth had been the Queen's tool to anticipate the

Mirror. Now that was no longer a functioning strategy, she would be the Queen's tool in Barsilay's bed, to create an heir that would rule both P'ri Hadar and Luz.

Kasfia said, "There is no other option for you. Either you agree and marry Ayleth, and I give you my word I shall help you raise Luz and defeat Tarses. Or else you must leave P'ri Hadar and never return, on pain of death."

There was, of course, no way for him to leave. The noose of his heirship had lain around his throat since the mark had appeared on his shoulder in the dungeon of La Cacería, and now it had tightened. He looked to the Peregrine, whose face was lined with strain, and at the old woman, who shook her head, either telling him to decline or else that he had no decent option. And he said, "Then I agree."

The wedding was to be held in two days' time, before the rise of the Katlav moon. Ayleth made it plain that she objected to the entire arrangement, but her hands were as tied as Barsilay's. He angled for a month's pause, but Kasfia guessed (rightly) that this was some plot to get out of the marriage, and said she would consider him an oath-breaker if he abandoned the original timeline. In fact, she told him, it was only due to respect for her daughter that she was allowing two days for the engagement. She ought to have insisted on the wedding the instant Barsilay agreed to it.

Barsilay, for his part, was forbidden to leave the palace during this time, but he was allowed visitors. He'd asked for Efra several times, but she was indisposed and the only messengers he was allowed were his guards, whom he did not trust. The old woman had left with the Peregrine, looking, Barsilay thought, a little silver around the temples, and had not returned, probably because she'd gone back to looking like an old mortal. Whether Naftaly was still in Aravoth, he did not know.

Worse... the first night of his engagement, he discovered that his rooms were warded to prevent him dreaming beyond them.

He'd sent word to Kasfia, enraged that he was still being treated as if he were inside her prison, and she'd replied (in a note carried by a shade) that the wards would be eliminated when he was married, and then spun some fabrication about this being a P'ri Hadari custom to abstain from the dream-world in the nights before a wedding.

He paced, and raged, and in one respect the palace was even worse than the prison: He could not speak to the other prisoners, and he hadn't seen the barest hint of the demon since he'd been released. Whether it was barred from the palace with magic or simply hadn't bothered to show up, Barsilay could not have said. But he took to leaving bowls of milk around his bedroom in the hopes that it might appear.

On the second day of his confinement, he had his first visitor, and it was Asmel.

He threw his arms around his uncle and said, "I feared I would not see you."

Asmel looked well enough, if a little strained. He was dressed in the clothes he'd been given in Zayit, which seemed out of place in P'ri Hadar where the fashions were so much more subdued, and men, in general, did not go about in such bright colors. Asmel's coat and trousers were pale blue—almost somber by Zayiti standards. Barsilay found he'd missed color in the dimness of the prison, and the familiar face of his only living family. He wanted, very badly, for Asmel to offer some advice, as he might have done when Barsilay was young and too much a fool to have heeded his wise uncle. He'd have liked the opportunity to reach back through time and slap his own face. Then things might have been different for both of them.

"I have been trying to get in since we had word of your ransom," he told Barsilay. "I only now was able to get inside the palace."

"I'm surprised they let you in at all, then."

"Perhaps they weren't meant to," Asmel said. "But I bribed a guard, and here I am."

"You have no money," Barsilay told him.

"It wasn't mine," he said. "Your old woman is now very rich indeed."

Barsilay did not ask how that had transpired. He said, "You will know, then, what I am about to do."

"I was told," Asmel said.

"Naftaly will never forgive me."

"Naftaly is no fool," Asmel said. "He knows what a king is and where his duties lie. It is unfortunate. I grant you this."

"It is more than unfortunate," Barsilay said. "What have you come to tell me, or are you here to hold my hand as I wait to begin my sentence?"

Asmel sighed and settled into the chair by the hearth. It had grown chilly outside, and a pair of shades had built a fire that failed to properly warm the large room. It did, however, create enough noise to mask their conversation from the hallway, particularly with some magical help from Asmel, who told him, "I have made a terrible mistake. And I don't know if there is any remedy for it." He explained how he'd given Elena part of the remaining shard of his safira, in the hopes she might reach Rafeq in the dream-world. Barsilay thought it had been a reasonable plan, despite how it had turned out.

"I'd have suggested the same, had I been there. What have you tried?"

"Al'qot was my first thought, having seen them on Naftaly. There was no response, no matter how many I placed, and I was worried I might be making her worse so I discontinued the experiment."

"There must have been a Zayiti doctor among the refugees?"

"There were two, but neither had any experience with mortals and I was rather afraid to tell them how she'd suddenly come by the extra magic. They'd no idea what to do. Unfortunately, the obvious person to help is Rafeq himself, and there's no way I could find him in the dream-world, even if he would speak to me. But he might speak to you, as Marah's nephew."

Barsilay sighed. "We were colleagues once. I will try, but I cannot dream in the room they've given me: it's warded."

Asmel was already making a circuit of the room, his hand tracing the wall. "These wards are very old," he told him. "I cannot break them."

Now that was odd—he'd assumed the wards had been created for him. Why else would Kasfia keep a room warded against dreaming in her own palace? The woman seemed a deep well of strangeness. "Rafeq will have to wait, then, but there is someone else who might help. I've been in contact with Saba."

"Saba! How?"

"There was a demon in the prison with me. He was a very able messenger."

Barsilay rendered a copy of the cypher in the air. "Saba was able to send me this."

"I don't know this cypher," Asmel told him.

"Nor do I, but there was a Zayiti in the prison who translated it for me. It is the antidote for decayed salt—the bezoar of a Leviathan. Saba must have developed it or discovered it by accident, for all the good it does anyone."

Asmel looked at the cypher a long time and said, "The Leviathan... That can be no coincidence. It is dead and washed up here only days ago."

Barsilay said, "No, that can't be a coincidence. And a bezoar?"

"I could not say. Efra should see this message, especially if it's a Zayiti cypher. Can you put this on paper? I will pass it to the Peregrine."

"I did try to send it to her already," Barsilay said, making another copy of the message on a leaf of paper he'd pulled out of the table. "But someone attacked the demon with a handful of salt. And now I haven't seen it since I was ransomed. I've been hoping it would find me again, to be honest. I'd have been quite lost without it down there."

"It sounds like you had a great deal to do," Asmel said. "The prisoners are with the Zayitis now. They speak very highly of you, and you did well to get them out. They want to help us, and I trust them more than I trust Kasfia."

"I don't trust Kasfia at all," Barsilay agreed, folding the slip of paper and handing it back to Asmel, who tucked it into his coat. "I can't believe I am doing this thing, Uncle. It is a nightmare I'm not certain I can endure."

"Most men shoulder their responsibility throughout their lives," Asmel told him. "You've had all yours thrust on you at once. It will not be easy for you, but at least you have been presented with a way forward—and no king marries for love."

"Still," Barsilay said. "Kasfia is older than the both of us together, and the Princess is clever. I fear my will shall be overrun by those two, and I will lose sight of what I need to do." He raised his eyes to his uncle's. "I am becoming what I must loathe, and I don't seem to be able to prevent it happening. Does the good we are trying to do outweigh that, truly?"

"Truly?" Asmel repeated. "I don't know. But the alternative is to do no good at all. Remember, Naftaly and Toba will be returning, and you've just ensured their safety. No one will try to take the book from them, nor the Ziz."

"No," Barsilay said. "Only myself, for whatever I may have been worth to them."

"You are maudlin."

"And if you'd wed the Infanta, Tarses would not be King of Rimon."

"She never intended to marry me."

"Perhaps," Barsilay said. "But that isn't why you refused."

"Are you angry that you are forced to make the choice that I would not? Marrying Oneca would have benefited only myself. Marrying Ayleth allows you to save the world—both worlds. You know this."

"Asmel," he said. "I am afraid."

Asmel said, "I know. So am I."

"You can imagine what Kasfia will do if I manage to sire an heir."

"Yes," Asmel said, a little uncomfortably. "Well. On that point, I think you should stall as long as you can."

"What, get so drunk on the wedding night I can't perform?" Asmel raised an eyebrow, but Barsilay said, "I have never been that drunk."

"Ah," he said. "But she doesn't know that."

"Hm. Then drunk every night 'til Luz is raised, is that it?"

"I've seen you drunk longer."

"That's presuming Naftaly and Toba return before I'm forced to sober up," he said, rising, because there had been a knock on the door. "I can't stay drunk forever."

He opened the door, revealing a shade who spoke in the voice Barsilay recognized as belonging to one of the Queen's men. "I was told the wedding wasn't for hours," Barsilay said.

"The Queen requires you for another issue," the shade told him. "It is unrelated to the wedding."

"I can't imagine what else she'd have to say to me today."

"It is concerning the agreement over the prisoners. There is some trouble."

Barsilay turned from the door. "What trouble can there be? I thought she'd already released them."

"Do you mean to argue with a shade?" Asmel muttered.

"Fine," Barsilay said. "I will go with you."

Asmel rose as well, and the shade said, "The Queen only wants to see you."

Barsilay did not much like the degree to which the Queen was dictating to him and felt he had better not let it continue. "My uncle comes with me, or I stay here and the Queen can come herself. Would that suit her better?"

The shade flickered—probably it was not able to consider a question like that—and went back down the hallway. "Just come," Barsilay told Asmel, and the two men followed a decidedly unhappy piece of magic down to a room he'd not been in before. He immediately realized why—the Zayiti prisoner was there, and the Queen would not want the entirety of her court present for this conversation. In fact, there was no one else in the room besides two guards and the woman he'd seen in the throne room with the flagon of wine.

Kasfia said, "This man says he knows you."

The man in question seemed to be meditating on the state of the floor. Barsilay said, "Yes," because there did not seem to be a need to lie.

"The prisoners do not have access to one another," she said.

"What is the problem?" Barsilay asked. "I was told there was some issue with our agreement, not my activities before I made it."

Kasfia snapped her teeth together hard enough that Barsilay could hear it across the room. She said, "He tells me he translated a message for you. It seems to have been something of importance."

Now here was an odd thing. Why would the Zayiti have given that information up to the Queen, whom he despised?

"Why did you not tell me of Tarses's new poison?" she demanded. "Or of the antidote?"

Barsilay said, "Since our only interaction has been to negotiate my release from your prison, it would seem it did not come up."

"You maintain you would have told me?"

"Are you accusing me of something?" he asked. "The new poison is deadlier in smaller amounts than salt, and it will kill mortals as well as Maziks. But since you guard for salt anyway, it hardly seemed urgent to mention it."

"And the antidote?"

"Is unobtainable," he said.

The Queen nodded, as if satisfied with this strange exchange. She said, "This man is refusing to leave the prison. He is asking to serve out his sentence."

"Why?"

"I care not why," the Queen said. "I care only that this breaks our agreement. Unless you will amend it and allow him to remain in my custody."

To the Zayiti, Barsilay said, "Why would you choose this?"

"The prison," he said, "is the void for cowards."

"Are you certain?"

The Zayiti nodded. Barsilay turned to Asmel, who whispered, "It is possible for a man to be too broken to live on, and also too frightened to die." Aloud, he said, "What is his sentence?"

"For thievery from the crown, one thousand years."

"What did he steal?" Barsilay asked, because that was not what he'd been told the man had done. But it would also not be the first time someone had been sent to prison on trumped-up charges.

"That is immaterial," Kasfia said. "Do you allow him his wish?"

"Do you understand, you will be alone there for a thousand years?" Barsilay asked the prisoner. "I cannot intervene for you again."

"I do," he said.

"Well then," Barsilay said. "I release this man from our agreement, that he may have his wish." He approached and set his hand on the man's shoulder, saying, "I hope you find what you are looking for down there. I will see you in a thousand years, if Hashem wills it."

"If Hashem wills it," the man said, and allowed himself to be led away.

Back in his chambers, Barsilay bathed before his wedding, while Asmel sat nearby, thumbing through books some earlier resident had left in the room. "Do you think it is really possible to be so broken?" Barsilay asked, his chin just above the surface of the water. He could not stop thinking of the Zayiti prisoner as he stared at the floor, and he wondered what Kasfia had done to make him reveal the contents of Saba's message. He supposed he would never know, if she'd threatened him with torture or even if she'd harmed him outright. But the expression he'd worn had been much the same as Asmel's after he'd lost the university and Marah, and spent months in Tarses's prison besides, before agreeing to accept the sigils of silence in exchange for Barsilay's own life. It was a thing they'd never discussed.

Asmel said, "It is not loss that breaks you so much as divorce from one's own self."

"Can that not be the same thing?"

"Of course it can," Asmel said. "But what I mean to say is the world cannot break you if you hold fast to your work. Attachments may be broken, even love, but the work always remains, Barsilay."

Barsilay laughed a little, rippling the surface of the water, and said, "I am glad you did not lose yourself in the mortal world, Uncle. But not all of us are so committed to our work as you."

"That cannot be so," he said. "Perhaps it's more that others misunderstand what their work is."

When Toba and Naftaly arrived in the citrus grove of P'ri Hadar, it was still daylight, and the midday sun shining through the trees was nearly blinding to eyes that had not seen such light in days.

Or had it been days? Toba found that she had no concept for how much time had passed; it might have been a week or three months. She had no idea how close they might be to the moon, and she was not sure if P'ri Hadar ran its affairs more like Rimon or Zayit, and how much traffic there might be through the gate. Without that knowledge, it really wasn't safe to stay in the grove.

They dismounted from the back of the Ziz, sliding all the way to the ground (which was a long way down) and Toba found herself landing in heap beside Naftaly. Nehama managed to land on her feet and stood stock-still, gazing up at the clear blue sky, whispering to herself, and then weeping.

Toba got herself up and put her hand on Nehama's back as the other woman sobbed, which she did for several minutes before she looked up and said, "I had forgotten the sun."

Then she tore off her clothes and stood naked before lying down on the dusty ground, laughing as the sun heated her bare skin. Naftaly looked uncomfortably away. The Ziz, unimpressed by this display, leaned down and began to eat the fruits off the citrus trees, one after the other.

"The trees will be bare soon," Naftaly said, still angling his body from Nehama, who had turned over and now lay face down, arms and legs akimbo, and was shouting into the ground.

Toba told him, "It doesn't matter, we can't keep the Ziz here if she's meant to be a secret. We don't know when the moon is coming. We'll have to hide her and then go off to find the others."

Naftaly craned his neck back and waved his arm vertically, saying, "Where is it you intend to hide her?"

"Citrus trees don't grow very tall," Toba said, "even Mazik ones, but there must be some taller trees nearby that might shield her. The scriptures talk about the great cedars…"

"Which were all cut down."

"Ours were cut down. Maziks wouldn't cut down trees, if they could avoid it. They don't build anything out of wood."

From the ground, Nehama said, "At one time, there was a great cedar wood south of the city. There would be no reason to cut it down." Rolling over and sitting up, she said, "The Ziz can probably see it."

"Yes, but we can't risk her flying there if we don't want her seen. We'll have to walk," Toba said.

And so, once the Ziz was done eating most of the fruit in the grove and Nehama had been talked back into her clothes, the three of them climbed back onto the Ziz and they made their way to the cedar forest of P'ri Hadar.

It took only a few hours to get there, by which point the sun had descended halfway down to the horizon; winter had shortened the daylight hours, and Toba squinted at the sky for some sign of the shape of the rising moon, but with the trees all around she could not see it. The forest was miles across, filled with Mazik cedars nearly as tall as the shortest trees in Aravoth.

Toba had wondered about the nature of trees since they'd come through the gate and seen the citrus trees in the grove. So much of

Aravoth had been forest, and though she knew the place was not truly as she'd perceived it, the trees had seemed entirely real. Were the trees in Aravoth the same manner of being as the trees in her own world? What did it mean, if they were? In her bag she carried the almond branch—she'd wrapped a little cloth around the cut end and wet it with water, but she would need something better to do with it soon.

Or would she? The trees in Aravoth grew without sun or rain. Maybe it did not mind being in her bag.

The Ziz cast her face toward the sky and clucked a little, sounding to Toba's ears like an enormous overgrown chicken. Naftaly must have thought the same, as he let out a bark of a laugh, and said, "I suppose she's missed the sun, too. Do you think she needs a nest?"

But the Ziz had already curled up on the ground and put her great head under her wing. "I think she's capable of making her own, if she needs one," Toba said. To Nehama, who had managed to keep her clothes and wits about her for the past hour, she said, "Will you stay with her? I don't want to leave her alone, but we need to find our people."

Nehama said, "She would prefer the boy."

This was probably true, since Nehama was the one who had suggested smashing the Ziz's egg—though Toba had no way of knowing if the Ziz had understood this. Still, Naftaly had people to see, and Nehama did not. "I think it must be you," she said. "It won't be for long."

"You don't know that," Nehama said. "You have no idea what you might be walking into. I have spent ten lifetimes alone in a forest. I have no will to spend another."

"Give me one day," Toba said. "Someone will come for you."

Looking to Naftaly for help, she said, "You owe me a great deal."

"We don't deny it," Naftaly said. "But you can't think we mean to abandon you. Give us a day to find the lay of things."

Nehama turned away and said, "Fine." So Toba found a few small rocks, inscribed them with the names of her friends, and used Elena's locator spell to determine the location of Elena, Asmel and Barsilay. Elena she found not far away, in a spot between the cedar forest and the sea. The others were in the city. "Why is she alone?"

she murmured. Naftaly would want to go to Barsilay first, but something about the distribution worried Toba.

"I think we should go there first," she said, tapping Elena's location. "It might be easier to find her outside of the city, and she can tell us where everyone else has gone."

Naftaly did not seem to think much of this suggestion. "I would speak with Barsilay first," he said. "He is the most likely to know what is happening. And you see Asmel is also inside the city."

"I know," Toba said. "But we don't know where they are in the city. We could wander for days trying to find them."

"Elena may be equally hard to find."

"I don't think so," she said, and sensed a greater argument brewing, and knew they had no time for it. "I will go to my grandmother. You go into the city. Meet me in the dream-world tonight, and we'll see who managed to learn more."

Naftaly nodded, once, but Toba said, "If you are going into the city, I think you should leave the book with me. It will be safer, I think."

Naftaly said, "I'm not inclined to part with it."

"If not for me, it would still be with Tarses," she reminded him. "I'm capable of protecting it."

"And I am not?"

"I wasn't implying as much."

"You were," he said. "But perhaps you are right; if we mean to keep the book from the Queen, outside the city is probably better than in." He took the book from inside his coat and handed it over. "Shall we set a time? Say three hours past sundown?"

"Three hours past sundown," Toba agreed. To Nehama, she asked, "Do you know how many hours' walk the city is from where we are now?"

Without turning around, she rather sulkily replied, "I can't recall."

"It's fine," Naftaly said. "I could see the wall on the way here; it isn't far."

It also wasn't far to the place Toba had seen Elena, and as she was coming from a higher elevation, she could see a settlement below her—a square village of sorts, with small buildings the color of sand having been pulled out of the rocky ground. There was some sort of demarcated perimeter around the settlement, and on the side she was approaching was a break in this, manned by two Maziks Toba recognized from their clothing as Zayitis. This must be where Efra had put the refugees, and Toba was a little chagrined it had not occurred to her to scry for Efra as well as the others. Why these people were out here and not in the city was anyone's guess. As she approached, the men guarding the perimeter sent a small flying creature into the settlement. By the time Toba had gotten there, Efra had also arrived.

She looked extraordinarily fatigued, and less pleased to see her than Toba would have liked, and Toba liked even less that she did not ask for any news of what had happened in Aravoth. Instead, she greeted Toba tiredly and led her into a relatively larger building in the center of the camp, inside which Elena lay on a low bed, asleep in the middle of the day.

"How long has she been like this?" Toba asked.

"More than a week," Efra said.

Toba knelt down and took Elena's hand, which was oddly warm. "Is she feverish?"

"I will let Asmel explain to you," Efra said.

"And where is he?" she asked, not a little angrily.

"In the city, " she said. "Attending Barsilay's wedding."

TSIFRA ARRIVED AT the city of P'ri Hadar on the eve of the full moon, having first walked, and then traded the jewels of the Queen of Sefarad for a horse which had collapsed en route, and then walked again. She was filthy from traveling but she'd made it in time for the gate.

She was not sure how she would find Tsidon hidden in the city while also keeping her promise to help Elena. Her orders from Tarses were, of course, the higher priority, but also nearly impossible to carry out. Tsidon would not be easily found, even if she knew the city, which she did not. The only point in her favor was the proximity to the winter solstice, which gave her a little extra time while the moon was up.

She had money left, which she traded for less conspicuous clothing and a few hours in an inn with a basin of wash-water. She could have used magic to alter her own things, but she wanted to save as much as she could for after moonrise. She did not even bother to heat her own bath.

The other issue was that she did not know where the gate would be on the mortal side, having not had access to a moon codex. She was weary and would have to find someone at the university to help her, and she was not very good at eliciting aid from mortals without threatening them. She knew also that she would be unlikely to get the information she needed as she was, so she did what many women before her had done in analogous circumstances: She disguised herself as a man.

In this guise she entered the observatory of P'ri Hadar and asked after the famous astronomer (not bothering to give a name), and once pointed in the proper direction, broke into his library and rifled his books 'til she found the one she needed. It would be helpful to have it, she decided, for future reference, so she put it inside her coat and walked out with it.

Then she left the observatory and went to where the grove would be at moonrise. At present, it was only a mostly barren strip of chaparral, so she made herself a meal with the lentils she'd brought with her and lay down to have a rest 'til dark. When she opened her eyes again the grove had appeared around her, fragrant and strangely humid. The gate had not appeared yet, the sun was not quite down, and so she ate a citron, and another. It was taboo to eat from the sacred groves, but she did not much care, and anyway someone else had been working on the fruit already… There were bare trees throughout the grove, so what were a few more pieces? She put a few of the citrons in her bag to make a change from lentils, and when at the appointed hour the gate flew up from the ground, she cast a time-keeper upon the back of her hand, an hourglass within her flesh, and then was ready to step through.

She knew Elena was near where she'd seen her in the dream-world, and that was closer to the gate than the city was. Healing her would not take long, she knew—all she needed was a little salt, and she had some in her bag. It was marked for Tsidon, of course, but she had enough to poison him twice over—which she looked forward to doing, but she would have to settle for killing him once. She set her toes toward the sea, and Elena.

NEAR THE PLACE she expected to find her, Tsifra found a settlement of Zayitis. They'd warded their perimeter with salt, which of course had no effect on her, and making herself translucent, she stole inside. She did not have time to search every building: She'd given herself two hours to pass through the gate and help Elena before heading for the city—enough time that she felt she could honestly tell Tarses she hadn't wasted any in case she failed to find Tsidon later in the night. So she listened for voices speaking, and presumed Elena would not be in one of the stone buildings filled with others who were awake.

Listening at every window, she made her way to the center of the settlement, to the largest building, and peered inside. There, she saw Elena, looking much as she'd seen her before, only with her eyes closed instead of open. The only other person present, Tsifra realized with a bit of surprise, was Toba.

She felt a little sour toward the other woman. Where had she been when her grandmother was stretched out alone on the sand of the dream-world, and why had she allowed her to risk her life with the safira anyway? Careless, she thought, with the person responsible for saving her life as a child. She wished she could have been the one to teach Toba to appreciate Elena better, but just then she would have to settle for luring Toba outside, because she did not think she would believe she meant to heal her grandmother, and in any case she could not risk being seen by the Zayitis.

She would only need a moment to get the salt into Elena, and so she cast a second-rate shade and sent it to knock on the door, giving it a reasonable rendition of Asmel's voice which asked Toba to come outside to measure the angle of the moon.

Toba looked very angry at this suggestion, and stormed to the door, throwing it open, saying, "That is what you have to say to me, after everything—"

She was cut short, seeing no Asmel on the threshold, and called him twice before she went out to find him. Tsifra slipped in through the window, making her way to Elena's bedside. The packet of salt was in her hand, and she whispered into Elena's ear, "I would mix this with water, but there's no time." And she poured the grains into Elena's mouth.

There was no immediate change, and she cursed herself for not asking the doctor how long this was likely to take. She ought to leave, she knew, before Toba returned. She'd done what she'd set out to do, and if the doctor's advice didn't work, that was hardly her fault. But then Toba, who seemed to be a little angry with Asmel already, came back not fifteen seconds from when she'd left, to see Tsifra crouching over her grandmother with the torn packet in her hand.

Tsifra rose slowly, her hands palms out. Toba said, very darkly, "What are you doing?"

It would look, of course, as if she were poisoning Elena. Tsifra said, "It's only salt—"

"Salt?"

"I spoke to a doctor—"

But then, a pair of Zayitis walked through the door: a tall woman accompanied by a man with a green earring. Seeing Tsifra, both of them threw up their hands. Toba shouted, "Wait!" but Tsifra hardly knew whether she was talking to them or to her, and the woman had sent a bolt of magic meant for her head. Tsifra threw herself sideways, while Toba shouted, "You'll kill her!" which probably meant Elena, and the woman sent another bolt of magic—which turned out to be a dagger that clipped her shoulder.

Damnation. She could kill all three of them, but it would slow her down, and Tarses hadn't asked her to kill these Zayitis, anyway.

He had ordered her to kill Toba, however, and here she was.

Beside her, Elena let out a rattling gasp. The salt was working. Only it hadn't been enough, and she could not use the rest of her salt, which was marked for Tsidon. The tall woman pulled a blade from her hip and rushed at her, and Tsifra concluded that this woman knew how to fight, and that there would be no stopping her without killing her.

Elena's eyes fluttered open, then closed again, and in that moment Tsifra carried out the most impulsive thing she'd ever done: She grabbed Elena around the waist and pulled her through the wall.

She heard an alarm go up, but only Toba would be able to follow where Tsifra was going and she was not fast enough to catch her. Tsifra ran toward the sea, arrows striking the ground to either side of her, and wondered that they cared not even a little if they hit the person they were trying to save.

No, she realized, they weren't trying to save Elena. They only wanted to kill Tsifra. She could hear Toba's steps behind her as she dodged arrows. Ahead of her lay the coast. Toba shouted, "Tsifra N'Dar, stop!"

Tsifra's body responded to the command before her mind had time to process it; it was as if she'd been turned to stone. In a panic, she reasoned that Toba had not ordered her to stop breathing—'til then, she had been holding her breath, and even her heart had stuttered a few times in her chest. She'd been given countless orders from Tarses since her childhood; she knew what it felt like to have her name used this way. But this felt quite different, and a good deal worse. Tsifra could hardly believe Toba had risked using her name—Toba's own name—in the hearing of the soldiers of Zayit. She took a few deep breaths and realized she could still speak, even if the rest of her was little more than a statue.

"I am trying to help her," she said. "Let me go. I can use your name just as easily. Don't play this game with me."

Toba said, "Please. Put her down. What happened to you? You were hell-bent on killing Tarses, and now you do his bidding?"

"I have no choice! Tarses murdered Atalef—the killstone was destroyed."

"And he sent you here."

"Yes, and if you're smart you'll leave now, before I remember what he told me to do if I saw you again."

"I can't leave you with my grandmother!"

"I am only trying to help her," she said. "You must trust me—"

"How can I?"

"Because she does!" Tsifra, still unable to move because of Toba's command, felt the pull of Tarses's order, and tried desperately to think of anything else. Elena's weight in her arms, the sting of the salt in the air, the cold sand beneath her boots. Elena was only in a thin shift and must have been even colder; the woman was a dead weight in her arms. As she looked down at her, Elena's eyes fluttered again. If Toba had her way, Tsifra thought, Elena would never wake up. But if she succeeded, if Tsifra saved Elena, then in that moment it would be as if she had been the granddaughter worthy of Elena's care.

Tsifra said, "Tsifra N'Dar, release me, then sit down, and do not speak again 'til I have gone."

Toba let out a cry of anguish, and said, "I release you," and then she sat down and wept.

Taking Elena into the sea, Tsifra dropped to her knees and cupped the cold water in her hand, pouring it into the other woman's mouth. The first three palmfuls ran back out of her lips, but on the fourth, she swallowed. Tsifra kept going, giving her draught after draught of sea water, 'til Elena began to cough and sputter, and then she sat up. Toba, only ten paces away, let out a cry.

Letting go of Elena, Tsifra got to her feet. This whole affair had been a mistake. She'd wasted too much time and too much magic, and now, without Elena's weight in her arms, Tarses's order was screaming in her mind and she was going to have to kill Toba. She made her arm a blade and walked out of the sea.

She heard Elena rise up behind her and felt a tiny blade against her throat. It would not be enough to harm her—Tsifra was too skilled—but then Elena's raspy voice said, "Tsifra N'Dar, you will not touch your sister. I will let you live for what you have done for me, but you must leave and never lay eyes upon her again."

Tsifra said, "It cannot work that way. My orders from Tarses are older; I cannot discount them, no matter what you say." She parried Elena's blade away with the tip of her sword, and turned back, and Toba was gone.

"How?" she demanded, but Elena said, "You had better leave. The Zayitis are not so fearful of the sea as you believe."

Tsifra looked again at the place where Toba had been, and there was nothing. From higher up the sand, she could see Zayiti archers taking aim.

Returning her arm to flesh, she left Toba and Elena behind and ran.

Chapter Thirteen

Naftaly had not considered, when he'd left Toba, that he spoke no P'ri Hadari.

He could understand a little of what he heard because there was some amount of Aramaic mixed in, which he'd learned (badly) when he'd studied. But mostly he was at a complete loss. Worse, he did not know exactly where Barsilay was in the city. His only clue was the vision he'd had of Barsilay's wedding, and he did not know if it had already happened, or if it was happening in the future. Glamouring his eyes, he set his steps toward the palace, which seemed the most likely place to find the heir of Luz. But he had no idea what he would say when he got there.

His mind was still a little muddled from Aravoth, and he could not help but question the landscape, the buildings, the people. Was this all real, he wondered, or was this all a concoction of his imagination?

Maybe he'd invented his entire adventure. Maybe this was all just a vision, and he'd open his eyes and find himself in his bed in his father's house, and he'd never met Barsilay or Toba at all.

At the door to the palace, which was cast from silver and featured trees laden with fruit made of golden stones, Naftaly stopped his rumination. There were guards, of course, and even if one of them happened to speak Rimoni, he had no idea how to talk himself inside. Why had he bothered to come on his own? Before he could think to speak, one of the guards said something to him, and not too gently, either. A hand on his shoulder turned him around, and he found himself looking at the Peregrine, who said, "He says none may enter today, because of the wedding of the Princess."

The Princess! And today, then. It was happening today, just as he'd seen it. The Peregrine did not bother to ask if he'd worked out whom the Princess was marrying, and he asked, "Can you help me get inside? Can you help me to see him?"

The Peregrine said, "I know you love him, but hear me now. Barsilay has given me a message: You should get as far from this city as you can, and now, before the moon rises."

Naftaly's mind went hazy, as if he were about to have another vision. "No," he said, "he cannot have said that."

"You must go," she said.

Naftaly would have protested again—surely the Peregrine could find a way inside, if anyone could. At least she could get Barsilay a message! He must know they'd returned from Aravoth, and with the Ziz. Even if he were married, even if he wanted Naftaly gone, he would want to know that. But the Peregrine had already vanished, and his coat was oddly heavy. Putting a hand in his pocket, he pulled it out again with his fist full of coins.

He put the handful of silver coins bearing an emblem of a citron tree back in his pocket and put his back to the gate. Had Barsilay really told her to do this? To pay him off and send him away? He could not believe it. He would not believe it. Unless, perhaps, this was the thing Barsilay had known he wouldn't forgive him for… Not the marriage, but the banishment.

His mind was going foggy and he ground the heels of his hands into his eyes, willing the sensation away. If Barsilay wanted him gone, he could tell him after he'd delivered the message about the Ziz. He took one of the coins in his pocket and used it to buy a bread roll stuffed with ground meat from a vendor on the other side of the plaza and sat down to eat it slowly.

Heartened by his full stomach, he resolved to find some other entrance, for servants, perhaps—not thinking that Maziks did not keep servants, and shades would not use a door. He hadn't enough magic to go through a wall, as Barsilay and Toba did, and these walls would probably not allow for such trespass anyway. The sun was growing low, and in his mind he heard Barsilay's voice again,

"Naftaly will never forgive me," and he put his head in his hands. For the first time since he'd woken in the pomegranate grove back in Rimon after losing Toba, he felt very much alone.

I am not alone, he told himself. My pockets are full of money.

He continued his circuit around the palace. Two guards could not be bribed. But one, guarding alone, might be. There must be another door someplace. And if there was no other door, he would find a low balcony, or a window, or some other way. He could get inside.

He'd come two-thirds around when he indeed found a second door—and this one had people coming into it. There were two guards manning it, most unfortunately, and the guards had a creature with them that might have been called a dog under different circumstances. It was nearly as big as a wolf but as red as a fox, and it had the same square-pupiled eyes as Mazik horses or Maziks themselves. The animal was perusing the goods that were being taken inside, and Naftaly presumed these must be things needed for the wedding, when a parcel was shown to the guards and revealed to be yellow silk.

Of course. If these Maziks were anything like those in Zayit, the Princess would want to be married in luxurious mortal-made silks, not textiles made by magic. The dog he could not account for, but it must have been there to sniff out some contraband. Or, more likely, salt.

Naftaly catalogued what else he might have on his person, besides the Peregrine's money. His clothes had come from Zayit, but they were not mortal-made (nor were they in particularly good condition, having been worn through Aravoth, up a massive tree, and into a magic lake).

But he still had his father's brass buttons.

He carefully plucked them off, two at each cuff and four down the front of his coat (which barely stayed closed without them). Taking them in his hand, he went to one of the guards, who looked perplexed at Naftaly's appearance with no shade or parcels. He pulled up what little Aramaic he could and, holding out the buttons, said, "For the Prince."

The guard exchanged a glance with his fellow and took a button and held it up to the dying sun. He asked a question Naftaly could not understand, and Naftaly nodded enthusiastically in reply. The other guard then approached with the dog, who seemed profoundly disinterested in either Naftaly or his buttons. Then they waved him past. As a gesture of goodwill, Naftaly tossed them each a coin as he went inside, and they replied with a cheerful word. He had no idea how much money he'd given them and didn't much care. He was inside the palace, and somewhere in this vast place was Barsilay.

Asmel was Barsilay's only attendant at his wedding, and this boded ill for all of them. The heir to the throne of Luz ought to have had advisors and kin and court, and instead all he had was one uncle. The Queen had also allowed him his ransomer, but she hadn't managed to turn up—perhaps her glamour couldn't be redone in time, or else she was having a bad day with her lungs.

The Peregrine had made herself rather scarce and Barsilay would have liked very much to know what she was doing. He hadn't had the chance to ask her about the King of Anab—whose assassination had been her last order from Tarses—but if she was here it was highly probable that he was dead. He ought to feel terribly guilty about that, seeing as he was the one who'd set her loose to murder him, but he felt oddly numb and detached.

He felt slightly less numb when he considered what to do about Naftaly. He would not be safe in Kasfia's court.

This was all a terrible mistake. He was turning his back on everything he'd learned from Marah and everything he wanted for himself, and making himself a pawn for Kasfia besides. A whisper in his ear asked him if this was really better than just letting Tarses take everything. Was he really so much worse?

Asmel helped a silent Barsilay into his wedding clothes. He had no crown of his own; Asmel had insisted he must have one, and crafted him a golden coronet set it with topazes made from magic. Barsilay had not wanted to wear it.

"If you do not," Asmel reminded him, "you are marrying her for nothing, and you will become naught but the Prince of P'ri Hadar."

He'd worn the coronet. His coat was golden and embroidered with the symbol of Luz, a great almond tree, with the other eleven trees set within its roots. His hair, which had grown overlong in prison, was trimmed, and his skin polished almost as much as his boots.

Then a Mazik, one of the Queen's retinue, came and told them it was time. Any further delay would mean marrying under a moon, which was as forbidden here as anyplace else. So they traveled down the stairs of the white palace and into Kasfia's throne room, in which there was a living canopy—a citron tree on the right had been made to grow together with an almond tree on the left. Barsilay came and stood beneath it, Asmel stood behind his shoulder. He tried to keep from willing himself to fall through the floor back down to the prison, in which he could at least have dreamed of rescue. In a moment, Ayleth would appear and he would drink wine with her and break a glass with her and sign their kit'bah, and then he would be expected, somehow, to consummate the whole business. Barsilay's tastes were far-reaching even for a Mazik, but in this case he was not sure he would be able to manage it.

Maziks were not quick to conceive. Probably he would be expected to perform that particular duty many times, over many years, before he was given his own heir, another king for Luz, and then he really would be just as terrible as he'd feared. Behind him, Asmel set a hand on his shoulder.

The Princess came, in a gown of pale-blue silk embroidered with green leaves and orange fruits; the work was mortal-made, and probably worth more than Asmel's entire alcalá. She wore no veil—he'd already seen her face anyway—and she came and stood beside Barsilay under the canopy. The Mazik leading the ceremony spoke. Barsilay was presented with very sweet wine, which he drank, and when he broke the glass under his foot it made a sickening crack he was sure could be heard all the way to the sea. He signed the kit'bah. And he was married.

The numbness that had descended earlier that day spread all the way to his fingers and toes.

He and Ayleth were ushered into a small chamber, where they were told they would have an hour before being taken to their wedding feast. Barsilay was not certain of the custom in P'ri Hadar, or what the Princess would expect during this hour. He was so tense his false arm vanished for a moment, and he hastened to bring it back before she noticed it missing.

She was a princess, he reminded himself. She would not be expecting affection from him. She would have anticipated a political union. Barsilay wet his lips, preparing to make some speech that might at least pave the way toward friendship, but the Princess said, "It was not in your best interest to agree to this."

The embers of Barsilay's speech sputtered out in his mind. "I'm sorry... What?"

"Do you know why my mother made this deal with you? Why she forced this marriage? She is out of options. She believes raising Luz will buy her time, and producing an heir to the thrones of Luz and P'ri Hadar will give her the power to rule over both."

Barsilay had understood all this, of course. He said, "Your mother was not the only Mazik out of options."

"So you understand."

"I do," he said. "What I have not yet understood is the nature of your task, all this past age. You were to help her manipulate the Mirror. I don't understand why you were not allowed to wake up." The Zayitis communicated with their part-mortal associates in the dream-world all the time, but at the end of the night they woke up and went about their regular business. Even the Courser was not made to stay asleep. He said, "Does Kasfia not trust you?"

"Kasfia trusts no one," she said. "Not so far as her crown is concerned. She did not want to risk anyone ever learning what I was doing. So she hid me away, and I was ordered to sleep and never wake."

"I'm surprised I could wake you at all then."

"Well," she said, "her order was for me not to wake myself. She didn't say someone else couldn't do it. I suppose it never occurred to her someone might come upon me down there in the prison."

Barsilay did not know what to say next, as he could not quite grasp Ayleth's feelings about the situation. She spoke of it so matter-of-factly and without malice that perhaps she had agreed to it, out of duty. He said, "Why did it have to be you?"

"The Queen trusts blood and little else." Her gaze went very far away then, and she said, "I was asleep for many years. I remember being ordered to dream. What came before that—my memory is hazy. It can only be because I was asleep so long."

"Perhaps your memory will improve now that you are awake."

"I suppose," she said. "Either way, understand: For all I have done, she sees me as a failure now, and you as an opportunity."

"To give her another heir, you've said. And your feelings on the matter?"

"Are beside the point," she said. "As are yours, now, too. I just wanted you to know."

"I suppose I should thank you for that much," he said. "But I do wonder one more thing, if you would not mind. Whose children are the half-Mazik agents living in the mortal city?"

Ayleth shook her head and looked away, and said, "I don't know."

Ayleth left not long after to change her clothing for the banquet, leaving Barsilay very much alone. He left the small alcove expecting to find Asmel waiting for him, and did not. Barsilay could not imagine under what circumstances his uncle would have left him to endure this. He had not a single person to cling to and found himself again questioning the wisdom of what he'd agreed to—he'd thought to make himself a king through his actions, but instead he seemed to have made himself Kasfia's permanent dependent. Worse, fathering an heir might well be deadly to him, but failing to do so would leave the marriage invalid, and then the Queen would have no obligation to him at all.

A shade appeared to escort him to the banquet but no sooner had he gone ten paces than from the other direction came a second shade escorting a man with his hands cupped in front of him.

"Naftaly," he breathed, and then he embraced him.

The numbness receded and his false arm vanished. It was a mistake to touch him in Kasfia's palace, but then what was one selfish moment in the face of everything else? "How did you get inside? Even Asmel had to bribe the guards."

Naftaly's face was very pale, and he held out—of all things—a handful of brass buttons, saying, "I told them I was bringing these to you."

It was then that Barsilay noticed that Naftaly's coat hung open over his chest. These were Naftaly's father's buttons, and he offered them in his cupped hands with an expression of veiled hope. Barsilay felt something inside him snap at the sight of Naftaly's heartbreak, and it was all he could do not to weep.

"Ah," he said, his voice breaking. "You beautiful creature." He embraced him again—the shade who had brought Naftaly had disappeared (Barsilay did not even know when it had gone) and they were alone. He kissed Naftaly's temple, and his cheek, and Naftaly said, "The Peregrine told me you wanted me to leave."

"The Peregrine?" Barsilay asked, because he had not seen her since he'd been ransomed, but then, before he could rationalize that he *should* make Naftaly leave—that if Kasfia learned who he was to him, he was in terrible danger, his eye caught a flicker of movement.

Ayleth had returned and was quietly watching her new husband with his hands all over a strange man in a coat with no buttons.

It was too late to pretend she'd seen something else, and he and Naftaly exchanged some glance of understanding. Barsilay's voice caught, and he said, "Ayleth of P'ri Hadar, this is Naftaly of Rimon."

Ayleth had taken in the glance that passed between her husband and this other man. She said simply, "If you love him, you should send him away from the Queen before she sees him. She will use him against you."

Screwing his eyes shut, Barsilay said, "She's right."

"No," Naftaly said. "I won't go. I've traveled through places you cannot imagine to be here, and I won't be sent away."

Barsilay pinched the bridge of his nose. "The Queen will hardly allow me to keep you with me."

Ayleth said, "Then tell her you have brought your own poison taster. She cannot object to that."

Barsilay recoiled a little. "No, I won't use him that way."

"The food will have been tasted already; it is only for show."

Barsilay looked carefully at his wife, whose face showed no sign of much of anything; whether she was concealing an emotion or had simply forgotten to have one he had no idea. Her manners were stilted, he'd noticed, and her speech less than fluent occasionally, probably from having been asleep so long. What did she wish from him?

Taking in his puzzlement, she said, "Remember that I did this for you."

It was both a gift and a threat, and Barsilay did not know what to say. He could not refuse. Then Ayleth took his arm, and together they walked into the banquet.

The wedding feast was held in the palace's great hall, which had a massive glass dome in the ceiling to allow for the viewing of the moon and stars at night. The sun was nearly down, and in the long room the light streamed sideways through tall, peaked windows. Light-stones lined the wall and had begun to wink on, and the table was heavy with fresh fruit and flowers. Shades hovered along the length of the room and Kasfia's advisors, the highest-ranking Maziks in her court, stood behind their chairs waiting for the Queen to take her place.

She entered, a small woman with light-brown hair walking just behind her. This, Barsilay knew, was Kasfia's poison taster. Asmel had told him she was said to be closer to the Queen than her own advisors, and the Queen went nowhere without her. Indeed, he recalled she'd been with Kasfia all three times he had seen her, sitting quietly in the background; 'til now, he had assumed she was simply a wine-pourer. She was given a chair behind Kasfia's left shoulder, and as the shades removed the golden dome over the Queen's plate, the woman ate a bite of every food there. Kasfia made a show of wiping the other woman's mouth with an embroidered cloth, and Barsilay picked up his wine, only to have Ayleth put her hand on his arm and lower the glass. "No one may eat or drink before the Queen," she said. "And she won't do either 'til she's satisfied there's no poison."

"Didn't you say the food was already tasted andd this was ceremonial?"

"Yes, it was tasted in the kitchen, but my mother's food is always tasted twice. Just wait."

The poison taster rose from her seat, bowed to the Queen, and then, while shades struck up on stringed instruments, began to dance, whirling and spinning as the food went cold. It was, Barsilay thought, the oddest custom he had ever witnessed. "The dance is to force her body to absorb any poison more quickly," Ayleth told him.

"Your mother must not be overfond of her."

"On the contrary. She has been at my mother's side a thousand years, and she loves her dearly."

"Your mother's love holds an interesting shape," he said.

The Princess smiled thinly. The poison taster bowed to the Queen and the assembled company applauded quietly, then the Queen put the first bite of food into her mouth, freeing everyone to eat.

The plates were so heavily laden Barsilay could not imagine a Mazik alive could have consumed all the food there—not even Toba, when she'd been making up for years of semi-starvation, could have managed it. In the center of each plate was a pigeon stuffed with a mixture of dried fruit and nuts, all soaked in wine, which left the bird a decidedly unappetizing shade of pink. The smell of the fowl was highly unpleasant, and Barsilay nearly laughed at the irony of his wedding dinner consisting of the food he most despised. Naftaly, who had been given his own chair behind Barsilay, took a bite of everything, which seemed like it would have been a full dinner under normal circumstances. Barsilay pushed the pigeon to one side and took a mouthful of some kind of root vegetable with a sauce made from citrons. He thought it was meant to be turnips. Since Naftaly did not have his own plate, he pushed the dish closer and let him take the greater portion of whatever he liked.

"You eat like a spoiled child," Ayleth said.

"You speak like a haranguing wife," Barsilay replied. Naftaly was eating with some enthusiasm, and he told him, "Eat all the fowl you want; I can't abide it."

"Couldn't you change it to something else?" Naftaly asked.

"No," the Princess hissed. "Do you have any idea how unspeakably rude that would be, at the Queen's table?"

He knew exactly how rude it would be, which is why he hadn't considered it. But with the Princess tweaking him over it, he felt overcome by a wave of contrariness. Meeting her gaze, he set his hand over the offending bird and turned it to a very nice trout. She muttered a curse at him, and he smiled and said, "I feel the same way," and lifted his fork.

"Barsilay, what is that?" Naftaly asked, pointing at the plate. Looking away from Ayleth's hardened expression, he saw that atop the fish were a spare handful of small granules… They might have been mistaken for some kind of grain, only Barsilay knew he hadn't made any. Leaning forward for a closer look, he pushed one with the tine of his fork. The way the light hit it, it might have been a fish egg. Maybe he'd made it by accident; a fancier meal than he'd intended.

Only then the Queen's poison taster began to scream.

She was doubled over and wailing, and then she cried out, "It burns!" Kasfia was on her feet, pale as a sheet of paper, and screaming at her men to do something, to find a physician. One of the men ran from the banquet, but the poison taster by then had fallen to the floor, and the screaming had stopped. Naftaly whispered, "Hashem have mercy." Barsilay leapt across the table, not sure what he could do, but since he was more a doctor than anyone available he felt he must do something. The poison taster was still alive, barely, and she met his eyes and said, "Help me."

Barsilay put his hand over her abdomen and could feel no flow of magic there. She let out a final, weak cry, and was still. The Queen roared.

Barsilay tore at the woman's dress, still not sure how he'd felt no magic in her belly at all. Her skin, under her ribs, had gone dark as charcoal. The poison had blackened her from the inside. He sat back with his hand to his mouth, his heart hammering. "Bring me my plate," he called, and Naftaly scrambled around the table with it as the rest of the company watched in mute horror. Barsilay prodded one of the grains on his plate, which gave way. "It's wax," Barsilay said. "Someone has suspended poison in wax to lengthen the time it needs to dissolve."

"Is this Tarses's new poison?" Kasfia asked tightly.

"It must be. There isn't enough salt here to kill like this," he said.

His eyes met Naftaly's. He'd used him to taste his food, his best beloved. "Naftaly," he whispered.

But the Queen had torn her necklace from around her neck, the pearl the size of an egg. "I have the antidote."

The room grew very quiet as all the Maziks present regarded their Queen, their eyes wide, their faces pale with the shock of what they had just seen. They would not know what Barsilay did—that the antidote was a bezoar of the Leviathan. They would not know how utterly impossible it was for her to have it in her hand. Someone had killed the Leviathan for this. Someone had known to cut the Leviathan open and take it.

"How is it," Barsilay said numbly, "that you have such a thing?"

But Kasfia was already holding it to her lips. Further down the table, the Princess was on her feet. For a brief moment, Barsilay thought he might be able to take the bezoar and give it to Naftaly. It was an instantaneous vision, and then the Queen said, to her daughter only, "Forgive me."

She swallowed the bezoar.

Everyone else in the room began to come out of their shock, and a great wave of weeping and shouting arose. How much time had passed between the poison taster's meal and their own? Kasfia set her hand over her stomach and seemed to decide there was no purpose in witnessing the poisoning of her entire court and her only daughter. "I will avenge you all," she said, and then turned and left.

She was nearly at the door when she, too, began to scream.

NAFTALY WATCHED KAFIA collapse and his eyes went strange, as if he were seeing the room underwater—or perhaps it was he that was underwater. He had the sensation of being in the lake in Aravoth, trying to guess which direction was up without the help of the sun. Then his vision shifted, but rather than clearing, it clouded over completely.

He was in a fog—drops of it were collecting on his skin. It was dusk and there was little light, but as the wind picked up the mist began to clear.

What he saw before him was a man as tall as Barsilay, dressed in silk that in the low light could have been either gray or blue, and which was spun so finely it rippled in the wind as if it were water. And here this became unlike any vision Naftaly had ever experienced, because the man was looking back at him.

Naftaly's visions were all the same in that he was an observer. He had never before been observed, and the sensation of it, of the man's eyes on him, was like falling from a great height. The man's face went rather shocked when he realized that Naftaly could see him, too. As the clouds blew by and the shadows moved off his face, his eyes were orange in the dying light. He'd seen this man twice before, in the olive grove of Zayit and at the oath-getting of the Queen of Rimon. This was Tarses. Only his hair then had been dark, and now it had gone as silver as Asmel's.

Tarses turned away from Naftaly, who could see now that they were on a hillside looking down over the sea, toward a peninsula with a great walled city. The city was burning. Tarses exhaled loudly and said, "I did not intend this." Then he reached out and grabbed Naftaly by the throat, pulling him closer to examine his face, saying, "I know you."

TOBA FOUND THAT even after her sister had gone, she had trouble getting up from the sand, as if Tsifra's command had somehow made her bones too heavy to lift. Elena, still soaked with icy seawater, staggered out of the surf and helped her to her feet.

"Grandmother—"

Elena was shivering in her wet clothes, and said, "You've come back."

Toba felt as if she hadn't come back; nothing was familiar in this place. Elena, at least, was still herself, and Toba leaned her forehead against her grandmother's and sighed, before lifting her hands to dry Elena's sodden dress, whispering, "Let me help you."

"I'm all right."

The sound of hooves on the beach distracted Toba from her task, and she looked up to see that Efra had ridden all the way to the shore, the horse shying a little on the shifting sand. "I need your help," she said.

"What's wrong?" Toba asked.

"Someone found a scroll just now—no one knows where it came from. It's written in my brother's cypher. I have to get to the palace."

"She's only just arrived!" Elena snapped.

"I may not be able to get in by myself," Efra said. "I need someone who can get through a salt-laced wall."

"Is it so urgent? My grandmother—"

But Efra said, "Asmel and Barsilay are both in the palace, and this is as urgent as anything I have ever seen."

Efra explained to her that Saba's true message had been this: *I've been forced to suspend the decayed salt in wax to make it slower acting. The Caçador plans to poison the heir of Luz and the court of P'ri Hadar. Assume anything might be poisoned. I am alive and in Anab.*

There was little time, Toba thought—if Tarses had someone with the means to poison the entire court, Barsilay's wedding to the Princess would surely be the best opportunity. She and Efra had departed immediately for the palace, but the moon was high overhead and Barsilay would be married already.

And Tsifra was ahead of them, too. Was she the intended poisoner? It stood to reason.

No, it couldn't be Tsifra. She'd been in the mortal world—she wouldn't have had access to Tarses's poison if Saba had been working with it in Anab.

The scars on Toba's arms were painful with her wish to grow another set of wings. She and Efra had a single horse between them, and they were so slow Toba could have screamed from it. Not only were Asmel and Barsilay in peril, she'd sent Naftaly into the city, too. *Fool*, she thought, *to let him go alone*. With any luck he might have gotten lost on the way. Or else the guards might not have let him in.

The handful of Asmel's memories she'd shared filtered through her mind, and she remembered herself on a beach, handing Asmel a periwinkle for his pain. She pressed her face into Efra's back against the wind, and the other woman called back, "Until we see them dead, we act as if they can still be saved. Do you understand?"

Toba understood, but she could also feel Efra's heart beating through her back as their horse raced up the road and past the looming wall, the moon bright on the sea behind them. As the city grew close, Toba felt her arms prickling again, and a strong feeling that she could be faster in the sky.

The city gate, when they got there, was closed. "What do we do?" Toba asked.

"Try to convince the guards to open it," Efra said.

"That'll take too long!"

Climbing down from the horse, Efra put her hand to the gate. "Salt," she said.

"That won't stop me," Toba reminded her.

"Then go," she said. "Quickly. I'll try to follow."

Toba made herself shadow and went through the closed gate. She ran down the abandoned street, and in the moonlight saw that some of her feathers had begun to grow back. *Not now*, she told herself. *There's no time.*

The feathers seemed to have other ideas, and Toba stumbled from the pain as they grew in a little, and then suddenly all at once. She tumbled to the ground, rose again, and decided to make use of her wings before she either lost them again or became a bird completely. She took to the air, willing herself higher. The guards on the palace wall were unable to see her—she was shadow still—and it suddenly occurred to her why Tarses had wanted her so badly, how easily she could become a monster, an assassin, a terror.

She flew to the roof, which featured a glass dome through which she could see a gathering in the room below… Many Maziks, celebrating the wedding of their Princess.

No, they weren't celebrating. Half of them were on the floor and weeping—and there was Barsilay, bent over Naftaly and screaming so loudly she could hear it through the glass. Scanning the room, she could see Asmel nowhere.

She slipped through the dome and glided to the floor, coming to rest before Barsilay, who looked up at her, his eyes wild with panic. She was too late.

"It's the decayed salt," she told him, in case he had not already made that assumption. "Can't you make them vomit it up?"

His voice shaking, Barsilay said, "It's encased in wax. The force of that would release the poison immediately. It wouldn't help."

"The poison has to come out!" she shouted. Naftaly began to choke, water coming up his throat and leaking out his mouth.

"Naftaly," Barsilay said urgently, his face as pale as it had been the night he'd lost his arm. "Naftaly, don't. Naftaly, look at me."

But Naftaly's eyes were closed, and he'd slumped sideways.

Barsilay was desperately running his hands over him, pressing magic into him in a nonsensical pattern. Nothing he was doing could possibly help, and after a few moments of this he looked up at Toba and said, "I've done this. I fed him poison, and I don't know how to save him."

Toba, too, was feeling desperate, and all she could think about was how much she wished Elena had been there with some last-ditch idea. Or Asmel, and where was he?

Maziks were dying all around them. Barsilay was screaming and shaking Naftaly, and Toba's mind went very quiet. I saved him before, she reminded herself. How did I save him before?

Toba smacked at the feathers on her arms that were resisting turning back to flesh. She was always turning into other things, and so seldom because she wanted to. Birds, fish. The first time she'd become fish, Barsilay had been there with her, at the fountain in Asmel's alcalá. It had been horrible, and worse when he'd made her swallow the fish afterward. She hadn't eaten any since; the feeling of them sliding down her throat was far too vivid. She'd felt them all the way to her stomach.

"The fish," she told Barsilay. "Fish can take the poison out."

"I don't see how eating fish—"

"No!" she shouted. Turning to Naftaly, whose face was soaked in sweat, she said, "Open his mouth."

"Toba!" Barsilay snapped.

"I know what I'm doing," she said, and from the palm of her hand she made a goldfish, as long as her finger, and while Barsilay swore, she slipped it down Naftaly's throat. Toba could feel it slide into his stomach, feel it swimming inside him while he opened his eyes briefly and looked at her in pain or shock, she could not have said which. She felt the fish swallow everything that had been in Naftaly's stomach, which left the creature much larger than it had been. "I'm sorry for this," she said, and forced it to swim back out of him.

Naftaly's eyes flew open, and he was left gagging and retching, while the fish—now twice the size it had been—landed on the floor, gasping for air. Toba felt it dying air and went down on one knee, and then she felt a searing pain that left her momentarily blind. She cried out, and the fish began to blacken on the floor, and then it was gone.

"Mother of monsters," Barsilay said, then called out. "You've all seen what she's done. Help yourselves. Help your friends." He turned to the Princess and made a fish of his own and forced it down her throat. The Maziks who were still alive made fish for themselves, and fish for those who lacked the will or skill.

Several died with the fish in their throats, too late to save them. But apart from Naftaly and Ayleth they were able to save some eight members of the Queen's court, while the Queen's dead eyes stared ahead as the moon passed over the dome in the ceiling. The great hall stank of the poisoned feast and of death.

Still weak from losing magic to the poison, Toba said, "Where is Asmel?"

"Not here," Barsilay told her. "He's safe so far as I know. How did you know about the poison? Who told you?"

"Efra translated the message," Toba told him, and then she wheezed, "Saba was made to suspend the decayed salt. He was warning you not to eat anything."

Barsilay sat back, rubbing the sweat off his face. "Efra, of course." He sighed. "I was given a different translation. A Zayiti I met in the prison here told me he could read it." Barsilay slowly got off the floor, which was littered with the bodies of so many of the finest Maziks in the city. "He's the one who told the Queen the bezoar was the antidote. Fools, all of us."

The Princess was still heaving great rasping breaths, but she turned to her guards and said, "Bring me that prisoner."

One of the guards hurried out. The room was filled with moans and weeping, and Toba was so weak from losing her magic to the poison she was not sure how much longer she would be on her feet. Barsilay, who had used his own magic to save more than one of the other Maziks, looked equally badly off, though Toba supposed he'd more magic to start with. There was one benefit to the loss of the magic—her feathers had all vanished down to the quills, and the pain in her arms was mostly gone. Instead, she was left with an itch that was difficult to ignore.

Naftaly, whose skin was a shade of gray that worried Toba a great deal, had opened his eyes but remained collapsed beside her as Barsilay made his rounds, checking on all of the surviving Maziks. The guards had blankets, and the two of them shared one as Naftaly sipped on some concoction Barsilay had given out to settle his stomach. "Barsilay is married," he told his drink.

"Yes, I know." She was existentially tired in a way she could not articulate, even inside her own mind. Elena had drunk salt and it had saved her; the Queen had taken the bezoar and died. It was all absurd, every bit of it.

After a bit, Naftaly asked, "Why fish?"

It took Toba a moment to realize he was speaking to her. "What?"

"The birds make sense. But I don't understand your affinity with fish."

Toba said, "I don't know. It's strange, isn't it? I don't suppose you have anything like that—some creature that you would rather be?"

"I'm less Mazik than you," Naftaly said. "I don't have the desire to turn into anything. Or at least I haven't got the aptitude."

"No. But you did know about Barsilay's wedding before it happened."

"Would have been more useful to know about the poison." He gasped a little and coughed. His throat was still spasming from either the poison or the fish. "I'm not suffering from the visions like I did, but I still can't control them. The Peregrine said—" he coughed again and continued, "The Peregrine knows Barsilay. They've eaten together plenty of times. She would have known what he liked, what he didn't. And she tried to send me away earlier today."

"She's here? In the city?"

He nodded.

If Naftaly were correct, they were facing something worse than a dead queen. Toba said, "If you think she was the poisoner, it means she's had recent orders from Tarses, and Tarses knows about the marriage."

She slowly got to her feet, intending to make sure Barsilay had drawn the same conclusions, when the guard returned with a disheveled man wearing Zayiti clothes—the prisoner, she supposed, who had lied about the bezoar. The man was dropped before them, chained hand and foot, and he looked up into Barsilay's face with an expression that was meant to be blank but instead read to Toba as guarded.

"Did you poison the banquet?" Barsilay demanded.

"I have been in prison all this time. I have done nothing there but sleep."

"You gave a false translation to the message I showed you," Barsilay said. "Why?"

The man said, "I only translated with the cypher I was taught. How can you claim otherwise?"

Toba said, "You could not have known the cypher for that message." To Barsilay, she said, "Saba never intended for anyone but Efra to translate it. That cypher was one Saba and Efra made when they were young."

The man kneeling before them had fair hair and dark eyes, and he seemed not to have noticed Toba before she'd spoken. His eyes lingered on her a moment too long, leaving Toba with an unwholesome feeling, and she shuddered.

"So you made the entire message up from whole cloth?" Barsilay asked. Reconsidering, he said, "No. If you couldn't read the message, how did you know about the decayed salt?"

Toba felt a dawning suspicion rise in her and strode closer to the prisoner, who looked down to the floor as she approached and examined him. Was he glamoured? Barsilay could probably tell better, but there was something about this man that made her viscerally uncomfortable, and she felt a strong compulsion to discover why, which she did in short order.

Barsilay had told her the prisoner had been a guildsman, and this man wore no earring. That by itself meant little—the Queen might have taken it before casting him into her dungeon—but his ear was not pierced at all. "This man is not from Zayit," Toba said, taking his face in both hands. She knew this man; he had tortured her for days, casting her into the void in her dreams fifty times or more. She felt it creep into her as she stood there, and felt again the rage, the despair at her own death. She wanted to kill him then, crack his skull between her hands like a piece of fruit. Instead, she forced magic into him as he grit his teeth. And when she let go, what was revealed was the face of Tsidon the Lymer.

Tsifra watched all this from the shadows of the banquet hall. Hadn't Toba done her a favor, that day? She wouldn't have to waste time hunting the man down. She could not see Toba—it was if there were a space her eyes just skipped over—but she knew from the others' speech and expressions exactly where she was and could guess at what she'd said.

And here was Tsidon. He gave Toba an acid smile and said, "My darling. I am only sorry you were not able to partake of the banquet that was planned for you." To Barsilay he said, "I don't know how you survived. But it won't be for long. Tarses is coming."

"Tarses has cast you out! What reason can you have to do his work?"

Tsidon raised his eyes to the moonlight above. "Tarses will have me back again. I have killed Kasfia for him. I have killed the Leviathan for him! He will see what I have done, and I will be at his side again in glory, the left hand of the new age." He smiled grimly at Toba. "You will die—everyone here will die. The world will burn." He looked to where the dead Queen lay. "And my hands have lit the flame."

Dear God, the man loved to hear himself talk. Tsifra stepped out of the shadows; her arm became a blade. She waited just long enough to make sure he knew her, and then she took his head—which hit the ground and rolled to the wall with a thump.

"Bastard," she said, stepping over his fallen body.

Tsifra touched a finger to his head, made it an apple as red as a pomegranate, and took a bite. And then another.

The others in the room gaped at her as she tossed the core aside. It was, Tsifra thought, rather gratifying. Barsilay held his arm out, shielding the young man on the floor beside him.

It would have been very easy to kill everyone present. But she was tired from running and forcing salt into Elena, and killing Tsidon had been enjoyable but left her feeling spent. "I made a promise not to kill you when I saw you," she told Barsilay. "I now hold that promise fulfilled."

She stepped over the bodies of the dead courtiers on her way to the door, when one of those she'd taken to be a corpse reached out a small hand and clasped it around her ankle. Leaping back, Tsifra saw a small figure belly-down on the marble floor, her face covered by a gray hood. How no one else had seen her, Tsifra could not say. But this was the Peregrine, and her face was the color of ash.

Tsifra knelt at her side. "What have you done?" she asked her.

"Carried out my orders," she said. There were tears running down the sides of her face as she lay there. Seeing Barsilay approach, she let out a little sob. "Forgive me."

"Tarses knew you helped Toba in the siege castle. You were caught."

"Yes," she said. "He killed all my Falcons—all of them."

Tsifra said, "No. No, he can't—"

"Then he told me— He ordered me to come here, tell no one. He knew about the wedding before it happened, before you left the prison. He told me to poison the wedding feast." Her breath hitched. "And then myself."

Tsifra said, "No, this cannot be. You are still alive."

The Peregrine gasped a little and said, "It's started already. I can feel it."

"I can save you," Barsilay said, holding out his hand, but the Peregrine shook her head.

"If you do, you ruin everything. Ayleth will never trust you again. And I can't return to Tarses."

Tsifra had seen the Maziks using the fish, but she had never thought to make herself another creature. Other Maziks often made parts of themselves into birds or bats to serve as scouts, but she had never done so; it felt dangerous, to send part of herself off where she could not protect it, and the fish Barsilay and the others had made to eat the poison had all died.

It was this small death Tsifra feared. She was strong and did not fear pain. But the death of that part of herself would be like dipping a toe into the void, and that terrified her.

The Peregrine's face was beaded with sweat; she would not survive much longer. *Who am I,* Tsifra thought, *to save all these people? First Elena, and now this.*

She made a small fish, blue as the sea, and slid it down the Peregrine's throat as her eyes went wide. She felt the poison, which had only just burned through its coating, flaming inside herself, and she only barely managed to force the fish back out before it shriveled and blackened on the floor. She felt the poison as if it were in her own body, and the tips of her fingers turned black.

The Peregrine had fallen unconscious. There was a pitcher of wine on the table, and immersing her burning hands in it, Tsifra said, "Is she alive?"

Barsilay looked at her as if he could not quite believe what she'd just done. Putting his head to the Peregrine's chest, he said, "Yes." Then, "Why did you come here, if not to kill me?"

"I was ordered to kill Tsidon," she said. "And I have done so."

"And now?" Barsilay asked.

"Now I return," Tsifra said. "If you care for her at all, send her back to Baobab. She will be safe there. For a little longer."

Tsifra set her hand on the Peregrine's cold cheek, and then she ran from the palace. She managed to make it through the gate just before moonset.

Chapter Fourteen

Asmel had meant to attend Barsilay's wedding banquet… In fact, his intention had been to walk directly there from the ceremony, along with the rest of the guests. But on the way to the hall, he'd found himself distracted by a statue he hadn't noticed before: a carving of a brightly painted Ziz in a corner of the corridor nearest the throne room. It was a strange place to put an artwork, in a forgotten corner, and an odd statue to be in P'ri Hadar, where the Queen had kept the real Ziz imprisoned beneath the palace. It had been very cleverly wrought—each feather bore individual barbs, and each barb had been individually painted in blues and greens. Even the talons were slightly translucent. The bird itself was shorter than Asmel, so it was not remotely to scale, but it was large enough to take up half the hallway, and he wondered that none of the other Maziks had noticed that it had not been there on the way inside.

It was a beautiful thing and also quite distressing. He passed a little magic inside it, to see if it were perhaps hollowed out and filled with something horrible, like a Cacería assassin, but it was solid stone. Turning to a guard who was filing past after the rest of the guests, he said, "Where did this come from?"

"That has always been there," the guard said.

"No," Asmel said, "it hasn't." But the guard paid him no heed and continued along, leaving Asmel alone with the stone Ziz.

"Well," he told it, "you're certainly something." He resisted the urge to break off one of the feathers for further examination, but did touch it to see if perhaps the entire thing were made of salt and camouflaged somehow.

It was stone only. As Barsilay was reasonably the only person he could ask about it, he decided he had better hurry to the banquet and pull him aside as soon as he arrived. He set off down the corridor, and turned left, as the other Maziks had done, and went down a hallway that stretched for what seemed like half a mile. Then he turned left again (the only possible way to continue) and found himself back before the stone Ziz.

All this way, there had been no doorway. Moreover, the original door he'd come through after the wedding was also gone.

He knocked on the statue with his fist. "Whatever enchantment this is will not fool me," he said. "Come out and face me directly, if you mean me harm."

If whoever had cast the enchantment had meant Asmel harm, he'd have fallen into a pit or been poisoned. Instead, the intent seemed to have been to separate him from Barsilay, and that was much worse. Asmel scowled at the statue, and set his hand on the wall behind it, made himself shadow, and passed through.

He came through the wall and found himself back in the hallway with the Ziz, only he'd come through the opposite side.

Asmel did not much care for being played a fool, and he found himself considerably less impressed by the beauty of the statue now. Raising a hand, he aimed a blast of magic, and the Ziz exploded in a cloud of pebbles, leaving Asmel coated in white dust. It had not, in fact, been stone. It was plaster, and Asmel was chagrined (and concerned at the state of his faculties) that he had not noted the difference. Moreover, it had not been entirely solid. What remained of the Ziz were the legs, still sticking up from the base. And inside one of these was a very small scroll. Unrolling it, there was a sloppily transcribed note, almost as if it had been written in someone's nondominant hand. It said, *The King of Anab is still alive.*

Wrapped in the scroll was a vial of purple liquid.

I would have to be mad, he thought, *to drink this.*

But Asmel was a scientist, and scientists are curious. So he carefully uncorked the bottle and went in for an exploratory sniff… at which point the liquid became a mist, and before he realized it had happened, he'd already breathed it in.

What a foolish thing to do, Asmel thought, and then he slumped to the floor, unconscious.

THE OLD WOMAN bitterly resented being left back from the wedding. How many Mazik weddings would she have the opportunity to witness? Surely there would be all sorts of magical splendor. And the food served at the feast would be beyond reckoning—pots of delicacies that never emptied, and so forth—with wine that tasted like lilacs poured into silver goblets.

The fact that it was Barsilay's wedding was also an issue, of course, but in her estimation it had only improved their situation. Barsilay would be a prince in reality, not just a king in some hypothetical future that might never come to pass. Naftaly, of course, would be devastated, but he must have known a man like Barsilay could not remain unmarried. As for the Princess's reaction to Naftaly, well, kings had lovers, and Maziks, dissolute as anything, probably had legions of them swarming about like flies. She imagined that the Princess might actually prefer her husband keep a paramour who couldn't become pregnant with a child that might one day displace her own heir. Presuming Barsilay's handsome face was not enough to engender a murderous jealousy…

Naftaly was also handsome, she reminded herself with a sniff. The Princess might fall in love with him, too, and together they'd shower him with gold and diamonds for the rest of his life.

Look at me, the old woman thought. *I've become so optimistic in my old age.* Or perhaps it was her brush with death from the decayed salt that had done it. In any case, Barsilay had been a prisoner, and she and the Zayitis had been living in a camp. Now Barsilay was the Prince of P'ri Hadar, of all things. And technically, she'd been the one to buy his way out of that prison. He owed her a favor.

And she'd not even been allowed to attend the wedding. She was too old to pout, she told herself. But that was exactly what she was doing.

The old woman was meant to share a small house in the camp with Elena and Asmel, only Elena had not been there since she'd been put to sleep by Asmel in a fit of idiocy. Since Asmel was at the wedding and the slumberous Elena was in Efra's house being stared at by guards, she was alone when she heard a commotion go up outside. Peeking through the door, she saw several of Efra's men running, and then there were the sounds of bowstrings.

Bother, she thought, and slipped her shoes on to see if she ought to be running away. The Queen would not attack on the night of her daughter's wedding, and the only other person with a reason to attack the Zayitis (so far as the old woman knew) was Tarses—and if Tarses were there, hiding in the house was not likely to do her much good. She managed to hear one of the guards shouting to the other, "They took the old mortal!"

She'd grown so used to thinking of herself as the old mortal that it took a moment to realize they must have meant Elena. But that made no more sense... No one from La Cacería could possibly even know who she was, let alone have a reason to kidnap her. Hurrying toward Efra's house, she found the door hanging open and no one inside. Listening again, she realized the commotion was coming from the direction of the sea, which was odder still, because the Maziks never went close to it. If Elena had been taken near the water, there was no one in the camp who could help her.

Tightening her shawl against the cold night air, she hobbled in the direction of all the noise and saw Elena down by the surf, alone. Turning to one of the guards, she said, "What's happened?"

"There was a spy, but she's fled," he told her.

"And why are you all standing there?"

With a shudder, he said, "She's covered in seawater. We can't let her back into the camp."

Of all the nonsense. "Can you give me one of your shadow-men?" she asked.

"A shade can't any closer to the sea than I can, mortal."

"Well, how close can it get, then?" she snapped. "Give me one and then go. I'll make sure the salt is gone. She can't be left alone down there, Hashem's sake, she'll freeze."

The guard gave her a very sour look, but conjured a shade. Turning to it, she said, "I want you to make me a hot bath and some privacy. A tent, maybe. As close to the sea as you can manage it."

"There is no water here to heat for a bath," it told her.

"Then go draw some!" she said, and went down to find Elena shivering at the edge of the water. "You've awakened," she said.

"So have you," she said flatly. "Look at us, both awake."

"What happened?"

"It was the Courser," Elena said. "She gave me salt, and it took the magic out of me."

"The Courser!"

"You are going to ask why she would have helped me," Elena said. "And I'm going to tell you that I don't know. But Toba was also here. They've returned."

The old woman's face lit. "Naftaly is here?"

"I didn't see him, but he's here somewhere. Toba's gone to the palace with Efra."

"And she left you freezing and wet down here?"

Her nose was running in the cold, and she sniffed and said, "I'm all right."

"You are not," the old woman said, helping Elena—who was shivering so hard she could barely move—up toward the small tent the shade had managed to erect. "No one ever thinks of us, have you not noticed? Asmel pumping you full of magic like stuffing a chicken, what did he think would happen?"

"Not this," she said. "Obviously."

She managed to pull off Elena's sodden clothes and put her into the steaming bath, which she sank into with a deep sigh, submerging herself once, then twice, to rinse the salt out of her hair. "Did you see anything interesting in there?" the old woman asked, tapping her own temple. "What is it like, the dream-world?"

"Like this one, but the stars move."

"The stars move here, too."

"Not like this. It's like they're blown about on the wind, like fireflies. But I went there to find Rafeq, and I didn't."

The old woman tried to imagine such stars... Well, such things were beyond her anyway. She could not manage to summon a similar longing to see Rafeq again. "I'm not sure that's much of a loss."

Elena scrubbed her wrinkled face with the hot water, drawing her knees up to her chest. She said, "Doesn't matter if it is or isn't, at this point."

"Then why do you look like that?"

Elena wiped the water from her eyes and said, "How do I look? Wet?" She scratched at her scalp and muttered, "My hair is still full of sand."

"As if you've suffered some grave disappointment. I know you were fond of him."

Elena gave no answer. She had been fond of Rafeq, the old woman knew, but if he'd had his way, if he'd managed to give her Marah's magic, she'd have died. Certainly that hadn't been his intent, but she'd have been just as dead nonetheless. He hadn't cared for her enough to test things out first. At least Asmel had only put her in a coma for a few days.

The old woman got some soap from the shade and proceeded to wash Elena's hair, which was so tangled from sleeping and saltwater she thought she might have to resort to cutting it off. Instead she got a comb from the shade and quietly set at the tangles, while the water slowly lost its steam. After a while, Elena said, "I had hoped to see my mother."

The old woman had not considered that might be possible, though of course she knew Elena was also somewhat Mazik. Elena went on, "I was like a corpse there. I could see but not speak, nor move. I could not go looking for her, even if I'd known how."

The old woman set the comb down. There seemed to be no adequate response to this admission. "The sand is out," she said quietly. Getting up from the edge of the bath, she balled up Elena's wet clothes, and then, without much consideration, handed them to the shade, saying, "Wash these too, will you?" and then the dratted thing vanished.

"Damn," she said. "They're so delicate. Do you ever think that? They wouldn't last a day in the real world. No wonder they can't stay there except when the moon is full. They'd stumble into someone's kitchen and it'd all be over for them."

Elena laughed a little, too. "Yes, that's very amusing. Except now you've dispelled the only shade we've got, and I haven't got any clothes."

"Oh," the old woman said.

ELENA WAS NOT sure how long it would be before she wanted to sleep again, but she knew it would not be that night. Toba, before she'd left, had left her a task of some urgency, too, and at first light, she put on the fresh clothes she'd gotten from one of Efra's guards—not the one whose shade the old bat had dispelled with salt, who would not speak to either of them, but one of the women who seemed slightly less offended by their mortality. She ate a little of the food that had been left for her, put on her boots, and left the camp, telling the guard at the perimeter she had an errand and was not sure when she would return.

"What do you mean, you aren't sure?" the old woman asked, trudging up behind her.

"I thought you were sleeping."

"I was. You make a lot of noise when you chew."

"My chewing did not wake you."

"It did. Where are you going? Into the city? I want to find Naftaly as much as you want to find Toba."

Striding away, Elena said, "I'm not going into the city. Toba asked me to attend to something in case she was delayed, so that's what I am doing. And it's a long walk from here, and you won't like it, so stay in the camp with the Maziks. You haven't eaten yet."

"I want to know where you are going. Every time you get it in your mind to do something on your own, you get into the most terrible trouble."

"I do not."

"Let's catalogue your many errors," the old woman said. "First, you decided to help the deSantoses with their hidden treasure, for which you dosed both myself and Naftaly with amapola, only for your plan to fail in spectacular fashion."

"That was not my fault," Elena said. "I didn't know Naftaly was part Mazik then. It would have worked, otherwise."

"The deSantoses had to run for their lives and we were left wandering in the mountains for days with no food," the old woman reminded her.

"I admit, that went badly."

"Then you got us lost in Zayit, and we wandered into an orgy."

"It was not an orgy!"

"Then you took it upon yourself to make the deadliest poison on earth. Which you lost track of."

Elena stopped short. "What is your point? I should have stayed home and tended my kitchen? I did try."

"My point is you get up to no good on your own."

"As you've pointed out, you were with me for all of those misadventures."

"Yes, but if I hadn't been there, things might have gone worse!"

Elena said, "How?"

"Well, you're still alive, aren't you?"

Elena sighed. "You don't want to be left alone with the Maziks."

Unhappily, the old woman said, "They move away when I enter a room, and half of them won't speak with me in Rimoni."

"Probably half of them don't speak Rimoni."

"I'm going with you. Where are you going?"

They were far enough from the camp that Elena assumed the Mazik guards would not be able to hear. She said, "Toba and Naftaly brought the Ziz back with them and left her in those woods. She has some kind of a guardian—Toba did not have time to explain much. But Toba promised to return to her in a day, and now she may not be able to. So I am going in her place."

The old woman walked at her side, craning her ancient neck back to gauge the height of the cedars in the distance. "The Ziz. Wasn't Naftaly concerned it might eat him?"

"Well, it didn't. He's very much uneaten. He went into the city yesterday."

"I still think we ought to find him."

"You go do that."

The old woman grumbled a little. Naftaly would have gone to the palace and she looked like she'd just crawled out of a crypt. She would need Efra's minions to make her look young again, and probably they wouldn't do it just because some mortal said please. Elena said, "I want to find Naftaly as well. But I promised to do this first."

"How long will it take to walk there? Couldn't you use your speed litany?"

"We haven't got a horse, you fool." Thinking this over, she said, "Perhaps I could use it on you. Let me climb on your back."

"I should have left you in the sea."

Their progress was hampered by the pace of the old woman, who needed to stop every ten minutes to catch her breath. It was absurd to take her. But Elena did not have the heart to do what it would take to make her go back. Anyway, after an hour or two, the cedar forest loomed before them… It was odd how it was so starkly delineated from the rest of the terrain, as if it had been artificially created by the Maziks. Or else, she considered, it had been preserved, and all the surrounding land had also been forest, and now this was what remained. There was some tale of a great cedar forest in one of Alasar's books with a massive guardian, a monster of some sort. She worried over that, a little. Only Toba had not warned her to beware of any monsters, apart from the Ziz.

They crossed into the forest, whose floor was bare from the shade of the trees, and breathed the air that smelled of cedar and moss and something Elena could only describe as magic. It was oddly quiet and Elena realized the strangeness was mostly because a forest ought to have birds, and here there were none. She stopped a moment to drink a little water—she was still dehydrated from too much sleep and too much salt both—and gave some to the old woman, who pointed out some gashes in the ground. A great animal had been there, and from the look of it, it hadn't been long ago.

Quietly, they followed what Elena presumed to be tracks, and it occurred to her that this had better be the Ziz they were following, or else the old woman was entirely correct and she really was leading them both to their doom. They'd gone some half an hour like that when she suddenly came to a stop. The old woman's eyes were huge, because she'd just noticed the same thing: The great tree trunks just ahead were not tree trunks. They were legs. And while the women watched, one of the great taloned feet reached up and scratched at the other knee, and then came back down to earth with a thud. Then the entire creature stuck its head down from the sky, stopping a few feet from Elena's face, and let out a shriek.

The old woman looked like she might faint. Elena hissed at her to be still. And then, from between the trees, came a woman as naked as the day she was born, her arms flung wide as if she meant to embrace them, and she called, "Mortals!"

The Ziz pulled her head back up, and the naked woman embraced Elena, who was too stunned to respond. Behind her, the old woman said, "I don't understand how this keeps happening to you."

Elena said, "Be quiet."

But then the naked woman—naked Mazik, Elena decided—released Elena and stepped back, staring at her face. And something in the expression was so familiar, she could not quite believe it. The eyes were different, and the voice, and the face as well. *She must be another descendant of Marah's,* Elena thought, *to be so familiar. That must be it.*

The woman had been speaking in the language of P'ri Hadar. But now, as she looked into Elena's old face, she whispered in Rimoni, "Grandmother?"

Elena could not quite speak. She did not know this woman. And yet, she would have known her anywhere. The voice, in that moment, was the same. The eyes, in that moment, were the same. This was the child who had lived at her knee, the woman who had run away with the Maziks, who had died with them. She reached out her wrinkled hand and touched her face. She could not say how old she was, but something in her expression had suddenly gone very young and wide-eyed, and she told Elena, "I remember you."

Chapter Fifteen

It took the rest of the night to sort out the aftermath of the banquet. The bodies of the dead were taken out, including the Queen's. In some last insult, she had vomited the bezoar before succumbing; this Barsilay gave to Ayleth for safekeeping, though Naftaly couldn't imagine why anyone would want it now.

Naftaly had no idea of the nature of Mazik funeral rites, or what might be done with the Queen in particular. A mortal queen might have been put in a mausoleum or given a monument, but the Queen had not planned on dying, and since Kasfia's ancestors hadn't been royalty, there was no grand family crypt awaiting her remains.

The Peregrine was a more difficult matter to attend to, as she'd murdered the Queen and much of her court. It had not escaped Naftaly that she had tried to send him away, and he presumed she had done something similar to Asmel, who still had not turned up. But he doubted that would be enough to sway the Princess, now the new Queen, whose mother had died in agony before her eyes. It also had the unfortunate effect of making Barsilay appear complicit in the poisoning of the court, as neither he nor any of his allies had died. It was probably better for his sake that Naftaly had been poisoned, even if he'd somehow survived.

Ayleth probably would have beheaded the Peregrine on the spot, but Barsilay had suggested she might know something about

Tarses's plans that could be gleaned—under torture, he implied but did not say. They moved her into the prison, into a cell Barsilay insisted must be lined with additional salt. And on the Peregrine's breast Barsilay himself lay a talisman, an orb the size of a grape, which was carefully laid in such a way that if the Peregrine moved at all it would roll off and trigger the ringing of a silver bell that Barsilay threaded around his own neck.

Barsilay found Naftaly in his bedchamber in the hour before dawn and embraced him, saying, "You should despise me."

"I don't," Naftaly said. "The furthest thing from it."

"Don't say that. I made you taste poison for me."

"You believed the food was safe."

"It doesn't matter what I believed! I fed you poison, and if it hadn't been for Toba, you'd be dead." He leaned back and held up his hand. "Don't say anything to console me. I don't want it. I acted rashly because I wanted you near me. It was unforgivably selfish."

Naftaly had been told not to console him, and so he didn't. He said, "I don't believe I traveled all the way through Aravoth just to listen to you berate yourself, Barsilay."

"For goodness' sake," Barsilay said. "What a self-indulgent bastard I really am. So tell me everything that happened since Zayit. Nothing much has gone on here, except I got married without telling you first and I'm the Prince now."

"Actually," Naftaly said, "I don't believe you are the Prince any longer."

Here Barsilay began to laugh a little hysterically, and Naftaly put his arms around him and said, "Forget I mentioned it. There will be time to deal with that in the morning."

But the sun was already making itself known out the window, and Barsilay said, "Lo, morning comes, beloved. Well, you wanted me king, and here I am, for all the good it does us." He wiped the tears from his eyes and said, "In a few hours, Ayleth will be crowned, and me along with her. But 'til then, I am yours alone."

Naftaly whispered, "Barsilay—"

But Barsilay put his thumb over his lips and said, "Naftaly, there is something I must give you." He leaned in close, and into

Naftaly's ear, he whispered, "My name, Naftaly Cresques, is Shi'vit Chal'mot."

Naftaly blinked in shock and said, "Why would you tell me this?"

"Because," Barsilay said, "if you see that I am aiming to do something terrible, you have the power to stop me. You are my conscience now, Naftaly. And I am your servant. Repeat it, so I know you remember."

Quietly, Naftaly repeated, "Shi'vit Chal'mot."

Barsilay closed his eyes and sighed.

"How many others have you given your name? Of your lovers, in your youth."

"None," Barsilay said. "And none after, either. This is yours alone."

"Shi'vit Chal'mot," Naftaly said again. "Would you like to kiss me hello, after all this time?"

Barsilay said, "That is not an order. But yes, I would."

"Shi'vit Chal'mot," he said again. "Kiss me hello."

"Well done," Barsilay said, and he kissed him hello 'til the sun cleared the horizon, and Ayleth sent for him to make him King.

IN ALL THE uproar in the palace, Toba was able to slip away from the commotion to figure out what had become of Asmel. That he had missed the banquet was a blessing, but it also meant something must be very wrong.

Finding an empty room, she took the pebble from her pocket inscribed with Asmel's name and spun it around. Odd, she thought. Not only was he in the palace, but he was close by. Was he hurt in some way? She tried again, to see if perhaps he was on his way to her, and she ought to just stay where she was. He was, however, completely still.

That could not be a good sign. She pocketed the pebble and went down the hallway to where the pebble had shown him, but there was no sign, not in that hallway, and not in the next one. Losing patience, she called his name, quietly and then loudly, and then she came around the corner again—the same one she'd just gone past—and found herself standing in the middle of a pile of rubble. At the other end of that hallway was Asmel, slumped in the middle of the floor.

"Asmel," she said, rushing toward him. He was not dead. She willed him to open his eyes.

Her voice—or perhaps the force of her will—caused Asmel to stir, and as she leaned over him he blinked a few times and rewarded her worry with one of his rarest smiles. He reached up and touched her cheek; she more or less fell on him, and he pressed his face into her hair. "Asmel," she said again. "Asmel, tell me you were not poisoned."

"I'm not poisoned," he said. "Well, not really. I was only dreaming."

"In the middle of the floor?"

"There was a potion I found—"

"You didn't drink a potion you found someplace!"

"Of course not!" he protested. "I smelled it, though."

She shook him a little. "If I'd done that," she said, "you'd be on me for stupidity the rest of my life."

"It was not my finest hour," he admitted. Then he leaned back, taking her in, and said, "What has happened to you?"

Toba could not think what he meant, but as he sat up he pulled back one of her sleeves, and then the other, his fingers tracking the red scars that dotted her arms, and tracing his fingertips over her throat. She had not realized there were more scars there, too, and as she became aware of them they began to ache, as if the nerves there had been waiting for her to acknowledge all the many tiny injuries they'd suffered. She said, "Aravoth is a strange place. But I am well, and I was successful." She was not sure how much she dared say in the palace of the Queen—even if the Queen herself was now gone—but Asmel seemed to understand, and said, "Well done, then. On both counts."

"What happened here? What is this mess all over the floor?"

"It was a Ziz. A statue. I exploded it."

Oh, of course he had. What a perfectly normal thing to do. And he'd said it so bluntly, too, as if this was what one did with a statue of a Ziz. *My, what a likeness,* and then: boom. "Why?" she demanded.

"It's difficult to explain." He waved at the wreck. "I have been trapped in this hallway all night. The statue was part of that enchantment. Look." He handed her a slip of paper, and as she read it, it disintegrated.

"Can this be true?" she asked.

"Oh, it's very true. I've just spoken with Yefet, and he's quite alive, hidden away with some of his advisors. The Peregrine was quite clear she'd killed him, though."

"Did you not ask him about that?"

"I was about to," Asmel said. "But then you woke me. I suppose if this was a test of her true intentions, she's passed it."

Toba did not quite know how to tell him what the Peregrine had done since then. But then the sun hit a window somewhere nearby, and as the light hit it, the ruined statue vanished, much as the paper had done. A doorway opened in the wall beside them. Whatever enchantment was laid here was only meant to last the night and had served its purpose. "I think I ought to get you to Barsilay," she said. "I would feel safer with us all together."

"Barsilay is safe?" he said, getting to his feet with Toba's help.

"He is," she said. "But a great many in this palace are not, the Queen among them."

TOBA AND ASMEL returned to Barsilay's suite, where they found him asleep in bed with Naftaly. Not a moment later, a soft knock came at the door. Toba was rather surprised to find the Princess on the other side in her dressing gown, with her hair loose down her back. She was not sure how Ayleth would feel about finding her new husband in bed with his lover, so she said, "I've just returned with Barsilay's uncle, but if you wait here, I can have him woken."

"I'm not here for my husband. I came to find you."

"Me?" Toba said. Inside the room, Asmel murmured, "You had better go with her."

So Toba stepped out, acutely aware she was in the same filthy clothes in which she'd fled Zayit. She was in the company of a Princess, and she hadn't so much as washed her feet or combed her hair. The door slid shut behind her, and she followed Ayleth to a much grander set of rooms, where a window overlooked a garden as magnificent as the King of Rimon's, with fountains that seemed to have come on at daybreak. Birds of all colors bathed in the waters, and in the center was a statue of a great leaping fish.

"These were my mother's rooms," the Princess told her. "I have none in the palace. Barsilay will have told you why."

"I'm afraid I haven't had any time to speak to Barsilay since I've arrived."

"I see," she said. "And what are you to him?"

"His cousin," Toba told her, which was, in fact, true. "His aunt was my foremother."

"In that case," the Princess said, "I will tell you that I have no rooms here because I have spent this entire age asleep in prison, in order to keep my mother from losing her throne."

Toba said, "I see."

"Do you?"

Toba did understand being an instrument of one's parent's ambitions, but thought explaining her relationship to Tarses was probably unwise. She said, "Did you agree to this?"

Ayleth said simply, "I must have."

"You must have?"

Ayleth said, "I don't recall agreeing. But I don't recall disagreeing, either."

This was a level of candidness Toba did not expect from a Mazik princess, and Ayleth seemed to be waiting for some further discussion. Toba said, "And with whom did you dream, in the mortal city, if I might ask?"

"Half-Maziks," she said, her tone again clipped, but her face betraying another emotion: She'd become attached to them. It was no wonder, after all that time. "Agents of the Queen, and therefore I have spent enough time with half-Maziks to know one when I meet one. The eyes are not quite the same. So I knew what you were when I saw you, as I knew Barsilay's lover. You are alarmed; you needn't be. You saved my life this night, and it is not a thing I am likely to forget soon."

"Is that why you wished to see me?"

"I am not explaining well," the Princess said. "The Queen is dead, but she was not the only Mazik who died tonight. Her vizier died. The general who commands her armies died. The treasurer died. And that isn't all. I have been asleep all this time. My mother did not bother to train an heir. Do you understand what I am telling you?"

Toba did understand, a little. Marah, too, had left her a great task and very little instruction, and the closer that task came into view, the more it worried her how unprepared she was. If not for Nehama, she'd never have got the Ziz at all. Ayleth's situation was a bit worse; there was no well-placed half-Mazik waiting to guide her toward being a queen. She said, "The government is in shambles. But why tell me this? Surely there is one of your mother's people you can trust."

"There isn't," she said. "My mother held this city together with a thousand stitches every day. I know what Barsilay thinks about the Maziks in the prison, or the way she treated the scholars… But P'ri Hadar has known an age of peace. Perhaps she killed or imprisoned a few to maintain that, but the alternative would have been another Rimon, a bloodbath in the streets again and again. You do not agree?"

"I don't know enough to agree or disagree," Toba said carefully. "But you seem keen to defend the woman who used you, if I may say, very poorly."

"She was less my mother and more my queen," the Princess said. "My own feelings are beside the point. But the fact is, this city cannot run without her."

Toba swallowed. "What about Barsilay?"

"Barsilay has his own agenda," Ayleth said. "And my mother was not the only Mazik in this city who remembers Luz. If it seems he is trying to assert himself, it will only make things worse. Listen, most of the people of P'ri Hadar don't even recall they have a princess; I haven't been spoken of in years, even in my mother's court. I barely know the names of my mother's advisors, besides the ones who are dead, and those I only learned in the past few days. I have not a single ally in this place, besides you."

"Me?"

"You saved my life. And at cost to yourself, too. You were weakened—I'd wager you are weakened still."

"I'll recover," Toba said. "And I don't think that makes me much of an ally. I just did what was reasonable."

"I will be crowned today," Ayleth reminded her. "There will be those who think this is a coup. They'll have no idea who I am. They'll believe me a usurper, and then they'll discover I'm unfit to rule. I'll be deposed in a fortnight, Toba, and whoever takes my place may not be so willing to help Barsilay with his plans."

Toba did not know what to say. Ayleth needed someone to teach her to be a queen, but all the kings and queens she knew of had been terrible. No, not all. Yefet had been a fair king, even Asmel had admitted as much, and he was still alive. Toba stared down at her filthy shoes, coated in ash from Zayit and dirt from Aravoth. She looked up, suddenly, and said, "There may be someone who can help you."

Tsifra made her way out of the citrus grove in mortal P'ri Hadar, drained and exhausted, and without enough magic to make herself any sort of structure she could safely sleep in. She found an inn, and after tossing a few coins to the owner, went upstairs to sleep on a mattress filled with straw of dubious cleanliness. Tarses would want to see her, after tonight. And even if he didn't, she was too exhausted to go on. She would sleep, she told herself, that day and that night, and then she would find a way to return to her hidden fleet at Dassos.

She opened her eyes to a different view than she'd expected. Usually when Tarses summoned her, it was to his place by the sea, where he channeled visions in the water beneath the swirling stars. But that night, he brought her instead to a mountaintop. The wind whipped her hair around her face, and far, far beneath, in the distance, she could see the city of Anab. How unlike him to change his pattern. She did not know what it might mean.

"Courser," he said. "I have been waiting for you, all this night."

The sight of him startled her. She had seen him only weeks before, and in that amount of time, his hair had gone completely white. He was slimmer, too; his cheeks hollowed and his lips thinned. If she hadn't known better, she'd have thought he'd aged.

Her position was much improved, but she was still not entirely sure she could safely comment on the fact that he resembled a man who had been long in prison, not the King Consort of Rimon. Still, her face must have given her away, because he said, "You are concerned."

She carefully asked, "Are you well? Is it your injury?"

Smiling with his thin lips, he said, "I have taxed my magic too much, but I need tools that only I can make." He cast an illusion of a horse and set his hand on its withers. "I will show you what I have done," he said. "Admire it."

It was a good-looking steed, with a glossy black coat, but otherwise it appeared unremarkable—'til she examined its face. There was something wrong about the eyes. The breath that came from its nostrils steamed the air, and when she touched it, the horse felt as if it were feverish. "What have you done to it?" she asked.

"I am surprised," he said. "Do you not sense the demon? No, I suppose this horse is only a dream. Still, I would have thought you would have seen it, if anyone could."

The horse was possessed. She clucked at the horse and it rolled its eyes. Tarses said, "You will have heard the lentil blight has spread to Erez. And it will be in Katlav before the winter is out."

"You've seen this?"

He smiled a little, which meant either he'd seen it, or he was facilitating the spread, weakening the southern cities before his army arrived. "I have agents in the south. The men in Tamar and Erez have been eager to join my army."

This was news to Tsifra. "I thought you believed the army of Rimon was sufficient?"

"There is opportunity to be had here, Courser."

"As you say. Then these horses are for the men in the south?" Tsifra asked.

"Some of them," he said. "Tamar is far and I may need to move those men quickly. These horses run fast as a flying eagle, and they never tire. They are indeed a wonder. Now tell me, where have you been?"

"I have been occupied," she said. "Carrying out your orders."

"You passed into the Mazik city, and back out again?"

"I did," she said. "Tsidon is dead."

His eyes narrowed. "How?"

"I took his head. There is no chance he survived."

"No chance it was a buchuk?"

"None," she said. She didn't want to mention that she'd eaten his head after removing it from his body—Tarses would find it distasteful. But she was pretty sure a buchuk wouldn't have enough magic to sustain itself once it had been killed and eaten.

"I see," he said. "Well done. And as you dispatched Tsidon, what did you learn of my Peregrine?"

Tsifra said, "She ate the decayed salt, as you ordered her."

"Are you sure?"

"Completely."

"You seem unfazed, Courser. Were you not friends?"

Tsifra kept her voice even as she said, "I do not have friends. My position precludes it."

"Yes," he agreed, "it does. You did very well, accomplishing all that in a single night. I am impressed."

"There is more," she said. "From when last we spoke. The Habushi fleet is sunk, just as you foresaw."

"And how many ships did you lose in that same storm?"

"One," she said. "The rest are safe."

"Very impressive," he said. "Very impressive. Return to your fleet and sail for Habush. It cannot resist you now."

"I will do as you say," she said. Then, considering whether it was safe to ask the question, she asked, "Will you have a new Lymer and a new Peregrine?"

Tarses said, "You are my only lieutenant now, my daughter." And then he did a thing he'd never done in all her life: He stepped forward and took her face in his hands and kissed her forehead.

She felt... odd. Warm, and yet not.

"Father," she said, because it might come out later, "Tsidon was trying to win his way back into your favor. He killed the Leviathan for you—that is why he took the Shamir."

"Did that nearly stay your hand?"

She hesitated, then said, "I had my orders."

"Are you worried now I wish that I had reconsidered? I am well aware of Tsidon's actions." He reached out and stroked her hair.

She said, "You knew all this already? That he was loyal? Why order me to kill him, then?"

He said, "Did it not please you, to kill him?"

Tsifra did not know how to answer this, if it was a trick. She said, "I don't know."

"That is a lie."

Tsifra said, "It did please me."

"Then you have your answer. That was my gift to you." He pressed his lips to her forehead a second time. "When I see you again, I shall give you many more. Whatever you most desire. Are there any others? Name them."

"Others I would kill? In La Cacería?"

He nodded once.

Her mind spun. She said, "I have no more enemies, Father."

"Good," he said. "That's very good. Now tell me, what else is it you might desire?"

"There is nothing," she said. "I am your daughter and I am Queen. I need nothing more."

Tsifra awoke in the seedy inn in mortal P'ri Hadar and touched the spot on her forehead that he'd kissed. She had no idea what to make of any of it.

Chapter Sixteen

Toba had been with Ayleth for a few hours, and Asmel found himself at loose ends. He was a scholar. None of this statecraft was meant for him—he'd patently ignored the workings of Rimon so far as he'd been able, at least until those workings had lost him his university. He would be no good to Barsilay on that front. That the Queen was dead cast things oddly for them; on the one hand, it was better for Barsilay not to be Kasfia's pawn, and on the other, the people of P'ri Hadar might well decide that the heir of Luz belonded at the bottom of the sea along with his city. The Queen of Luz had been broadly unpopular, but here, where her rule had been closer, they probably remembered her better, which was to say, worse. He was not sure how Kasfia's death affected Barsilay, and it worried him that he did not know.

That Ayleth was seeking advice from Toba was baffling, and implied Ayleth was not only unprepared for queenship but also, perhaps, either mad or exceedingly peculiar. In any case, Toba's task was raising Luz from the sea, not propping up the reign of yet another queen. The only issue with that, of course, was that Asmel was not precisely sure how to do it.

Asmel understood they needed the Ziz to fly to the middle of the sea to do the working required, but he was as to how to use their magic through the salt. Marah must have had a plan for that—she had plans for everything—but she hadn't told him about it.

Unfortunately the most likely person to have that information was Tarses, who had been Marah's confidant until he'd betrayed her.

He could not help thinking of the Leviathan, dead by Tarses's Lymer, and how that might be a bigger disaster than any of them knew.

The scholars of P'ri Hadar had been no help to him before, but with some encouragement from the crown they might speak to him now. When Toba returned from her meeting with Ayleth, he said, "Do you think she would write me a sealed letter to take to the university? Raising Luz is still an enormous undertaking. We're going to need help from somewhere."

"I will ask her," she said. "But I came to ask you about something else. You said Yefet was a good king. His people respected him."

"That's true," Asmel said. "But I'm not sure he's much of an ally, hidden away."

"I think he might be an ally to Ayleth. Listen, I've spent all morning with her, and you know what her life was under the Queen. She has no idea how to rule, and only half the court she needs to do it with. She needs someone who knows how to administer a city, and that isn't any of us. If we can bring Yefet here, he might be able to help her hold the throne. Otherwise, she's sure there'll be a coup before the next moon, unless Tarses gets here first. Either way, she can't hold the city together on her own. Do you know where Yefet is?"

"In the mountains north of Anab," Asmel said. "I don't know the precise location. But we have the book; we can bring him here easily enough. Have you mentioned this to Ayleth? She might think you are overstepping, or mean to replace her."

"She's absolutely desperate. She agreed right away when I suggested it. She has no other options."

"All right," Asmel said. "When did you want me to do this? I still need to talk to the scholars—"

"That can wait," Toba said, pulling the book from her satchel. "Go and fetch the King of Anab."

* * *

NAFTALY WOKE AT midday under Barsilay's arm with the sun on his face. He wondered that he hadn't woken earlier, it was so bright, and he could hear voices in the next room… Toba, and she was speaking Rimoni. He couldn't make out the other voice (Toba sounded particularly animated and was therefore projecting more than the conversation seemed to require), but he presumed she was speaking with Asmel. He hadn't the energy to try to eavesdrop. He knew the poison hadn't done any serious damage—else he'd have been dead—but he felt as drained as if he'd been ill for days. He rolled onto his back and was aiming to put his pillow over his face to block out the sun and Toba's voice when he noticed Barsilay was awake, too.

"Can you hear what they're saying?" Naftaly asked, because there seemed little point in going back to sleep now.

"King Yefet seems to be alive. Toba wants Asmel to go and get him, because Ayleth is incompetent."

"That's a bit harsh," Naftaly said.

"Only a fair assessment," Barsilay said, rolling face down, "from one incompetent monarch to another. They really ought to ask Efra, too. I don't know why it hasn't occurred to them."

"Oughtn't you to get up?"

"Not yet," he said. "They seem to have things in hand. I just want to stay here with you. What you've done— I can't really believe what you've done. Going into Aravoth and getting the Ziz. You did an impossible thing."

Naftaly felt unaccountably bashful. Moreover, he felt strange about the entire adventure, like Aravoth had somehow unmoored him. He looked at Barsilay face-on for the first time that morning and thought, *How much of what I know of him is real, and how much is only what my senses tell me?* Everything felt a little like a vision, both real and not.

"Are you all right?" Barsilay asked. "You haven't told me anything that happened while you were there."

"We found the Ziz."

Barsilay sat up on an elbow. "Why is it," he said, "that you sound like I do when anyone asks me about being in the Cacería prison?"

Naftaly said, "I don't know. I haven't any words for what it was like. It was strange and terrifying and I almost lost Toba, and I almost drowned in a lake I think I made myself, but I'm not even sure about that, either. Everything was vivid and unreal at the same time. And—and then there was the rest of it."

"The rest of it?"

He shook his head miserably. "I'm— I can't. I can't say more now. Even talking about it…"

"Don't talk about it," Barsilay said. "Not today. And I won't ask you about it again. But don't think it's because I'm not interested or don't think it's important." He kissed Naftaly's brow. "Is there anything you did want to talk about?"

"You mean your marriage?" He exhaled. "I'm not sure what there is to say. You're a king. You'll need—"

"If you say an heir, I'll smother you," Barsilay said.

"Ayleth will require one, too."

"Only if she isn't deposed in the next fortnight. Otherwise it hardly matters."

"But you do intend to help her?"

"So far as I'm able. But look, I don't know anything about how P'ri Hadar has been run. I don't know any of the people involved. I barely know the customs or the character of the citizens. She agreed to marry me because of what I might provide her in the future, if I become King of Luz. I may be able to help her stave off Tarses. But keeping the throne, ruling the city—I offer very little. And my presence is likely divisive besides."

"Or perhaps you aren't as divisive as you think," he said. "You freed all those prisoners. You think they won't talk about you in the city? Anyway, the people here will trust you better if they see you trying to help them, rather than skulking in the shadows."

To his pillow, Barsilay said, "I do not skulk."

Naftaly was already putting his feet on the floor and said, "I haven't had a bath in a month."

"All right," Barsilay said. "Let's clean you up and then let's go and help Asmel find a way to make land from the sea. But 'til then, I'm going to lie here and admire you. Does that suit you?"

"You know if Ayleth is deposed, the usurper will try to kill you, too?" Naftaly said, picking his clothes off the floor, and then discarding them again because they were much too dirty to wear.

Barsilay crooked his finger from the bed and the wardrobe at the other end of the room popped open, revealing several sets of clothes. "Wear something of mine. And yes, I do realize. All the better reason to allow myself a brief moment of pleasure before the axe comes down."

"The axe," Naftaly said. "Hashem's sake, I forgot. Last night, when I had the poison in my belly, I had a vision. I saw—I think it must have been Habush. It was burning."

Barsilay sat up straighter. "Habush is on the cusp of surrender. Ayleth said as much. Why would it be burned?"

"That was only part of it," Naftaly said. "I saw Tarses. And he saw me. It was as if we were having the vision at the same time." He blew out a long breath. "I think he might have recognized me."

Barsilay looked away and swore. "If you'd left when the Peregrine tried to send you away—"

"I might have had the same vision elsewhere," Naftaly said. "But he said he hadn't intended to burn Habush. He looked as surprised by it as I was."

"Tarses is the most deceitful man alive," Barsilay said.

"Yes, but either way Tarses has no interest in burning a city that's giving up. Something must change in the future, or else it's changing now, I don't know."

Barsilay leaned his elbow against his thigh and put his head in his hand. "I wish the Peregrine were still available to us."

"Do you think she'll wake up soon?"

"Soon? I don't know. But even if she does, I can only keep her alive for so long. I can stall the Princess, but ultimately she'll have to pay for what happened here. And when the time comes, it might be better if the Courser had just let her die from the poison."

ELENA WAS SO baffled by this person who seemed to be Toba, and also entirely not Toba, she hardly knew what to think. Her name, she learned, was Nehama, but she remembered being called Toba, in some dim past. She was very, very old, and remarkably like a child at the same time. She recalled Alasar, in some way, but did not remember having met Naftaly before Aravoth. She had not recognized the other Toba at all, and that was a puzzle.

What this implied, Elena could not begin to guess—if she were truly some reborn Toba, she had been reborn in a bygone age. Was such a thing even possible? The skeptical part of Elena's character struggled between what she wished were true and what she understood of reality.

Whom could she ask? Only the greatest of the rabbis could have guessed at such a thing. Either this woman was Toba and it was a miracle, or she was not and she was some sort of fraud.

But she had helped Toba—the other Toba—to bring the Ziz out of Aravoth. What reason would a fraud have to do that? Maziks could change their appearance. If Nehama wanted to pose as Toba, she could have killed the other Toba and taken her place.

Still, it was not in Elena's nature to believe in miracles.

Elena had encouraged her not to mention the possibility of a connection with Toba to the others, mostly because she was not sure yet if it were really true or what it meant, and also because it might tend to make her a target for Tarses.

Nehama, Elena noted rather quickly, was odd, and she herself hinted this might have been from too many years alone in a world that did not follow normal logic. She seemed to have forgotten the flow of linear time, for on thing. For another when they asked her questions, she often forgot to answer aloud. And certainly, she was not going to be presentable in any sort of public setting. Elena and the old woman would put her clothes on, and an hour later she'd have them off again, saying she wanted to feel the sun. She could not be kept in shoes, and the old woman would say, "Are you saying Aravoth has no dirt?" and Nehama would say, "I'm not actually sure if it has or it hasn't." The old woman pulled Elena aside after a while and said, "I don't know what we are meant to be doing here. Are we looking after the giant bird or the mad woman?"

Elena presumed it was both. But while she'd already raised two difficult children, she did not think she had it in her to do it again with this overgrown toddler, miracle or no. Particularly when she looked at Elena over lunch and said, "I miss men."

It was difficult to imagine Toba making such a statement—the child had never expressed the least interest in marriage.

"Let's not get ahead of ourselves," the old woman told Nehama, and then added to Elena, "If you happen to have any amapola left, perhaps you could just... take the edge off?"

"I haven't," Elena said.

"I don't normally talk this much," Nehama said. "It's just that for so long I had no one to speak to besides angels. And they don't generally reply."

"Don't they?" the old woman asked. "What are they like, then?"

"Wings," Nehama said, spreading all her fingers. "Eyes."

"I see," the old woman said. "I suppose you have a lot of chatting to catch up on. But let's steer clear of men 'til you've calmed down a bit."

Nehama looked a bit put out, and Elena said, "There will be plenty of time for men later." It was the exact tone she'd used with Toba, in explaining why she could not play outside in the rain.

The Ziz, at least, did not seem to need much minding. She ate whatever food they put together for her—and here was a conundrum, because none of them really knew what a Ziz ate. Nehama said she'd been eating fruit in Aravoth, but as the Ziz had been feeding herself all that time, she was not really sure what kind. The talons implied a more varied diet, but Elena did not want to hunt, and did not want to encourage the Ziz to do so, either, lest she start to develop a taste for meat she might have forgotten. The bird was nearly as tall as the cedars... Better to keep her eating fruit.

The day ticked by, and then, in the middle of the afternoon, a gate opened in the middle of the forest and through it stepped Naftaly. The old woman ran blubbering into his arms, where she stayed for several minutes.

"Are you all right?" Elena asked him over the top of the old woman's head, which was firmly planted against Naftaly's chest.

"A lot has happened," he said. "I am all right, and Toba is at the palace—I'm here to take you there. There is a place there for the Ziz now, where she'll be safe and guarded."

"The palace?" the old woman put in, lifting her face from

Naftaly's coat. "What about…" and here she passed her hand over her face a few times, emphasizing her appearance. "You know."

"The new Queen knows. Barsilay told her."

"The new Queen? What happened to the old one? The one I met?"

"I suppose she's dead," Nehama said, a little too happily.

"Did you know her?" Elena asked Nehama.

"No. Maybe. I can't remember. It was so long ago that I knew anyone. I might have known her. She was old?"

"The oldest living Mazik, Barsilay told us."

"No longer, it would seem," Elena said.

"Hang on," the old woman said. "Doesn't this mean the Princess is the new Queen? And wouldn't that make Barsilay the King?"

Elena blinked at her a little stupidly, and said, "Do you mean to tell me Barsilay is married to the Princess—the Queen—of P'ri Hadar? How long was I asleep?"

"I lost track. Did no one tell you this?"

"You are the one who ought to have told me!"

"I forgot you didn't know!"

"Is there anything else I might have missed?"

The old woman mulled it over and said, "I can't remember. Oh, yes, we ransomed Barsilay out of prison."

"I gathered that much, as he's married to the Princess."

"The Queen."

"The Queen," Elena breathed. "And remind me again, how the other Queen died?"

"Poison," Naftaly said, "which I shall also explain."

So the four of them passed through the gate, together with the Ziz. She seemed remarkably intelligent, by Elena's estimation, and perfectly capable of understanding a good bit of Nehama's speech (though not Elena's). "It sounds like Hebrew," Elena said, after Nehama had explained to the bird what they intended, and Nehama said, "It is the language of Luz."

"Are you of Luz?" the old woman asked. "Did you know Barsilay, when you lived there? Or his aunt?"

"No," she said. "Perhaps? No, I don't think so. You underestimate my time in Aravoth. When I went in, the Queen of Luz was still young in her reign."

"That was ages ago," Elena said.

"You are thinking it's a wonder I'm not madder."

"Under the circumstances, I think you're remarkably sane," Elena said. "But you'll need to mind yourself inside the city. Maziks can be unpredictable when it comes to divergence of behavior."

"Or appearance," the old woman said. "Keep your clothes on."

They passed through the gate and into the garden, which the Ziz seemed to admire, chattering to herself. Then she turned and saw the palace itself, let out a shriek, and reared back. Nehama called out to her, urging her to be still, but the Ziz seemed inconsolable and it was only through some magic of Nehama's they weren't all trampled.

She was imprisoned here, Elena recalled. "I don't think she knew where we were 'til now," she told Nehama. "Toba said she was kept in the dungeon for something like fifty years."

Naftaly said, "Nehama, tell her that Queen is dead, and the new one means her no harm."

She did, but the Ziz still looked as if she meant to fly away. "Swear on your name," Naftaly told her. "Tell her she'll never be confined against her will again."

"How can I make such a promise?" Nehama asked.

"The Queen has already promised it," he said.

"I have not met this queen! How do I know the worth of her promise?"

"Because Toba saved her life last night," he said.

So Nehama spoke again to the Ziz, who leaned all the way to the ground, the movement causing a rush of air, and put her face near Nehama's. She huffed a breath and then was still.

The Maziks had created a private garden for the Ziz, not far from the northwest wall. In the center was a tower reaching even higher than the city's wall, with a crosspiece set across the top and smaller branches encircling its length, giving the impression of an oddly crafted stone tree. In the base there was a doorway. Nehama opened this and they peeked inside, where there was a single room with no ceiling… In fact, the tree was hollow all the way to the top, so that they could see the insides of the branches growing out from the trunk. The Ziz flew to the very top, looked down on them, and let out a cry that reverberated in Elena's good ear.

"She can look out over the entire city this way," Elena said. "She's quite terrifying—won't she worry everyone?"

Naftaly, who by then had closed the gate, told them, "Ayleth wants her to be seen. She thinks it will be good for everyone to see that she is alive— Oh." He stopped because Barsilay had just come into the garden, dressed entirely in silk, a little thinner than last time Elena had seen him but otherwise looking like he hadn't suffered too much in the prison. Nehama's breath caught audibly at the sight of him, and Elena could not exactly blame her. Barsilay was absurdly handsome even for a Mazik—but she thought the Princess's good humor toward his infidelities was likely to extend only so far. Casting a stony glare at Nehama, she told her, "No."

Barsilay had ignored this exchange, and seemed to be mostly unaware of Nehama, too, as he told the women, "Ayleth has left this place for the Ziz and her companion, but if you will come with us I will show you where you can rest."

Nehama said, "Wait, her companion—"

But Barsilay was already walking away, and Naftaly had cast his eyes to the sky, like he would rather have been someplace else.

NAFTALY DID WISH he were somewhere else. Barsilay's reasons for the arrangements he'd made for the mortals made perfect sense—to him. And to Naftaly, too, after a fashion. Nevertheless, he expected this exchange to go badly and hung back while Nehama said, in his ear, "What did he mean, the Ziz's companion?"

Barsilay was already speaking. "So you see," Barsilay explained, "P'ri Hadar is not quite like Zayit. People here are not used to mortals, and you can hardly maintain a glamoured face all the time. I discussed this with Efra—"

"Efra?" Elena said.

"Yes, and we thought you would be safer outside of the palace."

"With Efra?" Elena presumed, "and the Zayitis?"

"Not with the Zayitis, no. We didn't think outside the city would be any safer."

"Speak plainly," Elena said. "Where have you put us?"

"Well, as I said, the Maziks here are not used to mortals—"

"You are putting us in the prison," the old woman said. "Aren't you? Oh—I can't believe this!"

"Not the prison! Not at all. So, we had to offer some explanation as to why the heir of Luz has two rather aged mortals in his retinue."

"He told everyone you were extraordinarily powerful witches," Naftaly said.

"Witches!"

"Yes," Barsilay said. "People here are a little worried over mortal magic. If they think you have any power, they're likely to stay away from you."

"Where," Elena asked again, "are we staying?"

"Ah," he said, "I was just getting to that. So, seeing as you are supposed to be witches, we have built for you a… a habitation to support that belief."

They had come, then, to another part of the garden, and as they turned a corner around a hedge, they were greeted by a small, round house with a roof that looked like it had been made of hastily assembled twigs.

"That," Elena said, "is a hut."

"Look at the base!" he said, pointing, and they realized that the structure itself rested on four posts that had been carved to look like animal legs.

"We are in one of the grandest cities of the world," the old woman said, "and you have put us in a *hut*?"

"It is safer, as you have no magic—"

"Is Naftaly in a hut?"

"Naftaly is often with me, and I am able to look after him."

"Is Toba in a hut?"

"Toba?'

"Don't be foolish," the old woman said. "Toba shares a bed with his uncle—of course he's not making her sleep in the damned garden."

Elena looked a little uncomfortable at this statement, but then Nehama said again, "The Ziz's companion?" like the greater meaning of that statement had finally occurred to her.

"They have put us in a hut," Elena told her.

"Oh-ho," Nehama said, "you get a hut?" She pointed back toward the other end of the garden, to the stone tree. "They mean to leave me in a great oversized chicken coop!"

"It's not a coop!" Barsilay said. "The Ziz can't be left alone, and as you and she have a bond—"

"She prefers Toba!" She turned to Elena. "I see how this is. You either share a man's bed or you sleep outside." She smacked Barsilay's shoulder. "Is that how it is to be?"

"Just wait," Elena said, "he'll have Ayleth out here, too. He doesn't want to share her bed, either."

Naftaly, then, had turned to slink back toward the palace. The old woman called after him, "And where do you think you are going?"

"I—"

"It isn't safe for you," she said acidly, twisting his ear. "Did you not hear that? The palace is a death-trap—boogeymen and horrors everywhere, Maziks jumping out of the cupboards to eat your eyeballs and shove red-hot pokers right up your nose. But this garden! This garden is safe. Here, we'll provide you with a place, too—would you like a bed in the mud?"

"It's temporary!" Barsilay called out, because Elena had taken off her shoe and hit him with it. "It's— It's—"

"Don't you dare laugh!"

"Give me a little time," he said. "Once they are better used to you, I will move you inside. I promise. I swear—stop hitting me—I swear on my name."

"Do you?" the old woman said.

"I do," he said.

"Fine," the old woman said, and taking Elena by the arm, they went into the hut and slammed the door. Nehama stomped off in the other direction.

"Harridans," Barsilay said, rubbing his shoulder.

Naftaly took his hand, and said, "Did it really have to be a hut?"

"Well," Barsilay said, "they'll get over it."

Naftaly put his arm around him and shook his head, still laughing. "No, they won't."

Chapter Seventeen

Inside the palace of P'ri Hadar, Toba had been given a room that she shared with Asmel not far from Ayleth's suite. The window overlooked the garden where the Ziz was kept, and if she leaned out she could see her perched on her false tree, gazing down at the city. The great tree had been Toba's idea, meant to remind the Ziz of the trees in Aravoth, with their stonelike bark the color of ash.

Toba put her almond branch into a pitcher of water and set it in the window. She had no idea what to do with such a thing, which was surely the most important object she would ever own (though it seemed somehow wrong to think of it as an object). It did not look as well as it had in Aravoth; the scent had faded, the blossoms wilted, and it generally seemed sickly.

At Nehama's suggestion, she fetched the man who was in charge of the Queen's garden, a Mazik called Natin, who seemed eager enough to see such a wonder as a branch from Aravoth and followed her up to her room.

He examined the branch with his eye an inch away, then touched it carefully. "You are right to be worried," he said. "It's failing."

"It cannot be allowed to die," Toba told him.

"It has plenty of water and sunlight," he said. "What it needs is to be grafted."

"Grafted? To another tree?"

"Is that not what you intended, when you took it?"

Toba hadn't intended anything. "What would you graft it to, then, another almond tree?"

"That would be the best thing to do," Natin said, "only there are none in the city."

"None at all?"

"They are quite illegal," he said. "Kasfia destroyed any that were growing here. I'm not sure where we could get one, to be honest."

"Could you not make a request to one of the other cities?"

He shrugged. "I would not take any living plant from Katlav, not with that lentil blight. Habush might have one, but I doubt it. Would you consider grafting it to something else? I have some very healthy persimmons."

"No," Toba said. "That feels wrong. Is there anything you can do for it now?"

"Hm," he said, taking his thumb and forefinger and pinching it between them. He gave it a little magic—Toba could see it flow through his fingers—and the flowers perked up a little.

"That helped," she said.

"It's a start," he said. "Give it a little magic whenever you can. I will see about finding you an almond tree. But you might want to make sure Ayleth will let me put it somewhere. I'd hate to go through all this just to have her cut it down."

Natin returned to the garden and Toba pushed a little of her own magic into the branch, which seemed not to have as much effect as Natin's. She would try again later, she decided. She had other concerns, foremost among them the recent arrival of the King of Anab.

King Yefet was looking very haggard when he came through the gate with his advisors; they had been in hiding for many weeks, and while they were all presumed dead, they were still in a great deal of danger. They'd often been afraid to sleep, and had escaped with very little food. They'd been waiting, Yefet told them, for word from Asmel b'Asmoda, the great astronomer of Rimon.

"Why would the Peregrine have chosen me for this?" Asmel wondered.

"Because she would have known you would stay with Barsilay,

and Yefet knew who you were, so it would have been more difficult to send an imposter. You've met him before?"

"Only once," Asmel said. "And that was long ago. I was visiting the university in Anab, and he came to hear my lecture. I'm surprised he remembers."

In any case, the Peregrine had managed to circumvent Tarses's instructions to kill Yefet, but only barely: She'd used magic to stop his heart, and once she was satisfied he was dead, she'd used magic to start it again.

It was, Yefet told them, something she had learned from a doctor in Zayit.

She'd revived him on the condition that he would swear his allegiance to Barsilay so long as he lived. Since the alternative had been dying in a more permanent fashion, he'd agreed.

Toba was not sure how Yefet felt about all this; Barsilay was the enemy of the man who had ordered him murdered and taken his city, true. But Barsilay had also set the Peregrine loose on him, when he might have stopped her.

Still, Yefet—once he was cleaned up and fed—seemed an understanding man, and so far as Toba could tell, he was not one to hold a grudge. In fact, he seemed rather grateful to have been pulled from the mountains where he'd been hiding with his men—some twenty Maziks, administrators, mainly—whose lives Yefet had thought might be at risk when Tarses's army arrived. Ayleth and her remaining advisors had explained the dire straits in which they found themselves, and Yefet had set about reestablishing the bureaucracy necessary to run a great city, combining duties where such things were possible, and inserting his own people where he thought they might be most useful.

All this was done with a speed that impressed Toba deeply. She had never expected to be impressed by a king. But Yefet was clever, he appreciated reason, and he was able to foresee problems that certainly would have eluded Ayleth—particularly when it came to making sure there appeared to be a continuity of rule, and that any positions that required interfacing with the normal people of P'ri Hadar were filled with familiar faces. "This already looks like a coup," he told Ayleth. "Whoever remains of your mother's people, put them where they are most visible. And order a new survey of the lands outside the walls."

"For what purpose?" Ayleth had asked, because she had just woken up and this was all moving very fast.

"Once you are Queen, you are going to hand out new adonates to the lesser sons of your wealthiest adons."

"What about an oath-getting?" Barsilay had asked.

"Not yet," Yefet had said. "It stinks of desperation and oaths can be broken." At that, he'd set down the pen he'd been using to write the list of Kasfia's surviving advisors who could be promoted, and those who were so out of their depth they would need oversight from Yefet's own people. "There is also the more pressing matter of your coronation."

"I've just declared a month of mourning," Ayleth said. "We ought to wait until that is over. We need—"

"What you need," he told Ayleth, "is a spectacle."

Ayleth's coronation was at noon the next day, and Naftaly found that it was indeed a spectacle.

The entirety of the city was out in the streets, all the way to the steps of the palace, which had been laid with illusions of citron trees so real you could smell the blossoms. The topmost step, which was more like a small plaza, was a semicircle mostly visible to those below. Barsilay and Asmel stood on one side of this with Naftaly behind them alongside Ayleth's advisors. Ayleth stepped forward, waiting for the crowd to quiet, and when it did, she was presented by her new vizier with her mother's crown, which she placed on her head. Then she placed a smaller version of this onto Barsilay's brow, as he bent forward to accept it.

Then the crowd began to scream, because flying through the sky from behind the palace was the Ziz. She circled three times before landing on the empty side of the dais. Nehama, on her back, slid down to the plaza beside her. The Ziz let out a shriek, and the people of the city went utterly silent.

It was a clever piece of showmanship, as if even the great Ziz had come to acknowledge the new Queen.

Ayleth stepped forward to address the crowd, a hand on her throat to project her voice. "Bear witness," she said. "The Leviathan is dead. But the Ziz survives, and she is with us."

The people whispered among themselves, still unsure. Naftaly caught a few phrases, thanks to the shade in his ear. Mostly, the people wondered what it meant—the return of two of the great beasts, one living, one dead. They were anxious, all of them. Naftaly could feel it, a great weight on the city.

Ayleth continued, "Every Mazik in this city was born under the rule of Queen Kasfia, who until days ago, was the eldest of us all. She was a fierce protector, for where else has a Queen ruled so long? What other city has been so safe for its citizens? There is none."

"Do you think she's going to mention Luz?" Naftaly asked in Barsilay's ear.

"She'll lose them if she does."

"But you will find in me a Queen no less fierce. No less protective."

Just then, the bell that Barsilay had hidden beneath his tunic began to ring; Naftaly could hear it even over the crowd, and Barsilay's eyes went a little wide.

"I shall show you, now, how I will protect this city. Here is the woman who has murdered your Queen. And now you may see how your new Queen addresses any threats to P'ri Hadar."

Two guards stepped out of the palace. Between them, in chains cast from glowing magic, was the Peregrine.

"Barsilay," Naftaly hissed, but Barsilay had already begun making his way to Ayleth's side, pushing richly dressed Maziks out the of the way as he went. He said something into her ear, which she ignored. "Ayleth," he said, loudly enough for Naftaly to hear, but she turned her back on him.

Naftaly met Barsilay's eyes across the dais, his face ashen. The colors around them seemed to drain away, like paint running in the rain, and everything seemed very muted. Naftaly shook himself. But nothing altered, and the noise of the crowd seemed also to fade. It all felt very unreal—the coronation, Ayleth, even Barsilay—and Naftaly had a strange urge to lie down.

Addressing the crowd, Ayleth said, "This Mazik is an agent of the Queen of Rimon. And today we send Oneca, and any who would stand against us, a warning. P'ri Hadar has not fallen with her Queen."

Ayleth raised her hand to one of the guards, who conjured an axe and lifted it. Barsilay's mouth was open—he must be shouting, Naftaly knew—and yet it was as if his ears were stopped with wax.

On the other side of the steps, Nehama looked up at the Ziz and said something Naftaly had no hope of hearing over the roars. And as the executioner's axe reached its zenith, the Ziz snapped her neck forward, took the Peregrine in her mouth, and swallowed her.

Naftaly thought he might faint. The crowd erupted in cheers so loud he was dizzy from the sudden return of noise. What had happened? The Peregrine had died while he'd stood there. And he'd done nothing, and he did not even know why.

He felt himself ushered back inside the palace, where the roar of the crowd was still dizzying. Barsilay was railing at the new Queen, repeating, "We never discussed this!"

"I don't need your permission!" she said. "I am the Queen, you are my consort, and don't forget it."

"But we agreed, she needed interrogation!"

"You were never going to get any information out of her," Ayleth said. "Yefet said we needed a spectacle."

"Yefet told you to execute her?"

"He did, and I agreed. I don't know why you're so upset—do you know how many Maziks that woman has murdered in every city?" She paused. "Unless you intended her to kill my mother?"

"Of course not. But she was useful."

"To you, perhaps. Not to me." She turned her back on him. "There are papers that require my seal. I have duties. And so do you, if you think you can perform them tonight." She left Barsilay staring after her.

"I can't believe this," Naftaly said.

"I can," he said. He glanced at Naftaly. "What I can't understand is your friend Nehama feeding someone to her pet bird."

Naftaly rubbed at his arms; he was unaccountably cold. "Maybe she thought... I don't know. I don't know why she would do such a thing."

"I intend to ask her," Barsilay said tightly.

"I will go with you," Naftaly said. The sight of the Peregrine's face was still behind his eyes. She'd been someone he'd trusted. More to the point, he'd thought she might be the one to kill Tarses, and now she was dead.

The two made their way back through the Queen's ridiculous gardens accompanied by a shade that seemed bent on attending them, floating along behind them carrying a ewer of water or wine or some other Mazik spirit. Nehama had taken the Ziz back to her stone tree; they could see the top of her head over the garden wall as she plucked oranges from the perfectly manicured trees and swallowed them whole. Nehama was sitting beside her on the ground, picking dirt from beneath her toenails when Barsilay approached.

She took in Barsilay, encrusted in silk and gold, and said, "Look at you, like the inside of a jewel box."

Naftaly was not sure if this were an insult or a compliment, and neither, it would seem, was Barsilay, who said, "The occasion seemed to call for it."

"Yes, well, I suppose the Princess had to convince all these people you were something important."

Barsilay looked less amused and more irritated and said, "I am the heir of Luz and the King Consort of P'ri Hadar."

Nehama remained unimpressed. "You are the heir of Luz because long ago the Queen birthed some bastard child who birthed some other bastard child who birthed you. There's little in blood but iron and water."

Barsilay looked a little startled. She said, "Do you disagree?"

Barsilay shook his head and said, "I know you gave that order to the Ziz, to swallow the Peregrine. But why?"

"Hm?" she said, looking up. "Well, from what I'd heard, she was being executed without a trial."

Barsilay said, "What?"

"Without a trial. Are there even judges here? Ayleth seems to be running things just like the Queen of Luz. Monarchy is such an abomination."

Barsilay went very still. "Where did you hear that?"

"Sorry to have insulted you. But it's a terrible system; things were better when we had the Judges. Anyway, I couldn't stand there and watch her get her head chopped off without any kind of trial or a judge or anything." She frowned at Barsilay. "Are you upset?"

"That the Peregrine is dead? Yes, I am upset that my friend is dead."

"Oh," said Nehama. "But she's not dead. Not yet, anyway."

"Are you saying she's alive in the Ziz's belly? How is she breathing?"

"Oh!" she said. "Right, it's probably time then." And she barked something at the Ziz, to which the Ziz responded by screaming in her face. Nehama repeated the word, the Ziz turned away, and then she gave the Ziz's foot a good hard kick.

The Ziz lifted her foot very delicately, as if she'd been grievously insulted, and glared at Nehama a moment. Then she opened her mouth and vomited up the Peregrine directly on top of her.

"Good grief," said Barsilay, as the two women untangled themselves, both coated in vomit and half-digested orange pulp. The Peregrine was coughing ferociously, and Barsilay tried to help her as much as he could without actually touching her. Naftaly took the pitcher of water from the shade who had been attending them and offered it to the Peregrine, who drank half of it before she began coughing again.

Naftaly found that he had to sit down.

"Who are you?" she asked Nehama. "Why did you…? I don't even know what you did."

"I saved you," she said. "Well, in a manner of speaking."

"Why?"

"If you'll forgive me, we've just been through all that."

The Peregrine leaned back on her arms and said, "Seeing as you kept me from having my head chopped off, I suppose I'll have to forgive you."

"Oh," Nehama said. "Good. Are you from Baobab? I always wanted to go to Baobab."

"Yes," the Peregrine said, her voice heavy with the exhaustion of just having been woken up from a coma and then eaten. "I'll take you there someday. If we don't all die first."

"Will you really?"

Ignoring all this, Barsilay said, "I did not know what Ayleth intended. I am sorry."

"I don't blame her," she said. "I did kill her mother."

"It was Yefet's idea," Nehama said helpfully. "The King of Anab."

The Peregrine said, "I don't suppose I can really blame him, either."

"You spared him!" Barsilay said.

"I did also kill him first."

"Yes," Nehama said. She gathered up some stones, tossed them into the air 'til they coalesced into a larger stone, and then set it on the ground. Stomping on it with her foot, it became a large tub, which she then filled with the pitcher she took from Naftaly, splashing it with her fingertips 'til the water level rose to the top. "I can see you're holding a grudge over that. Here, take your clothes off."

The Peregrine said, "I beg your pardon?"

"You're all covered with vomitus," she said. "Look, we're both women; Naftaly doesn't care—you're all right, aren't you?"

"I'm fine," Naftaly said, though he wasn't.

"—and Barsilay's already seen you naked."

The Peregrine said, "How can you know that?"

"Well," Nehama said, "I assumed." But the Peregrine had already removed all of her clothes, seemingly with magic, because one second they were there and the next they were gone, and Naftaly blushed and turned around. He heard her splash into the tub with a sigh.

"We're going to have to keep you hidden for now," Barsilay said. "If Ayleth finds out you're still alive, there will be trouble."

"For you," the Peregrine said. "She won't be able to catch me again." To Naftaly, she said, "I can't believe you're still here, and after I tried so hard to send you away."

When Naftaly, who still had his back turned, failed to give an answer to this, she added, "I take responsibility for poisoning the Queen and the others. Naftaly is not my fault."

Barsilay ignored this. "Nehama," he said. "Will she be safe out here with the Ziz? She won't try to eat her again?"

"No, I don't think so. And the guards won't come out here; they're too afraid. Besides the prison, this is probably the safest place for her."

"Good," Barsilay said. "Listen, if I don't turn up, someone will come looking for me." He hesitated and said, "Is there no food in Aravoth? Is that why you are so thin?"

"There is," she said. "But eating alone tends to curb one's appetite. I'm sure there were days I forgot to eat."

"Well, you won't have to eat alone now. You'll eat at my table tonight."

Nehama tilted her head sideways and asked, "What happened to the last people who shared a table with you?"

Barsilay made an inarticulate noise. Nehama turned to Naftaly and said, "Ought I not to have mentioned that? Is it rude to say obvious things?"

Naftaly said, "Perhaps another night might be better to introduce her to Ayleth."

"Nonsense," she said. "I'm ready now."

Barsilay said, "Not as you are—you're covered in digestive juices."

"Fine," Nehama said, and, fully clothed, stepped into the tub with the very surprised Peregrine, splashed around a little, and stepped out again. "And now I'm not."

"That hardly serves," Barsilay said. "And your dress is ruined. Even magic can't fix that monstrosity."

"Then make me a new one," Nehama said. "Something pretty."

"As you wish," he said, unclipping his cloak from his shoulders. Glancing at Naftaly he said, "Yellow, do you think?"

"Better not. Ayleth was wearing yellow."

"Will green do?" Barsilay asked her.

"I like green... Not like that. Darker. Darker. Yes." She held out her arms, as if expecting Barsilay to dress her himself, but he threw the thing at her and said, "You've been dressing yourself a thousand years, I'm sure you know how."

Stripping off her ruined dress, she stepped into Barsilay's, doing it up with some bit of magic, and looked down to admire herself.

"The bodice is a little low," she said.

"You claim modesty now?" Barsilay laughed. "All right. You are nearly presentable. Now remember, in company both of you will have to pretend to respect my title."

Nehama muttered something under her breath and Barsilay said, "Would you like to repeat that to my face?"

Nehama said, "Oh, no, I'm pretending to respect you."

Naftaly took her hand in his and said, "Pretend a little harder."

Tsifra did not bother to explain her missing ship when she returned to her fleet, nor how she'd managed to sail back without it. The truth was she'd made a small sailboat with magic and abandoned it on the far side of the island, but let her sailors think her return was a miracle. When her commander questioned her, she'd simply said, "You must lack faith, to ask such a question."

It seemed a good answer for anything.

She was exhausted from everything that had happened since she'd left the fleet, and from using too much magic to get back to it. Her sailors had made a camp slightly inland, where there was better access to fresh water, and once she'd made her men feel thoroughly damned for questioning her she retreated to her tent and fell immediately asleep.

She opened her eyes in a wood she had not visited before. The dream-world wind was as loud as the sea, and she pressed her palms to the trunk of the nearest tree to steady herself against the noise and the sensation of rushing air.

The tree was warm, and she pulled her hands back in surprise. Was it alive? She'd always believed trees in the dream-world were merely imaginary figments of the Mazik who dreamt them. Pressing her palm against the trunk again, she closed her eyes and felt the sap running below the surface of the bark. The tree *was* alive; whether she'd willed it so or it somehow existed on its own, she did not know.

What was the dream-world, really? What were the stars? She'd never been given to bouts of philosophizing, but just then she felt like some clever Mazik must have crafted an opinion on what all this was, on what it meant. There ought to be a book. Asmel could have told her, or that man she'd killed in Te'ena.

There were footsteps behind her and she was almost unsurprised to see that it was Toba with her in the forest. She hadn't called to her, she was sure. But the two of them seemed apt to be pulled together here. Most likely it was their shared name. "Why are you here?" Toba asked.

"I don't know," Tsifra said. "I simply am, but I don't understand how we can see one another, since your grandmother ordered us not to."

"We aren't seeing each other, in the technical sense," Toba surmised. "Since our eyes are closed. So I guess we could try to kill each other here, too."

"What would be the point?" Tsifra asked.

Toba said, "Did our father really order you to kill Tsidon?"

"He did," she said. "You are welcome, by the way. I'm sure you hated him as much as I did."

Toba did not deny this. She said, "You saved the Peregrine."

Tsifra went very stiff, because it would go badly for her if Tarses found out about it. At the time, the fact that she'd done it in front of a dozen Maziks had meant little to her. But Toba might someday be in a position to reveal it.

Toba said, "I won't tell anyone." She came a little closer. "I told you once that the heir of Luz can change a name."

"Only if he becomes king."

"You don't think he will?"

"No," she said. "I don't."

"So you would rather remain a slave to the Caçador than try to help the man who could save you?"

"My position is lately improved," Tsifra told her.

"He ordered your friend to poison herself!"

"Yes, and that's my point! The Peregrine did as you suggested—she threw in with the heir of Luz. She nearly died for it, and she's a more powerful Mazik than I shall ever be. If even she cannot beat the Caçador, then there is no hope I can. Your heir of Luz will be defeated, whether I try to help him or not."

Toba said, "Is that the true reason? Or is it that you enjoy being a queen?"

Tsifra said, "I owe you no explanation for my actions."

"I can imagine it, all those mortals fawning on you. What do they think you are? A witch? No, they wouldn't follow a witch, you'll have told them something else. An angel, then?"

Tsifra turned back to the tree.

"Ah, that's it. You've made yourself a false idol for them. This isn't about your fear of our father. You like being worshipped."

"I was an angel for them," Tsifra snapped. "But only for a short while. I haven't been so in a long time."

"You believe they love you."

"I don't require love from them!"

"You believe the Caçador loves you!"

"I am not a fool."

Toba crossed her arms over her chest and was silent. When she spoke again, it was to ask, "Why did you save my grandmother? Why would you care what happens to her?"

Tsifra rounded on her. "I don't know!"

"Our father wouldn't like it, if he found out, and I know you spoke to the doctor, too, and he wouldn't like that, either. You risked a lot to do it. I want to know why."

"What difference can it make to you? Are you not glad?"

"She is nothing to you! You've never even met her before. She's just an old mortal."

"You don't deserve her!" Tsifra shouted, and then felt rather abashed. Of course she was just an old mortal to her. What else could she be?

Why had she saved her? Surely she would be dead soon, anyway, even if Tarses did not kill all those fools in P'ri Hadar. Toba looked like she would have had an answer for that, but some movement pulled Tsifra from the dream; some noise in the camp, that was all, but it had been enough to wake her. She lay in her tent, breathing the damp air, and then thought, *since I saved Elena, maybe they will let the Peregrine live. That must be why I did it, as a trade.* She was sure they'd understood.

Chapter Eighteen

Barsilay changed out of his garish coronation outfit and into something that actually bent when he moved. The inside of a jewel box, that wretched Nehama had said, and she'd been entirely correct. Ayleth had made him out to be important, and instead he felt utterly absurd.

He was still angry with her and Yefet both, and could not imagine how he would get past it, even if they'd ultimately failed in killing the Peregrine. He'd expected Ayleth to have authority over him—P'ri Hadar was her city, not his—but he hadn't expected Yefet to trump him as well.

Tamping down his feelings was not one of Barsilay's greater gifts, but still, he knew he had no choice if he were to continue in his role. He'd known he'd have to make some concessions in taking a wife. He reminded himself that the Peregrine had killed Kasfia and tried to kill Yefet. That she was Barsilay's friend of long standing was a concern to no one but him.

By the time he was done changing his clothes, Asmel and Naftaly had finished describing the events of the coronation to Elena and the old woman while Nehama watched them from a corner. They stopped talking when Barsilay returned. "You look much better now," the old woman said. "But what did you do with that coat with the jewels on it?"

"Were you hoping to sell it?" Barsilay asked.

"I was just wondering," she said, with an affronted sniff. "I'm sure something like that needs careful laundering."

"Only if I ever intend to wear it again," he said. "I had better make an appearance at my own coronation feast. Has no one been by to get me?" A soft knock at the door revealed not the expected shade, but Toba.

"I thought you were with Ayleth again," Barsilay said.

"I was. I asked her to send me to get you rather than the shade." She put her fingertips to her temples. "I'm a little fatigued."

"What's she got you doing?"

"Every time something comes up, first she asks Yefet's opinion, and then she asks mine. Just now she wanted to know if I thought the Ziz should be moved to the front of the palace so everyone in the city could see her better."

Barsilay said, "If she's asking your opinion on everything, does that mean you knew what she meant to do to the Peregrine?"

Toba said, "She and Yefet discussed that without me. She probably thought I'd have told you. I'm sorry."

"There's no need," Barsilay said. "She's safe, for now. But I hope you didn't suggest the Ziz be moved."

"No, I thought it would be too difficult to keep her safe in public. Is the Peregrine with the Ziz? After she... you know?"

"She didn't actually eat her," Nehama put in. "She just sort of swallowed her a bit. For safekeeping."

Toba looked quite nonplussed, so Asmel took her arm and led her back down the corridor. The rest followed, the mortals on either side of Nehama. Elena never seemed to take her eyes off her.

The feast was nothing like the wedding banquet had been. There were two long tables in the hall, Barsilay heading one and Ayleth the other. Seated to her left was Yefet, and the rest of the table was made up of their respective advisors. She'd kept one seat open for Toba, who did poorly at hiding her disappointment but went to sit by Ayleth anyway. The room was sparsely decorated, due, he presumed, to the fact that the city was still technically in mourning for the late Queen.

He was more surprised when a shade set before him a plate of unchanged lentils. "What is this?" he asked, and the shade said, "As a precaution."

Against poisoning was the implication. If everyone had to change their own food, a poisoner would have to poison the actual lentils, which would be nearly impossible. Salted lentils couldn't be changed by magic, so it would require a rare poison, and one which could penetrate the lentils' shells as well.

Ayleth had made herself a large platter of some stuffed leaves, and she offered one to Toba. Barsilay rose out of his chair and spoke directly into Ayleth's ear. "There are two things you should know," he said. "The first is that using a half-Mazik as a poison taster is a terrible idea, since salt won't harm them. The second is that I will not allow you to use my friend this way."

Ayleth gave him a long look and said, "Was your own lover not tasting your food for you at our wedding?"

Barsilay had to close his eyes a moment to restrain his temper. "That was a mistake I grieve deeply."

"Is it?" she said. "As it happens, I was only offering a delicacy of P'ri Hadar to Toba because she has not tasted it before. I have already eaten it myself."

Barsilay bowed his head. To Toba, Ayleth said, "I thought you said he was charming. But if your cousin is missing you, go and join him. I have other companions tonight."

Barsilay returned to the head of his own table. Asmel, who made space for Toba beside him, had apparently created meals for those who could not change lentils, and the old woman was muttering about unseasoned food again.

Nehama said, "You must have said something dreadful to make Ayleth's face so sour when yours is so fine." She took a bite, which she chewed with her mouth open. "Did you decide to send her to the hut after all?"

Barsilay sat back in his chair and looked at Elena a long time before saying, "Do you have something to tell me?"

Elena said, "I don't."

"Really? Are you sure?" He sipped at his wine. "Because I have known a great many people in my long life—"

"Intimately or otherwise?" Toba put in.

He snapped his fingers and pointed at her impertinence. "Ah," he said. "There. You see? My point is made. I have known a great many people"—he smirked at Toba—"intimately *and* otherwise, and in all that time I have only known two so quarrelsome, so contrary, so quick to insult—"

Elena put forth, "Excuse me, but did your own wife not toss you out a window the hour you met her?"

Barsilay rubbed the back of his neck and said, "Yes, but she was much less clever about it." His eyes met Elena's. "Also, there is the fact that you look at her the same way you look at Toba. So I ask you, who is this woman Toba plucked out of Aravoth?"

The table went silent. Then Nehama, who was still eating as if nothing much had been said, asked, "You think I am Toba?"

Barsilay did not even know what he was asking. Of course she was not Toba. Toba—the original Toba—had died. But this woman who quoted his aunt and sounded so much like his friend… Something had happened in Aravoth. Aravoth, Hashem's sake, who knows what could have happened there? Naftaly still could not even talk about it.

"I'm not Toba," she went on. "But I think I was, once."

Asmel had gone pale, and he rose from his chair and excused himself. Barsilay waited a few moments before following him. He caught up to him down the hallway, where he was leaning against a pillar and scowling.

"Uncle—"

Asmel looked up sharply and asked, "How is it you noticed this when I did not?"

Barsilay said, "I live in the world. You live inside your own head. That's not an insult, Uncle, it's one of your better qualities."

"How is it?" Asmel said. He shook his head. "Toba is the woman I love."

"A declaration! From you?"

"Your charms are wearing thin with me. Or are my feelings so insignificant to you?"

Barsilay sobered. "I am sorry. I did not realize you were so distressed. Listen, it was Elena that gave it away more than Toba—Nehama—Toba. What do we call her? It's not important. If Elena hadn't behaved so oddly I'm not sure I would have picked it up. I might have just thought the universe had made a run on difficult women, and we happened to turn up several of them all at once. Apart from her snappishness, she's not really the woman we knew. Toba was young; this woman is older than you. She's older, nearly, than everyone, and you know that changes a person. She was Omer's apprentice before you were born."

"Before my father was born," Asmel said.

"Yes, that's true. If you compare the length of Toba's life to Nehama's, it's a very small piece. I would be surprised if she even remembered us."

Nehama, then, had joined them in the hallway, and she said, "I remember you. I remember... trying to drown you, I think."

"You didn't try very hard," Barsilay said. "And I'm sure I deserved it."

"You did. I remember that, too."

"You also died for me," Barsilay said quietly. "Do you remember that?"

Nehama turned inside herself for a moment and said, "No. No, I don't. But I think if I did that, you must have been very important to me." She met his eyes. "You were my friend. You were Toba's only friend. My only friend."

Barsilay took her hands in his, and she looked down and said, "That hand—it's not real."

"No," he said. "Your sister took that arm."

"The sister who killed me. Elena told me, I don't remember it."

"Yes, the same one. That's when you saved my life. You were very brave that day."

"Very stupid, Elena says."

"Well, there's often some overlap there."

Nehama laughed a little, then she put her hand to her mouth, as if she had not laughed in a very long time and had forgotten what it was. She turned to Asmel, who all this time was looking mystified and, truthfully, a little unhappy. "I remember you, too," she said. "But I think we were not so much friends. It's very muddled, what I remember. I know there were two of me, and it's hard for me to recall my feelings apart from hers. This must be making you very uncomfortable."

"No," Asmel said. "It's only..."

"I may have been in love with you," Nehama said. "At least one of us was; it might have been both, but that was"—here, she sighed—"very long ago. It feels like a very old dream, mostly forgotten. And you have your Toba."

"Yes," he said. "I have my Toba."

"Well then," she said. "I'm very glad that's all sorted." She took his hand. "Now, tell me of Omer. I want to know everything from when you last saw him." She pulled Asmel back down the hallway, as he said, "His library was destroyed—"

"No!"

"But he saved most of his books. Those dratted flame lizards are everywhere."

"Oh, he despises those! Did you know one tried to crawl into his mouth while he was sleeping?"

"That's appalling," Asmel said. "Is that true?"

"He was so upset he nearly washed his mouth out with seawater before I reminded him what was in the flask."

They continued their reminiscences, and Elena plucked at Barsilay's sleeve. "I thought it would be safer for her if fewer people knew," she said. "Seeing as Tarses might take an interest. She is still a half-Mazik." Barsilay was still watching the others make their way out of sight… The longer they spoke, the more animated they became.

"You were right," Barsilay said. "But I'm not sorry for having revealed it. It is a terrible thing to hide oneself. And look at her."

"She does seem better," Elena admitted.

"It's because they both knew Omer. He is a bridge between them, more than her life as Toba was, I think. They shall be great friends now. And you. You must be glad for this, however it has happened."

Elena said, "There aren't words for what I feel. For what has happened."

"No," he said, setting his hand on her shoulder. "There aren't."

NAFTALY HAD NEVER been able to dream of anyone besides Barsilay on purpose. He was rather embarrassed by this, both because it revealed his lack of control over his abilities, and because of what it revealed about his lack of self-control so far as Barsilay was concerned. Barsilay, of course, found this rather delightful. But it was also inconvenient, because Saba was trapped by Tarses and they needed a way to reach him, and now that Elena was no longer dreaming there was no one but Naftaly who could dream past the wards.

He lay in Barsilay's bed in the palace of P'ri Hadar—he had been moved to larger rooms, as King Consort—and on the other side of the wall Ayleth was waiting for her husband. A flagon of wine sat on the table, in which Barsilay had dissolved amapola he'd begged from Efra. He would drink it in a few moments, so that by the time he got to Ayleth's bedchamber he'd be asleep on his feet.

Just then, though, he sat beside Naftaly, his bare feet hanging off the edge of the mattress. Barsilay was telling him again that he only needed to concentrate on the man to dream of him, and Naftaly was telling him he'd been trying, and Barsilay suggested it might help if Naftaly imagined he wanted to make love to Saba rather badly.

"No," Naftaly said. "That would not help."

"All right," Barsilay said. "Then recall the man is all alone, probably being tortured, and with little hope of escape. Does this not seem a familiar tableau? Saba needs you. And just so your subconscious does not develop other ideas, I'm about to take enough amapola to drop a horse, which will prevent me dreaming completely. So don't bother looking for me."

Naftaly huffed a little. "This is insulting."

"It's important," Barsilay said, and then lifted his hand and cast an image of Saba on the ceiling. "Look at his face as long as you need to. That may help."

Naftaly did, and he was still looking at Saba's face when Barsilay set his hand on his forehead and sent him very quickly to sleep. For an instant, he was aware it was happening, and it felt very strange, like falling into the lake in Aravoth—the lake that had not been a lake. So similar was the sensation that he flailed a little, either his waking or dreaming arms or both, and was surprised when they found only air and not water.

He opened his eyes to a dim cell in a stone room. And on the floor was Saba. "It's you," he said. "All this time, I have been waiting—where have you been?"

"I'm sorry," Naftaly said, kneeling beside him. He did not look as poorly as Barsilay had in La Cacería's prison in Rimon, though he also knew Saba could be hiding his injuries. "I was—" He stopped himself. He was not sure what Saba might be forced to reveal under torture; better to say as little as possible. "I was elsewhere."

"I thought you might have forgotten me. I wasn't even sure the heir of Luz was still alive. I hear whispers," Saba told him. "The Hounds speak outside my door; I'm a dead man, so what's it matter what I hear? The Caçador is consumed by the lineage of Luz. He's got Hounds assembling pedigrees for all the heirs he's killed." He let out a noise that was something like hysterical laughter. "Can you imagine if it was *him*? If I wasn't trapped in this cell, I'd have dreamed myself to death already—"

"He's still alive," Naftaly told him. "Our heir."

Saba looked like he wanted to weep. "You can't imagine what it's been like, not knowing anything at all—nothing but rumors. Your old mortal came here, completely catatonic, and then nothing for days. Is my sister safe?"

"She is," Naftaly assured him. "And the old mortal has recovered. She's all right now."

"That's wonderful," Saba said. "I am not. Listen, do you intend to rescue me or what?"

So far as Naftaly knew, there was no plan to do so. They had the book, but the last time they'd used it to breach Tarses's prison it had gone very badly and Toba had died. He said, "It's safer for me not to tell you too much."

"There is no plan," Saba concluded. "Damn it all." He got his feet beneath him and stood. At least his legs appeared to be sound. "Perhaps if I tell you what is going on, it will light a fire beneath our heir of Luz. Here is what I do each day: I am made to push a small amount of magic into Tarses's mind—as I once did to you—to induce a very helpful vision. It isn't good for anyone, in case you were wondering, for Tarses to be having very helpful visions, and I would really rather not be doing this."

He'd gone rather shrill, and Naftaly reached out and touched his elbow. "He knows your name?"

"Of course he knows my name! He tortured it out of me the first day. I am a doctor, I have no great resistance to pain. I am not brave. I want to help people, that's all." He let out a shuddering breath. "So I gave it to him."

"That is no shame," Naftaly said.

"It is," Saba said. "But it's not important now. He has it, and I can't get it back. But there's more. Recently, he's been asking me about you."

This was no great surprise, of course. "We saw each other. In a vision."

"I'd guessed as much. Whatever he saw that day, it's changed him. He's become paranoid about the heir of Luz. He's pulling out his own magic to make beasts to serve him: demon horses that never tire, more flame demons. He's obsessed with recruiting from the southern cities and making sure the lentil blight spreads as quickly as possible. He's frightened."

"Of me?"

"Yes, of you! To see the future, it is no small thing, and he believed it made him unique. It is the basis for all of his beliefs in his own superiority. He's asked me about you, many times."

Naftaly's palms were numb from listening. He asked, "What have you told him?"

"As little as possible," Saba said, "but that's only because he's not asking the right questions. He doesn't know you're mostly mortal. And he doesn't know you're Barsilay's intimate, nor that you were the one carrying the gate of Luz around all this time. So for that, he hasn't sent anyone to kill you yet. But at some point, it will occur to him to ask these things, and I will tell him. So before that happens, and before I manage to give him the vision that shows him everything he needs to win, you and your handsome friend will have to either get me out of here, or you will have to kill me."

That night, Toba dreamed once again of herself.

Nehama was not really Toba anymore, that was what Elena had told her, but it had not seemed to her that Elena had really believed it. She did wonder, though, that Nehama had recognized Elena right away, and Toba not at all, in all the time they'd been together in Aravoth.

She supposed one did not spend much time looking at one's own face. But still, it confused her a little. They were near some dream-version of the palace, on the outer wall, looking south toward the cedar forest. Nehama was staring upward at the sky, and at Toba's approach, she said, "I missed the dream-world stars. I didn't think I would."

Toba stared upward alongside her. Nehama said, "I'm glad to see you here again."

"Do you remember me?"

"Toba Bet. Yes, I remember you, but probably not so well as you remember me. It was long ago. It's strange, isn't it? That so little time has passed for you."

"I don't understand what happened to you. Or why. Or how. The angels tried to explain time to me, and how it relates to the Mirror. They described it like rings on a tree, growing outward."

Nehama said, "That is more than they spoke to me, in all the time I was there."

"And I don't understand that, either. Why not simply help you back out, once you were trapped?"

"I have wondered about that for a long time. I can only presume that's where they thought I belonged."

"There's something comforting in that, isn't there? Because that implies that right now you belong here."

The connection that had existed between them, the sharing of thoughts and emotions and even their physical senses, was no longer there—much to Nehama's relief, if she were honest. But there was something, some vague feeling of knowing, of understanding. It was possible she was imagining it.

It was very odd. If, in some way, she was still the woman who had died, at one point there had been three versions of her. Herself in Aravoth, and the two Tobot in Rimon.

Or else time in Aravoth was so different that one could not even count it as existing contemporaneously with the regular world. She did not know. Time, there, had been muddled; even on her good days she'd often been confused. Still, she wondered. Toba and Toba Bet had shared a soul and yet been different. Nehama was and was not Toba. So who was she, really? What part of her was herself?

Or perhaps all that was different between them was less important; perhaps there was some truer aspect of all three that was shrouded in the superficial. Or perhaps it wasn't superficial at all, and it was memory—life—that made self. She only wished she could recall a little more of her own. Aravoth had made her past feel like an ancient mortal dream, mostly forgotten.

"There is one thing I do wonder," Toba said. "About your name."

"Is it the same as it was? The same as yours? No, it isn't. You told me yours in Aravoth. Mine is—"

"Don't tell me," Toba said. "There are too many Maziks who know my name. Better if no one knows yours."

"I wasn't going to tell you," Nehama said. "But perhaps I can safely show you a little. I feel I owe it to you." She held out her cupped hands, and in between them was a fish the color of starlight. Toba whispered, "Again."

"Again?"

"I have become this," she said. "Three times, and two of those were unplanned."

"I know what you are thinking," Nehama said, "and if you are worried you are still my buchuk, I can tell you that you are not."

"No," Toba said. "I am not. But there is something, still." And then—and she did not know why she did this, not then, and not later—she took Nehama's fish and swallowed it.

It was not real; *they* were not real. It was a dream-fish swallowed down the throat of a dream-woman, but Nehama gasped as she felt some strangeness within her own mind, within her own magic.

Before that night, she'd remembered bits and pieces: first Elena, the woman whose face she had watched as a baby, as a child. She'd remembered Asmel as the man she'd once loved, if only for a few months. But now, she remembered everything: a child, murdered in the Plaça del Rey; a hostage in the baths, sentenced to an eternity of pain; a book, hidden in an alcove.

She also remembered dying: her sister's arm a blade, Barsilay's blood on the floor, and for some small part of eternity… the void.

Chapter Nineteen

Naftaly thought that Barsilay took the news of this latest dream rather well. Barsilay looked at him a moment, said, "I understand," and then went back to eating his breakfast.

Naftaly watched him chew the salty cheese that he preferred, and then he said, "Excuse me," and left the room.

Naftaly handed his undrunk glass of tea to the shade who had been serving them and hurried after Barsilay. "Where are you going?"

"Stay here," he said.

"I won't. What are you going to do?"

Naftaly nearly bumped into Barsilay as he stopped short, saying, "I don't know. Something. I ought to be doing something, but there is just so much happening I barely know where to begin. I should speak to Ayleth... No, she can't help with Saba. I should speak to her anyway, because Asmel asked me to get a letter, and I haven't done that. And then there's the fact that not once since I got out of prison has anyone told me a single thing about what's happening in Habush!" He ran his hands over his face. "I've been King Consort for a few hours, and I'm already failing at it. Why did I think I could wake up and eat cheese for breakfast when the world is falling to hell?"

Naftaly set his hand on the small of Barsilay's back. "You aren't failing."

"Oh, I most assuredly am."

"Fine, have it your way," he said. "How is tearing your hair out in the hallway improving the situation?"

Barsilay said, "It isn't. But I don't know how to proceed—with anything. I feel like there is a whirlpool in my mind, and there are so many competing thoughts I can't grab hold of any of them."

Naftaly knew that whirlpool intimately. "Well," he said, "I've never been in charge of anything much in my life, but it seems to me you either pick the most urgent problem, or else you pick the easiest to solve."

"Right," Barsilay said. "Right, that's very reasonable." He glanced down at Naftaly. "All of these things are urgent." He straightened up. "Easiest to solve… Hm. I don't know if saving Saba is easy. It is simple, though."

"Is it? You have a plan for that already?"

"Not at all," he said. "But there is only one person who can save him, so let's start by going to see her."

The two men went back to the garden of the Ziz, which seemed empty except for the great bird herself. She greeted Naftaly by stretching her wings and chittering at him. "Where do you suppose Nehama is?" Naftaly asked.

The Peregrine stepped out of the shadow of the stone tree and said, "She went to go find something for us to eat. The shades won't come out here."

"Better for you that they don't," Barsilay said. "Are you all right?"

"You dragged yourself out of bed this early to ask after my health?"

"Hardly," he said. "But seeing as you did eat poison recently, it seemed polite to ask."

"My throat hurts," she said. "My belly feels poorly empty and worse full, but if you didn't come to express your concerns about my physical condition, I presume you are here to ask me to do something. I hope whatever it is takes me far away from here."

"It will," said Barsilay. "You remember Saba, the Zayiti doctor?"

"I do. He's the one who told me how I might stop and restart Yefet's heart."

"I suspect you know that he was captured by Tarses."

The Peregrine blinked twice and said, "I didn't know that. By the time I returned to Tarses from the siege castle, he had already decided I was a traitor. He told me very little, and I did not see much of Anab before I left. I'm sorry he was taken. I assume you think I can somehow rescue him?"

"As you said, you can't stay here."

"That's hardly the same as saying I should walk into Tarses's fortress."

"Then I shall tell you this," Barsilay said. "Saba is being made to enhance Tarses's visions."

"Ah," she said.

"The situation calls for some risk."

"This is more than a little risk," she said. "Tarses knows my name, but he also believes I'm dead. If I'm seen by anyone, I will be a danger to all of you." She seemed to make up her mind about something and said, "I will give you my name. Order me to kill myself if I am seen."

"I'm not sure that accomplishes much," Barsilay said. "Seeing as Tarses already ordered you to kill yourself, and here you stand."

"I doubt the Courser will be around to save me a second time," she said. "And if you want me to save Saba, we need whatever safeguards we can find. But I also think you can assume I may be compromised from the moment I leave. Until Tarses is dead, I won't return to you. If you see me again, it's because something has gone wrong."

"But how will you return Saba to us?" Naftaly asked.

"Tarses knows his name as well," Barsilay said. "He should stay away, too, 'til either Tarses is dead or else I am in a position to rename him."

"You will have a lot to do when you are King," the Peregrine said. "There are a lot of Maziks who would like their names returned to them. Many in Tarses's service would not be, under better circumstances."

"I'll remember that," Barsilay said, and she whispered her name in his ear, and then he whispered something in hers, and she nodded. "Good luck to you, my friend," he said, and then she was gone.

"There," Naftaly told Barsilay, feeling not a little pleased with himself. "That's done."

"Yes, that's done. But that was the only simple task I had."

"Then we return to what is urgent."

"Or perhaps to what is most unpleasant," Barsilay said. "I think I need to have a conversation with my wife."

It was the first time Barsilay had called her so in Naftaly's hearing, and it made him feel a little odd. "I think I should not go with you," he said.

"I think that's wise," Barsilay said. "I'll return you to my suite—I don't like the idea of you wandering the palace alone."

But when they returned to Barsilay's suite, Ayleth was already there, and she was very angry.

BARSILAY USHERED NAFTALY into the bedroom before turning to address his wife, who barely waited for him to shut the door before rounding on him.

"I have been looking for you all morning," she snapped, "while you've been off with your lover. I thought you agreed to marry me because you were concerned about Tarses?"

"That is precisely why I agreed to marry you, and I was not off with my lover, I was running an errand."

"What errand?" she asked.

"It's not important."

"An unimportant errand," she said, and sighed deeply.

"It might help if you told me why you were looking for me," Barsilay said.

"Right. I have been meaning to speak to you since the coronation but…" She got up and walked around the table, wringing her hands.

"What's the matter?" Barsilay asked. "What's it got to do with Tarses? You've heard something."

"The opposite," she said. "Let me explain. How to explain…"

"Ayleth," he said. "It's all right."

"No," she said. "Please don't interrupt me. I can't claim my thoughts. Ah. Yes. So when you first arrived, Tarses had only just taken Zayit, and he was in the process of moving on to Anab."

Barsilay inclined his head, because she had asked him not to interrupt.

She continued. "On that same day, my mother sent a squadron of troops to help Habush secure the Saharon Bridge."

Barsilay did interrupt then, saying, "I didn't know that. She told me—"

"I know what she told you, but she did send them. And the problem is, all the Maziks capable of reaching them in the dreamworld are now dead."

Barsilay stood up. "But you must have contacts in Habush."

"I have no contacts anywhere. I don't know faces or names, only titles, and that does not help me. The head of the diplomatic corps is dead, our spymaster is dead, and I have no way to know what happened to those soldiers."

"So you have no idea if Habush still holds the Saharon Bridge?"

"I have no idea if Habush still holds itself!" She slapped her hands down on the table. "I don't think you can understand how badly I have been prepared for this role."

Barsilay looked a little chagrined and said, "Go on."

"I need someone to go to Habush and remake those connections."

"You've discussed this with Yefet, I take it? Surely he has connections in Habush."

"He's unwilling to do anything that would reveal he's still alive to anyone outside the palace. But he felt that sending the King Consort to Habush would be a show of faith on our part."

That was not entirely unreasonable. And while Yefet had made a number of interesting choices lately, Barsilay could travel via the gate of Luz and be there and back in a day. It was unlikely Yefet would be able to get up to anything in that amount of time. He said, "I will go. But I will take Naftaly with me."

"Because you believe he isn't safe here?"

Of course he didn't think he was safe there, but he said, "Naftaly might have some insights that could prove useful."

She said, "Take him with you, if you like. But when you return, I would like your word that you will spend one night in my bed and not his."

Barsilay said, "As you say." As she left, Asmel was on his way in, and Barsilay swore under his breath. "I forgot to speak to her about your letter," he said. "Let me go after her—"

"No," Asmel said. "I went without it and spoke again to the Maziks at the university. The gate must be replaced exactly where it came from. I went to inquire about using their maps." He sighed painfully. "Kasfia destroyed them all. There is no map in the entire city that shows the precise location of Luz or her grove."

"I can get us close."

"Not close enough," he said. "I need a map, and a good one."

"You must have had some back in Rimon?"

"I can't vouch for anything in my collection since we left," he said. "Zayit is ash, Habush is cut off, the southern cities are shut down by the blight. There is one person who will have those maps, though. Omer will have them."

"You told me his library was burned."

"He saved much of it, and if he hasn't got a map, our next best hope is Omer himself. He was an astronomer in Luz for generations. He might be able to use the stars to plot the proper position." He reached out and took Barsilay's hand in both of his. "And there is the matter of a promise I still need to keep. I told Omer I would rescue the Maziks from Te'ena, and I don't intend to forget them."

WHILE THE MAZIKS were inside the palace squabbling over who was to get the first turn with the book and the mortals were asleep in their hut (because they were, after all, rather old and extremely tired), Nehama found herself the caretaker of the Ziz. It was not difficult work—her task seemed to be to ensure the Ziz neither ate anyone nor flew away, which she seemed disinclined to do anyway—and otherwise she wandered the garden and tried not to muse on all that she'd remembered. She ought to be able to keep this all in perspective, she told herself. Her life as Nehama had been so much longer than her life as Toba. She'd been in Aravoth much longer than she'd been in the void. Nothing she remembered was more than a butterfly's brief flitting across a blossom: one day, in a very long season. And yet, she probed the memories. She found she could not help it.

She'd been quite surprised to discover that the gardens of P'ri Hadar were kept not by shades but by a Mazik, a man named Natin, who was somehow always sunburned—despite the fact he perpetually wore a hat that, when he knelt on the ground to tend his plants, made him look very much like an overgrown mushroom.

Natin was thoroughly displeased about the sudden appearance of a giant bird in his garden, whose main mission—according to him—was to either trample or eat his very well-kept flowers.

"You there," he snapped at Nehama, the first day she lived in the garden with the Ziz. "Disheveled woman."

"I have a name," she protested hotly.

"I don't care. Keep your creature out of my persimmons."

"She's not in your persimmons!"

"Look at her right now!" he shouted, pointing at the Ziz, who had found a persimmon tree and, in attempt to eat the fruit as quickly as possible, was taking off entire branches at once.

Shouting and waving her arms, Nehama managed to get her to leave the tree alone, and Natin clucked over it like a mother hen. The damage was considerable; the persimmons, as in most Mazik gardens, were ornamental and could not be picked without damaging the tree. And that wasn't even considering what she'd done to the limbs.

"Look at this," he grumped, meaning the trampled flowers all around. "She's like an overgrown goose."

"She's had a hard time," Nehama said. "You must be patient."

"She's giving me a hard time," he replied. "She ate an entire apple tree this morning. The whole thing, down to the ground!"

"I am sorry," Nehama said. "I did not realize. I will try to pay her better mind."

"Well," he said. "Fine."

"Maybe if she had her own garden?" she said. "Things she could have to herself that wouldn't trouble you?"

"She already has a third of my garden," he said. "Not that anyone asked me."

"It isn't yours," Nehama reminded him. "It belongs to the Queen."

"The Queen admires it from her window," he replied, "I'm the one that makes it grow. It's mine." He mused on this a minute and said, "What does she like?"

"The Queen?"

"The Ziz. Is there a fruit she likes? Or something to gnaw on, like a dog with a stick? I don't know what Zizim do."

Nehama thought on this. In Aravoth, she had mostly seen her eating large fruits, due to her size. But there were no trees in the ordinary world that produced fruit anywhere near that scale, so far as Nehama was aware. "She likes big things," she said. "Melons, maybe."

Natin pondered this and said, "She could eat melons without destroying any trees. I have some seeds that will grow quickly with a little magic. But you will have to be the one to keep her from stomping on them or eating them too early." And he went off into the little shed in the corner with the roof made from growing vines, and handed her a packet of seeds, saying, "Here."

"I don't know what to do with these," Nehama admitted.

"You plant them," he said. "You dig holes"—he indicated his finger to the second joint—"like so, and you put one in at a time, and you add water and magic, and poof!" He waved his fingers. "Melons."

"I'm sure there is more to it than that."

"There isn't," he said. "That's why gardening is mostly done by shades."

"If that's so, then why are you out here working in the sun?"

"Because I'm better than a shade," he said. "And my mother was a gardener, and her mother, and her father. And the Queen—well, the old Queen—respected a pedigree, so here I am."

Nehama watched him return to his work. He was tidying a patch of little purple flowers, which had become littered with dried leaves from the taller plants around it. "You're still here," he pointed out.

"Did you ever think about doing something else?"

"Like what?"

"I don't know," she said. "Something."

He said, "No."

"So you enjoy it?"

"Yes."

She watched him another minute and said, "In that case, could you help me plant these melons for the Ziz?"

He turned around and looked at her then. She smiled. He took the packet back from her hands, walked over to the Ziz's portion of the garden, and planted the seeds.

After he left, she wandered the rest of the garden for a while, considering things. Everyone was very busy, and here she was, doing nothing much. In one corner was a great floating ball of quicksilver that reflected the colors from the plants all around it, and she stared at it, mesmerized. It reminded her strangely of Aravoth, all those misdirected colors, and as she was lost in her reverie, Natin returned. "The Queen had me install it," he said. "Kasfia, not Ayleth. I've never liked it much."

"Any particular reason?"

"It's like a game," he said. "Playing with your eyes. I don't think gardens need such things."

She turned to him, in his mushroom hat, and said, "A game—because it plays with your perception?"

He shrugged.

She said, "Watch the giant goose for me, would you?"

"I will not," he said, but Nehama was already walking away, and she said, "It's only temporary!"

IT WAS QUICKLY decided that taking turns with the book was not a reasonable option, and Toba insisted that the book ought not to be taken out of P'ri Hadar if it could be helped. "There's too much that could go wrong," she'd argued. "And certainly the book should not go to Habush when we don't even know what's happening there." The safest place to open the gate was the cedar forest, where the height of the trees would conceal much of the streak of light, avoiding attention from the people in the city.

When they went to use the book, they discovered a note on it written by Nehama. It said, *Gone out, open a gate for me at dawn in two days' time.* And then, further down the page, she'd written,

Left a book in Omer's library, red leather binding, six fingers high. Please return to me.

"Of all the things," Toba muttered. "Gone out. Gone where? And now she wants you to find a book with no title?"

"I will look for it," Asmel said. "Don't trouble yourself."

"I'm not," she said. Then, "Gone out!"

So Toba opened a gate for Asmel into Te'ena, with the understanding that he had a single day to gather up any surviving residents and their most irreplaceable belongings. Then Toba would open a second gate for them to return. Asmel turned to her, sitting on the ground with the book open before her, and said, "I shall bring you a gift."

"A gift?"

"From Te'ena. Who knows if any Mazik will ever go back there? Once the gate has been returned to the firmament, it won't be so easy to come and go." He kissed her. "I'll return tomorrow."

Te'ena was, of course, exactly as it had been. He had Toba open the gate to the fig grove, since it was the only part of Te'ena she'd gotten a good look at on their trip there, and he made his way to the central plaza where Omer had found him the last time. Shading his eyes and looking at the sky, he noted how much lower on the horizon the sun was than it had been in P'ri Hadar. It was expected, of course; he was so much farther west. But still, he wondered if anyone before had experienced such a thing, to have effectively gone back in time. What a curiosity.

A few of Te'ena's flame lizards peeked out from behind the rubble of Omer's house, and the boldest among them flew closer and pecked at Asmel's boot. "Be gone," he said, and with a puff of magic, blew the creature back to its companions.

There were footsteps behind him, and there was Omer, a smile on his face that Asmel had not seen since the two of them—and the world itself—had been much younger. "My dear friend," he said. "And with your magic. And if I'm not much mistaken, you just came through a gate in the middle of the day."

"Indeed, all three," Asmel said, and clapped his hands on Omer's shoulders. "I have come to take you back with me—all of you. You are needed by the world again."

Omer began to laugh a little and then with so much force that Asmel worried for him. "Of course you need me. What can I do for the world today, old friend?"

"Actually," he said, "we need you to help us restore the gate of Luz."

"Luz is at the bottom of the sea."

"Yes, I know," Asmel said. "And we're going to raise it."

"That is impossible," Omer said. "None of us can penetrate the sea with magic."

"Impossible for you or me," Asmel agreed. "But there are others with us possessed of skills we lack. And we have the Ziz."

Here, Omer went very still. "The Ziz? But you told me the Ziz was in Aravoth."

"She was, and we retrieved her."

Omer's eyes were glassy. "Your companions, they ventured into Aravoth and returned?"

Asmel said, "Yes."

Omer let out a short breath and said, "I don't suppose you saw any sign of the half-Mazik who was lost there? I'm sure she could not have survived, but some trace—"

"Nehama is very much alive," Asmel said. "She is with us in P'ri Hadar. We will do this thing. I feel it in my bones, Omer."

Omer wiped his eyes. "Nehama," he said. "Nehama is with you?" Asmel nodded, and Omer said, "Then we had better hurry up."

OMER AND THE other Maziks made a list of their most important belongings—books, nearly all, since everything else could be recreated—and these were packed into chests and parcels tied with fabric, whatever each Mazik was able to generate most quickly. None of them slept that night, and sometime past midnight Asmel recalled his promise to Toba. She would be amused by one of the flame lizards, he thought, but it would be cruel to remove one from its fellows, so instead he made his way to the beach, nausea setting in a little along the way.

She might not understand the significance of a gift of something from the sea, which among Maziks could only be taken in person and not made by magic, and only obtained through some degree of pain besides. He walked an hour, as close to the water as he dared to go, admiring the shells in the moonlight. *All wrong,* he thought.

Finally, he found what he was looking for: a periwinkle. And he put it in his pocket.

When he returned, he found Omer outside in the plaza, gazing up at the stars, probably contemplating leaving Te'ena forever. Asmel still felt the pangs of his own exile, but he, at least, might hope to return home one day. "Did you go to the sea?" he asked Asmel.

"I did." He showed him the periwinkle. "I was looking for this."

"Ah," Omer said. "I see. I am glad you have found some measure of happiness, after everything that has happened. After Marah." Squinting up at the moon, he asked, "What do you suppose she would say, if she knew what we were doing?" He sighed. "I don't suppose there are many of us left from the old order. Is Rafeq with you, by chance?"

"I'm afraid Rafeq met his dreaming death only recently. Were you friends? I did not know."

"Us? Hardly. We were colleagues. Marah was the only person he ever liked. Still, I'm sorry he's gone. With Tarses's betrayal, I suppose I am all that is left of ha-Moh'to."

Asmel had wondered when this conversation might be necessary. He said, "Not quite. Barsilay has survived."

"Your nephew, of course," Omer said. "I had not thought of him. He was cast out; perhaps you wouldn't have known."

"I knew," Asmel said. "It was for this that he survived the Fall. Marah sent him to me in Rimon."

"Has he been with you all this time? I'm glad to hear of it. He was a well-meaning boy."

Asmel said, "Yes, he is that, for all his faults. But there is something more you must know about what we are doing. We are raising Luz to repair the firmament, to replace the gate, but something else will happen when we do this."

Omer glanced over to him rather darkly. Asmel told him, "Barsilay is the heir of Luz."

Omer said, "I don't know whether to laugh or weep."

"I've done both," Asmel said. "Omer, he isn't the youth you knew. He's accomplished things I never dreamed. He's a good man."

"That's beside the point—a good king is still a king!"

"Would you rather it were Tarses?"

Omer turned away. "You speak as if there are only two alternatives."

Asmel said, "Omer, you are my oldest friend, so hear me when I say this: All the time you have been trapped here, I have been living in Rimon, where Tarses has been the next thing to King, and he means now to rule all the world. He's burned Zayit, he's taken Anab. Soon he will have Habush. And I tell you, his rule will be a horror unlike anything you have ever seen. Barsilay is headstrong and he can be heedless, but his heart is kind. He will try to do right, and he wants no part of kingship."

"So you ask me to choose the lesser evil."

"No," Asmel told him. "I ask you to choose our only hope."

THE NEXT MORNING, as the Maziks prepared to gather all their worldly possessions in the middle of Te'ena's fig grove, Asmel remembered Nehama's book. Turning to Omer, he described it, but the other man looked a little baffled. "A book with no title?" he said. "I wouldn't have packed it."

Asmel frowned. He had promised Nehama, only to forget. It was a remaining symptom of his time without his magic—his memory was not exactly what it had been. "Go ahead to the grove and ask them to hold the gate," he said. "Just give me a few minutes."

He went back into Omer's library, which was all a mess of cast-off items. Old books, deemed redundant or otherwise unvaluable, littered the floor in stacks, while others were sideways on shelves. *What a bother*, he thought, and cast a pair of shades to help him look through every shelf, every stack. Through the doorway, he heard Omer calling to him. "Just go," Asmel told him. "I'll come in a moment."

But Omer came inside himself. "I won't leave you combing through all this like a rat," he said. He cast what looked almost like a firefly and described the book to it, and off it flew, through the stacks, the shelves.

"You never taught me that bit of magic," Asmel said, a little incensed.

"I certainly did."

"I would remember."

"It's the first thing I teach anyone! I think…"

Asmel would have argued further, but by then the firefly had lit on something on an upper shelf and then winked out. "It's found it," Omer told him, and called the book down to him with a finger before handing it to Asmel.

It was smaller, even, than Nehama had told him, and if the cover had once been red it no longer was. He was set to put it in his pocket, but then Omer said, "Can I give it to her myself?"

"As you like," Asmel said, and together, they ventured to the gate. The rest of the Maziks, of course, were already gone, and Omer turned to look at the area one last time.

"Will you miss it?" Asmel asked.

"It is a strange thing when your home is also your prison. I don't want to miss it. But I know that I will." He stepped through the gate, and Asmel followed, the last Mazik ever to set foot in Te'ena, and the city was left to time and the flame lizards.

RIGHT AFTER BARSILAY saw Asmel through the gate to Te'ena, he returned to his rooms to have something to eat for the first time since he'd woken. P'ri Hadar, he'd decided, was exhausting. Everyone in the entire city seemed to be on edge; either the government was about to collapse, or Tarses was going to arrive with his army, or—and this was currently his own belief—both at the same time. If Yefet hadn't been there, Barsilay suspected the city would have fallen in on itself already. Thankfully, the man was quick to act, putting out fires before they began smoldering. He could only hope to be half so able an administrator.

He could only hope to live so long, he thought, finishing the dregs of his wine. It was mostly water, by his own making. He couldn't afford to dull his wits. Though he deeply wished to, even for five minutes. Naftaly was resting in the next room, still tired from the poison; Toba had mentioned checking in with Efra; and the two old mortals were off doing old mortal things—sleeping, probably, or arguing over whose joints hurt worse. He was alone, and did not like it, and then from the next room—Ayleth's room—he heard raised voices.

The voice in question was not Ayleth's. It was Yefet's. Barsilay frowned, trying to make out the argument, and then realized that another man ought not to be in his wife's bedroom in any case. Pushing back from the table, he got up and threw open the door to Ayleth's suite.

Ayleth was standing while Yefet sat at his wife's breakfast table, a sheaf of papers in front of him. The two stopped whatever disagreement they'd been having, and Yefet looked more than a little startled to see Barsilay in the doorway.

"I was told you were indisposed," Yefet said.

"I was," Barsilay said, gesturing behind him. "These are my rooms." He started to ask Ayleth about the presence of a man in her bedroom, then recalled the sleeping man in his own bed, and stopped himself.

This hadn't sounded like a lover's quarrel, however. He raised an eyebrow to Ayleth, who said, "In this particular matter, I will defer to my husband."

Yefet looked slightly displeased. He said, "Barsilay is not King here."

"No," she said, with a little more venom than Barsilay had heard her use with Yefet. "But as he has more experience with Tarses than either of us, I trust what he will say. Go on. Tell him what you came here to ask me."

Barsilay looked between them. "Am I to understand you came to the bedchamber of the Queen to discuss state business?"

"The matter is sensitive," Yefet said. "You'll understand when I explain. You have a gate. A gate that opens to any place at any time."

"Yes," Barsilay said, "I'm quite aware."

"A wonderous thing," Yefet said. "A wonderous and terrible thing. And yet, I do wonder how you choose to use it."

"We chose to use it to rescue you from halfway up a mountain in Anab," Barsilay said.

Yefet smiled. "Oh, do not think me ungrateful. Far from it. But since then, you have been using it to take the Maziks off Te'ena. And you are going to visit Habush. But what I do not hear is that you are using it to kill Tarses, and I do not understand why. You know where Tarses is. You have a way to get to him."

"He wants us to send an assassin," Ayleth said. "One of my soldiers. I have told him no. But if you think it is wise, I will reconsider."

Barsilay sat down on the chaise at the foot of Ayleth's bed. "Tarses is guarded—it would be pointless. We'd only be sending a man to his death."

"Then send another! And another!" Yefet slammed his hand down on the silver-inlaid table. "His Alaunts may stop one assassin, or five, or ten, but they won't be able to stop them forever—"

"Do you imagine we have an infinite supply of soldiers?" Ayleth asked. "How many do you find acceptable—fifty? A hundred?"

"More than a hundred of your soldiers will die if Tarses brings his army to P'ri Hadar."

Ayleth said, "When Tarses brings his army to P'ri Hadar, we will be so much the worse if we have already sent our hundred best soldiers to their deaths. This war cannot be won in the shadows."

Barsilay held his hands up. "Yefet, Tarses will certainly be warded. We know he is in Anab, but we don't know precisely where, and even if we did, he's the most guarded Mazik alive. What you are suggesting—it cannot work. He will have planned for it. You will be sending good men to die in vain."

Yefet leaned back in his chair and stared at the ceiling. After a moment he said, "This war cannot be won in the shadows... And yet you loosed an assassin to kill me. The same assassin, as it turns out, who killed Kasfia and half her court." To Ayleth, he said, "You are making a mistake in deferring to him on this. He doesn't understand what is at stake."

Barsilay said, "My city is beneath the sea because of Tarses. I understand very well. But as you object to my judgment, let us walk through your scenario. Let us say Tarses's location has not been warded. We are able to open a gate to the very room where he is drinking his tea. A best-case scenario, correct?"

Yefet only waited for Barsilay to continue, so he did. "So we have your best case. We pick one of Ayleth's soldiers, the best swordsman in P'ri Hadar, and we send him through that gate. There are ten guards in the room with Tarses, and this swordsman is such a fighter that he kills five of them before he's run through. So, all right, you say. We send another man. A great swordsman, loyal to the bone, and he goes through the gate, and since this is still your best case, Tarses has not replaced any of his guards; now he has only five. And this man, he's not quite the swordsman his dead fellow was, so he only kills three guards before he, too, is killed. But, all right, you say. We send another. Only now... Hang on, Tarses knows we are opening gates to try to kill him. So this time, as soon as the gate opens, he sends his own assassin through. Or perhaps he sends three assassins, or ten. And Tarses's assassins are far deadlier than any here, and now we have a real problem." Barsilay walked over to Yefet and set a conciliatory hand on the other man's shoulder. "You are correct. I have never been a king. But I have known Tarses all my life, so hear me when I tell you: This cannot work."

Yefet slowly got out of the chair, giving Ayleth a nod, and said, "I withdraw my request."

Chapter Twenty

Naftaly woke to find Barsilay standing at the window, looking out to the garden. The Ziz was on her perch, singing one of her little songs, and around her some smaller songbirds had joined in. The resulting sound was unlike anything Naftaly had ever heard—beautiful but odd, like a cacophony of pleasant sounds all jumbled together.

"Are you all right?" Barsilay asked, when he saw that Naftaly had woken.

"Much better now," he said. "You look like you could use a turn at a rest, though."

"A rest," Barsilay said. "What I need is a bath—a real bath. Not some little tub in my room. I have never seen the palace baths, but there must be some benefit to being King Consort. I would like to boil my brains while a shade rubs oil into my feet."

Naftaly had avoided the baths when he'd been in mortal Rimon, lest his eyes linger where they should not, and he usually went early in the morning or late at night on the rare occasions he did go. But if Barsilay wanted a proper bath, he ought to have one. "Let's go then. Surely they can spare you an hour."

"An hour?"

"They'll scarcely miss you."

"Hm. That's rather what I'm afraid of," he said, looking back in the direction of Ayleth's rooms. "All right. Let's find someone who knows where they are."

* * *

THE PALACE BATHS were on the lowest level, on the other side of the garden. Naftaly found that he could barely tolerate the caldarium, it was so hot, and sat on the edge while Barsilay immersed himself again and again, going so far as holding his breath and putting his head under.

"When you said you intended to boil your brain, I did not think you meant it."

"Oh, yes," Barsilay said. "My head shall be a boiled egg in a moment. It's all that I've dreamed of… Ah." He put the head in question under water again, and came up and splashed Naftaly, who said, "I don't know how you can stand it."

"It isn't that hot."

"The yolk between your ears has gone completely solid."

"Bah," he said. "It's delightful." He leaned back and allowed himself to float belly-up in the steaming water. "Naftaly," he said, "what do you think of Yefet?"

"Yefet? I've hardly spoken to him, but Toba says he's very competent. What do you think of him?"

Barsilay's eyes were on the ceiling, which was painted with a replica of the night sky so real they might have been outdoors. He said, "I find him reasonable and decisive."

"That seems like a positive impression. Why are you asking me this?"

Barsilay pointed his toes toward the ceiling and said, "I don't know."

"You have misgivings about him?"

"No," he said. "No, none. He's the only thing holding the city together. Wouldn't you agree?"

"That's twice you've asked me about him," Naftaly said. "What is it you are really getting at?"

"Nothing," Barsilay said, sitting up. "We owe him a great debt is all."

"And that worries you?"

"Why should it?"

"You are the one asking the question!"

Barsilay stood, letting the hot water pour off him and said, "My brain is thoroughly boiled. Let's move on."

"Barsilay—"

He kissed him. "I'm too hot. That's all there is."

The shade that had been attending them covered them both in filmy robes, and they followed it into the tepidarium in the next room, which was completely open to the garden on one side, laden with flowers that left the air heavy with their scent. The pool was in the shape of a crescent moon, with fountains at either end. In the middle of this sat Yefet himself, leaning back over the edge while a shade combed oil through his hair.

Naftaly came up short at the sight of him, and Barsilay's phantom arm, which he hadn't bothered with 'til now, made a quick reappearance. "Forgive us," Barsilay said. "We don't wish to intrude on your solitude."

"If I wanted solitude, I'd have bathed in my room," Yefet said. "I needed a respite; I'm sure you feel the same."

Barsilay handed his robe back to the shade and lowered himself into the water, leaving Naftaly to follow rather awkwardly. There was a bench of some sort along the side of the pool, and they sat on the opposite side from Yefet. Barsilay had asked the shade for a massage, but as it approached he held up a hand and said, "My hair instead, I think."

The shade poured a small cupful of warm oil onto Barsilay's head and began to massage it into his scalp as he sighed.

"If you'll accept some advice, you ought to be careful where you flaunt yourselves," Yefet said, his eyes still closed. "Ayleth is half in love with you. You'd be wise not to make her jealous."

Naftaly looked between the two men, both of them with their eyes shut. Barsilay said, "Ayleth is not prone to jealousy, so far as I'm concerned."

"You think she isn't falling in love with you? She was very quick to accept your counsel upstairs."

"Because it was the reasonable course."

"Hm, yes. But that is not why she did it. She accepted your decision before she knew what it was. Did you not notice?" Here, he opened his eyes. "You are fortunate. Not every wife is so agreeable."

"You are angry," Barsilay said. "About your plan to send the assassins, or about the Peregrine?"

"I'm not angry about either," Yefet said. "As you have already said, your course was the more reasonable on both counts. My desire for vengeance got the better of me, I suspect. Don't think too much less of me."

"I don't," Barsilay said. "Far from it, I understand."

"You are too kind."

"Only grateful. You have done much here. No one could have asked for a better ally."

"Hm," Yefet said. "You flatter me. But I have been thinking—you are planning to leave for Habush tomorrow. Ayleth has no one with experience in Habush, but I have. Do you know Eitan? Surely you've met him?"

"No," Barsilay said. "I don't believe so."

"Ah, well, he is one of my best men, and he's been to Habush many times. When Abishai claimed power, Eitan led the delegation to affirm our trading ties. He'll be a great asset to you; I'd like to offer his service."

Barsilay said, "I was under the impression you did not wish to reveal that you or your advisors were still alive."

"I went back and spoke to Ayleth after you left, and she convinced me it was past time to let that go. Tarses will find out I am alive eventually. It makes no sense to let fear prevent us from making use of me and my men. With your permission, of course, I will ask Eitan to go with you and make the introductions. But I think it best you still go in person, to shore up the ties between Habush and P'ri Hadar, now that Kasfia is dead."

"You are probably right," Barsilay said. "And I thank you for the use of your man. I could certainly use him."

"Then I shall send him to you." Yefet stayed the shade with its comb. "That's enough." Rising from the water, he said, "Truly, you are gracious." He allowed the shade to put his robe on and bid a very polite farewell.

The shade had finished with Barsilay and poured heated oil over Naftaly's head, only he hadn't exactly been expecting it and half of it went down his face. He wiped it away while Barsilay rubbed a kink out of his own neck.

Decisive and reasonable, Barsilay had said. And wasn't he? Conciliatory and polite, too.

"Is there such a thing as too polite?" Naftaly mused aloud, taking some of the leftover oil from his scalp and rubbing it into Barsilay's neck. He could still get his massage, now that Yefet was gone and unable to note the shade working around Barsilay's missing shoulder, but Naftaly wanted to do it himself.

"You mean Yefet?" Barsilay said, stretching his neck to the other side. "Ahh—too hard—I think that's how men are in Anab. It's a very civil place."

"Is it?"

"So I've heard."

"You've never been there?"

"Not in this age, no. You don't like him?"

"Yefet?" Naftaly mulled it over. Did he like him? What wasn't to like? The man was as perfectly civil as one could be, and under very trying circumstances, too. He supposed his concern was that Yefet really ought to hate Barsilay more than he did, but that was hardly a fault, being too composed, too rational. Too reasonable and decisive. "He's exactly as you say."

Barsilay turned and smiled, taking the comb from the shade and tossing it aside. "I'd like some real wine," he told the shade, and then the two men sat in the bath for another half an hour, taking what little respite the world had left them.

Tsifra's voyage from Dassos to Habush was not long, though it did require a traversing of the Rosh ha-Tannin, the narrow strait that opened to the Bahat Sea, beyond which lay Habush. Good sailors, which she had in droves, would have no trouble navigating the narrow passage, and she expected to arrive there in a few days with fair winds.

As she sat in meditation, considering what she was meant to do when she got to Habush, and how this time she would neither burn the city nor behead their Sultan, one of her men came and beckoned her above deck. She followed, annoyed with the interruption, and found that as far as the eye could see there was nothing but fog. "We've had to drop anchor," the captain told her.

The mist was so thick she could not even see the railing from where she stood, and it made her deeply uncomfortable. "How long can weather like this continue?" she asked.

"I would not expect more than a few hours," he said.

Only it was quite a bit longer than a few hours, and by the time the fog cleared it was fully dark. Still, at least they could safely sail; the sailors knew how to calculate their position by the stars. So they sailed slowly, but progressively, all night. Then, as the dawn broke, Tsifra—who had 'til then remained on deck—saw that the fog had returned.

"It will burn off in a few hours' time," the captain told her.

"Is this normal, two days running?"

"The sea," he told her, "is fickle, Majesty. At least we haven't had another storm."

Tsifra was inclined to agree, but then as soon as darkness fell, the fog receded again. This is magic, she realized, and then slowly turned a circle on the deck. Toba must be there, and because of Elena's order, there was no way for her to see her. There could be no other explanation. So she put pen to paper, drawing what she believed to be a reasonable likeness of her sister, took it to the captain, and asked him to find this woman among the fleet, because she was a witch.

"There are no women but yourself, my Queen," he told her.

"Look anyway," she said, and he took the drawing and withdrew.

She did not know how he meant to search the other ships, but when he returned—she did not know how long afterward; time had little meaning in the fog—he told her again, "There are no women among us."

How would she search for Toba herself, when she could not see her? She reasoned that if Toba were glamoured she might be able to find her somehow, as she'd been able to see her in the dream-world. But leaping from ship to ship was bound to engender questions she could not answer, so she waited 'til it was fully dark again, made herself shadow, and leapt to the next ship in the fleet.

None could see her, and she searched above deck and below, and found nothing, and leapt to the next ship, and the next.

It was too slow to search this way, and she was growing increasingly agitated. The fleet was sailing again, using the stars, and she could not stop the nagging sense that this was what they were being made to do—to travel only at night. She moved on to the fourth ship.

In this one, there was a sailor in the stern of the ship, tall and slim and casting his eyes heavenward. A navigator, was Tsifra's first impression. And then the man turned his face to Tsifra and, even in the near darkness, she could see a feminine face and Mazik eyes. But it was not Toba's face that looked back at her, nor did she have Toba's carriage nor manner of moving.

"Who are you?" Tsifra said, her voice low. She had made herself visible now, and the nearest sailors exclaimed at her sudden appearance. "Go elsewhere," she snarled at them, and they were frightened enough to comply. "Who sent you here?"

"I go where I like," the Mazik said, lowering her hands to her side. "No one sent me. Oh, that's interesting. I do remember you."

Tsifra took a step closer and said, "I do not know you."

"No? I suppose not. But I know you." She cast her cloak to the deck of the ship, saying, "You're the one that killed me."

Chapter Twenty-One

Barsilay concluded, after only a little consideration, that if he was going abroad to look into a matter of military significance, he needed someone with some military experience. So in addition to a half dozen soldiers—who had come with the reference of the lower-level commander who had survived the wedding banquet—Barsilay concluded that the best person to accompany them to Habush was Efra.

After much negotiation, Barsilay had persuaded Ayleth to allow the Zayitis to move into the city, where they would have the protection of the wall. Efra had been fairly busy trying to integrate her people into the fabric of the city, which was no easy feat because the place was already solidly occupied, and the wall could hardly be extended to the west. Extending it eastward was a possibility, but the P'ri Hadaris who were consulted maintained the matter would have to be studied, because they could not risk compromising the integrity of the wall if Tarses were to show up with his army.

Instead, the Zayitis had been sandwiched into the existing quarter where the guildsman had made their homes with their families, and the buildings had been expanded vertically to make space for them. The consequence, of course, was that the Zayiti quarter towered over the surrounding area, and the native inhabitants were not pleased either by the structural or social changes in their city.

Which is to say that when Barsilay asked Efra to take a brief trip to Habush, she was understandably angry. Barsilay had anticipated this, of course, so rather than going himself to ask, he'd sent Naftaly.

"She likes you better," Barsilay had said.

"She does not. She thinks I'm just some mortal."

"You made all those mines for her," Barsilay reminded him. "And her brother was very fond of you."

"Her brother found me an interesting case study."

"He liked you!"

"You can stop trying to convince me," Naftaly said, because he'd already wrapped himself in a heavy woolen cloak against the winter air. It was a good piece of cloth, smelling like newly spun wool. Had it been made by magic? "Do Maziks keep sheep?" he wondered aloud.

"What?"

"I'll return soon," he said.

He found Efra in the Zayiti quarter, tearing her hair out over a great stack of papers.

"Naftaly," she said. "Some disaster?"

"No disaster," he said, but that was not entirely true. He explained that they'd lost contact with Habush in general and the squadron sent to reinforce the Saharon Bridge in particular. "Barsilay and I are using the gate of Luz, and he would like you to come, as you are the most experienced military commander in P'ri Hadar."

"That's probably the case," she grumped. "But I'm also up to my ears trying to keep my people from ending up on the wrong side of the rest of the city. I can't leave."

"But the bridge," Naftaly said. "You understand the strategic importance. If we can hold that, Tarses would have to go all the way 'round the Tsafon Sea. It buys us a great deal of time. Maybe even a year, Barsilay said. Is that not worth a day of your very valuable time?"

Efra looked at him levelly. Naftaly said, "Please."

Efra called in one of her men and had a brief conversation in Zayiti. Then she got up from her desk and said, "Let's go."

* * *

THE SAHARON BRIDGE was the greatest feat of Mazik engineering ever constructed.

It had been built by the Maziks of Habush in the time of Luz, as their city had become a trading hub linking the northern and southern cities. At that time, Habush had been a city without a sea, but it had been a city of varied elevations. The lower lands had been used for farming lentils; the upper were where the adons lived very comfortably. When the time had come to build a proper road, there had been a debate as to where to construct it, because the lower part of the city was more difficult to access with horses and carts, but the upper part was separated by what was, at the time, a dry isthmus—a broken ridge that towered over the valley below. Spanning this would require a bridge that would be considerably more expensive than simply requiring travelers to go down one side of the valley and up the other.

However, it so happened that the Queen of Luz had been traveling to visit her western holdings when her favorite horse had fallen descending to the lower road, laming itself. She had been notably furious. Several Maziks had died. And she had announced, to the residents of Habush, that they had better spare no expense in building that bridge, if they knew what was good for them.

It had taken some ten years to connect either side of the ridge, several miles north of the city at its narrowest point (this location, too, had been the subject of some dispute, as the adons wanted it built further south, so visitors would be directed into the city itself—but economy, in this case, had won out). There were some two hundred Maziks involved in the construction, and it was afterward known as one of the greatest wonders of the world—and one of the most beautiful, too. Carvings at either end had once featured almond trees, and all along the span was the repeated motif of the phases of the moon, repeating twelve times from one side to the other. The entire bridge was shaped like a crescent, arcing up over the valley below, and it rested on stone pillars that had been pulled in one piece directly from the ground below.

So solidly was it constructed that on the day that Luz fell and the waters rushed in through the firmament, washing away the lower portion of Habush—some third of the city—the bridge itself remained. The newly independent Habush wasted no time in instituting a toll on every Mazik who crossed it—this was borne, on the main, by the traders of Zayit, and tended to explain some of the latent animosity between the cities. The almond tree finials had been replaced with quinces, and the phases of the moon carved along the span had long ago worn away in the salt air, but the bridge persevered.

Only one thing changed: While the bridge was high enough above the water for Maziks to safely cross it, they found it deeply unpleasant to do so, as one might find wading through mud even in a good pair of boots. Most Maziks preferred not to do it a second time if they'd done it once. For this reason, the eastern and western halves of Habush were mainly administered by distinct entities, though the city shared one king, who lived in the east and had reportedly only been to the western part of the city three times since his reign had begun.

NAFTALY, BARSILAY, EFRA, and Yefet's man Eitan, together with some of Ayleth's soldiers, stepped through the gate onto a hill overlooking the city, a spot Asmel had picked because they would be able to survey the area easily and without being seen. Naftaly came through just behind Barsilay, and it took him a moment to get his bearings; he'd not expected to see quite so much of the sea in three directions. It seemed an absolutely improbable place for Maziks to have built a city. Of course, he reminded himself, the sea had not been there at the time. It was a wonder all of Habush hadn't been lost in the Fall along with Luz.

The Saharon Bridge was below them, and Naftaly could hardly believe the sight of it. It extended some hundred feet above the sea, and seemed like a cross between the Roman bridges Naftaly was used to seeing in Sefarad and the arced bridges that crossed the canals in Zayit. It was made of weathered gray stone that looked almost blue in the light. To the south of them, where the strait was slightly wider, was the city of Habush itself. They were on the eastern side, and from where they stood Naftaly could see the wall extending around the city. He knew the western side had its own fortifications, but Naftaly could not see them. The quince gate was on the eastern side of the strait, slightly inland from the rest of the city.

"I think I should proceed into the city," Eitan told Barsilay. "Find out what is happening there, and make your introductions."

"Go," Barsilay said. "Pick two of Ayleth's soldiers to go with you."

Naftaly had not taken his eyes off the bridge all this time. It reminded him oddly of the tree in Aravoth and his garden path, an impossible passage across nothing but air.

"What can you see?" Barsilay asked him.

"Nothing," he said. "I see nothing."

"How many soldiers did the Queen send?" Efra asked.

"Fifty, I was told. They were meant to supplement Habush's own Bridge Guard. They weren't supposed to hold it alone."

"I see no soldiers," Efra said. "I see no horses, either."

"It's possible they are concealed from our current position," one of the soldiers said. "We need to get closer."

"Carefully," Efra agreed, and they descended the hill, approaching the bridge.

There was minimal cover along the peninsula; the winds were strong and the sea air made the Maziks scowl. Naftaly walked a little ahead, as the others wrapped their cloaks around their faces. The bridge, now, was close enough that Naftaly could see it arcing up ahead of them. Efra said, "I believe the King Consort should stay here. I will go ahead with Naftaly—we will move more quietly if there are just the two of us. I can hear you all wheezing in the salt."

Barsilay looked as if he might have objected, but said, "Go quickly, then."

Efra put her hand on Naftaly's elbow, made them both shadows, and together they crept around the curve of the road.

There were still no soldiers anywhere that Naftaly could see. But ahead of them, where the land met the bridge, was a great pile of stones, at least twenty feet high. Efra stopped moving and pulled

Naftaly to a halt beside her. No part of the bridge's structure appeared to be broken, so Naftaly could not see where the stones might have come from.

"A ruin?" Naftaly whispered.

Efra knelt and picked up a pebble. Setting it on the palm of her hand, she flicked it with her finger toward the stones, sending it ricocheting across the pile.

There was a grinding sound, and the pile began to move. Efra grabbed Naftaly and ran back a dozen steps before forcing them both to the ground as the pile of stones took the shape of a stone behemot—not unlike the one Tarses had used in Zayit—which lifted its head to the sky and trumpeted, a sound like shrieking metal.

A little further down the bridge, Naftaly could see another behemot lift up and trumpet back. And then, in the distance, there was another trumpet, and another, so quiet he could barely hear them over the sound of the wind and the sea.

"Let's go," she whispered, and they returned to Barsilay.

"I saw," he said. "Any chance those beasts belong to Habush?"

"If these belonged to Habush, we'd see the regular complement of archers out here, and there are none."

Barsilay said, "If Tarses is already here, then where is his army? Are they already in the city?"

"We'd have seen signs of that," Efra said. "He's sent people in advance, to take the bridge."

"We'd better get into the city," Barsilay said. "We need to find the King."

Only when they arrived at the gate of the city, they found it open and unguarded. The streets themselves were deserted. And when they got to the palace, King Abishai nearly fell on his knees in front of Barsilay and said, "You have to save us."

Toba stood on the edge of the sea, looking out to the western horizon. Three days' ride, Barsilay had told her, was the distance between Luz and P'ri Hadar. This presumed a restful pace and stops at the many splendid inns and such along the way, but even so, it was a distance of many miles. To raise the city and the land surrounding it would be a feat she could not quite imagine.

But that would be a disaster, she reminded herself, not to imagine it. She altered her perception, envisioned herself walking west to a second city, rising from the sea.

Still, she could not quite make herself believe such a thing were possible.

With her were Asmel, Elena, and Omer—Nehama still not having returned from wherever she'd gone. It made little sense that she'd told no one where she was going, but Nehama was not used to accounting for her time or actions. Toba found Omer rather fascinating; his mannerisms were similar enough to Asmel's that Toba thought he might be mocking him, 'til she realized Asmel had probably learned them from Omer in the first place.

Also on the beach was the Ziz, which was being ridden by the two Maziks, who preferred not to set foot on the sand unless necessary. Toba had wondered if the Ziz herself might be affected by salt, but then the bird had waded into the surf—while the men on her back called out for her to stop—and eaten a great wad of sargasso.

They were there to conduct a series of experiments, to see the best way to raise Luz from the bottom of the sea. Toba, Asmel, and Elena had bounced several suggestions between them, from the absurd (making a magical anchor and simply pulling the ground up—this had been the old woman's suggestion, which is why she'd been left behind in her hut) to the improbable (causing a series of boulders to roll into the sea, thus raising the height of the seabed—this had been Elena's). The latter had also been deemed a mostly useless theory. Where would all the boulders come from? And how would they rebuild a city on top of a giant pile of rocks?

After listening to the others debate their respective theories, Omer broke in, saying, "There is no Mazik alive who could raise the seabed—not a thousand Maziks could do this." He slid down from the Ziz's back and approached the women. Then, taking a lentil from his pocket, he fisted it, opened his fingers again, and revealed a yellow blossom. "Our magic—or even mortal magic—cannot create something from nothing. We only alter what is already there. To raise the seabed would require creating more land."

"This is why Marah knew we needed the Ziz," Asmel surmised, and Omer said, "Just so."

"I don't understand," Elena told them.

Omer smiled in the manner of an old teacher who was about to offer an important lesson and said, "You are aware of the three great beasts, made at the beginning of creation? They are quite different than us." Here he put his hand to his own breast and then touched Elena's shoulder. "Our magic is inside us, our will or our learning. The beasts, they drink the magic of the very world."

"So you are telling me the Leviathan drinks the magic of the deep, and so on?"

"And the Ziz of the firmament. Such magic is almost incandescently powerful. The tiniest breath of it would overwhelm all the magic a Mazik possesses." He patted the great bird's flank, and she turned and chittered at him in response. "We did experiments, back in Luz, to see if a Mazik could absorb the magic of the firmament by ingesting it from the Ziz."

"They ate parts of the Ziz?" Toba said, aghast.

"Only her feathers!" he said. "And only very few, because more than one would nearly kill you—it would be like ingesting the magic of a hundred safiras."

"More than one," Elena mused. "What could be done with just the one feather?"

"Not much," he said. "But there was one thing we discovered. It seemed to give you some temporary immunity to the use of your name."

"It made a Mazik impossible to command? That does sound useful."

"Not permanently. But from what we saw, it gave a Mazik the ability to escape a single command." He shrugged. "It was only a limited test, however. The Ziz, as it turns out, was not keen on being plucked like a chicken. Ah," he told Asmel, "you remember Shimon? He was the Ziz's favorite."

Asmel said, "Shimon of Habush? When I knew him, he only had nine fingers."

"Yes," Omer said. "If she didn't like you, she took more than one."

"Hang on," Toba said. "Are you saying the Ziz's magic can create things?"

"It has that potential," he said. "But she would not know how. A Ziz has unimaginable latent powers, but they are latent. She was not designed to use magic as we were."

Toba felt the air in her lungs and thought, *I too, have drunk the firmament.* She said, "I believe I could channel her magic."

And there was birthed a new idea: Use the magic of the Ziz to increase the number of particles beneath the immediate surface of the seabed, lifting the bed itself.

A small-scale trial was to be attempted, to see if the theory was even workable. After Toba coaxed a little magic from the Ziz, she practiced on the bare sand, asking the wet layer beneath the dry surface to expand itself. It was a difficult process because the wet sand was soaked in salt, which inhibited her magic rather badly. But she could feel it doing *something*, and through the sand she could hear it hissing, and the air above the sand seemed to be heating.

The surface of the sand, however, did not change. Elena, who was watching all this, said, "Something happened. I could hear it." She tapped her good ear. "Did you heat the water in the lower layers? It sounded almost like a hot spring."

Toba scowled at the sand. "I think that might be what happened, but it isn't what I was trying to do at all."

"What if you tried a more direct approach?" Asmel called from the back of the Ziz.

"I'm already standing on the sand," Toba said. "Are you suggesting I burrow underground like a gopher?"

"That might work," Omer said. "Could you try that?"

Toba looked at the ground beneath her. Elena said, "That might be a bad idea. There's a lot of salt down there—what if you couldn't get back out?"

She was right, of course. But it did give her a less extreme idea. Making her arm shadow, she pushed back her sleeve and plunged it into the sand to the shoulder.

"Are you all right?" Elena asked, because Toba's face was etched with strain. "Should I pull you out?"

She could feel the salt, but it did not inhibit her magic nearly as much as she had feared. Still, she was glad she was not bodily down in it. She closed her eyes and felt the particles of sand around her hand and thought, *Wouldn't it be wonderful if there were more of you?*

She felt the sand heat and heard the same crackling as before. Asking it was not quite right. She needed to do more than imagine it happening, too—instead she told herself it was happening, had already happened. And then, she felt her hand being pushed upward, further and further, and when she opened her eyes again, she was atop a small hill of sand.

As she pulled her arm out, Omer and Asmel began asking a lot of questions at once. How much magic had she used? Had it been painful? Could she have used magic, did she think, to extend the length of her arm?

Toba, however, felt herself rather tired, and sat down hard on the sand. Elena gave her some water and smoothed the sweaty hair off Toba's forehead, saying, "That was well done."

"It did work," Toba agreed. "But there was no water over that sand, and that was as much as I could do on my own."

Still, it was better than they had hoped. The theory, at least, was sound. They decided the next test was to see if Toba, now that she understood what needed to be done, could do it without submerging her arm. This worked, in a more limited fashion. The next test would involve her increasing the mass of the sea floor through the sea itself. For this, they took to the Ziz—not so far as Luz would be, but over the shallows—and she flew in a lazy circle while Toba cast her magic at the sea to no effect.

"This can't work," she said. "I'm having to do this over too great an area because the Ziz is moving."

"Yes, but there will be an even larger area when we do the actual raising of Luz," Asmel reminded her. "What if you had more magic?" He put his hand on Toba's bare forearm, pushing his magic into her, and she tried again. But still, she felt her magic hit the surface of the water and then nothing further. "I can't do it," she said. "Even using some of the Ziz's magic, I can't penetrate the water. We'd need some way to move it, and I can't imagine what that might be."

Omer clapped his hands together, once, and pronounced, "The Leviathan. The Leviathan could do it, if we could summon her."

The others went quiet, and he continued, "She could make a whirlpool as great as anything, all the way down to the seabed... Why are you all so dour?"

Elena, blunt harbinger of bad news, said, "The Leviathan is dead."

TSIFRA TOOK A step back from the woman in front of her. The wind had picked up and the smell of salt was strong in the air, and the deck of the ship had become markedly less steady.

She did not know this woman. It was true, Tsifra had killed a lot of people, and she could hardly be expected to recall all their faces. But this woman she would have remembered. And further: "You appear exceptionally unkilled."

"Don't I?" she said. "To everyone, it seems." She began circling clockwise toward Tsifra, who was forced to back up to keep the distance between them. "I've found that makes things easier. So when they ask me if I remember dying, I always tell them no. But to you I'll tell the truth: I remember it perfectly. I remember death. And I remember you giving it to me. I wore a different face then. I was much younger. Do you remember now?"

Tsifra was having trouble keeping the distance, because the other woman was moving in a way she did not quite understand; sometimes one of her steps was a step, and sometimes it felt more like three. How was she doing it? Tsifra had to leap up onto the railing of the ship, and then leapt back to the deck again, further away. "Who are you?" she demanded.

"I am insulted," she said. "That you do not recall your own sister."

This could not be the buchuk... No. The other Toba, the one she'd spent so much time with in Sefarad—she had been the buchuk. The original Toba had died. There could have been no saving her. The other Mazik made her arm a blade.

Tsifra quickly said, "Tsifra N'Dar, be still."

The other Mazik laughed. With her remaining hand, she let her cloak blow away into the sea, and she said, "So you do remember."

She leapt at her then, across the deck of the ship, sword flashing in the light of the waning moon, and as her sword met Tsifra's, she snarled, "But that is not my name any longer."

Tsifra parried the blow—harder than any she could have conceived coming from Toba—and ducked behind the mast. Toba, somehow, was already there, her sword coming at her. This was no dance. Toba meant to kill her.

"I was so young, then. All I wanted was to save my friend, and you gave me no mercy. But I am so much older now." She delivered a stroke that nearly took the top off Tsifra's head and left her blade embedded in the mast. "I see how weak you really are."

She kicked Tsifra savagely in the chest, and with the wind knocked out of her, she went down on her back. Toba was on her then, straddling her chest, her sword-arm to Tsifra's neck, and she said, "Die, then, and be damned."

Tsifra did not close her eyes to her own death. She felt the sword press into her skin. For a moment, she actually felt very peaceful.

Then… nothing. Toba's face was a mess of strain, but something—some inner process Tsifra could not imagine—held her back. She swore and stumbled back a few steps. "Tsifra N'Dar," she began, and Tsifra knew she was about to order her to do something. Drown herself? Swim to the bottom of the sea?

She never knew what Toba meant to tell her. An arrow from above caught Toba in the shoulder, then another, and several stuck in the deck around her. When the second arrow struck the arm that was also her sword, Toba leapt over the side of the ship.

Two of her sailors came running to Tsifra's aid, lifting her up and demanding to know if she was well, and who the intruder had been. "A witch," Tsifra said. Then, "A demon. A ghost."

A ghost. She ran to the side and looked down to where Toba had fallen. But there was no sign of a woman, only, rising to the surface, a dark shape. The sailors began to scream. She was, somehow, a sea monster—the men cried it was a Leviathan—and then she rammed the ship.

The deck lurched, and there was the crunching of wood. She'd breached the hull, and now she came around again, as the entire ship went sideways. "The angel!" her men cried. "Pray for us!"

But there was no angel, only Tsifra herself, as frightened as she'd ever been. She could flee, she knew, jump to another ship. But if Toba meant to sink the entire fleet, what could she do? Toba struck the ship again, and it began to list further.

"We're taking on too much water," the captain called. "Abandon ship!"

The sailors began to scramble, calling to one another, and then there was a final impact that ripped the ship in half.

The ship went completely over, and Tsifra found herself in the water, scrambling for something to hold on to. Before her, the Leviathan came to the surface: a great fish the likes of which Tsifra had never seen. And in the darkness, its great orange eye met hers.

In the eastern sky, the sun had just touched the horizon, and Tsifra could see her sailors swimming away to the nearest ship, begging for rescue. The Leviathan emitted a sound that echoed in Tsifra's ears.

Not twenty yards away, a gate opened directly into the sea.

Toba turned toward it, made the noise again, and swam through it.

The sailors of the next ship collected Tsifra, who was so chilled they thought for certain she would freeze to death. She was mute from shock and it was an hour before she could move again, by which point she heard the men arguing up on the deck. Throwing off the blankets in which they'd wrapped her, she went up to ask what was wrong—besides, of course, the loss of one of her ships.

"Majesty," her captain said, "you must forgive us."

"That was hardly anyone's fault," she said. "No one could have saved that ship."

"No," he said. "Look." And he pointed north, where she could see land in the distance, and clinging to the coast, a city.

They had sailed two nights in the wrong direction and come all the way back to Anab.

Chapter Twenty-Two

Habush, Barsilay had explained to Naftaly, had endured more turmoil than most of the Mazik cities over the course of its existence. First, it had been cut in half during the Fall. Then, much more recently, it had been laid siege to and sacked by Zayit, which had divested the city of most of its treasures (which, unfortunately, had thereafter been burned when Zayit was lost). And, most recently, only some forty or fifty years prior—Barsilay was a little light on the details—there had been a coup and Habush's king, the king who had ruled since the Fall of Luz, had been replaced.

Naftaly, of course, was only a tailor and not well attuned to the workings of the greater world, but he knew that in his father's lifetime Habush had gone from being the seat of one empire to the seat of an entirely different one. The people living there, he presumed, were the same. But much about the city had changed. His knowledge of the area was fairly limited to how these regime changes affected the Jews, and he knew that at the time of Habush's fall most of the Jews had left, but subsequently others had repopulated the city—and the Sultan himself had sent the ships Naftaly had seen at Merja, transporting Jews into the new empire, where he hoped they might engage in useful activities like trade.

Mazik Habush's regime change had been slightly different. In general, Mazik geopolitics tended to be simpler than Naftaly was used to, in light of the Maziks' extreme longevity and limited population. So, while Mazik Habush had acquired a new king at around the same time the mortal city had gone from an emperor to a sultan, the Mazik King was himself of Habush. The takeover had gone along these lines: Abishai, an adon from the western side of Habush, had launched a coup in which he and his supporters had fired munitions from the western wall across the narrow strait, blowing a hole the size of a behemot into the eastern wall. This accomplished, Abishai had killed the prior King, exiled most of the remaining court to Anab, and replaced them with his own people. The scarlet quince flower—the symbol of the eastern half of the city—had been replaced with the white quince blossom of the west as the emblem of the city proper, and on the main, life had continued as normal—except that they had lost some third of their fighting force in the coup, and, moreover, regime change is expensive. Fortunately for them, around this time the Queen of P'ri Hadar began sending tribute to the new King as an antidote to what she foresaw in the mirror. Of course, the King of Habush did not know this, but was disinclined to look a gift horse in the mouth—which is to say, he took the money and promptly spent it. The Habushis collected their tolls for the use of their bridge, Abishai administered as well as could be expected, and things went on as well as they did anyplace. Or at least they had, up until a week ago.

King Abishai had to be put into a chair with a glass of wine before he could explain what had happened, and there was hardly anyone left in the palace who could do even these things. After Eitan introduced them, Barsilay sent him and the P'ri Hadaris out so that Abishai could speak without the stress of an audience.

"Where is your court?" Barsilay asked him, to which the King replied, "Half of them have fled. They heard what Tarses did in Zayit, and they are terrified."

"Anab is whole," Barsilay reminded him.

"Anab surrendered after their king was murdered," he said. "I don't presume Tarses will let me live even if I do surrender, and most of my advisors are in the succession. They think he'll kill them, too. Yefet hadn't any heirs."

"And you have scads," Barsilay surmised. "You're right, he probably would kill them. But let's begin at the beginning. Kasfia sent you some fifty men. Did they make it here?"

"They did," he said. "And we appreciate P'ri Hadar's efforts on our behalf, believe me, but it wasn't enough. They were with the Bridge Guard when the stone behemots arrived. By the time I knew an attack was happening, it was already over. Our entire force was gone, wiped out. The only survivors were those who retreated to the city so we would know what had happened."

Barsilay and the others were quiet. "The behemots—how many Maziks are among them?"

The King looked slightly perplexed. "There are none, so far as we could tell. Only the behemots."

"The behemots are created and maintained by magic," Barsilay said. "There must be Maziks down there, even if they are concealed."

"It hardly matters," Abishai said. "We'd never get close enough to defeat them in any case. The Saharon Bridge is lost. My city is lost. I don't—"

"Stop," Barsilay said. "Stop. We won't simply leave you here to be murdered." To Efra he said, "See what you can do to help them organize an evacuation when the gate reopens tomorrow. We'll take them with us to P'ri Hadar."

Efra said, "Should you not consult the Queen? What if she objects?"

"I am the King Consort," he said. "I'm not entirely without authority."

Efra said, "That's not correct in the strictest sense," but Abishai had already risen from the table, saying, "Thank you. Thank you, I shall gather my things." And he hurried from the room. Efra turned back to Barsilay and said, "P'ri Hadar can't accommodate any more people. You know this."

"What is my alternative? Leave them here to die?"

"Remove those in the succession, and leave the rest to surrender the city!"

"I won't distinguish who is important enough to help and who isn't," Barsilay said. "When Tarses comes across that bridge—"

Here, Naftaly's vision went strange. He'd been sitting already, but the floor seemed to be calling him, and he found himself sliding sideways 'til Barsilay caught him, calling his name. But he was already elsewhere.

He could see it then, Tarses at the head of a great army of mounted Maziks crossing the sea under a star-filled sky. So many Maziks, and behind them... they had great carts filled with wooden crates. Were they lentils? The moon was bright and they rode across the sea like it was nothing to them at all, even with the wind blowing the salty air into their faces. Once on the other side, Tarses raised his sword and shouted to his troops, "Even the sea is no barrier for us!"

Naftaly's eyes snapped open, his cheek was down on the table, and Barsilay's hand was on the back of his neck. Across from him on the table was a cat made of smoke, and the cat said, "The best beloved is awake."

Naftaly was sure he was still stuck in some vision, but Barsilay said, "It's all right, this is one of the prison demons."

"Prison demons," the cat muttered, affronted.

"He only just arrived."

"You only just left the palace," the demon told him. "We could not get near you, all this time. Wards, everywhere, and we your friends. Why did you never break them?"

"I didn't know about them," Barsilay said. "Naftaly, are you all right?"

Naftaly's head felt woolly and he was drained, like he hadn't slept in a few nights, but when Barsilay asked if he was all right, he said, "I saw Tarses crossing the sea." He sat up.

Efra said, "Then whatever we do here doesn't matter."

"No," Naftaly said. "I saw him crossing the sea. But the bridge he was using was not the Saharon Bridge."

The demon laughed.

Barsilay said, "He was using a different bridge?"

"That's not possible," Efra said. "There is no way for him to build another bridge. No Mazik could do it."

"His Courser," Naftaly said. "She could do it."

"One half-Mazik, working alone? I don't see how it could be done," Barsilay said.

"I am telling you there will be another bridge!" Naftaly said sharply. "The Saharon Bridge has ornaments and the one I saw had none, and the landscape was different. The Saharon Bridge is beautiful. This was not." He exhaled a shaky breath. "It wasn't the same bridge. Tarses builds another, somehow."

The weight of this settled on them for a moment.

"Could you tell where it was?" Barsilay asked, and Naftaly shook his head.

Efra, who seemed to have accepted the truth of Naftaly's vision at last, said, "There are only two reasons Tarses might cross elsewhere. Either we ourselves have retaken this bridge, or we have destroyed it."

"Then we must destroy it," Barsilay said. "I don't think we can retake it, in the face of what we've seen."

"Would it be any easier to destroy it?" Efra asked.

"A gate opened in the middle of it ought to do the trick," Naftaly said. "It worked on the behemot in Zayit."

Barsilay was frowning, and he waved his hand over the surface of the table, making a map. "Here is Anab," he said, touching an area on the coast that lit up under his finger. "Here is Habush, and here is P'ri Hadar. Where else could he cross?"

"At the Rosh ha-Tannin," Efra said, touching a place much further south, where the Bahat Sea narrowed. "It can be no place else. It's closer to Anab. It shortens his route. But listen, if we destroy the Saharon Bridge, he'll be coming directly to P'ri Hadar with his army. Are you sure you want this?"

"If we destroy this bridge," Barsilay said. "We will know exactly where he means to cross. There is no way he could have foreseen Naftaly's vision. We will ambush Tarses at the Rosh ha-Tannin. He will never get to P'ri Hadar."

Since she had drunk half the sea under the Courser's tender ministries, Elena had gone back only to her ordinary dreams. She dreamed of things she'd seen during the day. She dreamed of Alasar, and she dreamed of Rimon, and she had a rather uncomfortable dream about Omer that she would never admit to in public.

All this to say, she was very surprised when she opened her sleeping eyes on the night Naftaly and Barsilay left for Habush and found herself back in the dream-world.

It was a very different experience this time, as she was able to move about. She wasn't sure where she was, but it was not the beach she'd been trapped on before. The stars seemed about the same, though, and she'd spent enough time staring at them that she was pretty sure she recognized them. But were the stars the same everywhere in the dream-world? They weren't real stars. At least she didn't think they were. She made a mental note to ask Asmel.

She was in a forest of very tall trees and someone nearby was singing some old folk song she hadn't heard in twenty years. She followed the voice to where a woman sat at the foot of one of the trees, feeding birds from the palm of her hand.

It was her mother. As old as she'd been when she'd died, but as she rose from the ground she moved without the constrictions of arthritis, her posture regal as it had been when she was young. She approached Elena as if she were expecting her, and she embraced her warmly.

"Mother," Elena said.

"I was told you'd found your way here," Beladen said. "I'm not surprised."

"I'm not sure I will ever be able to get here again," she said. "There was an experiment, but it failed."

"Doesn't look that way to me," Beladen said.

"I have so much to tell you."

"I'll have heard most of it. The dead are rather chatty. We've nothing but time, you know." She took Elena's arm, and together they walked through the trees, all types she did not recognize.

"Where is this place? It looks nothing like the waking world."

"The dead make their own pockets here and there," she said. "The living are wearying."

"For me, too," Elena said, and Beladen chuckled.

"Tell me, how is your grandchild?"

"You told me you'd heard about her already?"

"I know the story. I don't know how she's feeling."

"Overwhelmed," Elena said. "Though she hasn't said so. Frightened, I'd imagine. I wish I could carry her burden. I did try."

"You did what you could," Beladen said.

"I fear I've not done enough."

"Every mother fears that. And every grandmother."

"I didn't do enough for Penina."

"No," Beladen said. "Neither of us did enough for Penina. You for not shielding her, me for not warning you strongly enough. But self-recriminations do nothing to help the child before you."

"I know it," Elena said. "But I fear I'm repeating old mistakes."

"You probably are. We are creatures of pattern, all of us." She patted Elena's shoulder. "You do the best you can, knowing it's inadequate, but you keep at it, and you fail, and it haunts you."

Elena closed her eyes. "It wants to consume me, some days."

"I did not raise you to be so self-indulgent," Beladen said. "Put it in your pocket and go on."

"I am trying," Elena said.

"I know you are. Did you not risk your life coming here looking for answers?"

Elena shrugged a little. "Compared to saving all the world, my life seems a small enough price."

Beladen rolled her eyes. "You don't give two figs for saving the world. You only want to save her."

Elena made no attempt to deny this, but she said, "I failed in any case. I was supposed to find an old friend, and I can't."

"The dead are very difficult to find," Beladen said. "We come and go. We aren't stuck in the same part of the dream-world like you are. You think I stayed in Rimon all this time? But someone was looking for you, and they managed to find me. And here I've found you, too."

They came, then, to a great tree, with a door set in the trunk. The latch looked like a great pomegranate, carved from the wood of the tree. "Whose house is this?" Elena asked.

"Oh, it's mine," Beladen said. "I suppose I don't really need one, but I like to have someplace cozy to come back to, sometimes. The stars can be exhausting if you stay under them too long."

Beladen opened the door. Inside, tinkering with an apparatus made out of what looked like spider silk, was Rafeq.

He dropped his work at the sight of her. "How are you here?" he asked. "Beladen said she heard a rumor, but I didn't believe her. You ingested a safira?"

"Part of one." Her limbs began to shimmer a little; she was losing the dream, and it took all her concentration to keep herself from waking up. Back in the waking world the old woman was snoring, and Elena willed herself to ignore it. "It didn't work, not really, and we had to destroy most of the magic with salt... Listen, I haven't got much time left. I need to ask you about your flame demons. The Caçador has them. He used them to burn Zayit."

"The Caçador?" he asked. "No, he cannot have mine—flame demons burn themselves out, they don't last more than a few days. If he's using flame demons, he's making more of them himself."

"Is there some way to defeat them?"

"Once they've been created? You have to wait for them to extinguish themselves or else submerse them in saltwater. Tell me, where is he getting the demons?"

"He's been pulling them out of the dream-world. In the Gal'in."

"Of course," he said. "They're so numerous there." He met her eyes. "Someone will have to go there and stop him. What have you tried?"

She said, "Nothing."

"Nothing!"

Here Beladen smacked him. "You've only just told her what she has to do, of course she hasn't tried anything, and anyway, she's only got a little time before she wakes up! She needs someone who can stay longer in the dream-world."

"Yes, yes, of course," he said. "And I'd do it, too, only demons are not overfond of me. On account of my work."

"Yes, but that was when you were alive," Elena said.

"Do you suppose they'll prefer me dead?"

"It's not as if there's anything they can do to you now."

"There is," he said. "I still feel pain. I just can't die again."

"Now hang on," Beladen said. "My daughter risked death and worse to find you. And you're refusing to help because you're afraid of a little discomfort?"

"They are capable of rendering more than a little."

"Stupid Mazik!" she said, and then, of all things, she took off her shoe and slapped him across the shoulder with it. Probably she'd have liked to have hit him in the face, but this was as high as she could reach. "Stupid"—she slapped him again—"cowardly, wicked—"

"Madam!" Rafeq said. "You are testing the limits of my patience."

And here, she reached up and twisted his ear. "I don't care about your patience. I don't care about you! You'll do as she says because I've been dead a lot longer than you, and I have friends here, and we can hurt you just as much as any demons."

Rafeq pinched the bridge of his nose between his fingers. "The temper seems to be in the blood," he said. "And if you were not the descendants of my dearest friend, I would tell the lot of you to go rot in hell. But you are. Most unfortunately." He held out one hand to Beladen and one to Elena. "We'd better hurry. You are looking more transparent all the time."

Elena looked down at herself and realized he was correct, but as she took his hand, the three of them went rather sideways, and when her eyes focused again, they were in the mountains, under the trees. She'd been in the Gal'in before, and knew he'd somehow brought them all the way there.

She was a little alarmed. "I was told I could not dream this far from my body," she protested. "I can't be here."

"The dead are not so constricted, and I'll send you back before your body misses you," he said.

The trees had come alive, and from them descended a flock of demons, too numerous to count. They swirled around them, whispering, "Rafeq the magic-giver."

The demons' wings swirled the air around them, which went cold as frost. One of them drew very close to Beladen and let out an unworldly shriek. "Salt-slinger!" it wailed, and then the rest of them joined in. "The defeater!"

"You never told me you defeated a demon!" Rafeq said, a little incredulously.

"Well," Beladen said, "I forgot."

"There is no salt here, Salt-slinger."

"I have no quarrel with you," she said. "We're here to help you. More to the point, *he's* here to help you."

The demons grew very excited and began flapping and shrieking again. "The Caçador? You can defeat the Caçador?"

"Indeed I can't," he said. "But I can keep him from taking any more of you and feeding you fire."

"Our young," the demons said. "He is taking our young. He makes a flame, a special flame, and our young are too foolish to resist it. It is too beautiful."

"Too beautiful?" Rafeq mused. "Does it look like this?" He cast a flame in the palm of his hand and held it up.

"No," they said. "No, no, the Caçador's flame is much more beautiful. Much more tempting."

Rafeq frowned at the flame and the color shifted, first to blue, and then to white, as if it were a ball of light. "Yes!" they cried. "Yes, that is his flame. It is so beautiful, do you not see? Some he feeds the flame, and others he feeds to horses."

"Horses?" Elena asked. "Whatever for?"

"To make them faster, he feeds us to the horses. They run swifter and never tire. He has taken so many of our young for this."

Elena did not like the sound of possessed Mazik horses; the regular ones were bad enough. Rafeq extinguished his fire, and the demons settled a little. "What if I made a flame of my own? A safe flame, that your young could visit? Would that be enough for them to ignore the other?"

The demons hissed to each other, and then said, "Yes. We think so, yes."

"Then is there someplace hidden, someplace the Caçador could not find me while I did this?"

"Wait," Elena said, as the demons flew off. "Do you intend to stay here?"

"I must," he said. "The flame will extinguish itself unless I keep casting it. I will have to stay here until the Caçador is defeated."

The demons returned, circling around them. "We have a place for you, Rafeq of Katlav. It is underground and you are dead. The Caçador will never find it. Go there now, before he returns."

"A moment longer," Rafeq told them. He took both the women's hands in his. "Will you return her to P'ri Hadar?" he asked Beladen.

"I will help you send her back. But my intention is to stay with you, and tend your flame."

Rafeq's face softened. He said, "You would do that for me?"

Beladen huffed. "Of course not. I do it because that bastard murdered my grandchild, and I will oppose him however I can." To Elena she said, "Send him to me, won't you?"

"I would prefer to send him to the void," she said. "But I will take whatever opportunity presents itself."

"When that opportunity comes," Rafeq said, "know that my will is with you."

She smiled. "'Vengeance and two lentils is worth the lentils.' Did you not tell me that once?"

"Well," he said, "perhaps not in this case." He squeezed her hands. "I still think you would have made a very good Mazik."

"She's fine as she is," Beladen said.

"Yes. Yes, I think so. If you happen to dream again, come and find me. I want to tell you about my theory—"

Elena opened her eyes to her bedroom ceiling in P'ri Hadar.

"You were talking in your sleep," the old woman said.

"What was I saying?" Elena said, rubbing at her eyes.

"You said I love you. Who were you dreaming of?"

"My mother," she said. "And an old friend."

IT WAS TOBA who had made the gate to retrieve Nehama from wherever she'd gone, and she was very slightly put out because doing so had meant she had to delay beginning that day's experiments while she returned to the forest. She opened the gate and waited, and waited, and was about to shut the dratted thing and try again later when what came through was not Nehama, but a sea monster that sailed over the top of Toba's head and then hit the ground with an impact so loud it shook the trees.

Toba slammed the book shut before something else could come through and then wondered if she should have tried to push the creature back where it came from, before it died on the forest floor. What a thing! Then, while she was puzzling this over—and puzzling over why the gate had opened in the middle of the sea when she'd been opening it to Nehama's position—the giant fish began to shrink, and in a handful of seconds she was looking at a very wet, very angry Nehama.

"You couldn't have given me a quarter of an hour more?" she said. "I was in the middle of something important."

Toba sputtered at her. "I had no idea what you were doing, because you didn't tell anyone! You just left with a note, 'Open a gate for me at dawn in two days' time,' and that was all! Well, now I've done that, and you're most welcome… Did it not occur to you I ought not to open a gate into the sea? We're lucky the water didn't come gushing through!"

"Hm," Nehama said. "It didn't, did it? I hadn't thought of that."

"You hadn't—"

"I hadn't planned to be in the water myself, either," she explained.

Toba could hardly believe this line of explanation, and she shouted, "You were a giant fish!"

"Plans can change. It happens to everyone."

"Really," Toba said. "To everyone—you mean sometime tomorrow I might just think, you know what this situation calls for? Fins!"

"Don't be absurd," Nehama said. She seemed to be bleeding from one arm, and she set her hand over the wounds, which glowed a moment with the magic she was using to heal herself. "You know that isn't what I meant. Life calls for improvisation. Otherwise what use are you?"

What use, indeed. Toba said, "Look, what were you doing before you decided to improvise with a little swim?"

"Buying some time," she said. "Also, I was trying to return a favor to our sister."

It took Toba a minute to realize whom she must mean. "The Courser—you killed her?"

"I did try. It turns out that I can't, most unfortunately. Though

I suppose she might have drowned after I destroyed her ship. We won't know for sure 'til we see her again. Or rather we don't."

"I can't see her in any case," Toba said. "My grandmother gave a rather ill-thought-out command. We can't see each other."

"You mean physically?"

"Just so."

"Oh. Well at least she can't kill you, then."

"That was the original intent. Tell me, can all Maziks change into giant sea creatures?"

Nehama said, "What an absurd question. What do you suppose would happen to a Mazik sea creature swimming in salt water?"

Toba felt a little embarrassed. "I'm very tired," she put forth. "I spent all yesterday doing experiments with Asmel and Omer."

"Omer is here?" she exclaimed. "Where is he?"

"I left him with Asmel, near the—"

But Nehama had already taken hold of Toba's horse, and Toba had to shout at her to stop so they could ride together. The two men—and Elena—had been left in a pavilion they'd made near enough to the beach for easy access but far enough back that the Maziks were not impacted by the salt. Inside, Omer and Asmel had constructed a model, with the city was on one side of the table and the sea on the other. Asmel was fiddling with a pair of calipers to mark a diameter offshore she supposed was meant to show the position of Luz.

Nehama slid off the horse and then stopped, as if the sight of Omer had caused her legs to cease functioning. He looked up and dropped the pen in his hand, and said, "Nehama." He ran to her and clasped her hands in his. "I'm sorry," he said, weeping. "I'm so sorry I never came for you."

Nehama was unable to speak in the face of her teacher and could only sob at the sight of him. Toba herself felt a strange affinity for the man—she, too, felt like she could almost remember him, as if the memories were strangely out of reach, an odd sensation of déjà vu.

When Nehama was able to speak again, she told Omer, "You would have died if you'd come, and you did not even know I was still alive there. Even if you'd had another half-Mazik, there's no navigating out of that place. They'd only have been trapped, too."

"Nehama," he said.

"I'm all right." She put her own hands over his. "I am sorry about Te'ena. But we're going to set this right now. I can feel it."

Toba sidled up to Asmel, who was looking unhappy, and said, "What is it?"

"It's just... the area we have to raise is a little larger than I'd planned. We found some old maps in Omer's collection. I'd remembered Luz slightly closer than it was."

Toba said, "I have a feeling we've been given a solution. You said we needed a Leviathan."

"Oh," Nehama said. "Do you?"

Omer said, "It would have helped, but she's dead."

Nehama looked a little dark and said, "Only for a minute."

Chapter Twenty-Three

Naftaly wondered if it were possible for a Mazik to have a stroke, as the vein in Abishai's throat was throbbing so violently it was visible across the table. He wouldn't need Tarses to kill him at this rate. Naftaly pushed a glass of wine at him, and he took a swig and then grimaced, saying, again, "Absolutely not."

This was his response to their description of their plans for the bridge. "If we destroy it, Tarses will burn the city in retaliation. It will be as it was in Zayit."

"Your wall will protect you," Barsilay said. "Tarses had no artillery in Zayit, and your wall is higher than theirs. He won't be able to launch anything over the top."

"Our wall," Abishai said, "has a gaping hole in it!" He stormed around the table. "I ought to know. I'm the one who put it there."

"That was years ago!" Barsilay said. "Why haven't you repaired it?"

"That side faces the sea," he said. "We have been repairing it, but the work is very slow. It's about halfway closed now, but it's not enough. I can't let you destroy the bridge." At that, he'd gotten up and stomped out of the room.

Barsilay sat back and looked to Naftaly. He had seen the city burning, so he knew what the King described was most likely what was about to happen. They would destroy the bridge without Abishai's permission, and then Tarses would burn the city. It was the logical conclusion of his visions. But there was still one needling thing that troubled him. He said, "Tarses said, 'I did not intend this.' I keep wondering what he might have meant."

"I think it should be obvious," Efra said. "He'd much rather keep the bridge and the city. He burned it because he had no choice."

"But he did have a choice," Naftaly insisted. "There is a hole in the wall. Even with the bridge destroyed there would be no reason for him to burn the city when he could simply take it. So I am thinking, what if he isn't the one to burn it?"

Barsilay said, "Are you suggesting that *we* burn Habush? How does that help anyone?"

"No," he said. "No, no. Listen. Maziks are capable of making things look other than they are. That demon, Atalef, he glamoured a river to fool Asmel and Toba. Why not make Tarses think we burned the city to prevent him taking an easy target? Let him think you are that ruthless."

"You are suggesting glamouring an entire city—it isn't possible."

"Atalef glamoured the entire night sky!"

"We can't glamour it forever," Efra said. "Even if it were possible."

"It needn't be forever," Naftaly said. "If Tarses thinks the city and the bridge are both gone, he has no reason to send anyone to poke around and see if it's still burned, and he'll be focused on the Rosh ha-Tannin. It will be a long time before he realizes he's been tricked, and by then Habush will have had time to finish fixing the wall."

Barsilay made eye contact with Efra. She said, "So in this plan, who is it that is glamouring the city 'til the wall's repaired? It will require a lot of magic. And we return to P'ri Hadar in a matter of hours."

Naftaly said, "I don't know about that part."

There was a whisper in the corner. It was Barsilay's demon, and it had uncoiled itself and stretched, then sent out a half dozen clawed hands to idly knead the air. "Have you been listening to all this?" Barsilay asked it.

"We are always listening, Heir of Luz. We can do this thing. It would be payment for what your friends are doing in the Gal'in. While they keep Tarses from our young, we will keep Tarses from this city. A favor for a favor."

Barsilay said, "What friends have we in the Gal'in?"

"Your dead friends," the demon said.

"Dead?" Naftaly asked, but Barsilay cut him off with a glance, as if to say, *We'll figure out which dead friends these are later.* He asked the demon, "Can you really glamour an entire city? That is beyond what I have known demons to be capable of."

"Demons are capable of much," the demon said. "It's that we don't much care. We can do it. But is this the favor you want? It is a very great one. It will be very boring for us, to make the city appear to burn so long." The demon swirled a little and said, "It would be more amusing to burn it in reality."

"No," Barsilay said. "Don't do that. Let me discuss this with the King. It is his city; he ought to have some say."

And so Barsilay explained this to the King. "You will remain in Habush. Your throne is secure, the city will be safe, and when this is over, I will send people to repair your bridge. The only thing I ask in return is fifty archers to serve with us at the Rosh ha-Tannin."

Abishai went very thoughtful for a few minutes. "Entrusting the safety of the city to demons is what you are suggesting."

"This particular demon is known to me," Barsilay said. "And furthermore he owes me a favor I am willing to use to save your city. Will you accept my help?"

The King looked out the window at the city below. He said, "I will."

Asmel knew the layout of the bridge well enough to open a gate onto it, but not with the degree of accuracy required… The destruction caused by the gate itself would be fairly narrow, and if it were opened over one of the struts, it might not create the necessary structural failure. So the gate would have to be opened directly to the position of one of the Maziks, and that, of course, meant one of them would have to be on the bridge when it collapsed.

Barsilay was the logical choice for this because the demons could hardly let him fall into the sea and perish, but as the demons reminded him, he was large and heavy, and—more importantly—missing an arm, which made him more difficult to hold on to.

The demons could not truly be trusted with Efra, whom they disliked by virtue of her heritage (Zayit being the city that had banished most of the demons to the Gal'in in the first place). The demons suggested Naftaly instead. "He is lighter than the rest of you," they said. "Let us take the best beloved. We won't let him fall into the sea."

Naftaly insisted this was for the best, in any case. "If I do fall in, the sea water won't kill me."

"The fall would kill you," Barsilay insisted. "I think it must be me. They can't let me die."

"They've already said why that won't work!"

"Yes, and it's very convenient for them."

"They have no reason to want me dead," Naftaly said. "I've never done a demon any harm."

It was Naftaly, then, that approached the Saharon Bridge, with a demon on each shoulder. He was not sure if it was two different demons or the same demon twice, but in either case they could be best described as a pair of ravens, their talons sharp in his skin. "Must you cling so tightly?" he whispered to them.

"Would you like us to hold you loosely, when the bridge falls?"

"We aren't even on the bridge yet," he told them.

"We are practicing."

The demons had made Naftaly a shadow. On his arm, emblazoned on the inside of his wrist, was an hourglass counting down to the time Asmel would open the gate—Asmel himself had its twin, as they had arranged this in a dream. Naftaly's heart hammered, and one of the demons hissed in his ear, "The behemots will hear your heart, best beloved, and crush you if you can't control it."

He took a breath and tried to still his nerves, reminding himself that of course the behemots could not actually hear his heart. Or at least he did not think so.

He had left his boots behind, the better to walk quietly, and he approached the eastern end of the bridge, where the rubble that was the first behemot lay. It was not, as he'd believed, entirely still, but contracted and released, as if it were a slumbering creature and not a pile of animated stones. Somewhere, some Mazik was controlling the thing. He had no idea where he might be hiding.

He passed the first behemot, onto the bridge. It made no sign of noting Naftaly's coming nor going, and he exhaled when he was well away from it. There was a second he would have to pass at the quarter point, and then a third at the center of the bridge.

He walked for several minutes, the sea below loud in his ears, and came to the second behemot, dormant as the other had been. He crept past this one, too; again, it did not stir. The demons held him so tightly he felt a talon pierce his skin, and fought the urge to push it off. That same one nipped a little at his earlobe, and he jerked his head away and continued.

He'd gone several more paces when, behind him, he heard the stones begin to stir.

At some point on the way, he'd walked through sand and left a trail of half-formed footprints behind him.

The behemot, now fully risen, began to trumpet. In his ear, the demons said, "We must fly now!" and he began to run. The behemot behind him took a moment to turn around, and then it began to give chase. He knew, from seeing one in Zayit, he could not hope to outrun the thing. On his shoulder, one of the demons let out a shriek, halfway between breaking glass and the cry of an angry bird.

Then they lifted him and he began to fly toward the center of the bridge, where the remaining behemot had already awakened.

The hourglass on his wrist had only seconds left... He'd walked too slowly. All of the behemots were storming toward the center of the bridge, and one was now blocking his path. Behind him, the two eastern monsters were terribly close. And the center creature was only feet away. "Stop," he told the demons. "We're going to—"

At the last moment, the demons lifted him higher, carrying him over the top of the beast. And then Naftaly saw what must have been glamoured before: the Mazik commanding the thing, riding on its back. His gaze briefly met Naftaly's as he passed within feet of the other man, and Naftaly thought, *At least one of us is about to die.*

"Where?" the demons asked. "Here?"

The exact center of the bridge was decorated with a circular frieze, now mostly worn away, depicting the crest of Habush, and Naftaly pointed to it. "Just there," he said, as the behemot he'd passed turned and ran back toward him. He landed directly on the trunk of the quince tree. The behemot was nearly on top of him, and the hourglass on his arm had already run out. Asmel was late.

He threw his arms up over his head, and then, only feet away, the gate opened.

The bridge crumbled to stones almost immediately. The behemot tumbled into the sea after it; its rider tried to leap to safety and failed. The demons lifted Naftaly into the air as the ground fell out beneath his feet, and the gap widened as the bridge collapsed all the way to the next strut. The two behemots on the eastern side had been running at him with such speed they could not stop before they themselves went into the growing chasm.

The gate closed, and the destruction abated. What was left was some thirty feet of open space with nothing but sea beneath. The demons deposited Naftaly on the solid part of the bridge, and he sat down, rather hard.

On the western side of the bridge, the riders of the two remaining behemots unglamoured themselves and began firing arrows. One landed not a foot away from Naftaly, and he dove sideways at the sight of it.

Getting up, he said. "Carry me!"

"Why?"

"Because they are shooting arrows!"

"We are tired and your legs work," they said.

So Naftaly ran 'til he was sure he was out of range, and then a little farther besides. "Get off," he told the demons. "My shoulder is in shreds."

"You are very sensitive," the demon told him.

"Yes," he said. "And you are not exactly gentle."

"If we were, you would be dead."

"I think you have something else to do now," he reminded them.

"Already?"

"I'm afraid so."

"But you have not thanked us for your life."

"Thank you," Naftaly said. "For my life."

One of the demons produced a face that looked for all the world like Barsilay's, and it kissed him, its lips as cold as the sea below.

"Goodbye, then, best beloved," the demons said, and while Naftaly reeled on his feet they flew off toward the city.

The city really did appear to be burning. Naftaly and the others watched it from the entrance to the bridge.

"They will sing songs about what you did today," Barsilay told Naftaly. "For the rest of your life you will be the Hero of Habush."

"I destroyed their bridge; I hardly think they will thank me."

"Barsilay is right," Efra said. "There will probably be a statue of you someplace. I imagine they'll make you out to be taller."

Naftaly only shook his head. Technically Asmel had destroyed the bridge, and the demons were the ones concealing the city. He'd done very little besides come up with the plan. He said, "Asmel will be opening the second gate soon, if he isn't late again."

"Was he late?"

"He was," Naftaly said. "I was almost crushed because of it."

"I'll have a word with him," Barsilay said, but he was smiling, his arm draped over Naftaly's shoulder. A few feet away, the gate opened again. Efra said, "Back to my paperwork, I suppose," and strode toward it. The soldiers of P'ri Hadar—who, Naftaly thought, had proved entirely useless on this entire quest—passed through first, save Eitan, who told the last remaining man, "Send word the King Consort will remain behind for now."

The man looked between Eitan and Barsilay and said, "For what reason?"

"We can hardly trust the demons to keep the city hidden, can we? We should stay long enough to make sure it doesn't reappear while Tarses's men might still be in the vicinity." He clapped the man on the shoulder, saying, "I think five days ought to do it."

Barsilay said, "Now hang on—" But the soldier, who seemed to have some view that Eitan was speaking with authority, had already passed through the gate.

"We never discussed remaining here," Barsilay told Eitan. "If you had such an idea, you ought to have discussed it with me."

"My apologies," Eitan said. "When Abishai suggested it this morning, I thought it seemed prudent."

Efra, who had been about to step through the gate, asked, "When did you speak to Abishai?"

"Earlier," Eitan said. "It doesn't matter—"

Barsilay said, "Abishai never said anything of the sort to me. Listen, I trust these demons to carry out their task." Turning to Naftaly, he added, "Let's go."

"Wait," Eitan said.

"I don't take your orders," Barsilay told him, and then Eitan produced a blade and stabbed Barsilay through the heart.

Naftaly could hardly believe what he'd seen, it made so little sense to him, and at first he thought he must be having a vision, or else he was simply having a failure of perception. The ground felt like sky and the sky felt like water, and then, as Barsilay collapsed into Naftaly's arms with the knife sill in his chest, Eitan pulled a second blade and came directly at Naftaly.

He had no time to defend himself, on the ground with Barsilay bleeding out in his arms, but Efra drew her own sword and parried Eitan's long knife out of his hand.

"You are a dog," Eitan told her, "to be loyal to such a master."

Wordlessly, Efra slashed the man's throat. He fell by Barsilay's feet, dead with his eyes open.

"Efra," Naftaly begged. "Efra, I don't know how to help him."

Efra tore open Barsilay's shirt. "Pull it out," Naftaly begged.

"Wait," she said. "He'll bleed out if we do it too quickly." She applied her hands to the area around the blade and began to pass magic into the wound. "I will do my best to repair the damage as you go, very slowly." She closed her eyes. "I wish Saba were here. Start," she said. "Go so slowly you feel as if you aren't moving at all."

"Will this work?" Naftaly asked.

She said, "I don't know. Saba explained it to me once. Go. His heart isn't beating."

Naftaly set one hand on the knife and then the other, because he was unsteady and the blade was caught on Barsilay's ribs. He moved it as slowly as he could, and still Efra snapped, "Too fast."

He waited to the count of three and only *thought* about moving the knife. "That's it," she said. "Again." He again pulled the handle so slowly it seemed absurd, and she nodded. "Again."

They moved like this for so long Naftaly could not imagine how Barsilay could survive without a beating heart. But at the end, the knife was out, and he flung it away. Efra closed the flesh in Barsilay's chest and then set her hand over the wound and pressed in so much magic Barsilay's entire body jerked. She set her hand there again, feeling, and then nodded.

"Did you start his heart?"

"I did." She sat back hard, wiping her brow with her bloody hand, and laughed rather hysterically. "Saba showed me once. With a chicken."

Naftaly put his hands on Barsilay's cold body and began to weep. "Why?" he said through his tears. "What reason can Yefet's man have to kill Barsilay? Yefet's sworn allegiance to him, hasn't he?"

The knife had fallen near Efra's feet and she kicked it away, saying, "I don't know. Look, the gate is still open, Asmel must be questioning the soldiers. You had better hurry and warn the others, and Barsilay can't be moved just yet."

"I won't leave him."

"If he needs more help, better I'm with him," she said. "I will ward the two of us to keep him safe, from everyone but you."

"What if something happens to me?" he asked. "We don't know what's going on beyond that gate!"

"If something happens to you, it can only mean P'ri Hadar is lost to us. Now go, Naftaly, before the gate closes."

Naftaly took one last look at Barsilay on the ground and ran toward the gate, but all he could think about was Barsilay's blood on his clothing, on his hands—*I can smell it*, he thought. *This is what Barsilay's blood smells like, like a pocketful of old coins.* By the time he reached the gate, his mind was so muddled he could hardly remember where he was going. Instead of stepping through, he fell into the gate, landing on his knees, and when he looked up he saw blood on the ground all around him. Beside him, torn from the ground with its roots exposed, was an olive tree.

The course of Barsilay's asssault seemed to him to go something like this: First, some crazed Mazik came at him with a knife, which he somehow interpreted as an attack on Naftaly, and by the time his mind could wrap itself around what was actually happening, he was feeling the edges of the void creeping in around him.

This was what had nearly destroyed Toba, and like Toba he fought it every moment, the unendurable dread, the terror, the nothingness of it.

But only for a few moments—or a few hours? What was time, in the void?—because then the darkness gave way to stars, and he was in the dream-world. Someone had saved him. He set his hand on his dreaming chest and felt no pain, but somewhere in the waking world someone was stitching him back together. He hoped they knew what they were doing.

He felt exceptionally odd and thought at first it might have been from the injury, but then he realized the magic within him was not his own. Efra, most likely, had pumped him full of her own magic to save him, which was certainly the only reason he was able to dream at all. When he'd lost his arm, he hadn't had enough magic to dream for weeks. He wondered how long her magic would keep him here, before he faded back into the dreamless sleep of the mortally wounded.

He was near the place where, in the waking world, Habush would have been. But there was no dream-world bridge—no need for one—and the place where the city should have been had gone entirely dark. The demons had been cleverer than he'd given them credit for. They'd even managed to glamour the city here.

His mind tried to find its way to Naftaly, to tell him he was all right, but of course Naftaly was probably awake. So he turned back to the water again and looked for a place to rest. Even dreaming, he was weary.

But as he approached the shore, he found he was not alone. Out of the darkness stepped Tarses, his face oddly conciliatory, his hair white as Asmel's. "Hello, old friend," he told him.

They had been friends once, but not since the turning of this age. The weight of Tarses's betrayal never left Barsilay's mind for long. He said, "You must be under some strain, for your hair to look like that."

Tarses's eyes narrowed, and it seemed to Barsilay that he'd

forgotten to mask his hair in this dream. Something must be very wrong indeed for his hair to have turned, and for him to have forgotten to hide it. Smoothly, he added, "What business have you in Habush?"

Tarses smiled and inclined his head. "None, now; you have seen to that. But I am not here for Habush. I am here to see you."

"Truly?" Barsilay asked. "Do you wish to call off your invasion and return to Rimon with your forces? Would you like my blessing? You may have it."

"I had something else in mind," Tarses said. "We are rational men, the two of us. It was you who understood the threat the Mirror posed. It was you who suggested how to fight it."

"Tearing out the gate did nothing to stop the Mirror," Barsilay said. "And I never would have suggested it had I any idea what would happen after."

"As you say," Tarses said. "Yet, I think the world is better for what you did. I know you to be a man of wisdom—"

"Your compliments mean nothing to me. I'm not the callow youth I was."

"You are not, which is why I wish to propose we cease our hostilities. An alliance would benefit us both—would benefit the world."

"An alliance," Barsilay said. "You are laying waste to all of Mazikdom!"

Tarses gestured to the place where Habush ought to have been. "Have you done differently? Burning Habush rather than allowing me to claim it—I would not have thought it of you. But let me make my proposal. I have no desire to spill a drop of blood more. I have a daughter, both clever and wise. Marry her, and you may become King of Luz."

Marry his clever, wise daughter. At least he wasn't suggesting the homicidal one. Barsilay said, "As you well know, I am already married."

"That is easily dealt with."

"You intend to murder yet another Queen of P'ri Hadar? This isn't inspiring me to trust you."

"She needn't die—we'll need someone to carry out the will of

Luz in P'ri Hadar. Divorce her. Or declare the marriage invalid, since I happen to know you haven't consummated it."

Barsilay made an effort not to react to this last statement—Tarses couldn't know that. He said, "Your reach exceeds your grasp, Tarses. You do not know so much as you believe. And you must believe your chances very poor, to consider such a thing."

"Not so," Tarses said. "I only care for the lives of the Maziks in all the cities that stand between us. Mazik life is precious to me. All I have ever wanted, in all my life, is to spare us from the Mirror. I have seen what's coming, Heir of Luz. If you had seen it, too, you would thank me for what I am doing. Ask your seer, if you like. If he is all you believe him to be, he can tell you what will happen. Marry my daughter, and I will help you mend the firmament. Let me rule in your name. And no one else will die—not here, not in the mortal world. There will be naught but peace between us."

For a brief moment, he did consider it. Toba would make a better queen than he a king, certainly, and if there were anyone who might find a way to thwart Tarses it was she. It bought him time. It bought the world time.

But as he tried to imagine this new world, where Tarses lorded over him, he could not imagine for a minute that Toba would consent to marry him as she'd once consented to marry Tsidon (though he imagined he was immensely preferable). Toba wouldn't put herself in a position to be Tarses's pawn. He said, "She would never agree."

"My Courser has never failed to carry out my commands before."

Barsilay felt his bile rise. "You would have me marry the woman who took my arm?"

Tarses's face went slack. Barsilay's temper was lost, now, and he said, "She never told you that? She never told you why?" He pulled open his shirt, revealing the mark of Luz. "This was on my shoulder, once. 'Til she removed that arm, so that you would not learn the truth."

"Why?" Tarses growled. "Why would she want to conceal that?"

"Because she was asking about ha-Moh'to. She was asking about the killstone." He put his face near Tarses's. "Because she wanted to kill you."

"You lie."

"Perhaps," Barsilay said. "Either I am telling the truth and she will betray you the second she is able, or I am lying, and if you ask her about it you will make her hate you. And as I'm keeping count, you are growing rather thin on allies."

"I am wed to the Queen of Rimon."

"We're very far from Rimon, Caçador. And I would rather burn every city from here to Tappuah than allow you to rule two worlds."

His eyes opened on the shore in Habush. Efra was prodding at him, and she said, "You survived."

His shirt hung in tatters; what hadn't been sliced in the attack had been cut away later. Glancing down at the left side of his chest, he noted that the mark of Luz was still there on his waking body, too.

"That was the first thing I checked," Efra said. "Your heart stopped for several seconds. I wasn't sure if that would cause the mark to pass on." She sat back and wiped her forehead with a bloody hand. "But you're still the heir."

"Yes," he said, sitting up—a feat which proved enormously painful. "For now."

TSIFRA DID NOT stop trembling all that day. The fleet dropped anchor back at Anab, because she did not know what else to do. That Toba had survived, that Toba had become the monster she'd seen, was terrifying. She could not tell Tarses what had happened. But she did not know how else to explain why they were not already at Habush.

That night, she was called again to Tarses. He had lost more weight even since the last time she'd seen him; the tendons in his neck stood out against his pale skin, and there was a strangeness in his eyes she had not seen before. He said, "I expect news of Habush's surrender."

Tsifra only went very quiet. In truth, she was too afraid to speak. "I am sorry, Father," she said eventually. "The weather did not hold and—"

"The weather? You are Mazik, Courser. The weather is no concern of yours. You may create whatever weather you wish."

She said, "I was unequal to the task. Forgive me."

Tarses turned away from her, as if trying very hard to control his temper. When he spoke again, his voice trembled. "Where are you? Where is the fleet?"

"Forgive me," she said again. "The fleet is once more at Anab."

"Anab!" he snapped, turning back to her. "Did the weather cause you to travel in a circle?"

"I was poorly led," she said. "My navigators—"

"Do they live?"

She took a breath. "They do—"

He turned away again, clenching and unclenching his fists and said. "Kill them. Kill them and find someone else."

"But—"

"I don't care where you find them! Surely there are navigators in Anab?"

"I will do as you ask, and sail for Habush at once."

"No," he said. "No, I have changed my mind. Leave Habush. It is useless, now. Sail for P'ri Hadar, and when you get there, use these. It is the last of them."

He then revealed a silver chest she had not seen before; either he had only just conjured it or else she'd been too frightened to notice. She approached to take the chest, and then pulled her hand back, because it was hot as flame. She looked to him in shock. "I cannot take these across the sea," she told him.

"You will make a chest lined with lead," he said, and offered no further explanation. "And at the next moon, I want you back in Mazik Anab. You have work to do here."

"But how can I take the fleet to P'ri Hadar and be back by the moon?"

"Tsifra N'Dar," he told her, "open the chest."

She opened the burning chest and was caught in a whirlwind of flame that woke her at its touch. When she opened her eyes, her small house burned all around her, and she knew he'd given her an impossible task.

Chapter Twenty-Four

While Naftaly and Barsilay were attempting to save Habush (or destroy it, depending on one's point of view), Toba stood on the beach south of P'ri Hadar, together with Nehama, and contemplated the feat they were about to perform.

It was Marah's own task, the task she had left to her heirs, and it would be Toba and Nehama's to complete at last. When she thought of it, the pinpricks in Toba's arms began to itch again, and she scratched them so hard she left bruises.

Nehama would hold back the sea, the Ziz would channel the magic of the firmament, and Toba would stand between them.

"We need another test," Nehama said.

"There isn't time for another test. Once the Saharon Bridge is destroyed, Tarses will be coming directly here," Toba reminded her.

It would have been better, they knew, to raise Luz in both worlds at the same time. But there was only one Ziz, and only one Leviathan. They had argued about where to begin, in the mortal or Mazik world; Omer had argued the mortal world should be first, to make use of the Mirror. But Toba had insisted the Mirror did not work that way, and, in fact, so long as their will was strong it did not matter where they started, the second raising would be easier.

Asmel remained unconvinced, and he worried for Toba, channeling the Ziz's magic from the bottom of the sea. He insisted on passing Toba some of his own magic, wanting her as strong as possible, and he gave Toba so much that she had to make him stop before he weakened himself. He also handed her something small that fit in the palm of her hand—a periwinkle.

"Wait," he said, taking a strand of his hair and making it into a silver chain he threaded through the center of the shell. He put it around her neck.

To Nehama, Omer said, "I am eager to see you become a Leviathan. Could you always do that?"

Nehama only smiled in response.

The Ziz took wing, toward the open sea, much further out than in the tests they had run before. Asmel had measured the distance by triangulating the position with the highest tower of the palace and the sea cliffs further south. Nehama had marked the spot in her own mind, and when the Ziz arrived there, she leaned forward and whispered something in the Ziz's ear.

The bird went utterly still, her wings extended fully to either side. She was hovering on the wind that rushed beneath them, holding her up as if she floated.

The demons had used their magic to call the wind, Toba recalled. But this was something different… a magnitude of power Toba could not have imagined. The wind was so strong all around her it felt like a solid thing, like a manifestation of the firmament itself, and Toba felt lightheaded and breathless, trying to force it into her lungs. Nehama looked over her shoulder at Toba, waiting for a signal, and Toba told her, "Go."

Nehama leapt from the Ziz into the sea, becoming again the great fish as she touched the surface. She slid into the water as cleanly as if it were glass, and then her tail, silver-blue, sent a plume of droplets skyward. Nehama swam down into the depths, creating a whirlpool that opened a passage all the way to the bottom of the sea.

On Toba's arms, feathers had begun to burst through her skin. She felt the magic in the Ziz beneath her, and felt it ache through her bones.

Behind her, Asmel whispered, "Tsifra N'Dar, go and raise Luz from the sea."

She willed her mind away from the firmament and leapt from the Ziz, giving herself wings of air—wings that, this time, were covered in feathers as blue as those on Toba's arms. She descended through Nehama's whirlpool, which was louder even than the wind had been, and lighted on the seabed. The sand below her feet was soft and she knelt down and sifted it through her fingers, hoping the bite of the salt would keep her mind from the call of the sky.

In the middle of the whirlpool, near where Toba stood, there was part of the ruin of a building. Gray brick covered in barnacles. This had been Luz, this very spot. Marah had lived here, and Barsilay and Dawid, and so many others who had died in the sea the day that Tarses tricked the sages of Luz into pulling out their gate, and now she stood there again.

She plunged her hand into the sand.

The other she extended to the sky.

The Ziz still floated above her on the wind she commanded, and as Toba's magic met hers, the Ziz released the magic of the firmament to her in a flood. Toba gasped from the shock of it, so much magic that her skin glowed, and her feathers, too; the light shining so brightly through her that she thought it might turn her to ash.

She willed the sand, once soil, to grow, to extend. She told it, "Rise."

The seabed lifted all at once, beneath her hand and all around her, so great was the Ziz's magic. Her ears rang from the noise, and her body was aflame. She went down on her knees, closed her eyes, and thought she would burn away from the inside, like one of Tarses's flame demons.

From over the wind, she heard Asmel's voice shouting, "Tsifra N'Dar, stop."

She opened her eyes.

She'd come above the surface of the sea, so that even kneeling on the ground she was looking down at the water, at a newly formed coast. She lowered her arm and pulled her hand from the sand, and could do nothing but breathe the still air that felt too thin to be real.

Nehama walked through the waves, her skin still the silver of the Leviathan, and said, "Well done." The Ziz landed in the center of the new land she'd just made, and Toba realized not far away was a grove of trees—all dead. They were the almond trees of Luz. Further away were the assorted ruins of some buildings: the shell of what once had been the palace and part of a wall.

"Don't get down," she warned the men. "The ground is full of salt."

"Look what you have done," Asmel said, his voice awed.

Toba's voice sounded like birdsong as she said, "It was the Ziz's work."

NEHAMA STOOD ON the ground that had once been her home and felt as if the world had turned itself over, as if she had just witnessed the birth of an age. Omer and Asmel, on the back of the Ziz, had been stunned into silence. She approached one of the ruins, the remains of the foundation of a house, with stones littered all around it. In the midst of these, there was, of all things, a shoe.

Toba was still on the ground, blue feathers down both arms, and glowing faintly from the Ziz's magic. She hadn't become a Ziz again—not yet—but she was very close, and there were no angels here to turn her back.

Approaching the men on the Ziz, Nehama said, "Toba cannot do this again. It isn't safe for her."

Asmel said, "Can you do it, if you make a buchuk?"

Very honestly, she said, "I don't know."

Behind her, Toba had risen. "I can do it again. I must. A buchuk would not be strong enough."

Asmel said, very gently, "Toba—"

"Don't tell me I am a buchuk!" she snapped. "I have not been so for a long time, you yourself have said as much." She rubbed at her arms, and much to Nehama's relief, the feathers began to fade, fizzling away like embers from a fire. "This is my task, Asmel."

"If Asmel had not called you back," Nehama said, "there would be a mountain here and you would probably be dead, and Asmel cannot go with us to the mortal world."

"We'll wait for the next moon," Omer said.

"We can't wait for the moon!" Toba retorted. "I will be fine. I understand what to do now. I will do it." To Nehama, she said, "You were the one who bequeathed me this task when you died. You cannot take it from me now."

Nehama looked to Asmel, who was very quiet. Then he said, "Tsifra N'Dar, you must have five days' rest, before you go to carry out your task. When the land in mortal Luz looks just like this, you must stop. And then return to me."

Toba said, "I will." At that, Asmel's command must have taken hold, though perhaps more extremely than he'd intended, and she slumped down, asleep.

Then Asmel told Nehama, "Take Elena with you."

THE THREE WOMEN had their rest, and when Toba awoke they took the Ziz through the gate, leaving the book in the care of Asmel.

The landscape of the mortal world was so much the same that Toba had to look back at the gate behind them, to make sure they'd really passed through. There, in the distance, was P'ri Hadar, larger in this world, its wall higher.

Toba felt far from Rimon in a way she had not in the Mazik city, in which the land on the other side of the ocean was still not her home. Somehow, looking out across the mortal sea toward her birthplace made her feel unmoored, as if the distance were grounded in reality, and had not been so before. Elena, beside her, was looking the same way, wearing a wistful expression Toba did not recall seeing on her face before. "Are you thinking of Grandfather?" she asked, and Elena sighed a little and said, "Yes."

Anchored some distance from where they stood, was a ship. A speck in the water was a rowboat, and someone was coming ashore.

Elena said, "Why is there a ship anchored here and not at the harbor?"

Nehama said, "Could it be pirates?"

"No," Toba said, pointing out at the horizon. "Look."

In the distance, she could see the tops of masts coming into view. A host of ships. The Ziz, beneath them, let out a cry. It was the Sefardi fleet.

The person in the rowboat was on the beach now, too far away to be made out. But then there came a sound like fire and breaking glass, and a host of flames erupted into the sky.

"Hashem help us," Elena whispered, as the fire began taking on a new form: a Ziz of flame. And then the creature flew away toward P'ri Hadar.

The real Ziz let out a shriek, and in a gust of wind, flew after it.

Chapter Twenty-Five

Nehama called out to the Ziz as she flew toward the flame demons, begging her to come back. The Ziz was a creature of primal power, but she wasn't immortal. Tarses had killed the Leviathan already. He might have found a way to kill the Ziz, too.

"Don't use her name," she told Toba, setting a hand on her arm. "We can't risk whoever came in that ship hearing it."

"But she might be killed!"

Nehama could think of no way to help. The Ziz was already banking around the demons, putting herself between them and the city. She beat her wings, blowing them back toward the sea.

Inch by inch she pushed them lower, 'til they were only feet from the water, not far from where the mysterious ship was anchored. The wind was so strong the ship began to roll with it; in a moment, it would capsize.

The air was heavy with salt; the demons were shrieking from it. The person on the beach—the person who had released the demons—was screaming at them to fight, and lifted her hand, sending a gust of wind in the other direction, trying to counter the Ziz.

It was useless, of course. But one of the demons broke off from the others, thrown forward by its fellows and the wind made by the Mazik, and managed to fling itself into the Ziz's wing, where it clung to her feathers.

The Ziz let out a great cry, and in a final beat of her wings, forced the remaining demons into the sea. But her wing was still aflame, the air filled with the stench of burning feathers, and she fell from the sky, crashing into the beach.

The Mazik who had been there only a moment ago had vanished.

The Ziz lay on the sand, her wing continuing to burn, and Nehama ran to her, Toba and Elena close behind. The demon that had its burning teeth in her wing was spreading quickly; soon her entire body would be alight.

"Can you get up?" Nehama urged the Ziz. "If you can get to the sea, you can save yourself."

But the Ziz was in too much pain from the flames and from falling from the sky and only keened heedlessly.

"Nehama," Toba called, but the other woman had already run halfway into the surf, rough from the Ziz's magic, and then took a breath and knelt, the water coming up over her head.

She released her breath all at once, a bubble of magic that caught the sea and made a wave half as tall as the Ziz herself, sending it toward the beach where it crashed over the top of the splendid bird. Elena was nearly dragged out to sea. Toba, grabbing her with one hand and the Ziz's splayed-out leg with the other, managed to catch her.

Nehama came up coughing from the water and staggered back toward the Ziz, who had given up her keening and was now only crying. But her ploy had worked; the flames were out. Searching along the Ziz's wing, Nehama could see it was missing half its feathers and many that remained were charred black. The skin beneath was white in places. It was a terrible injury.

"Will she live?" Elena asked quietly.

"She has the magic of the firmament to heal herself," Nehama said. "I think she will live, but she cannot fly. And look." She pointed out to the horizon, where the ships were growing closer; where before they'd only seen the tops of masts, hulls were now visible. It was a huge fleet, she could not even count the ships.

Toba, soaked to the bone, said, "We can't wait. We'll have to do it without her."

"How?" Elena asked.

"I will be the Ziz," Toba said.

Elena cried, "No!"

Nehama told her, "Apart from the effect that will have on you, we cannot raise Luz that way. We need you to do the working at the bottom of the sea, and you can't be there and in the sky. You yourself said a buchuk couldn't do it."

"I said your buchuk couldn't do it," Toba told her.

"But yours can? How can you channel the firmament as the Ziz and sustain a buchuk at the same time?"

"If I am channeling the firmament, I can sustain a hundred buchuks."

Nehama shook her head. "I am much stronger than you are."

"Right now, yes. When I am the Ziz?" Her feathers had already come back and were spreading up her neck, so greatly did she want this.

"You may not be able to turn back," Nehama told her.

"My buchuk will be my anchor," she said. "If a part of myself remains, I will be able to turn back."

"And what if that doesn't work?" Elena asked.

"Then you will use my name," she said. "There is no time."

Toba's eyes were very strange, as golden as the Ziz's, and she reached her arms wide, then wider still, and then another Toba stepped out of herself. The first Toba—the real Toba—let out a sound like a screaming bird. Her face lengthened, and her clothes fell away to reveal a body covered in blue feathers that grew to tremendous size, no longer remotely human, but a second Ziz. She leapt into the sky, leaving the others behind.

The fool. The utter fool. She was not even the one who knew where the whirlpool needed to go, and now Nehama was going to have to swim there and that was going to cost them time. "She's coming back," said Toba's buchuk, her own voice strange, and Toba lit on the sand just long enough for Nehama and the buchuk to climb on her back.

"I think you should stay with the Ziz," Nehama told Elena, and then they flew over the breaking waves, out toward the open sea. The fleet was nearly upon them, so close Nehama could see the faces of the sailors looking on in amazement at the great bird flying in their midst.

"Here," she told Toba. "Stop here."

Toba caught the wind, as the Ziz had done; Nehama had not really believed she could do it 'til then.

The buchuk looked at her and said, "She is truly a Ziz. There is no distinction between them."

"That isn't possible!"

"You know that it is," she said. "Go."

Nehama let herself fall from Toba's back, her mind spinning, and knew she would not be able to hold back the sea with the muddled clarity she had just then. It did not matter if Toba was truly a Ziz or not, she told herself. They had already done this once. If the angels had told the truth—if the Mirror worked in both directions, under the right circumstances—then this would work. She slipped into the water, and she made a second whirlpool.

She could not really see through to the center, but she knew the buchuk was there because she could see the light of the Ziz's magic—Toba's magic—even through the whirlpool, through the depths of the sea itself.

She could feel the seabed rise. This, for Nehama, was the hardest part, keeping the whirlpool alive while she herself was forced to pull back to make space for the rising land. The sound of the ground breaking the surface echoed underwater, and in a moment she felt her whirlpool begin to collapse.

It was done. Toba had done it.

Letting herself become a woman again, Nehama stepped through the water and onto the newly dry shore. The buchuk was before her, one hand in the sand, one to the sky, her eyes closed. The ships that had been near enough to Luz ran ashore on the land that Toba and Nehama had raised, so many ships that Nehama could not count them all.

Realizing that Asmel's order to stop once the land had been raised could not work if Toba's eyes were closed, she said, "Toba, open your eyes."

The buchuk opened her eyes, gold as the Ziz's, and said, "I am my task."

She blew apart in a sea of sparks.

Above, Toba circled the new land, coming to light beside Nehama, who told her, "Tsifra N'Dar, change back."

Toba turned her eye and looked at her, chittering in the language of the Ziz, and did not alter herself at all. Damnation, Nehama told herself. But the beached fleet was still nearby, and in a moment there would be armed men everywhere. "We have to go," she told Toba, who allowed her to climb back up on her back, and together they flew to Elena and the real Ziz, who now had her eyes open and was watching Toba with something like amazement.

Tsifra watched the woman who may or may not have been Toba escape with both Zizim and Elena, who seemed to look back at her. Whether they intended to stay in the mortal world or return through the gate did not much matter to her. Tsifra's mission was of limited scope, and she was not terribly interested in anything beyond that.

Her orders were fairly simple: Lay waste to P'ri Hadar.

But that was before she'd lost half her fleet, which lay beached on this new shore—hulls broken, masts at odd angles. The other ships, farther back, had managed to keep themselves away. Her men had mostly survived, but there could be no naval battle for the city now. She would have to regroup and attack by land, and quickly, too, before P'ri Hadar realized what had happened and took advantage of the situation. Already the men on the destroyed ships were being moved to those that had remained unscathed. Her commanders met and suggested a retreat to further down the coast, where they could offload and prepare to attack the city by land.

Tsifra did not know how the women had done this impossible thing, but it seemed to her that Toba's cleverest move had been making a second version of herself.

Or perhaps that's what she told herself because she, too, was a buchuk.

She did not know if she'd survive long enough to carry out the attack herself—she had been made to lead the armada here, and she had done so, calling a wind so swift they'd come all the way from Anab in days. The sailors were amazed by her, by their speed, but from here on out, the men might have to carry on without her.

The real Tsifra had remained behind in Anab, waiting for the moon, to carry out Tarses's more important order: Create a bridge at the Rosh ha-Tannin and burn Mazik P'ri Hadar to ash.

THE BLOOD ON Naftaly's hands was still wet as he struggled to focus his eyes. There had been an olive tree, he knew, but now he saw Habush burning once more, and then P'ri Hadar, subsumed by a rainstorm he was sure would flood the city. He'd seen so many cities in his mind's eye: Tamar, starving; Habush, aflame, and now P'ri Hadar drowning. He saw other cities, too, he did not recognize: a city filled with soldiers, a city on a mountain, all its streets deserted.

After some time, his mind took him back to the dead olive tree, its trunk smeared with blood. This was no city; it was a desolate land devoid of life. But something about the landscape was distressingly familiar, beyond the olive tree that had first caught his eye.

It was Zayit... He was in the olive grove. The remaining tree had been destroyed, that was why he hadn't recognized it... No, that was not why.

Where were the mines?

Detonated. The ground was littered with the detritus of exploded amphoras and scattered bones and scraps of cloth.

Tarses had marched Maziks into the minefield. Naftaly bent to look at a length of bloody cloth that might have once been a hood or scarf, the same gray cloth the Peregrine often wore.

Ahead of him, the gate opened, and a quartet of men stepped through, carrying a wooden litter, and on the litter were several crates. They set the entire apparatus on the ground and went back through the gate, and Naftaly drew close to look. But he knew what was in the crates even before he peered into one with a cracked lid: They contained cannonballs full of salt. And the men came through again with another litter and set it down, and returned again with another, and another.

Naftaly jumped at the sensation of someone taking his hand, and turned to see that Tarses was at his side, his white hair loose and blowing in a breeze that had stirred the ash on the ground. "Fascinating," he said, "that we should see something that has already happened. Do you often see the past?" Naftaly struggled to pull his hand back, but Tarses held fast, asking, "Wouldn't you like to see what happens next?"

Naftaly had decided, after their last shared vision, that he would not speak to Tarses if he saw him again, lest he reveal more than he ought to. He pulled his arm, but Tarses responded with a hard tug sideways. Naftaly stumbled into him, his vision blurred, and when he looked up again they were someplace different.

A city by the sea, but not P'ri Hadar. And it seemed a new city, too, based on the whiteness of the stone buildings that rose up from the ground and nearly sparkled under a midday sun. Maziks bustled about, dressed in blues and purples, past blooming trees—blooming almond trees.

The corner of each building featured an almond tree, cleverly carved into the stone. This was Luz. But was this the Luz of the past, or a future city?

It could not be the past—there'd been no sea there before the Fall. He was seeing some future version of the city rebuilt, and Tarses's face had gone very grim. Pulling Naftaly's hand again, he walked up a set of stone steps into a domed building that must have been the palace; the guards wore white-and-silver livery. He was looking for something, Naftaly knew, and he must not be allowed to find whatever it was. But he held Naftaly fast, and he was not sure how he could break Tarses from the vision even if he managed to wake himself up.

Down a long corridor, with windows all along one side. A door opened at the far end and out rushed a Mazik woman in white and silver, carrying a cushion made of deep-purple silk. On the cushion rested a crown that resembled a silver almond branch twisted in a circle, with white blossoms set with pearls. The woman passed directly beside them, so close that Naftaly could see that there was hair caught in the crown, long strands that caught the light. The hair, like the crown, was silver.

Tarses's face, serious 'til then, slowly softened into a smile, and he pressed his mouth near Naftaly's ear and whispered, "Barsilay is not King."

Naftaly felt a deep sense of loss and rage well up within him, so potent that he gave one final pull and wrenched himself free of Tarses's grasp, stumbled, and then saw before him an open gate and staggered through.

He nearly tripped over Asmel upon exiting and collapsed on the ground beside him. "What in the Name is happening?" Asmel asked. "Why do you look like that? Where is Barsilay?"

Barsilay—Barsilay was near death, but Naftaly found himself unable to speak, his throat felt as if he'd breathed ash in his vision of Zayit. Omer passed him some water, which he drank. "Ayleth's soldiers told us you were staying in Habush another five days," Asmel told him. "But I tried opening a gate to Barsilay and it wouldn't work. You're the only one I could find."

Naftaly coughed and rubbed his face—he hadn't been so ill after a vision in months. "Wait," he said, "five days? Are you telling me it's been five days since the soldiers returned from Habush?"

Omer said, "It is distressing that you don't seem to have been aware of this."

Naftaly looked down at his hands, his clothes. The blood on them—Barsilay's blood—was still wet.

"Naftaly, where is he?" Asmel asked, closing the book, extinguishing the gate. Without its brightness, Naftaly could see P'ri Hadar in the near distance.

"He was attacked by one of Yefet's men." Taking Asmel's hand, he said, "He was alive when I left him, but badly hurt. Efra said she would ward them both from anyone besides myself, so that I could confirm it was safe to bring him here."

"Then you should do so," Asmel told him, handing over the book.

"We can't," Naftaly said. "We don't know what we might be bringing them into. When was the last time you were at the palace?"

"We're on our way there now," Asmel told him. "We've been at Luz all this time, and we sent the soldiers back to the city without us when they came through and said you'd been delayed. If Ayleth knew about a plot to murder Barsilay, her soldiers would have taken the book from me when they had the opportunity, I think."

"Then it might not be too late to warn her," Naftaly said. "Can you get an audience with Ayleth?"

"She has no use for me," Asmel said.

Naftaly said, "Then perhaps she will see me."

After riding the rest of the way to the city, the three were greeted at the gate by ten mounted guards from the palace.

"Well met," the lead guard said. Asmel nodded and the guard continued, "What business do you have, so late in the day?"

"I am to meet the Queen," Asmel said.

"On this day? I do not think she will see you. She is lately with her husband."

Asmel did not much like the sound of that, as Ayleth's husband was still in Habush. He said, "If that is so, then I certainly have business with him."

"And what makes you think he would want to see you?"

"I am Barsilay's uncle," Asmel said. "He will see me."

"Barsilay of Luz is dead," the guard told him. "The Queen has taken for herself another husband. Our new King is Yefet of Anab."

Asmel went cold. The guards were armed with blades and bows both; he'd never seen them arrayed so, and it boded very badly for all of them. Backing his horse away a step, he said, "If Barsilay is dead, we have no further business in your city."

The guard said, "Actually, we were sent to come looking for you, Asmel of Rimon."

"Me?" Asmel asked, and Omer moved to put his own horse between them.

"Where is the gate of Luz?"

"The gate of Luz?"

"The book," the guard said. "It is the property of the Crown."

"It is not," Asmel said hotly. "It belongs to no one."

"It belonged to the heir of Luz and he is dead. His widow claims it as her right."

There was no point in arguing the legality of this, but Asmel was prepared to do it anyway as the guards drew their swords. There was no cover anywhere nearby, and there were three of them and ten soldiers, all armed. Their horses would be no faster than the ones the soldiers rode.

Asmel held up a hand and, very suddenly, the entire road was pitch dark. The setting sun, the lights at the gate—all of it extinguished. Pulling Naftaly from the saddle, Asmel dragged him away soundlessly, Omer following behind them. Nearby, the guards set up flashes of light that were immediately extinguished, then swore and tried again.

The darkness would not last more than a few minutes, but it would be enough to get them well away from the guards—only where was there left to go? The book, inside his coat, was hot against his breast, and he felt a strong impulse to read it.

He mustn't, he knew. Not yet. The guards would see; they were much too close. They'd only gone a few hundred feet.

And yet—the gnawing desire began to grow within him. No, he thought, it was not a desire, it was a need, acute as anything he'd ever felt. No one had ever used his name against him, and some small part of his mind (the part that was not consumed with wanting to read the book) wondered if this was what it felt like.

But that could not be what was happening. The only Maziks who had ever known it were his own mother, Marah, and Toba; the first two were dead and Toba was in another world. The recipient of a named command had to hear the order for it to work. Or so he'd always been told.

The book, somehow, was already in his hands, and he realized he had gone still. "Why did you stop?" Naftaly whispered in his ear.

"I must read this," Asmel told him, though it was still pitch black and Naftaly would not be able to see the book. As he opened the cover and set the book on the ground, he realized the pages were dimly self-illuminated. He'd never noticed that before. A curiosity.

Omer said, "Asmel what are you doing?"

But Asmel was already reading. "Stop him," Naftaly told Omer. "Has he gone mad?"

Omer reached for the book, but Asmel held out a hand and pushed him back with a puff of magic as he read. Omer turned to Naftaly and said, "Someone's used his name."

"There is no one here to use it, besides us," Naftaly said, and then swore, because the soldiers had seen the light coming from the book and were riding toward them.

The gate opened directly in front of them, lighting the area as brightly as a full moon. The soldiers shouted and began firing arrows; Omer managed to knock one of the riders from his saddle with a bolt of magic, but then the riderless horse reared wildly and fell, taking Naftaly down with it. Whether he'd been pinned beneath the animal or simply knocked over, Asmel did not know, because through the gate came the Ziz.

The archers were still firing. Asmel heard Omer shout as he was hit, and the Ziz screamed, lifted her talon, and slammed it into the ground with such force the trees around them trembled. The soldiers' horses bucked; some were thrown, and as the Ziz began to charge them, some simply fled. Asmel felt a pain in his arm and realized that he had been struck and had blood running down his sleeve, and he clapped one hand over the injury as with the other he slammed the book shut. The Ziz was calling out nearby, so close he could smell her, and he reached out a groping hand in the darkness.

"Asmel," came a whisper—a female voice, perhaps Nehama's—and then there was the sound of great wings, and the Ziz's talons around him, and she flew off with him into the darkness, leaving the book and the others behind.

He called out to her in the bit of the language of Luz he remembered, and when that did not work, took to smacking her toes with his fingers. "The others are all still back there," he shouted. Of all the things, he was arguing with a bird. "Put me down!" The Ziz gave no indication she'd either heard or understood, but he was quite certain she was capable of both. "I'm bleeding all over you!" he screamed.

This, at least, seemed to get the creature's attention, and she descended. She'd taken him south, and the sun—now that either Asmel's spell had worn off or they'd travelled beyond its reach—was beginning to set over the sea behind them. He only hoped the others had managed to escape before his cleverly constructed darkness had faded.

The Ziz set him on the ground and landed beside him; she, too, had been struck by the archers, and had two arrows embedded in her breast. "Blasphemy," he muttered, ignoring his own injury, and pulled them out, reaching to set his hand over each of the wounds and knitting them back together—which he found he did rather badly, his own magic not being up to the task of repairing a creature like the Ziz.

She snapped at him with her beak, discouraging any further efforts, and he sat down hard and put his hand over his own wound. It had bled like the devil but seemed otherwise unserious, and he began working the inner layers of flesh back together with magic. "We have to go back," he told her again. "The others are likely in a great deal of trouble—you know that, don't you? Naftaly fell, I don't know what happened to him. Omer was struck—why save me?" The Ziz had never shown him the slightest interest. She was known to be rather partial to Toba, in fact, who was presumably still back at the wall.

Asmel craned his neck back as he sat on the ground taking her in, and only then did he notice the subtle differences... The feathers a slightly different shade of blue, the eyes a different shade of gold. And this bird was smaller than the one he'd seen before, though not by much. She stood, watching him quietly, and cocked her head to the side, waiting, it seemed, for him to come to some obvious conclusion.

"Toba," he said. "Of all the things." He got to his feet and stepped closer, setting a hand on her feathers, probing with magic. But she didn't feel like Toba's magic. She didn't feel Mazik at all. It must have been she who'd compelled him to open the gate, though he couldn't understand how that was possible; a mystery for another day. "You can't turn yourself back? Or you don't wish to?"

The bird twittered at him a little, and he sighed. "Before all this, I never ordered you to do anything," he told her. "Not even when I probably should have." As a point in fact, he'd never used anyone's name—not that he knew so many names, but he'd never used his wife's, never used Barsilay's. It would sully him, he felt, to do so. But Toba had barely been able to return from her time as a flock of ordinary birds, and this was something much more profound. Every moment she remained a Ziz, drinking the firmament, was a step down a path from which she would never be able to return. He whispered, "Tsifra N'Dar, return to yourself."

The Ziz looked at him through her great gold eye and did not change at all.

He leaned forward, resting his forehead against her feathered breast, and felt her great heart beating within her. She leaned her head down and placed her beak on top of his head, so gently all he could feel were the edges of her feathers. He said, "I don't know how to help you."

She lifted her head suddenly, clicking her beak, then nudged him when he failed to note what had caught her attention. He turned to see what she was looking at just in time to see the gate close to the north.

Someone, at least, had survived the attack. He had not seen a second gate open, but they could only have gone to the cedar forest. It was the safest place left to them that didn't mean leaving Asmel and Toba behind.

Or as much of Toba as remained. "Let's go," he told her.

Chapter Twenty-Six

Naftaly's ankle had snapped under the weight of the fallen horse. It had rolled off of him, so he was not pinned, but he had been unable to do anything besides slide himself out of the way, dragging Omer along with him.

As Asmel's magical darkness faded, Naftaly could see that Omer was much worse off than a broken ankle, with an arrow beneath his collarbone. He was gasping for air, and Naftaly did not know whether to pull the arrow out or not, since Efra had told him it might cause a man to bleed to death.

He was also worried he might be hallucinating, because for a moment, before the gate had closed, it had seemed to him that there were two Zizim. "Where are Asmel and Toba?" he managed, as Nehama approached and exclaimed over Omer, who was now unconscious. Spreading her fingers around the arrow, she pulled it out with her other hand. Even with her magic pouring into the wound, there was an unsettling amount of blood.

Elena, who had picked the book up from the ground, said, "Toba became a Ziz again and can't turn herself back. When she saw Asmel, she took him and flew off."

"She just left the rest of us here?"

"I'm not sure how much of her mind is intact," she said. "But if she recognized him, it's a better sign than we've had so far. What the hell is happening here? Weren't those Ayleth's men shooting at you?"

"There's been a coup," Naftaly explained. He willed his mind away from the vision of the crown with the silver hair, and what it might mean. Barsilay was still alive. Efra was protecting him. Still, emotion caught his throat. "Barsilay is alive, but not here, and we don't know whether Ayleth is involved or not."

Nehama said, "We'd better get out of here, then. We're right next to the wall, there will be other soldiers here any moment." Setting her hand on Naftaly's ankle, she added, "This has to be set before I can heal it. It will have to wait." She took the book from Elena and opened it, setting it on the ground.

"Wait," Naftaly said. "The old woman is still in her house in the garden. We have to get her out."

"If there's been a coup, we can't risk taking the book into the palace," Nehama said.

"Then I'll go on the Ziz! She can fly me over the northern wall."

"She can't fly at all—look at her!"

Naftaly took in the Ziz's burned wing and wanted to pull his hair out.

"There's no time for this argument!" Nehama snapped.

"Then open a gate to the garden, and I'll go on my own!"

"You can't even walk!"

"You must *think*," Elena told him.

"I am thinking! I am thinking you mean to abandon her!"

"Naftaly, you can't help her!" Elena cried.

The sound of hoofbeats from the city was unmistakable, a death knell for the old woman. "Please," he said quietly, as the tears climbed up his throat and through his eyes, and Elena said, "Damnation."

But Nehama had already opened the book and begun to read when she suddenly shut it again.

"What's wrong?" Elena asked.

"It's dusk. If we open a gate to the cedar forest, they'll be able to see it all the way from the city—it will be a beam of light pointing at our exact position. We can't risk it. And the Ziz can't fly there."

"We'll have to go someplace else," Elena said. "Habush?"

"No," Naftaly said. "Tarses has men watching Habush. And do you mean to abandon Asmel and Toba, too?"

The hoofbeats were growing close, and Nehama said, "I will send the Ziz back into Aravoth. She'll be safe there—"

"I have a better idea," Elena said. "Give me the book." And she began to read quickly, 'til a gate opened. Rising, she turned to Nehama and said, "Send her through."

Nehama said, "Where are you sending her?"

"The Gal'in," Elena said. "The demons there will protect her until she's healed."

"Are you sure?" Nehama said. "The demons—"

"She is their friend," Naftaly said, through his tears. "They told Barsilay so."

Nehama set her hand on the Ziz's injured wing. "You have done all you can," she said. "Go and free your children."

The Ziz leaned down and met her gaze. Then she carefully plucked one of her smallest feathers and presented it to Elena, who asked, "What does she want me to do with this?" as the Ziz stepped through the gate, and Nehama closed the book.

The soldiers from within the city were close enough now that Naftaly could smell the horses, and Elena, pocketing the feather, put her arms around him and made them both into a large stone as Naftaly held his breath. He could no longer see Nehama or Omer anywhere.

The soldiers arrived only moments later, stopping where Elena had just opened the gate, turning in a circle. "They must have gone through the gate and taken the book with them," one of them said. "There will be hell to pay. Come on."

They turned and rode back into the city. Nehama, curled up on top of Omer, let herself be seen again. "Let's go," she said. "Can you carry him?"

Elena was already hauling Naftaly's arm across her shoulders and said, "I've done it before."

They returned to the forest, where they found Toba the Ziz curled up asleep and Asmel sitting in front of a small wooden house he'd made to keep out the cold. Omer had woken and lamented having forgotten to return Nehama's book from Te'ena (which in all the strain of raising Luz, he'd forgotten about until that exact moment) and then losing it in the scuffle, while Nehama told him to stop his caterwauling because it hardly mattered. Asmel had—very painfully—set the bones in Naftaly's ankle while Nehama knit them together. They made a meal which they ate in silence, and then Naftaly went back outside; the little house was too warm, with too many people in it, and it left him feeling very cold and alone.

The old woman was probably dead already, her body, too, cold and alone. He would never again see her wrinkled face. She had been dearer to him than his own grandmothers, who had died before he could properly remember them. She had followed him to the other side of the world, and fussed over him, and he'd never so much as said thank you.

The near-full moon was bright in Naftaly's eyes, so bright it seemed for a moment like the sun, and he winced and held his hand up against it. His latest vision came rushing back to him: P'ri Hadar in a deluge of rain; the gate of Zayit stripped of its mines; the crown with the silver hair.

"Naftaly?" Nehama asked. "Are you all right?" She put her hand to his forehead, which was wet with perspiration.

"I had a vision," he told her, "when I came through the gate from Habush. Tarses has the gate of Zayit. The salt—there is so much salt." His eyes burned as if he could feel it, and he wiped at them. "I think that's how he killed the Falcons. He ordered them to walk into the minefield."

Nehama sat back on her heels and exhaled, "No."

He did not tell her about the crown with the silver hair, and he would not tell Barsilay, either. It was one more piece of bad news, bad luck. He could hardly imagine that only a day before—no, it had been five—Barsilay had been calling him the Hero of Habush. He itched to open a gate to him; it had been much too long since he and Efra had been left behind. But bringing them back would probably be even worse for them.

Naftaly suddenly looked up from the fire and said, "Oh, no. Asmel—I forgot. Before we left Habush, Barsilay had a plan. Tarses is making a new crossing at the Rosh ha-Tannin. We were supposed to ambush him there, together with a force of archers from Habush. They are promised to do so." He closed his eyes. "Ah," he sighed.

"There's nothing we can do," Elena told him.

"But the Habushis won't know the army of P'ri Hadar isn't coming," he said. "And even if they realize, they've already promised to attack."

"This is the least of our problems."

"They'll all be killed!" Naftaly snapped. "I have to warn them."

Everything was very quiet. Omer said, "Perhaps you shouldn't."

"Why?"

"Habushi archers rarely miss. Even fifty could do a lot of damage."

"Before they're overrun, you mean."

Omer said, "It might be enough to weaken his forces before he gets here. It might be the only chance we have."

Naftaly looked to the others—to Elena, who had a mind for such matters—to see if she would disagree. She saw his eyes on her and said, "I don't know. I don't know if anything we do matters anymore."

"How can you say that? You raised the sea in two worlds!"

"Yes! And for our troubles we're being hunted," she said. "Like always. It is always this way—it will always be this way!"

It was silent then, and Naftaly did not know how to reply. Barsilay had nearly died in his arms, and since then he'd seen Maziks crushed and flayed with arrows. His old woman was trapped inside the palace, unless she'd already been murdered, harmless as she was. His eyes welled.

They had saved Habush, but they could not save themselves. They had done the impossible, raised a city from the sea, and still, they were in the forest, warming their freezing bodies before a fire, just as they'd done so long ago in Rimon. There was a circularity to it: They were hunted, they did the impossible, they were defeated anyway.

The exhaustion of it wore away at him.

But still, when he closed his eyes that night, he tried to dream his way to Barsilay in Habush, finding instead an empty place where the city should have been. On his shoulder lighted a demon, who said, "Best beloved, you should not be here. The city is hidden, even from you."

"Where is the heir of Luz?" he asked. "Where is the Savia?"

"One does not dream," the demon told him. "The other does not sleep."

"But they are alive?" Naftaly asked.

"They live," the demon said. "You must go, though, lest someone else sees you who should not."

Naftaly tried to master his feelings. It didn't matter, he told himself, if he could see Barsilay, so long as he were alive. And he had something else to do, anyway. "I must see the King," he began. "I have a message for him."

"You cannot go in," the demon said. "It would destroy the illusion if we let you. But we might give him a message."

"I have nothing to trade you for the favor."

"We will do it, because we like you."

That was less comforting than it might have been. "How can I trust you to do this?"

The demon moved to his other shoulder. "We know already of your news. Your army does not come." The demon pecked at his ear. "But there is more. Tell us?"

Naftaly found himself too numb to stop the demon nibbling at him and said, "It isn't only the army the Caçador is bringing across the Rosh ha-Tannin. He also has the salt of Zayit."

"Ah," sighed the demon. "A conundrum. If we tell the King, it will save his archers. But if the archers are left to fight, they will weaken the Caçador. He brings salt to P'ri Hadar. Don't you wish to slow him down?" Naftaly had already made this decision, but with the demon questioning him he found he began to equivocate once more.

The demon asked, "Do you want us to tell the King of Habush? Or shall we not?"

Naftaly took a deep breath and said, "Tell him the heir of Luz releases them from their promise."

THE OLD WOMAN was very cross, because the shade the Maziks allowed her to keep with her to do things like make food and draw bathwater had vanished overnight days ago.

She still had food about, since she always kept a little extra squirreled away (a habit from her begging days), but she was beginning to run low, and that morning the ewer that filled itself with water whenever she tapped on it was nearly dry.

Elena, too, had been gone for days because it was too cumbersome to travel all the way to the sea and back every day, and they were all living in a tent or something else the old woman wanted no part of. She never went into the palace if she could help it, and she was feeling slightly put out by the lack of attention and very put out by the lack of fresh food. She'd just worked up the gumption to go find some Mazik to shake her fist at when she realized that her door had been sealed from the outside.

This really was insupportable; first she'd been banished to the hut, and now she was trapped inside. She beat on the door, and then kicked it, and then went to the window and discovered, on the other side of the curtains, that it had been closed in.

She had the sudden sensation of having been buried alive and muttered a prayer under her breath. And then, a pair of hands emerged from the floor, grabbed her ankles, and pulled her under the house.

There was a lot of screaming and flailing then, but the Mazik who had pulled her into the space left empty by the four horrible carved animal-leg posts insisted he meant no harm and had not been the one to lock her in the hut—and, in fact, that he was Barsilay's friend and had only come out to check on her because of some stories that were being passed around.

"Barsilay's friend?" she asked. "What did you say your name was?"

"Tarek," he said. "I was together with Barsilay in the prison, and I know it was you who ransomed him." He was a broad-shouldered man with dark hair cropped short for a Mazik and fingernails bitten to the quick, as if he hadn't gotten over the habit he'd developed while locked away. He spoke slowly, as if he were still not exactly used to it, and quietly, as he went on, "I've heard… things, and some of us wanted to make sure you were all right."

"Things—what things? Is Barsilay all right?"

"He is reported to be dead," he said, only a little gently.

"Dead!"

"We believe it isn't true. There is another rumor that one of Ayleth's soldiers was with him in Habush just a few days ago. But the day after he was declared to be dead, Ayleth married Yefet. She hasn't been seen in public since. He claims to be acting in her name."

"Doesn't sound like it, if no one has seen her. Could she be dead?"

"She's not," Tarek said. "As a matter of fact, we found her. But she won't speak to any of us. She doesn't trust us."

"What makes you think she'll talk to me?"

"Because," he said, "you are a witch."

Of course she was. Gnarled joints, wrinkled face, liver spots: What else could she be? The old woman sighed heavily and said, "All right. Take me to the Queen."

Ayleth had been returned to her tower in the prison, together with her advisors—those from P'ri Hadar, of course, as those who had come to her from Anab were all supporting Yefet's coup. They were completely isolated—the place had been newly warded to prevent their dreaming, Tarek told her—and though they were being fed, they looked the worse for strain.

The former kings and queens of P'ri Hadar who had been imprisoned with Barsilay hadn't entirely trusted Kasfia to keep her word; many of them assumed she would arrest them again the first chance she got (which, to be fair, she might have done if she had not immediately been poisoned). Some of them, taking a cue from the rats in the prison, went into a room not far from the kitchen, which was known to be above the prison, and chiseled a hole in the floor that could be used for an escape attempt, if it were needed later.

It also made a good way back into the prison, which was useful if one's Queen was being held there against her will.

Tarek used his magic to pull the old woman through the hole in the floor (much as he'd pulled her through the floor of the house), into the prison, through the floor again, and then through yet another hole. By this time the old woman was feeling rather nauseated and very claustrophobic, and she wondered how Barsilay had managed to stay sane in this place. The man must be tougher than she'd given him credit for. She resolved to tell him, if she ever saw him again, which at that moment seemed a doubtful prospect.

Tarek took her into some giant chasm of a room, in the middle of which was a stone tower that resembled a head of garlic on a massively tall pedestal. The whole place smelled like a room that had not been aired in a thousand years, and it was cold and damp besides. She imagined the poor Ziz down here with no air or sun. Fifty years, had it been? It was criminal, and she thought very uncharitable thoughts about Kasfia, and then recalled she was dead, and felt a little better.

So deep were her ruminations that she caught her foot on a piece of loose stone which must have decayed in the damp, and nearly landed on her nose—Tarek being a dozen paces ahead, annoyed, like most Maziks, by her old-woman pace. She stopped to rub at her ankle, and then noticed that stuck beneath the stone, which must have fallen from the ceiling, was a feather.

It was about the length of her smallest finger, and blue as the Ziz—it must have only just grown in when it was lost. She knew better than to pick up random objects after that business with the Peregrine and the rock, but it was so pretty, and so blue, she felt she could not help herself and plucked it from beneath the rock before hurrying to catch up with Tarek.

"It's you," Ayleth said, upon the old woman's entrance through the window. Looking at her a little suspiciously, she added, "The witch."

"The very one," the old woman said.

"Did Barsilay send you?"

"I don't know where he is," she admitted. "Nor Toba, nor any of the others you doubtless would prefer to me, but here I am. I have been told Barsilay's alive, however, which makes you guilty of some things."

"You think I wanted to marry Yefet?" Ayleth snapped. "I had little choice."

"So he married you and locked you in here, and now he's

running the city by himself," the old woman said. "But I don't understand how he's able to do any of that. He's an outsider—no one in P'ri Hadar has any loyalty to him."

"He has names," Ayleth said, dropping her voice. "I don't know how. I certainly didn't give him mine, but he knows a lot of names he shouldn't, and for those he doesn't, he simply tells everyone he's acting on my behalf."

"That's no good," the old woman said. Turning to Tarek, she said, "Couldn't we just kill him?"

"Not easily," he said. "He's very well guarded, and he would be anticipating an assassination."

"Hm," she said. "What about your half-Mazik friends in the mortal city? There's a full moon soon—couldn't they come and help you?"

"They are forbidden ever to come through a gate," Ayleth said. "They cannot come here."

"Ever?" the old woman said. "But Kasfia's dead—surely any order she gave them must be null by now."

"Her death has no bearing on the command," she said.

Turning again to Tarek, the old woman asked, "What about the demons in this prison? They are loyal to Barsilay."

"We saw them when Yefet brought us down here," Ayleth told her. "Yefet told them he'd have the entire prison salted if any of them came in here again."

"Damnation," she muttered, and Ayleth said, "Listen, can't *you* do something?"

"Me?" she sputtered.

"You're a witch! Surely there must be some trick you could do."

Hashem's sake—why did she have to be the witch? Elena, at least, could have passed for one, if she wasn't really one already. She had all those little spells, and a clever mind to boot. All the old woman had were achy joints and bad posture.

Well, if they all thought she was a witch, she supposed she had better find a way to become one.

Only she had no magic, which was not a useful thing in a witch. What else did witches do? Mischief, that's what. The problem she'd always had with the witches in stories was they so often seemed to act out of nothing short of boredom. They kidnapped children and dragged them into the sea—and then did nothing but gloat. Or they turned babies into puppies, because it was amusing. The Witch of Endor, well, at least she might have learned something useful communing with the dead, but mostly the witches were up to no good because they were very clever and the world had given them nothing better to do.

Mischief, hm. She asked Ayleth, "I don't mean to be terribly crude in front of all these people, but on your wedding night did you happen to... perform your... duties, so to speak?"

Ayleth made a very sour face and said, "Indeed not. But he will think I did."

"How did you manage to get out of it?"

"I found a jar of amapola by Barsilay's bed," she said. "I poured it in Yefet's wine, then once he was asleep I tore my nightgown and smeared blood on the sheets."

"So he believes he was simply too drunk to remember," the old woman said. "And he also thinks you were a virgin."

"Neither is true," the Princess said, a little smugly. "But yes, that is what he likely believes."

The old woman tapped her lip with her gnarled finger and paced about. What a scene... All of the Queen's advisors locked away and useless, and looking to her like she might be able to save them all.

Turning to Tarek, she said, "I need a puppy."

Chapter Twenty-Seven

Tsifra was not sure if her buchuk would survive her return to the Mazik world, but in truth, she hardly cared. The buchuk's task was relatively simple and could be carried out by her commanders. They would be only too happy to destroy P'ri Hadar on her behalf.

Her own task could be performed by no other. On the night of the moon, the very instant she stepped through the gate, she called for her horse and rode all night from Anab to the Rosh ha-Tannin.

A mortal horse could never make the trip in one night, and even a Mazik horse could only go twice as far without rest. But Tarses had created something entirely new: a horse with a demon in its heart. It could run forever without tiring, twice as fast as a normal horse, and in battle it showed no fear.

The demon would kill the horse eventually; she'd seen it once. The horse collapsed, foaming at the mouth, as the demon flowed from its nostrils like curling black smoke and then escaped back to wherever it had come from. It was not a pleasant thing to watch, but when Tarses had gifted her one of his precious steeds, she had accepted it. They were relatively few in number (most having been sent to the southern cities), and Tarses—to his anger—was nearly out of demons, so there would be no more when these were dead. For now, she rode her horse all the way to the Rosh ha-Tannin, the wind biting into her face.

The army was already camped there, waiting for her. Tarses came out of his pavilion to greet her, his face serious. "Courser," he said. "Are you ready?"

Of course she was not ready... She'd just ridden some four hundred miles in a single night, the buchuk had drained a non-inconsequential amount of her magic, and while crafting a bridge over saltwater was possible for her, it was still not going to be easy.

She risked anger if she complained. But he would be angrier still if she collapsed in the middle of making the bridge and drowned in the sea below. "I need rest," she said, in a tone she had not used with Tarses before, and he seemed displeased.

He allowed it, though. "How much rest do you require?"

"Let me see the crossing first," she said. "Then I will know better."

She was testing him, and he knew it, but she was so tired she could barely control her temper. Next she would tell him to build his own damn bridge. He brought her to the place he'd intended, the end of the long island. The strait itself was narrow enough that she could see the other side, even in the dark, but still, it was a great deal of work for one person. Under better circumstances, she would ask for a month to do it.

Tarses would not give her a month. She said, "What about your doctor—can he not help me recover more quickly?"

Tarses's face went very dark, and he said, "He is not among us."

"You left him in Anab, when you ride into battle?"

"Do not ask me about him again, Courser."

Was he dead, then? Had Tarses killed him? He could not have escaped; such a thing was impossible. No one had ever escaped from Tarses, besides Barsilay—

"You have seen the crossing," Tarses said.

Tsifra took her mind from the doctor. It made no difference to her, whether he were alive or dead. She had a bridge to build, and she was so exhausted she could barely keep on her feet. "I need a hot meal and ten hours' sleep. And my magic alone will not be enough. I will need more than I have if you mean me to do this quickly."

Tarses said, "You may have mine. Go, then, and eat and rest."

She returned to Tarses's pavilion, unsure of his behavior. He was neither as warm as he had been in her dreams, nor as disdainful as he'd been for most of her life. It almost seemed like he was watching her, waiting for something.

It mattered very little, just then. Some shade gave her a meal of simmered lamb and watered wine, and she ate until she thought she might be sick, and slept until the sun was high overhead. Her dreams were hazy and unformed from fatigue; she only heard bits of the dreams of those resting around her—men who were eager to steal the treasures of P'ri Hadar, or others who wanted to go home and sleep in their own beds.

One voice, some Hound she had known to be one of Tsidon's better men, whispered a tale to his companion. As Tsifra had not taken proper shape, she was not seen, and what she overheard was this: Tarses, the Hound said, had developed an obsession with the lineage of Luz. He'd had the very man assemble a pedigree for all the heirs the Peregrine had killed.

What he was looking for Tsifra only wondered, but she had a sneaking suspicion he was trying to guess at who the next heir might be after Barsilay, if he died. But the Peregrine herself had never been able to guess at that. It was all so far removed from the original line at this point, it might have been anyone. She suspected he was hoping the next heir would be someone he could better control, or else someone he could easily kill. Or, perhaps, that it might be Tarses himself. He was capable of such grand ambitions, certainly. Was it possible? Who could say?

When she rose, she was still tired.

But she went to the edge of the Rosh ha-Tannin with Tarses by her side. She could not, alone, build a bridge anything like the one in Habush—this one would be simple, largely flat, and entirely utilitarian. A strong storm might cause it troubles. But it would be high enough over the water that Maziks could safely cross.

He took her hand in his, and she felt the magic pass into her, as he stood tall and very proud. She expected him to retreat to firmer ground, but instead he said, "I will stay with you, 'til your task is done."

There were only two reasons, so far as she could see, for him to remain with her as she worked. The first was that he wanted his troops to believe he was the creator of the bridge—that later, he would tell the tale of the building of this crossing, and it would be him that had made it possible, and her contribution would be lost in the telling. The second, and this only occurred to her once they'd been on the bridge for quite some time, was that he was testing her, to see if she meant him harm. She could not do anything directly. He'd ordered her never to harm him when she'd been barely old enough to hold a knife. But out on the bridge, it would be very easy to create a plausible accident. He was waiting to see if she would do it.

She kept up her work, stopping only to take a little water. She and Tarses exchanged not a word, and she wondered if hewould do more than watch her every move.

Her answer came when they were halfway across. It had begun to rain, making the entire process much more unpleasant. As she'd turned to gather her sack of stones, Tarses said, "I will carry it a while," and leaned over to pick up the sack. The sole of his boot caught in a crevice and he reeled backward.

Tsifra's bridge had no railing at all; it was an aspect they had neither the time nor the materials to craft. If she did nothing, Tarses would fall backward off the bridge and into the sea.

She reached out and grabbed his arm, righting him: a reflex, she supposed. Tarses smiled at her.

Artifice, she suspected. But if she'd let him stumble, he'd have killed her—not on the spot, but once the bridge was complete. He doubted her in a way he had not done since Zayit. Someone had planted a seed of suspicion in his mind.

The bridge was finished as the sun lay low on the horizon and they returned to the troops to gather their forces. Then the entire army rode across the sea with sabers held high, their faces bright with power, led by Tarses on his demon-stallion. The sound of hooves on the stone bridge was so loud Tsifra could scarcely think through it; there were so many more soldiers than she'd realized.

When they were on the other side of the sea, Tarses raised his sword again and shouted, "Even the sea is no barrier for us!"

The men cheered, but Tsifra seethed, and she vowed vengeance on whomever had tried to turn her father against her.

* * *

THE OLD WOMAN's instructions to the Princess were simple: tell Yefet she had birthed the puppy, and then insist they call on Barsilay's very powerful mortal witch for help.

This she did the very next day, and the old woman found herself brought to the prison by one of Yefet's men. She found Yefet with Ayleth in the tower… The Queen's advisors were absent, and she had no idea where they might have been taken. Ayleth held a swaddled puppy in her arms; Yefet stood beside her, his face white with anger or shock.

"What has happened?" the old woman asked, folding her arms. "Why have you called me here?"

"My wife," Yefet said, "has birthed this thing."

"It's lovely," the old woman said flatly. "I do like a wet nose on a baby."

Yefet seethed. He said, "I only knew my wife three days ago—how is it she can have given birth in such a time? And to a dog!"

The old woman made a show of examining the dog. Its eyes, to her surprise, were normal (by her standards at least), and not the square-pupiled shape she had come to expect of Mazik-world creatures. It wriggled in Ayleth's arms and let out a little yip. "This is a curse," she said, "and there can be only one cause."

"What? What curse can there be?"

"Your wife is already married to another man," she reminded him. "Her womb has therefore cast out its contents—as you see, the product of her sin."

"Barsilay is dead!"

"He is not," the old woman said, though of course she'd had no way to confirm it. He'd better be alive, the damned Mazik. "The evidence is before your eyes. He is cuckolded, but very much alive."

"He is hardly the first man to be cuckolded."

"Your wife is a Queen twice over," the old woman said, "and you swore an oath to support Barsilay, if what I've heard is true. Did you think the actions of a Queen of two great cities and an oathbreaker would have no consequences?" She held up a finger. "But there may be a way for me to undo this terrible thing."

"Undo the curse?"

"Certainly you don't mean by murdering Barsilay?" Ayleth gasped.

Here, the old woman knew she would have to be very careful. Yefet was no fool. If she asked him to do something obviously to her benefit, he would see through the entire thing. She said, "That would not help now, in any case, as this child was conceived while you were married to another man. Killing him after the fact wouldn't alter that. The sin is done."

"I won't listen to this," Yefet said.

"You could simply let things stand," she replied. "All the world will say that King Yefet fathered a dog, but there are surely worse things. May I then return to my hut? I have bones to boil."

The vein in Yefet's neck stood out a great deal. He said, "How would you break the curse?"

"Break it?" she mused. "Hm. Cursed is cursed. But I could move the curse to another."

He looked a little doubtful. "Can you?"

"Such things are done all the time," she said. "But I think you will have a little trouble finding one of your subjects willing to allow their baby to be turned into a dog."

"I will find one," he said.

"All right," she said. "But in the meanwhile, there are certain objects I will require to cast the spell."

"What objects?"

"A drop of blood from each of you," she said. "A fillet from a freshwater fish, charcoal from a recent fire. And of course I will also need the Queen to sign a Get."

Ayleth's mouth popped open a little at the mention of a divorce—she had not expected the old woman might trick her, too, but she could hardly say no under the circumstances. The favor Barsilay would owe for ending his marriage was incalculable. Well, he already owed her an incalculable favor for getting him out of the prison, and he'd repaid her by sticking her in a hut. Really, the man was insufferable.

Ayleth smiled just a little and said, "But the Get would not be official unless Barsilay could be presented with it, would it?"

"It is a symbolic act," the old woman said. "All mortal magic is based on symbolic acts, surely you must know this. Bring me all these things, together with the baby you wish to carry your son's curse, and I will do this for you."

"You would do this," Yefet said, "without payment?"

Oh, dear. Of course a real witch would demand payment. What would be reasonable? This sort of thing should command a hefty price, and if she undersold herself it would look like an obvious trick. She said, "I had not yet come to that part. As payment I require the bezoar of the Leviathan."

Yefet cocked his head. "It failed to save Kasfia. Has it some purpose?"

"Only to me," she said. Of course it served no purpose. It was pretty, though.

"I will do all that you ask," he said. "Give me a day and return here when I send for you."

"Of course," she said. "I will await your messenger."

It was just past sunset the next day when Yefet's man came again to the old woman's garden hut, and she returned with him back to the prison tower.

Ayleth held the puppy in its swaddle, but now Yefet held in his arms a wailing baby. The old woman felt slightly uneasy at the sight of it and was quite concerned by what Yefet had done to obtain it.

"I have all that you've asked for," he said.

"The bezoar?" she asked, and he presented her with a box that might have been carved of a seashell. Opening it revealed the bezoar on a bed of white silk. Satisfied, she set the box aside. "The Get?" she asked, and Yefet handed over a scroll. She unrolled the document and realized her mistake—she had no way to read it. "Do you swear to me, on your name, that this is as you've said?" she asked Ayleth.

Yefet looked a bit confused at the sudden mistrust, but Ayleth said, "I do swear it."

She put the scroll aside and said, "Very well. That goes at the last. For now, make a fire with the charcoal you have brought, put the drops of blood onto the fish and cook it, then feed it to the dog."

When all this had been accomplished, Yefet looked at her and said, "Is this the point at which the curse is transferred?"

"Yes," she said. "But there is one more thing that must be done."

"You mentioned nothing more!"

"It is only a trifle," she said. "Another symbolic act. Since the curse was made by the Queen's adultery, it can only be transferred if someone further commits adultery against her."

Yefet said, "You wish me to send someone to seduce Barsilay?"

Of course this was the logical conclusion. She wobbled her head a bit and said, "Seeing as that is impractical, there is another option. The infidelity could be yours."

Yefet's face went very stony. "And whom am I meant to carry this out with? You?"

The old woman said, "I wouldn't dream of such a thing. It is a symbolic act, my King, it needn't be quite so graphic as you are thinking. A kiss should be enough to serve for the spell."

"A kiss," he said. "I kiss you, and that is all?"

"Yes," she said. "That is all."

So Yefet set the wailing baby in its cot and approached the old woman.

She had never imagined kissing a Mazik. And if she had, it would not have been this man. He bent down to her, and as he did, she put her hands on either side of his face, kissing him as hard as she could.

He reeled back, screaming, his mouth reddening, and he wiped it with his sleeve as he fell to his knees. "Salt," he gasped.

"Yes," she said. Then, all around the room, the former kings and queens of P'ri Hadar, who had been hidden all this time, stepped forward from the shadows, raising their hands. Yefet, weakened by the salt, looked up to Ayleth for help. "My honored wife," he said, and she replied, "I am not your wife and you have no honor."

The Maziks all around the room cast their magic at Yefet, and he cried out, and in a flash he was transformed. In the spot where he had been, all that remained was a small gray stone.

The old woman swiped at her own mouth, which she had coated earlier in salt mixed with chicken fat. The dog had begun to bark, and the Princess rose from her bed and took the crying baby in her arms.

The old woman sighed and said, "Whose baby is this?"

"It belongs to the wife of one of my soldiers," she said.

"Oh dear," the old woman said. "I hope we haven't upset his mother too badly." She took the baby and handed him to Tarek saying, "Won't you please return him right away?"

"Of course," he said. "But Yefet is still very much alive. He won't stay like that more than an hour or so."

She picked up the stone and said, "I won't need an hour."

Ayleth had given the old woman an escort of four riders, who brought her as close to the sea as they could before leaving her to walk the rest of the way. As she hobbled across the sand, she took the stone from her pocket and told it, "You know, I'm sure in some other life you might have been a good person." She had come to the surf now, and she felt the water soaking her toes through her shoes. "I'm sorry to do this," she said, "but you tried to kill my friend."

She sang the first five verses of the Shir HaMa'alot MiMa'amakim.

And then she cast King Yefet into the sea.

Tarses ordered his army to a halt to rest their horses—particularly those pulling the carts holding the salt munitions, which were exceptionally heavy. Tsifra took the moment to drink a little water. She'd worn herself to the bone building the bridge, but she reckoned she'd better stay in her saddle 'til Tarses gave her leave to dismount. He was exultant from their crossing; it would be the stuff of legends for all time. He would be the King of Luz, Tsifra was sure. He had brought his entire army across the very sea—he might as well have had a crown set on his brow by an angel. He would be more than a Mazik to his men, more than a Mazik to those in the cities they conquered.

Tsifra wondered how much of his success was from the Mirror, and what she had already wrought in the mortal world.

Something flew past Tsifra so close it brushed her cheek, and she nearly fell sideways off her horse.

"That was a demon," she told Tarses, who had also seen it, and then the thing circled the assembled force faster than Tsifra had known a demon could move. When it reached the center of their formation, it let out a shriek that made several of the soldiers cover their ears.

It was calling something, she suspected, and then atop the ridgeline above them she saw mounted soldiers. Scores of them. Horns sounded in the distance, and even in the dim light Tsifra could see archers pulling their bowstrings.

"Hold your positions!" Tarses called. "It is a glamour!"

"Are you certain?" Tsifra asked.

"The outriders would have seen a force this size," he said. "Hold steady."

Tsifra made her arm a blade and prepared to shield Tarses, who said, "There is no need."

She heard another horn, the sound of shields being flung into position ahead of them, and then the sound of arrows—one was heading directly for Tarses. Tsifra leapt from her saddle, knocking it from the air with her blade, only for it to fizzle out of existence the instant she touched it.

From the ground, she turned and saw other arrows evaporate on impact, again and again. From up on his horse, Tarses said, "Your protectiveness is noted, but as I told you—"

The sound of arrows again, but this time from the rear of the formation, and here Tarses cried out, "Look to the salt!"

Tsifra had to climb back into her saddle to see what was going on. The troops on the ridge had vanished. But there had been a second, smaller force she had not seen. Archers, wearing no colors, dressed in clothes dark as the earth, and they had shot into the rear of the formation, where the carts that held the munitions were kept. The horses reared up and the Maziks who had been leading those teams found themselves thrown to the ground.

The rear guard turned to fight, but the demons—there were several now—flew screaming at the horses, which ran eastward along the coast.

"They mean to steal the salt!" Tarses roared, but Tsifra saw something else—the demons were driving the horses ever closer to the sea. She spurred her own mount, but there were too many soldiers between her and the carts—she could have killed them for being in her way—and arrows were flying all around her as she raced toward a goal she knew she could not meet. Ahead of her, the demons succeeded in forcing the horses into the sea.

Then, as quickly as they had appeared, the archers vanished. She shouted at the rear guard to keep firing into the attackers' last position, since they could not have gone far, but then the arrows fired by archers behind them also fizzled out like sparks from a dying fire.

The entire force, front and rear, had been glamoured by demons.

Tarses was seething in a way she had come to fear, and out of long habit she sought to direct his attention away from herself. "They cannot have known we meant to cross at the Rosh ha-Tannin," Tsifra said. "It's impossible."

"They knew," Tarses raged. "Our enemies have a seer among them." He held up a hand and made an illusion of a young man's face—a young man Tsifra recognized. He'd been with Barsilay in P'ri Hadar. Naftaly, they'd called him. Toba had saved his life.

Then, unaccountably, Tarses began to laugh. "Tsifra N'Dar," he said, sending a cold dread down her spine, "I have seen the Fall of P'ri Hadar, and it is not with salt we win the city. Ride ahead now. Open the city to my army. But let Barsilay replace the gate of Luz in the firmament."

"The gate? But did you not wish—"

"He shall replace the gate, but he will never be King. I will be King of Luz."

Tsifra said, "But the succession—"

"It does not matter if I am in the succession! I am of Luz! If enough heirs die, it will come to me. It must—I have seen it!"

Without thinking, Tsifra said, "You will kill every surviving Mazik from Luz 'til the mark comes to you—how? You have no Peregrine. You have no Falcons!"

He grabbed her by the throat and said, "I will make more Falcons."

Tsifra's eyes watered as her breath went stale in her lungs. "Father," she wheezed, and he released her.

"Go," he said. "Open the way for us, as I have foreseen, and take from Barsilay his vision. Kill his seer."

Chapter Twenty-Eight

In the heart of the cedar forest, Naftaly was too restless to sleep with the full moon shining overhead. Elena was beside him, snoring quietly, and he recalled Barsilay telling him how much he enjoyed the incidental sounds of other people since his time in the Cacería prison. Naftaly found himself hoping that Barsilay was resting comfortably and that Efra might be chattering beside him. It was difficult to picture it. She didn't seem the type to make unnecessary noise.

He must have nodded off at some point, because he woke to the sounds of hooves—many hooves. Elena had her hand on his arm and was whispering, "We need to hide."

Nehama put her hand to the Toba-Ziz and glamoured her to resemble a boulder, and the others followed suit, becoming stones and trees, in turn.

The hoofbeats grew even closer and then stopped. Naftaly had closed his eyes, and he cracked them, barely—enough to see a dozen black horses in the livery of P'ri Hadar. At their head was Ayleth, and behind them was a small carriage. The Queen dismounted and approached the golden conveyance, holding up her hand.

The hand that took hers appeared rather gnarled. Naftaly sat up a little, earning him a tweak of his ear from Elena. And then out of the carriage stepped the old woman.

No one moved, sure this might be some trick. But then the old woman rapped her knuckles on Elena's forehead and said, "I've seen this stone before, you old cow."

Naftaly forgot about being a rock. Leaping to his feet, he embraced her so swiftly he nearly knocked her off her feet, and he kissed her cheeks again and again, saying, "I'm sorry."

"Hashem's sake, for what?" she said, patting his face.

"For not saving you," he said.

"Didn't need saving," she said with a sniff, and he said, "I know. You're always the one saving me."

She patted his hair some more, while Asmel asked, "What has happened? What about Yefet?"

"King Yefet is at the bottom of the sea," Ayleth said. "Your witch is very powerful indeed."

"Is she?" Elena said.

"I learned it all from you," the old woman replied.

"We should return to the palace," Ayleth cut in. "Now that Yefet is gone, it is the safest place for us all. But first I must ask, where is my husband?"

While Naftaly opened a gate back to Habush and the others readied themselves to return to the palace with Ayleth, Elena and Asmel held back with Toba, who seemed to be meditating on the sky. Elena took the feather out of her pocket and tried to think what to do with it. Could she use it to turn Toba back, somehow? There was magic in it, she could feel it, but she had no idea how that helped.

Asmel said, "I already tried using her name. There was no effect. It isn't that she doesn't wish to change back. She simply can't." He took note of the feather in Elena's hand. "The Ziz's?"

"Yes, and she made a point of giving it to me. I'm trying to figure out why. Maybe Toba needs more magic?"

"I gave her the rest of my safira already," he said.

"But this is different, the magic of the firmament." She tried offering the feather to Toba, who turned her head from it. "Is there something you can do with it?" she asked Asmel.

He took it in his hands and ran his fingertips over it a few times. "It is beyond me," he said. "This magic. Omer told us it could be used to counter a command, but I don't see how I could use it to force her back."

Toba closed her eyes and began to sing a little—sadly, Elena thought. "There is someone who has more power over Toba even than you," she said.

Asmel said, "If I understand your meaning, recall that the Courser has already been ordered to kill her. You stopped her last time. You may not be able to stop her again."

"I don't think she wants to kill her."

"It doesn't matter what she wants. You know this."

"Doesn't it?" Elena asked. "If magic is intention, then why shouldn't she be able to disobey a command? I've never understood that."

"I don't know," Asmel said. "It is a mystery, like the Mirror."

"Toba said there was no Mirror."

He blew out a breath. "There's *something*," he said. "You've seen it. Maybe we misunderstood how it worked, but there is no denying that actions that happen in one place have consequences elsewhere."

"Yes," Elena said. "And I've been thinking about that, too."

Asmel did not ask what she meant. She thought he probably knew, as old as he was. She said, "I'm the one who put the amulet on Toba."

"To save her life," he said. "If you think that gives you some responsibility for what Tarses has done with the Courser, I don't think it does."

"Perhaps," Elena said. "But I did take Toba's will from her, just as Tarses did with the Courser." Taking the feather back from Asmel, she said, "I think I know what to do with this. Do you intend to stop me?"

Asmel said, "Either you will succeed, or she will kill you."

Elena answered, "Then I shall succeed."

BARSILAY, ALL THIS time, had been recuperating in a small house Efra had made not far from where he'd fallen, sleeping a mostly dreamless sleep and occasionally fussing when Efra woke him to pour some broth down his throat.

"You lost too much blood," she told him, when he complained. "I can't let you sleep so long without drinking, or you'll never heal."

"I suppose I'm lucky," he grumbled. "If I can't have Saba to look after me, at least I have his kin. Thank you."

"My brother is a very good man," she told him. "Or he was, once."

"He is," Barsilay insisted. "You will see him again, I believe."

"How?" she said. "Tarses will use him until he can't, and then he will kill him. He has no hope of escaping."

Barsilay sat up rather painfully. "I haven't told you this, but I sent someone to rescue him—someone Tarses believes to be dead."

"Do you mean the Peregrine? I thought—"

"I'm sorry for not having told you before. I thought it better it wasn't known she was still alive."

"No, you did right." She leaned back against the wall of the hut. "I miss him terribly."

"I can make you no promises," Barsilay told her, "but I'll tell you this: I saw Tarses in a dream just after I was stabbed, and he didn't look like a man who was being cared for by a doctor like Saba. His hair was white as Asmel's."

Whether that gave Efra comfort was difficult to say, because it might also indicate that Saba was dead. But he rested and drank the broth he was given, and then, when he'd decided he could stand to lie about no longer, a gate opened and there was Naftaly, who brought them to the palace garden of P'ri Hadar.

They walked past the arcing fountains, along the sunlit paths. "Are you really recovered?" Naftaly asked him.

"It only twinges when I cough," Barsilay said.

"I wish Saba were here." Naftaly pulled Barsilay to a halt. "I need to tell you something. It's about the Rosh ha-Tannin. When I saw that we could not get the army there, I sent a message to Habush to call off their attack. I told them they'd all be killed."

"How could you have sent a message to Habush? Even I couldn't reach it, and I was just there. It's completely cut off. Did you somehow find the archers?"

"No," Naftaly said. "I tried to dream to Habush. But when I couldn't, I left word with your demon there."

"The demon?" Barsilay said.

"You trusted him."

"I did, but…"

"Did I do wrong?" He sighed. "The others said I ought to let them continue the attack, weaken the army before it gets here. But all those men might have died, if they thought P'ri Hadar was coming."

Barsilay said, "I don't know what I would have done in your place. I won't gainsay you now, Naftaly. You did what you thought was right."

Naftaly found little comfort in that. "The demons might not have relayed the message anyway," he said. "Perhaps they came to the same conclusion: It was in the best interest of the heir of Luz to let Habush attack."

"I don't think demons make those sorts of plans," Barsilay said. "But this demon did seem to like you. Perhaps he did what you wanted for that reason alone."

They'd come inside and made their way to Ayleth's private suite, where she was sharing a glass of wine with the old woman. Barsilay said, "When did you become such friends?"

"Did you not tell him?" the old woman asked Naftaly.

"I hadn't yet—"

Ayleth said, "She saved the city from Yefet the Usurper."

"How?" Barsilay asked, in a tone that was too incredulous to be polite, even to his own ears.

"Witchcraft," Ayleth said, and the old woman laughed, got up from her overstuffed chair, and shuffled her way to the door.

"Where are you going?"

"To enjoy my new rooms," she told them. "Sorry, by the way. I heard they were yours 'til now."

"My rooms? But those are for the King Consort—"

"And you aren't that any longer," the old woman said, handing him the scroll she'd been holding in her lap. "Here."

"What is this?"

"Your divorce," she said, taking Naftaly's arm. "Escort me, won't you? I'll show you the new carpet I had put in."

Barsilay perused the scroll, and said, "You signed this?"

"She tricked me," Ayleth said. "You don't have to accept it, though."

Barsilay went quiet. "I don't wish to cause offense. But I agreed to the marriage because I wished to do good and felt it was my only option."

"If you accept the Get, I will still help you," she said. "But I would like to know precisely what you object to."

"Not you, certainly," he said. "I have no wish to be married at all."

"But you must produce an heir."

"Not if I can help it. But in any case, it seems very unlikely now that I will succeed in becoming King at all. Tarses is coming. Efra—my Zayiti general—she's had word that Tarses has crossed the Rosh ha-Tannin already, and is on his way here. And it is worse."

"Worse?"

"He has been recruiting in the south for some time," Barsilay said, "in light of the lentil blight. He has demon-possessed horses that run twice as fast and never tire, and there are stories in Katlav that some of those troops are on their way here."

Ayleth closed her eyes.

"There is one hope left, my Queen, which I have not told you of 'til now. Once the gate is restored, and I am King, I inherit the power to change a Mazik's name."

She looked up to him. "Is such a thing possible?"

"It is," he said. "Tarses has many in his service who would rather not be. With new names, they become free."

"Your Peregrine," she said. "That is why you didn't wish her killed. I am sorry. I did not know, when I had her executed."

Barsilay smiled at her. "Fortunately, you failed that day."

"But—the Ziz—"

"The Peregrine is alive and hiding. She cannot come here while Tarses has her name, nor can she harm Tarses. But she is waiting, and others like her."

Ayleth said, "I understand why his people might be inclined to hate him. My mother, too, kept a codex of names, I recently learned. Mine was in it."

"She wrote them down?" Barsilay said, aghast, because writing down another Mazik's name was an almost unheard-of violation. Even the slightest chance of exposure was too terrible to contemplate.

"It was how Yefet was able to cause so much trouble. He found it, somehow."

"Or someone gave it to him," Barsilay said.

"That had not occurred to me," she said. "It should have."

"Where is that codex now?"

"I burned it," she said. "It's gone. And all the men of Anab are in prison now."

"Are you sure they are secure?"

"Oh yes," she said. "I made sure the prison was well shored up after your fellow prisoners broke into it to rescue me."

"Did they?"

"Former kings and queens," she said. "I suppose it will be a step down when I make them all adons. But first we will have to live long enough to see it happen."

"And so who is administering the city now?"

"We are managing," she said. "It turns out the Zayitis are very good at paperwork—oh, I've forgotten. I have a book the soldiers found by the gate." She handed it to Barsilay. "I haven't looked at it, but it's certainly old and looks like it might be important."

Barsilay flipped through the small volume. It was a journal, and by the writing it must have been Nehama's from back in Luz. What a treasure. He turned to a page halfway through, which featured a single entry: *Omer is a fink*. He closed it and said, "I'm sure Nehama will be glad to have this back, just as soon as I'm done with it."

"Do you intend to read it?" Ayleth asked.

"Oh," he said. "Yes, I do."

IN THE GARDENS of P'ri Hadar, Nehama was surprised by Natin's response to her return—which is to say there was a spring in his step that had been decidedly absent before. It was the fact that the Ziz was gone, she decided. And the hut, which had also been a particular bane of his, had been removed.

The melons he had planted had done well in the absence of the Ziz tearing up their vines, and in the past few days Natin had also planted a series of walnut trees. These, he explained to Nehama, he'd intended as the Ziz's gnawing trees, because their branches could endure a bit of hassle so long as she were gentle. As the Ziz was gone, he now planted some low-growing flowers among their roots, something he explained would pair well with the scent of the walnut blossoms when they came in.

Nehama, when she had spare moments, took to following Natin around, peppering him with questions about what he was doing. Tidying seemed to be his main occupation, but he spent a great deal of time checking things with magic, or giving magic to a plant that looked like it might have had too much sun. Sometimes he created a shade to help him with the watering, but mainly he did the work himself, and his hands were very calloused and usually dirty. The sight of his wide-brimmed hat among the pansies in the morning gave Nehama a little thrill she could not explain.

He was, Nehama decided, the most singularly joyful person she had ever met. Every new fruit or flower brought him wonder; every minor nuisance seemed an opportunity for him to puzzle out a solution, and when he found it he often clapped to himself in delight. He smiled when he spoke to the plants as if they were old friends. He was like an artist—his palette was flowers and trees and fountains and ponds.

One day, while she was following him at his work, he handed her what appeared to be a paintbrush. "If you are going to hover," he told her, "then you can help."

"You want me to paint something?"

"Of course I don't want you to paint something," he said. "You see those flowers there?" He indicated a small grove of low-growing trees with flowers the color of strawberries. "These are normally pollinated by dvrim, but there aren't so many here now."

"It's winter," she reminded him. "Perhaps that's why."

He turned to her. "P'ri Hadar has winter-loving species of dvrim, I would have expected you to know that, if you grew up in Luz. I'm sure they had them there, too."

Nehama could not remember if there had been dvrim or not.

In any case, she'd spent most of her formative years in Omer's observatory, not a garden. She said, "So you are doing the work of the dvrim?"

"Those flowers are male, and those are female," he said. "You take the paintbrush and move the pollen from one to the other."

"There must be some way to do that with magic," she said.

"It works better if you do it this way," he said.

"Why?"

"It just does. The tree prefers it."

She took the paintbrush and swiped the inside of the flower, where he showed her. The flower smelled of berries, and she laughed and told him so. The sun was warm even in the winter air, and Natin corrected her twenty times 'til she laughed so hard she had to lie on the grass, and she looked up at the sun 'til he came to stand over her. "Should I be worried?" he asked, and she said, "There is dirt in my hair."

"There is always dirt in your hair," he pointed out. "I think the last time it saw soap Luz was topside and you were in a library someplace, terrorizing someone else."

She sat up. "I don't know what to do."

"You could cut it," he said.

"It would look horrible."

"It looks horrible now."

"You could be a little kinder!"

"Oh," he said, "is that what you wanted? All right. Your hair resembles that bed of snake vines under the hazelnut trees by the southern pergola."

She harumphed. "If it were yours, what would you do?"

"I would never let it get like that."

"Never mind," she said, and he replied, "I would cut out the worst of it, and see what else could be saved." He cocked his head to the side. "Are you asking me to do it for you? There will be Maziks in the palace who know how to make hair look nice. I only know plants."

Nehama said, "Please do it."

Natin took his gardening shears and passed his hand over the blades to make them smaller and remove the sharp points from the end, then he ran his calloused hands over her hair a few times, muttering about its state, and cut off the entire length. Then he worked in several smaller snips, taking out the remaining mats that could never hope to be brushed out, and when he was done, he sat back and she put her hands in what was left of her hair. It was very short, and she was not sure what it looked like, but did not much care. Her head felt light enough to float off like a soap bubble. "No more snake vines," she said. "I think it's more like… like the ferns in the northern corner."

"The ones in the shade garden under the cherry trees? You know them?" he said.

"Of course I know them. You were just fussing over them yesterday."

"Hm. My grandmother planted those."

"I had no idea such small plants could live so long."

He looked up at the sun and took off his hat to ruffle his own hair under his fingers. He pulled a few lentils out of his pocket and made some of the honeyed pastries that Nehama liked, and passed one over, saying, "Many things can live a long time if they're cared for well. Others are just hardy. Like snake vines."

"I thought you hated those vines."

"They'll take over if you let them," he said. "But you have to have a deep respect for anything that good at staying alive."

"Ah," she said, "the gardener likes a metaphor."

"I do not," he said gruffly. "I'm only talking about vines; I don't know what you think I'm saying." He got up then. "I have to weed below the southeast fountain."

"Wait," she called after him, and he stopped. This close, she could see creases around his eyes. She'd been about to hand him his hat, when she said, "You have wrinkles!"

"It's the sun," he said. "You have them, too."

"It's the age. Also, my father was mortal." She handed him the hat. "Here is your hat that does nothing." He took it and set it back on his head, and then hesitated.

"I said I was going to weed below the southeast fountain," he told her.

"Oh," she said. "Yes, you did say."

He did not move.

She said, "Did you need help?"

"I don't *need* it." He squinted up at the sun again—see, this was what was causing the wrinkles. "Don't you have stars to measure or something?"

"They can do without me for another hour," she said, and jaunted off toward the southeast fountain.

Tsifra was two days' ride from P'ri Hadar when she had to stop and rest her demon horse, which seemed to have reached the end of its endurance. Her father had claimed the beasts could run forever; she wondered whether this was an exaggeration or more hubris on his part. Either way, the animal had slowed its pace considerably.

She dismounted and poured some water into her hand and let the creature drink, watching her all the while with one of its great strange eyes, as if the demon itself were looking back at her.

Probably that was an accurate description of what was happening. *Did you know Atalef?* she wanted to ask, but if it had, it might not be to her benefit. Anyway, the demon horses did not seem to speak as demons did. Apparently the marriage between the two beings did not improve the horse's intellect. Though she supposed that, too, might be for the best. A horse with the cleverness of a demon might be inclined to throw her off or worse. Mazik horses were untrustworthy enough with their occasional taste for meat. She thought the mortals had a better idea, riding herbivores, even if they were slower.

Leaving the horse to graze, she decided to scout ahead a bit. She'd seen no sign of the army of P'ri Hadar, but she knew there were spies about, and probably some of them were Zayitis, watching her even as she stooped to examine some tracks in the dirt—a fox, most likely, or a wild dog.

The winter sun was too bright in her eyes, 'til a shadow passed over her so intense she had to look up to see what could be causing it.

It was the Ziz, her wings blocking the sun.

Tsifra considered whether it would be better to hide or face what was coming directly, but as the creature descended, she could see that riding on its back was Elena.

If Barsilay had sent an assassin, he'd picked a strange one. Or perhaps the best one of all, since Tsifra would not be expecting it.

Still, she found she wanted to see the woman who had sought her out as she was on her way to lay waste to the city she and her friends were protecting. The Ziz landed gently on the ground and Elena slid off her back.

A moment later, Tsifra's horse fell down dead.

"Oh dear," Elena said.

Tsifra stewed a little and kicked at the ground. "Are you here to kill me?" she asked, and Elena laughed.

"No," she said after a minute. "You think they'd have sent me for that? You can't be killed with salt, and that's really the only weapon I can wield."

"You've killed with salt?"

"I have," Elena said, so matter-of-factly Tsifra was almost surprised. "But most Maziks die a little more easily than you."

"They do," Tsifra said. "If you aren't here to kill me, what is it you want?"

"A deal," Elena said.

"For what?" Tsifra said, laughing a little herself. "I am Queen of mortal Rimon. What can you offer me?"

"Very little," Elena said, "but I think you will want it, nonetheless. I need you to command your sister. And in turn, I will give you what I can of your freedom."

Tsifra scoffed. "That is impossible. You think you can order me to disobey my father? There is no command you could give me that could do that. Will you order me not to see him? Not to hear him? It won't work."

"I don't intend to use your name."

"Then what?" Tsifra asked. "Will you take me home with you? Feed me sweets and comb my hair, as Toba promised when we were young?"

Elena looked rather taken aback. Tsifra said, "I'll spare you the trouble. Take the Ziz as far away from P'ri Hadar as you can get.

Across the desert, to the end of the silk roads. Just go east and don't stop 'til there's a thousand miles of salt between you and my father."

"It wouldn't help," Elena said. "What I need to save her from isn't Tarses. It isn't even you—this is not the Ziz. *This* is your sister."

Tsifra looked at the great bird, the height of four Alaunts, and said, "How?"

"I think you must know," Elena said.

Her name, Tsifra presumed, but she did not understand how or why. Tsifra had never been one for transforming herself into more than weapons. She'd told herself she lacked the knack, but now she wondered… Why could she not do these things that came so easily to Toba?

"You are wondering if your father did something to you," Elena guessed. "Honestly I don't know. I suspect he might have. He would not have wanted to risk you becoming this."

Tsifra felt strangely empty. She said, "She can't change back?"

"No."

"And you think I can do something for her?"

"You know you can—you felt it when she ordered you to stop on the beach in P'ri Hadar. You nearly died that day. You can command her in a way the rest of us can't. It won't matter if her mind knows how to change back or not. She will do it."

"What if she doesn't want to change back?" she asked. "She seems content enough to me."

Elena said, "If she did not wish to change back, she would not have come here."

Tsifra said, "What if I don't wish to change her back?"

"That is the deal I spoke of." Here, she put her hand in her pocket and pulled out a feather as long as her hand. "This is from the real Ziz."

The feather glowed, almost imperceptibly. "It is a token," Tsifra said. "I have no use for such things."

"It is not a token," Elena said. "It contains a breath of magic from the firmament. You were there, at Luz. You know what power it has. It is an older power, an elemental power. It takes nothing to wield it, no will, no mastery. It simply exists."

That had been Tsifra's buchuk, not Tsifra herself, but she had seen through the other's eyes that day. She knew what they had done with Luz. As she leaned in to examine the feather, Elena said, "The magic it contains will be enough for you to resist an order from your father."

Tsifra's eyes met Elena's, searching for any sign of deception, and found none.

"What makes you think I want to break with any of my father's orders?"

Elena said, "Because you've already betrayed him. You tried to kill him, and it's only a matter of time before he finds out. You saw what he did to his Peregrine. He will order you to kill yourself." She held out the feather. "But you will have this."

"Even if that were to happen, he would only kill me another way—and you might not be interested in my salvation if you knew what Tarses has already ordered me to do. You ought to be trying to hasten my death, not trying to prevent it."

Elena sighed. She said, "This is as much freedom as I can buy you."

It was more freedom than anyone had ever bought her. Tsifra took the feather in her hand. The magic running through it—if it even could be called magic—was unlike anything she'd ever felt, and she raised it to her lips.

"Not yet," Elena said.

No, not yet. But Tsifra brushed the barbs of the feather against her lip. It felt like life, whatever was inside it. She carefully tucked it inside her coat, and then she said, "Tsifra N'Dar, be as you were."

The Ziz raised her face to the sky and let out a final cry, then vanished in a cloud of sparkling magic. Even from a distance, Tsifra could feel the magic of the firmament being released. But there was no sign of Toba, and she looked to Elena, wondering what had happened.

"Thank you," Elena said quietly, and took off her wrap and covered—nothing. Seeing Tsifra's expression, she said, "She is here. Apparently my order still stands. I suppose you could test the feather now, but I suspect you'd rather take my word for it."

She took the bundle in her arms and approached the body of the dead horse, settling the knot of fabric that was Toba in the crook of the saddle.

"What are you doing?" Tsifra asked.

"I am sorry about this," Elena said. "But I'm too old to walk all the way back."

The horse was suddenly very much standing, and Elena leapt onto its back with more speed than Tsifra thought she could muster.

"How—" she stammered.

"Try not to kill anyone," Elena said, and kicked the horse into a run.

Tsifra watched her race back toward the city, taking a swig of what was left her of water. She ought to be mad as anything; the woman had tricked her with a third-rate glamour and stolen her excellent horse. Instead, she felt something else, a bubble of something that might have been admiration. This was tempered with the knowledge that Tsifra was about to go and destroy the city in which Elena and Toba were living. It made no sense.

It made even less sense because Elena could have killed her anytime she wanted, and she'd even told Tsifra how it could be done. All she would have had to do was use her name.

Chapter Twenty-Nine

Naftaly, in the wake of all that had happened, found he could not sleep. Elena had returned with Toba only hours before, and something about the look in her eyes left him feeling decidedly uneasy, as if it would take very little to put her back to being a Ziz. Barsilay had declared her healthy, but Naftaly had noticed him giving her a good dose of his own magic during his examination, which implied she wasn't, really.

"She's exhausted," Barsilay had told him after. "But she'll recover."

Naftaly wondered about it, and when he went to say goodnight to the old woman—his new habit, since Yefet's coup—he asked her own opinion.

"I've seen people survive worse," she told him as she climbed into bed. "But I expect she won't be herself for a while."

He pulled the blankets up to her chin and kissed the top of her head. "I will see you tomorrow," he told her, and she closed her eyes.

He and Barsilay (who was no longer King Consort) had been moved to lesser lodgings, which meant they were further from Ayleth in smaller rooms that also, thankfully, had a little more privacy. Their new bedroom connected to a small interior courtyard, and Barsilay had wandered out there and fallen asleep on a bench. Naftaly covered him with a blanket and went out for a walk.

The soldiers who had attacked them had not understood that their orders came from a usurper and so could not be blamed for what they'd done. Still, Naftaly was nervous in their company, and hurried past whenever he could. The night air was very cold and Naftaly had not dressed for it, so he shivered in his coat and turned to go back, just as he saw Efra on the other side of the palace, hurrying on top of the wall.

She saw him and waited. There were steps nearby, and he climbed up to the wall himself. The moon was still near enough to full to light the ground below, and from up there he could see the way to Luz stretching out toward the south. It was desolate; there was little but sand and scattered ruins, and it was hard to imagine that people had once lived there.

"Are you admiring your beloved's city?" Efra asked, seeing him looking out.

"Admiring," Naftaly said. "I'm not sure."

"Ah. You're thinking it was not worth the effort." She nodded. "It's not much at the moment, I'll grant you that. But once the gate is back, people will want to live there again."

"Why? Do they not have cities already?"

"Not all of them do," Efra reminded him. "And it's in the nature of Maziks to build cities around the gates. Look at Erez—up on top of a cliff. And yet it is a wonder. I assume you've never been there?"

"No," he said. "I've never even imagined it. Is it really on top of a cliff?"

"It makes a very good natural fortress," Efra said. "If Tarses ever gets that far, he'll have a time with it, famine or no."

"You think he will get there?"

She said, "I think if Tarses arrives at P'ri Hadar with the salt stores of Zayit in tow, there will be little any of us can do to stop him. The walls won't hold. Barsilay and Ayleth both know it."

"But you are Maziks," Naftaly said. "I've seen you build walls in a day! Can't you just… build a second wall?"

"Around the entire city? There isn't time. And anything we could put up would be knocked down straightaway by his behemots—we saw that in Zayit. Besides that, I presume he'll have cannons this time."

"He didn't have munitions in Zayit," Naftaly reminded her.

"No," she said. "But it stands to reason he'll have built some, now that he's seen them used. What is waiting on the other side of the Zayiti gate is salt-filled cannonballs."

"But surely there is no infinite supply," Naftaly said.

"It doesn't have to be infinite. He just needs one to blow a big enough hole in the wall that Tarses can march his soldiers through. You were there in Habush, and the hole in their wall was much smaller than what Tarses can make with a salt munition."

"There must be something to be done, to make it harder for him." He turned to look at her. "What are you doing on the wall in the middle of the night, by the way?"

"Oh," she said. "Trying to think if there's something to be done."

He laughed a little. "If Elena were here," he said, "she'd say the first thing to do would be to name all our assets."

"That's fair advice. Well, we've got the gate of Luz, that's a big one. We have several people who can handle salt. We have a standing army that is large but untested. And I can't think of anything else. The city has no cannons and very little in terms of salt stores."

"Well, there's the sea. That's a salt store, isn't it?"

"I suppose it might be for you, if you were willing to boil the salt out of the water. If you start now, you might have enough salt to kill four or five soldiers before Tarses gets here."

Naftaly thought on that for a moment. The salt in the sea was one resource. But the water, perhaps that was another. He thought of the lake in Aravoth, and his garden path, and how Nehama had turned his face to see the tree as horizontal. He closed his eyes and imagined the sea horizontal, as if it were a river flowing into the sky.

"Could you make it rain?" he asked. "A lot?"

"Rain?" she asked. "That wouldn't stop a Mazik, it will just make him cranky."

"It wouldn't stop a Mazik," he said. "But mud will stop a behemot."

Toba was rather numb and not entirely conscious as they rode back to the city of P'ri Hadar, tucked in front of Elena on the fastest horse she had ever ridden. The wind in her face was too much like flying, and she wept a little at wishing to feel the sky in her veins again.

"Hush," Elena told her.

Toba quieted, not because of Elena but because she had no strength to weep. Her memories, since they'd raised Luz, were hazy, as if they were someone else's completely. As the Ziz, she had been both herself and not. And she'd wanted to turn back, and also not.

That it had been her sister to change her... She did not know how she felt about it. She was grateful, but it was another debt between them, even if Elena had traded on the Ziz's feather.

Still, when she found herself back in the company of all her dear ones, she was glad to be herself again. She allowed them to put her in a tub of hot water, where Elena washed out her hair—what a strange thing, to have hair on one's head—and then she was dried and fed, at which point she realized she had not eaten all the time she'd been a Ziz, and was in fact very hungry, and she was delighted when Barsilay kept piling bigger and bigger platters of food in front of her. She ate until she was sick, because the taste of food seemed to help her feel connected to her own body, which only felt half hers. Asmel wrapped her in blankets 'til she was so hot she thought she might faint, and put her to bed, wrapping himself around her, pressing against her so she would remember to stay herself. Then at last, lulled by the sound of the driving rain outside, she'd slept.

She was worried, a little, that she would dream of her sister again. But instead, when she opened her eyes, the sun was beginning to rise and it was like no time had passed at all in a sleep so complete she might have been wearing her amulet again.

Leaving Asmel in their bed, Toba ventured outside. It had rained so hard the ground was sludge beneath her feet, and while it had let up, drizzle still caught in her hair. As the sun came up and the rain sputtered out, she asked Naftaly to open for her a gate to Luz.

Walking along the strange piece of land that had been reclaimed from the depths, she stepped over various loose stones and other random debris—both city and sea-based. Eventually she came to the derelict almond grove, and let herself touch one of the trees, hoping, in a childish way, that it might be alive somehow.

It was not, of course.

Nearby, Nehama had built some kind of aqueduct-like structure to siphon the water from the still-open rift back to the sea.

Unfortunately there was no way to do this on the mortal side, as that gate moved with the moon. Toba imagined the moving rupture would eventually carve a channel into the new land. Even with Nehama's waterwork, both sides would be underwater again before long.

Barsilay had come down even earlier; he was sitting atop the remains of what was left of a stone wall, and he hopped down to meet her.

"With all the rain," he explained, "I thought I should come down, now that the salt has washed off the surface."

"It's still in the ground," she said. "You ought to be careful."

"I can feel it a bit," he admitted. "I don't know how we'll go about getting it out. A problem for another day, I suppose. Are you all right?"

Toba was not, really, but she said, "I seem to be." Barsilay looked doubtful, but she added, "Does anything at all look familiar?"

"Does this wasteland remind me of home?" He laughed, sadly. "No, there is nothing here that resembles Luz as it was. And, of course, you know there was no sea there." He waved his hand westward. "This was all fertile valleys and farmland, as far as the eye could see. It was extraordinary. You could ride a horse all the way from here to Rimon, did you know?"

"Sounds hard on the horse," Toba said.

"It wasn't a fast trip," he said. "But it was possible. You could walk from Tamar to Rimon in a few days! Katlav—" His eyebrows knit together. "Katlav and Anab used to have a caravan between them. I went on it once, with Marah. We bought books in Katlav, and then in Anab she wanted to show me the artwork the Maziks had imported from mortals. Can you imagine?

"It wasn't even a particularly long journey. We just went, like it was nothing. There was no picking your way past the salt flats between Katlav and P'ri Hadar, covered head-to-toe so you don't breathe poison when the wind blows the wrong way. No paying half your fortune to cross the Saharon Bridge." He looked down at his boots. "The world was very different then."

"It will be different again soon," she reminded him. "Or perhaps it is already. Are you not King now?"

"Since the land has returned? I don't know. What makes me King? Do I simply declare it?"

"You could try it," she suggested.

"I'll give it a go," he said, and hopped up on the wall. Putting his head back he shouted, "I, Barsilay b'Droer, claim my place as King of Luz. There, do you think that's done it?"

"Do you feel different?" she asked.

"I really don't. I don't think it worked."

"We could test it," she said.

"Test it? Like I could order you to do something, as your King?"

"You could change my name," she said. "I've been thinking about it all morning. It is the only thing that will keep me as I am. And you know I would prefer not to share a name with the Courser. I always hoped you could save me from that."

Barsilay nodded somberly. It was no small thing, to give up the name Marah had given her, and Barsilay would understand that better than most. He asked, "Do you have a preference?"

"I think you have to choose it," Toba said. "That seems to be part of your kingly responsibility."

"All right," he said. "Let me think. Ah." He took her face in his hands, leaned forward and said, "Your new name is Ystehar Amit."

She looked at him a minute. "But that was Marah's name."

"I know. I thought— I thought it might help you, somehow. Say it back."

She whispered, "Ystehar Amit."

"Do you feel any different?" he asked.

Toba closed her eyes and felt around the edges of her own magic, which still seemed so foreign she could not tell if anything had changed or not. "Not really."

"Let's test it," he said. "Ystehar Amit, go up to the palace and change out of your very ugly dress."

"My dress is fine!" she snapped. "Oh."

"It didn't work," he said. "I am not King. Should I be concerned or relieved, I wonder?"

Toba was not sure either. She said, "Is there some rite or other? Does someone have to put a crown on your head?"

"Well," he said, "the stories about Luz were that an angel came through the gate and set a crown directly on the Queen's head. But I'm not sure how true it is, and there's no one alive who was there."

"Maybe it won't require anything so dramatic," Toba said. "It could be all the salt in the ground that's blocking your ability to rename me."

"I don't know how we could test it," he said. "But you've given me another idea for trying to weaken Tarses. If I were to offer amnesty to any of his people, a new name and a fresh start, I'd wager the Peregrine isn't the only one interested. If any of the southern recruits were made to give up their names, they might go home if they thought they could."

"True, but how would you tell them?"

"Whisper it into the dream-world, and hope someone is listening," he said, squinting into the rising sun. "I asked Naftaly to give me an hour, and it's nearly up."

"Yes, he told me that when I left." They turned and began the walk back toward the place where the gate would open, and she added, "I left Asmel a note I'd be back by breakfast. He'll want to talk about how we should proceed in putting the gate back at the next moon. If we're still alive then."

"Well," he said, "as your King, I command you to not die."

"I'll do my best," she said.

Elena had moved to the King Consort's suite along with the old woman, and found that she rather liked being a witch, if this was what it brought you.

The old woman, of course, was the one everyone whispered about, but Elena did not envy her success. The Maziks did not know the truth of her dubious exploits, and she doubted they would be so terrified of the old buzzard's great and terrible power if they understood she'd fooled Yefet with a dog-baby.

It was, she had to admit, a pretty good trick.

The dog in question had taken to running around Ayleth's rooms, where it was tended to by its very own shade. It had originally been found in a pile of trash someplace in the city, and the Queen thought it was bad luck to put the dog back, given its role.

Toba seemed mainly to have recovered from her transformations, but still, Elena worried. She'd always been an introspective child, but it seemed her trip into Aravoth had closed her off further, and now... it felt to Elena like some part of her was still the Ziz.

Or maybe those were just the musings of an old woman who knew she was being left behind. The child she'd raised had, in truth, died back in Rimon. Nehama was someone else. This Toba, too, had become someone else. And there was Elena, following after both, looking to catch glimpses of the girl she'd loved.

Her mother had been right to call her self-indulgent, and she reprimanded herself. Put it in your pocket and go on.

Elena found Ayleth in her rooms alone, having left her advisors for the day. On her table was a model created by magic—a very fine topographical map underneath, and then small depictions of soldiers and horses and so forth on top. According to the model, Tarses had left the Rosh ha-Tannin behind and was racing toward them as they spoke.

In the south something was happening at Katlav; there were masses of tiny silver soldiers surrounding it. "Barsilay said something about recruiting troops in the southern cities," Elena said. "But they are awfully far away."

"Efra tells me he's been recruiting in Tamar and Erez for months, and those troops are already en route. Katlav, now, is losing their harvest. There will be recruits made there soon, too, I'd wager."

The old woman had come into the room and frowned at the table. "So these new soldiers, does Tarses know their names? Is that how he controls them?"

"I don't know," Ayleth said. "The real issue is the blight. No one knows how to prevent it spreading."

"So if there were lentils in the southern cities, he would not be able to recruit there," the old woman said. "Is that right?"

"It would be more difficult for him. Famine is a potent motivator."

"Then end the famine," the old woman said. "If they need lentils in those cities, send them."

Ayleth blinked in surprise. "There aren't enough lentils in P'ri Hadar—"

"The mortals have lentils!" Elena said.

"You do have the money," the old woman said, "because I'm the one that gave it to you. I ransomed Barsilay with enough silver to feed those cities three times over, I'd wager. You have the money; you have the gate of Luz."

"What if it doesn't work?"

"What's it matter then? Tarses is about to empty your treasury anyway."

Ayleth said, "Mortal P'ri Hadar won't have enough lentils for so many cities. It will require looking elsewhere."

"Fortunately you have a trade guild living in your city," Elena said. "The Zayitis will help you. They'll know where to buy lentils. And they probably have mortal agents in most of the cities you'll need to deal with."

"But we can't use the gate outside of the moon."

"We can," Elena said.

Ayleth looked again at the old woman, whose opinion she seemed to value rather highly these days. "Do you really think this is the best course?"

"I think men with empty bellies do terrible things," she said. "And if you fill them, they will probably stay home."

THE STONE TREE that had been the Ziz's home in P'ri Hadar had been removed. Natin had begun the process of replanting the area, installing cherry trees that bloomed the same day, crimson flowers that smelled like honey, and some white-spiked blossoms Nehama had never seen before among them. In the hole that had been left when the tree was removed, Natin had put in a second pond, and in the middle of this he installed a golden statue of the Ziz herself, wings extended as if she were about to leap heavenward.

Nehama came and stood there often, regarding the still waters and the golden Ziz. Natin found her there one morning, and set down his bucket of tools, saying, "You must miss her. You were together a very long time."

She did miss her, but not in the way that he meant. It was easier, in some ways, to let go of Aravoth now that the Ziz was not there as a constant reminder. It struck her that her life was turning another corner. She felt very old; her memories of Toba had left her feeling older still. Someday, the Ziz would feel as far away to her as Rimon did. "Natin," she said, "I came here today for you, not her."

"For me?" he asked.

"Listen to me," she said. "Tarses's army is coming. You shouldn't stay here."

He laughed a little and rubbed his hair, pushing it back under his hat. "And where would I go?" he asked. "I have worked five hundred years in this garden."

"You could go to Baobab and then return when it is safe."

"And when will that be?"

Nehama had no ready answer, and so she gave none.

"I thought so," he said. "And when Tarses comes to Baobab, what then? Nehama, if I leave and his troops come here, they will tear out everything I have done, because that is what armies do. They'll pour salt in the lotus pond. They'll rip out the walnut trees we planted for the Ziz—I can't bear it. I'd rather go to the void myself than see it happen."

"Don't say such things."

"It's the truth. I love everything here as much as a man loves his wife. Would you ask a man to leave his wife to save his own life?"

"You have no wife," she pointed out.

"I am sure you are educated enough to understand the metaphor," he said. "No, I have no wife."

"Why?"

"Because I am content as I am. I am a man of simple pleasures. I enjoy the sun. I enjoy the rain, and the dirt, and the smells of things that grow. And most Maziks do not so much enjoy those things as I do."

Nehama said, "I enjoy them."

"Yes, well. Aravoth made you a little mad, I suppose."

She laughed. "Only you would prefer a mad woman. Tell me again how I am like one of your snake vines."

"That was your hair I was comparing, not you," he said. "Anyway, it's grown out rather nicely now."

"Rather nicely?" She touched the ends of her hair, which had not really grown out much in the days since he'd cut it, but it had begun to curl in new ways she wasn't used to without gravity tugging it straight.

"It's lovely," he said gruffly, and she leaned in then, and kissed him, and his eyes went very wide and then he kissed her back. She was surprised to discover that it seemed he had wanted to kiss her for some time, because he took her sleeves in his fists and did not want to let go. "Nehama," he said. "I am a gardener."

"I know who you are," she said.

"You were alone a very long time."

"I was," she said. "I have been many things in my life. I was a scholar, and I was a cursed child, and I was the heir to the wickedest man in Mazikdom, and then I was alone. But what I have never been, in all that time, was content."

"You are content, in this garden? I would have thought you were itching to return to your studies and your books."

"Why can I not have both?" she asked.

Natin squinted at the sun again; it was endlessly endearing. "Nehama—"

"I will cast every ward I know," she said, "every glamour to protect this garden, so long as you are safe. Please. I know you love it; I love it, too. Let me protect it for you."

He closed his eyes and pressed his forehead against hers. He said, "Don't waste your magic, if you need it to protect yourself."

"So you'll go, then?"

"No," he said. "I stay in this garden. But I will let you glamour me with the rest of it. Make me something wonderful, and then when this is over, come back and wake me. I shall be waiting."

Nehama did not like this answer, but the look on his face told her this was one argument she could not win. "Close your eyes," she told him, and she made him fall asleep, in his beloved garden.

Then she warded the entire garden so that anyone walking into it would immediately find themselves walking out the other side, like the double gates in Aravoth.

Chapter Thirty

Toba had been taught by her grandmother that one always solved a problem by beginning with a list of one's assets. If one was facing an army, for instance, one considered the size of one's own force, the available weapons, and who the cleverest strategists might be.

They had many such problems to face, and it wasn't so much that they had no assets, but that their assets were being spread increasingly thin. Tarses's army was coming; Toba had seen it, in fact, when she'd flown west with Elena. Mounted men and behemots and archers, more than she'd been able to count. They had so little time left... Time, it seemed, was their most rapidly diminishing asset.

If Tarses arrived before they repaired the firmament, they might never have another chance, certainly not without having to raise Luz a second time. Only they didn't know precisely how to put the gate back, and there was no time for hypotheses or tests.

They had no time for arguments either, but that seemed to be all they were good at. After days of what felt like going in circles, Toba found herself once again in her own room in the palace, which she and Asmel had repurposed into a study with a great square table beneath the window, together with Asmel and Nehama and Omer and Naftaly... It was too many people, she thought, and the conversation kept breaking down before any truth could be uncovered.

Asmel was saying, "I had always reasoned that if we simply opened the gate in the right place at the moon, it would return itself to the firmament."

Naftaly said, "But that would be like laying a patch over a garment without stitching it down, wouldn't it?"

"Are you making an analogy between the firmament and… And a pair of trousers?"

"I believe you've been making that analogy all along," Naftaly said. "Haven't you always referred to the hole in the firmament as a tear?"

Asmel looked very crossly at him, and Omer laughed. "The boy could be right," he said. "Don't look so angry."

"I'm not angry," Asmel said. "Only frustrated. If that doesn't work, I don't know what else we could do. Unless Naftaly has a needle that will pierce the sky?"

Naftaly smiled a little sheepishly.

Really, this was getting them nowhere. Toba wished that Elena had been there (rather than working with Ayleth and Efra); she would have found something useful in all this bickering. She felt like she could not think for it all, and found herself longing for the peace of the firmament and the wind in her heart.

She shook her head vigorously; that line of thought was even less useful. Asmel, thinking she was telling him no, gave her a puzzled look. "It's noisy," she said. "I am thinking. You all sound like squabbling chickens."

Nehama barked a laugh, which certainly sounded like a chicken, and Toba wanted to throw something at her. She closed her eyes. *Assets,* she thought. What were their assets? Dawid had left them the book.

"The answer must be in the book itself. There must be something we've overlooked. Instructions or… something along those lines."

Asmel said, "The sages who created the book didn't intend to die… They assumed they would be able to put the gate back themselves at some point in the future. So why bother writing down instructions?"

"Not necessarily," she insisted. "Tarses told them the Queen was going to attack through the gate at the moon. The sages were mortal, and that threat could have lasted past their lifetimes."

Asmel said, "You have read the book as much as anyone here. Have you seen something in it that I have not?"

"No," Toba said, "I haven't, but I also wasn't looking. Let's look again, all of us. Maybe one of us will see something in the text. Sages always write in layers."

"Layers," Nehama said. "Gematria, you are thinking?"

"It could be," Toba agreed. Taking a piece of paper and a pen, she began converting words to numbers, going one line at a time, effectively making a second book.

"Move over, and I'll do the left-hand pages while you do the right," Nehama said. "It will go faster."

"Do you know the letter-values?"

"Here, I'll show you." And she quickly summed up the values of the letters, writing them in a neat column.

Her penmanship, Toba noted, was quite different from her own. It might have been that she wrote with her left hand, while Toba generally preferred her right. Or maybe it was that her first written language had been different. Or that her hand itself was larger—

"Toba," Nehama said. "Do my calculations match yours?"

She gathered her thoughts. To be obsessing over her penmanship, honestly. "They match," she said. "We should continue. It might take a long time to find a pattern." To the men, she added, "I don't think you can help with this."

Naftaly said, "I don't even understand what you are trying to do," and stood up. "I'm going where I can be more useful."

Asmel said, "Surely there must be something I can do."

"There is," Toba said. "Make us some more paper."

They spent days pouring over the book, which took longer than Toba had hoped because they kept having to pause for Ayleth's people or Efra's, who were in charge of obtaining and distributing the lentils, to use the gate. At first Toba and Nehama tried a straightforward approach to their analysis. When that yielded no results, they tried adding the values of each letter spelled out phonetically, and then tried transposing the first and last letters, copying the book so many ways the table was littered with stacks of paper, their hands were black with ink, and then Toba sat back and said, "This is a fool's errand. We're applying a Hebrew system to a book written in Mazik."

"It's written in Hebrew characters," Nehama said.

"The sages had no reason to conceal this information," Toba insisted. "They wanted the gate replaced." She pushed back from the table and let out a curse of frustration. "We are making this too difficult," she said. "We are thinking like mortals."

"The book was created by mortals—that was your entire argument!"

"Yes, but I'm rethinking it. Dawid was half-Mazik," she reminded her. She had seen Dawid in the dream-world, only once. He knew she was trying to put the gate back—he'd given her the name of the book, to help her find it. He hadn't given her anything else. It could only be that he didn't think she needed anything else.

Could it be so simple?

She whispered the name of the book and said, "Tell us how to repair you."

The letters in the book began to light—not all, but several on each page—and Nehama, still covered in ink, took up her pen and began to copy them. They were left with a single page of writing, which Nehama passed over to Toba, saying, "You've done it."

Toba, reading the page in Nehama's careful handwriting, said, "The sages left us a spell."

There were eight of them who met in Toba's study: Toba and Nehama on one side of the square table; Asmel and Omer to their left; Barsilay and Naftaly to their right; and Elena and the old woman on the side closest the window. Toba said, "We've finished studying the book, and it does contain instructions for replacing the gate. We were correct about one thing and wrong about others. First, the most pertinent piece of information: We don't need to wait for the moon."

"No?" Asmel asked. "Are you sure?"

"It's in the text. From what we can tell, if we replace it outside of the moon, it should gradually close and then reopen as normal the following month. If we do it during the moon, it will stay open the rest of the night. We can do it either time."

"That's very good news," Omer said. "We might be able to do this before Tarses arrives after all."

"You said there were multiple things we were wrong about," Asmel said.

"Right," Nehama said. "Better if I just describe what it tells us. Three people are required to stand in the place where the gate ought to be in the three worlds, all reading at the same time. That will be enough to restore the gates, but not to link them together. For that, there is a separate spell—a mortal spell. Meaning intent won't be enough to cast it, and it looks a little picky when it comes to intonation and such." She sat back. "And that's all."

"Oh," the old woman said. "That's all. How comforting."

"Well, that's not all," Toba said. "We have to discuss the implications of what we are about to do."

"You mean the fact that Tarses is coming with his army, and we are about to dispose of our greatest weapon and our best chance of escape?"

"Well," Toba said, "yes."

Barsilay tapped his fingers on the table and said, "If we don't put the gate back, we could lose the book again."

"I agree," Asmel said. "And if P'ri Hadar does fall, no one will ever get a second chance to replace the gate. The sea will continue to rise. Luz will be underwater once more, and soon other cities will follow. Whether we beat Tarses or not, we must do this now."

Naftaly said, "What about evacuating the city? Taking out everyone but the soldiers before Tarses gets here?"

"Where would they go?" Barsilay asked. "Tarses has the north. The southern cities have their own troubles, and Habush is cut off."

"What about the outlier cities?" Omer said. "Those are safe for the moment. People might rather send their children to Baobab than leave them here."

"I will propose it to Ayleth," Barsilay said, and rose. "The spell takes three people?"

"Yes," Toba told him.

"Then it will be the three of you," he said, indicating Toba, Nehama, and Naftaly. "You had better start learning it."

* * *

NAFTALY SPENT SEVERAL hours with Nehama and Toba learning to recite the spell under Elena's tutelage. Toba seemed to have a good hold of it right away. Nehama, on the other hand, was used to Mazik magic and kept slipping back to doing the work inside her mind rather than with her tongue, and Elena had to force her to stop more than once.

"Your will cannot do this for you," she said.

"I am saying it as you tell me," Nehama had insisted, but her intonation had been off, and Elena had made her start over. Naftaly, too, had to be schooled so often he thought he might weep from Elena's constant corrections. Ultimately, he and Elena had gone off to find a quiet corner once she realized he was being made anxious by Toba and Nehama watching him.

"I'm not sure I can do this," he said, once they were alone. "I'm no scholar."

"Naftaly," Elena began, and then she sat down and sighed. "I'm tired."

"I'm sorry," he said. "Let me work on my own."

"No," she said. "I'll be all right in a moment. But I want you to recall whose book this is. It is not Toba's book, or Nehama's book, or even Barsilay's. This is your book. When you had to choose between it and a free passage to Anab and comfort for the rest of your life, you chose the book. I'm sure it hasn't forgotten."

"You speak as if it had some feeling about the matter."

"It has a name," she reminded him. "Is it so strange to think it might have memories, too?"

Naftaly had not considered such a thing—but he'd always felt like the book was somehow alive. It was warm, and it felt less like an assemblage of papers and more like an old friend.

"No," he said. "It isn't a book at all. It was never a book. It only seems so to us right now. We aren't turning the book into a gate—it is a gate." He stood up and put his hand to his mouth, whispering, "We misperceive."

There was a commotion outside in the courtyard just then, and turning to the window, Elena said, "There are riders."

"Ours?"

"I can't tell. There's two of them, and that horse has smoke coming from its nostrils." Naftaly went to the window to look out with her, just as the horse in question, muddy halfway up its legs, collapsed.

"Hashem's sake," she said. But that rider and the other—who Naftaly recognized as one of the wall guard—were speaking to the men at the door, who allowed them inside. Before they could decide how much of their attention this demanded, the door to their room burst open and in walked Barsilay, who said, "I've just left Efra. She's had word that Tarses's southern force never actually left Katlav."

"Never?" Naftaly asked. "Are they deserting him?"

"It's unclear whether they are deserting him or just stalling to see what will happen here. But we anticipated them moving north past the salt flats days ago, and they haven't shown up. She sent people to see what had happened and found his force milling about outside of Katlav."

A shade appeared in the doorway behind him and said, "The Queen requires you."

"Me? Now?"

"Yes," the shade told him.

"Is this to do with the riders who just arrived?" Elena asked.

"Just come with me," Barsilay said.

The three of them followed the shade back to Ayleth's study, where a Mazik with dusty hair—the one whose horse had died, Naftaly noted—was drinking draught after draught of water. He rose as they entered and demanded, "Are you the heir of Luz?"

Barsilay went very still, and Ayleth said, "It's all right. Repeat what you just told me."

The man sat back down, drank more water, and said, "My name is Othnel. I was sent from Katlav to find you."

"And you've done so. Go on," Barsilay said, because the man had stopped drinking long enough to have a fit of coughing.

"You sent word to the cities in the south that you would send lentils, 'til the blight had passed."

"We did," Barsilay said. "If you came from Katlav, you will have seen that we have delivered them already."

The man hesitated again. "They also say you will change the names of any who have given their name to Tarses. I would like you to prove it."

"Prove it," Barsilay repeated uneasily. "I'm afraid I cannot do so until I am made King—how many of you are there?"

"Many," Othnel said. "There are many of us. The blight came fast, and then the stores went bad—no one knows how. All our lentils moldy in days, first in Tamar, then in Erez, now in Katlav. We were starving in the streets. So Tarses sent agents with a deal, names for lentils—enough to feed our families 'til next spring. We were desperate."

"I understand," Barsilay said. "No one holds any in the south to blame. I am sorry we did not offer help earlier."

"We asked for help earlier!" he shouted. "We sent word to Zayit months ago, before it burned. They had the money! They had the money, and they refused!" He slapped his hand down on the table. "They deserved to have their city burned."

Barsilay said, "Focus your ire instead on Tarses. It was likely he who caused your lentils to go bad in the storehouses."

"There are those who said so," he said. "They are all dead now. Listen, no one in the south wants war with P'ri Hadar, we want only not to starve in our cities. When Tarses ordered us here, you had already sent help, so we looked for a way out of our agreements. You saw the horse that brought me here—it is infected with a demon. Our entire force was outfitted with them. When Tarses ordered us to ride to P'ri Hadar, we killed them all." He nodded toward the window. "Except that one, so I could come here, and ask you to help us."

"I will," Barsilay said. "I swear it. As soon as I am able."

"As soon as you are able? And when will that be, tomorrow? Next week? Why do you wait?"

Naftaly watched Barsilay turn himself inside out, because he could give no answer as to why he was not already King. "It didn't take," did not seem like a reasonable explanation. Finally, he said, "There are further things I must do. Steps I must take to ensure my place within the mandate."

"Then I suggest you take them now," Othnel said. "The rest of us are compelled to come here, even without those horses. We are slow, but we will arrive eventually. Be sure you are ready to help us when we do."

A horn sounded outside, and Ayleth rose from the table. "That's the wall." To Othnel, she asked, "Did you see anything on your way here?"

"No. But I rode from the south," he said, rising too.

Another horn, and another, and then a woman ran into the room and said, "We just had word from the Zayiti spies. Tarses's army will be here by morning."

Chapter Thirty-One

Elena was on the wall with Efra, standing back while she and the Queen's commanders discussed reconnaissance and how best to proceed. The army of P'ri Hadar was stationed in front of the city already but had not yet been ordered forward to attack. This seemed like a mistake to Elena, who would have thought it more prudent to keep the enemy as far from the city as possible, but she guessed the Maziks had some idea what they were doing.

"I suppose it prevents them sneaking in from behind," the old woman said in her ear. "The P'ri Hadaris only have to fight in one direction, and they can retreat into the city if they have to."

"Who said you knew anything about military tactics?" Elena asked her, though she supposed she was probably correct in her understanding. Still, it was not what she herself would have done. If you've got an enemy, you keep it as far as possible from whatever you are trying to protect.

In this case, that mostly meant Ayleth. She had given the Maziks the opportunity to take themselves and their families out of the city, and those who had not stayed to fight had mostly fled to Baobab, leaving few ordinary citizens behind. What those Maziks would do if Tarses ever got to Baobab was a problem for a later time.

Ayleth, too, had been encouraged by her people to go, based on the volume of monarchs Tarses had already extinguished (depending, of course, on whether you counted Yefet among this number). If the city did fall, she would almost certainly find herself without her head. But she had insisted on staying, which again Elena found ill-advised, seeing as she had no more knowledge of military strategy than the old woman, and probably not as much general sense.

No one, of course, asked Elena's opinion on any of this.

Efra had a few of her own people with her—Maziks whom Elena presumed had been part of her wall division in Zayit, and they had sent bats out to scan the area. One of them turned to Efra and said, "It's a smaller force than we were expecting. They must have had to leave troops behind to garrison Anab."

"So we outnumber them?"

"Yes, but only just." A second bat returned to Efra's other soldier, who told her, "I haven't seen any cannons yet."

The Queen perked up at this. "Can that be right? Naftaly said Tarses had access to your entire stockpile of salt. Weren't you expecting cannons?"

Efra frowned. "We were."

"Is it better or worse that you don't see them?"

"I'm more worried he has them hidden," Efra said. "But you know what else I don't see? Behemots."

This was likely because the entire area around the city was thick with mud; only that morning had the Maziks stopped it raining. That, she'd been told, had been Naftaly's idea. She wouldn't have thought he had it in him.

The army was in view now, even to Elena—countless men on horses, Tarses at the fore. She did not see his Courser with him, but that meant little. The army of Rimon halted before they came into range of P'ri Hadar's archers up on the wall. Tarses rode forward alone into the breach, 'til he was close enough that Elena could see his face. "I will still accept your surrender," he called. "I do not seek the blood of any Mazik. Live in peace, beneath the banner of Rimon."

Ayleth turned to Efra and said, "Shoot him."

Efra sputtered a bit, because this was obviously against some Mazik code of warfare, but Ayleth said again, loudly enough to be heard on the entire wall, "Shoot him!"

Arrows began to fly. Tarses's horse reared up, and he seemed to meet Ayleth's gaze for a moment before riding back at such speed the Maziks could not hope to catch him. Once he was back to his line, the Maziks of Rimon began to charge.

"You should get off the wall," Efra told Ayleth. "This is about to become extremely unsafe, especially once those cannons come out."

"If he has cannons," Ayleth asked, "why isn't he using them?"

That was a good question. In Zayit, the cannons fired a mile out, and Tarses was well within that. Turning to Efra, Elena said, "I don't think he has any."

"But the salt—"

The armies had engaged, coming together in the mud with the clashing of blades. Efra ordered the archers to hold 'til they had a clear shot. Below them, Maziks died, and screamed, and horses lay in the field. And then, from behind Tarses's own forces, came another volley of arrows—not meant for P'ri Hadar's troops, but for Tarses's.

"What just happened?" Ayleth said, peering over the edge of the wall. Efra pulled her back as a bat lighted on her shoulder and said, "Archers—nearly fifty."

One of the other Maziks said, "They wear the livery of Habush."

"Habush!"

"What's happening?" asked the old woman.

"Habush has sent archers," Elena told her.

"The ones that Naftaly prevented attacking at the Rosh ha-Tannin?"

She assumed so, and they were good archers, too. Tarses's troops were doing poorly between the army of P'ri Hadar and the archers of Habush. Ayleth said, "They will lose, and badly."

"My Queen," Efra said again. "Cannons or no, you should go."

"I want to see this," she said acidly, then she set her hand to her throat and called out, "An adonate to the man who slays Tarses b'Shemhazai!"

The fighting continued for some time. Elena kept her eye on Tarses, who seemed invincible on his demon horse, riding down any on foot and swinging his blade at any mounted man who came at him. His men, though, were being cut down all around him.

"I don't understand," Elena said again. "He's not even trying to breach the wall."

And then, there was a hideous creaking sound. "What is that?" the old woman asked.

"Hashem help us," Efra said. "That's the gate. Get men down there!" she shouted. "Now!"

"What's happening?" Ayleth asked.

"The magic that was holding the gate has been breached," she said.

"They aren't anywhere near the gate!" Ayleth protested, pointing down at the fighting armies.

"It's being opened from the inside," Efra said, and then, below them, there was the groaning of iron.

"It's that rider from the south," Ayleth said. "The one that vanished."

It was possible, Elena knew. But her gut told her a different tale. This was Tarses's Courser. She did not know how she knew, but she felt it deeply.

There was a slam of wood meeting stone, and the wall itself trembled. "It's been opened," Efra said. Elena looked out again to see Tarses's troops streaming into the city.

Toba, who had 'til then been blessedly absent from the wall, came running up just as several of the other soldiers went past. "Grandmother," she said, "I'm leaving."

"Leaving!"

"We're going to Luz before it's too late," she said.

"How? There are soldiers everywhere!"

"The others are waiting for me," she said. "I said I had to see you first. I didn't think they'd breach the wall before I got here."

Elena was stricken. It wasn't safe for Toba to stay where she was, nor was it safe for her to go back. "The city is full of soldiers!"

"Wait," Ayleth said. "I don't see Tarses any longer."

Efra turned to scan the field, and said, "I don't see him, either." To one of her men, she said, "Did he ride into the city?"

"I'm not sure, Adona—"

Elena worried that Tarses had vanished the precise moment Toba had appeared on the wall. "Toba, you must go *now*," she urged.

"I'll give her an escort," Ayleth said. Turning to Efra, she said, "I need three men to get Toba to the north wall, and quickly."

"I'm going with you," Elena said.

Toba, who had just been surrounded by three tall Maziks, said, "You are safer here with Efra."

"I'm not staying with Efra!" Elena insisted, and began following her, breaking into a run.

"Wait," called Efra. "I need someone who can touch salt!"

Stopping to push the old woman in her direction, she said, "Take her!" and then dashed after Toba, down the wall, and toward the north wall, where together with the others they opened the book and made a gate to the city of Luz.

TSIFRA WAS SURROUNDED by the dead who had tried to prevent her opening the gate—so many she had to step over them all as she went back into the city itself.

She had been hidden there for days, watching in the shadows as Barsilay's companions (with the exception of Toba, whom she could not see) worked the problem of the gate of Luz. She had nearly slain Naftaly the moment she'd arrived, but then she had realized, as she listened, that he was a necessary part of their plan. They needed someone to affix the gate to the mortal world, and they all seemed to agree that Naftaly was the best person to carry out this task. So she had stayed her blade, which had been ready for his throat 'til then, and waited for Tarses's army.

Meanwhile, her buchuk was in the mortal city, leading the Queen of Sefarad's army in their crusade. She had been with them when they'd landed some miles south. She'd been with them when they'd marched to the walls of P'ri Hadar, and though she felt the magic of her buchuk beginning to fade with time and distance, she'd felt her as she'd left her troops that morning, riding to the ruins of Luz, where even then she lay in wait for Naftaly to restore the gate.

They would do it now, Tsifra knew; they'd have no choice but to act then. Once she'd opened the city gate for Tarses's troops, she made herself invisible and slipped back inside the city. From there she followed Elena to the north wall, and when she and the others passed through the gate to Luz, she slipped through with them.

* * *

EFRA FINALLY MANAGED to convince Ayleth to get off the damn wall, essentially by taking her by the arm and dragging her away. The old woman followed, as quickly as her short legs could carry her, partly because wherever Ayleth was being taken was probably the safest place in the city, and partly because Ayleth called after her.

She had developed a fondness for the old woman, despite her having tricked her out of a husband—though the old woman supposed she'd hardly been out much, Barsilay being exceptionally handsome but more than a little unavailable. He wasn't even a king, really. Ayleth could hope to do a little better.

She howled at Efra to wait for the old woman, and once they concluded that was an impractical solution to the necessary haste of the moment, one of the guards simply put the old woman on his back and ordered her to hold on. It was, she thought, horrifically undignified.

The wall extended most of the way to the palace, so they went along the perimeter 'til it was in sight, then Efra crafted some sort of temporary bridge leading to the palace's roof. Seeing what was intended, the old woman asked, "Isn't the palace the first place they'll look for her?"

"There's salt in many of the walls," Efra said. "It's the only secure place we've got."

"Shouldn't we leave the city altogether?"

"And be caught in the open?"

At this, a volley of arrows sailed toward them, and the Mazik carrying the old woman overbalanced getting out of the way and fell to his knees. He looked sideways at the old woman over his shoulder. "Are you quite all right?" she asked, and he replied, "Get off now."

She slid off. Beside them, Efra had thrown Ayleth to the ground and fended off the arrows that had come from the eastern wall. One of their number had been hit in the leg; Efra pulled out that arrow but the soldier was still too lame to be any help to them. Efra ordered him to find someplace safe to hide, and the rest of them continued, 'til they found a spot on the roof Efra seemed to have predetermined, and then the four of them went directly down and into the room below. "How did you know that was where the salt had been left out?" Ayleth asked.

"I studied the schematic," Efra said.

"There's a schematic?" Ayleth demanded. "I can't believe this."

"No one told you?"

"No!" She screwed up her face then said, "I suppose that means you have some idea where we're going."

"Kasfia made sure there were a few interior rooms with salt throughout," Efra told her.

"Of course she did."

"There's one not far from here."

"Not to be rude," the old woman put in, "but couldn't we do that thing where we go invisible or look like rocks or something?"

"I'm no good at glamours," Ayleth said.

"I could do myself, but no more," Efra answered. She looked to the broad-shouldered Mazik, who said, "I can look a little thinner if I concentrate."

Of all the foolishness. The old woman was in the palace of P'ri Hadar hiding from murdering soldiers with the three most useless Maziks on earth. She should have gone with Elena to Luz. At least those Maziks knew how to do things. Efra said, "I don't think the soldiers will be in here yet, but we should be careful." She eyed the old woman. "And quiet."

Oh, dear. Had she said any of those things out loud? She didn't think so. But at her age, it was sometimes hard to recall.

They came around a corner and directly into a pair of Tarses's soldiers. Efra flung Ayleth behind her, and she and the man who had been carrying the old woman engaged them in a flurry of blades that was over very quickly. Efra was unharmed, but the man had taken a blade to the side. Efra tore his shirt open and swore; the wound was already blackening.

"There was salt on that blade," the man ground out.

Looking to Ayleth, Efra said, "You'll have to help me carry him. I'm not going to leave him to die in this hallway." So they began to walk, slowly, with the man between them. The old woman, however, stopped to look to the bodies of Tarses's men.

"What are you doing?" Efra hissed. "Come on!"

But the old woman wanted to see if they had anything useful. She could not really wield a blade, so those she ignored, but one of the men had a pouch at his hip, and when she put her hand in it she realized it was full of salt. She untied it and took it with her, hurrying after the others who had left her behind.

She followed them into an unassuming room with a wooden door, which Efra closed behind them. It appeared to be a storage cupboard with shelves at the back holding spare linens. Efra did some magic business to the door, and the old woman took her pouch and poured a line of salt across the threshold.

"Where did you get that?" Efra asked.

"Dead soldiers," she said. "There's more, don't worry."

Efra responded by looking worried indeed, but then she had to turn her attention to the man's wound, which was much worse than it had been a minute ago. "It's a slash," she said. "So the salt isn't deep, and it's still bleeding, which will flush some of it out. I'm going to extend it a little and wash it out. This will hurt."

"Wait," said the old woman. "Wash it out?"

"I have to get the salt out of the wound," she said. "Bring me some water."

"But won't that make it worse? It'll expose more of the flesh to the salt."

"Do you have another suggestion?" Efra said. "Are you going to pick out every grain with your fingers?"

The old woman had no reply to that. Ayleth had handed Efra a flask of water, and she poured it into the man's wound while he gritted his teeth and tried not to scream.

"Do you feel it's out?" Efra asked him.

"I can't tell," he said. "It hurts the same as it did."

She and Ayleth exchanged glances, which told the old woman this was not good.

There was a sound at the door, and here, the old woman knew, was where a glamour would have been helpful. A locked door meant someone was certainly inside the room. If they'd made themselves look like piles of laundry, they could have left the door unlocked, and the horrible Mazik on the other side would have gone about his merry, murdering way.

Instead, the Mazik kicked the door in, and realizing there was a line of salt on the floor, drew his bow and aimed an arrow at Ayleth.

Chapter Thirty-Two

The Mazik at the door curled his lip and fired his arrow. Efra managed to block it and sent out a surge of magic that left a scorch mark on the wall behind him. The old woman scrambled for the door as he pulled out another arrow—this one he aimed at Efra herself, who had pushed Ayleth flat to the floor.

She wished she'd kept one of the blades after all. The man had another of his arrows knocked aside, and then he dropped the bow and pulled something else out of his pocket: a small silver sphere. Efra looked to the old woman and said, "If you're going to do something, do it now."

She had no idea what was in the sphere, but she stepped into the doorway, and the man flung the device directly into her face.

Salt exploded all down her front and into her eyes, which burned like the devil, but she managed to wipe her face on her sleeve and lick her lips. "Do you have some meat to go with that?" she asked his stunned face, and then she reached into her stolen pouch, pulled out a handful of salt, and blew it directly into his eyes.

He reeled back, screaming with his hand over his face, and fell to the floor. The old woman slammed the door and turned around. "We can't stay here," she told Efra. "This isn't secure at all!"

Efra was badly shaken but managed to get herself and Ayleth up. The man—he had a name, the old woman was sure—was very quiet. His wound was not any worse, but he said, "I can't move any further. I'm sorry, Savia."

"Where else can we go?" Efra asked Ayleth.

"You're the one who's seen the schematic," she answered. "I have no idea where else. Maybe she's right: We should try to get outside the city."

"It's too late for that now," Efra said. "We've already seen three of Tarses's men in the palace; there must be others."

The old woman mulled this over and said, "They won't think to look for her in the prison. I don't know how to get there from here, but there's a way in through the floor outside the kitchens. That's how I got in there before."

"I ordered that sealed," Ayleth told her.

"We'll unseal it," Efra said. "It's out best option."

Efra left the rest of her water with her injured soldier. "If anyone comes in again, pretend to be dead," she said, and he laughed a little, before closing his eyes.

"All right," she said. "Let's go."

DESCENDING THROUGH THE hole in the floor (the old woman was never sure exactly how Efra re-opened it) was not much nicer than it had been the last time, especially since Efra managed to drop her before she was all the way to the floor below, and she landed in a heap of sore joints beside Ayleth.

Efra cast a somewhat dubious glamour to conceal the hole in the ceiling, leaving them in darkness while Ayleth struggled to make a light source from one of her earrings. "Let me," Efra said, tapping the gem with her fingertip, illuminating a room which was unaccountably filled with shadows.

"Don't move," Efra said, as the shadows—on the floor and in the air both—began to swarm, swirling so that they seemed to dance. The old woman was thinking of the remaining salt in her pocket when the demons began to whisper as they changed from cats and bats and ravens into unformed smoke and back again.

"Ayleth!" the demons hissed. "Ayleth has returned! Our beloved Ayleth!"

The old woman stopped herself reaching for the salt. "Your beloved?" Ayleth said. "I am no one's beloved, least of all yours."

This seemed a questionable tack from the Queen, whom the old woman thought ought to have been agreeing heartily to be anyone's beloved with the palace above them all full of assassins. Efra drew closer to Ayleth, and the demons let out a wail. "She forgets," they lamented. "She forgot us a long time ago, just as she forgot our friend Dawid."

"Dawid?" Ayleth said. "Dawid half-Mazik, who escaped with the book?"

"Yes, our friend Dawid—our friend who you forgot!"

"I forgot?" Then, "Was it you demons who helped him escape?"

All of the demons joined together in one common shape then, like drops of water becoming a puddle. This singular demon took the shape of a large gray cat, and it put its paws on Ayleth's dress, pulling itself upright until it was looking her in the eye. "No," it told her. "It was you."

Ayleth said, "Me? I don't think so."

"Putting that aside for a moment," the old woman said, "can you protect us in case any of Tarses's soldiers find us down here?"

"We will protect the beloved Ayleth," the demon told her, turning its gaze only briefly from the Queen. "We are used to protecting important things. Protect the Ziz, protect Habush, protect the children."

"The children?" Ayleth asked. "What children?"

"Perhaps it would be better if you just tell her what she's forgotten," Efra said.

"We can't," it told her, returning its paws to the floor and stalking a circle around the room. "She would only forget again. This was the order of the Queen, that she not remember. Even now, she's forgotten that she freed Dawid, and we've only just said it."

Ayleth looked a bit vague around the eyes, and said, "I don't understand."

"There must be something that can be done," Efra said. "Some way she can remember. Every command has a loophole—how else did Yefet betray Barsilay?"

"She can help," the demon said, casting its eye at the old woman.

The old woman did not know how to break it to Ayleth that, in fact, she was no witch at all, but then the demon said, "Give her what you have in your pocket."

"In my pocket?" she said, and then put her hand inside and took out the feather of the Ziz. She'd thought of it as a good-luck amulet, but now she handed it to Ayleth, who held it in her fingers.

"What should I do with it?" she asked.

"Eat it," it told her, "and remember."

She took the feather between her lips and closed her eyes. When she opened them again, she said, "I told you to protect them. Before my mother ordered me to sleep— Oh. Oh, I remember." Looking to the old woman, she said, "I found the book, hidden in my mother's study. I used it to visit him here. I was caught the night he escaped. I did not know yet I was pregnant." She looked to the demon. "Is he still alive?"

"He despaired," it told her, and she closed her eyes and turned away.

"The children," she said. "Do they know?"

"They know who their father is," the demon said. "But not their mother. We tell them, they forget, we tell them, they forget. It is the Queen's command, that they should not know."

"Can't you bring them back?" Efra said. "They could be of help to you now."

"The Queen ordered them never to come back here," Ayleth said. "I remember that."

"'Never step outdoors under a moon,' that is what she told them," the demon said. "But right now there is a gate open and no moon, beloved Ayleth. They are watching it, even now. They are very close."

"How can you know that?" Efra asked dubiously.

"Because we are with them. Should we bring them through the gate?"

Ayleth said, "Yes."

Luz in the time of the Queen, in the time of the Judges before her, had been three days' ride from P'ri Hadar. Toba and the others had come there in an instant, using the gate of Luz in this way for what Toba hoped would be the last time. Naftaly had been the one to close the book, once they had arrived, and he gently picked it up and kissed it, as if it were an old friend.

They stood amid the dead almond trees, the ground littered with the debris of the ruined city. The sea was at their back, and in the distance, Toba could imagine she heard the armies of Rimon and P'ri Hadar clashing at the city's gate.

"Keep your mind here, not there," Nehama told her. In the grove, Omer had spread out his map, ancient and yellowed, and with Asmel he triangulated the exact location where the gate had once opened, checking it three times.

When they were satisfied with their work, Toba turned to Naftaly and said, "Give me the book."

"No," he said. "Don't call it that. If that is what you see, that is all it will ever be."

Toba's mind turned over a little, and Nehama reached out and put her hands on either side of her face, turning her toward the sea. "What do you see?" she asked.

"The sea," Toba told her. "The horizon."

She tilted Toba's head sideways, so that the horizon became vertical and said, "And now?"

The sun hit the surface of the sea, and the horizon, in Toba's eyes, became a gate.

She took the gate of Luz from Naftaly and began to read.

She hoped she had managed to get it in the right place in the mortal world by willing it to open in the spot of the rift. If she hadn't, the tear would be repaired in Mazik Luz but not in the mortal world, and there, the water would continue to rise. But she had no tool for placing it correctly other than her own will, and so she summoned whatever resolve she had learned in Aravoth and opened the gate.

Naftaly stepped forward to pass into mortal Luz, but first he leaned in to whisper something to Barsilay that she could not hear, and to which Barsilay replied, stricken, "No, do not ask me this."

Naftaly said, "I have asked already."

"Naftaly," he said. "Please."

Naftaly kissed him and stepped past Toba into the gate.

Nehama, then, stepped into Aravoth, where she saw that the plume of water that stretched into the sky was, in fact, two; twin rivers gushing with the waters of the firmament, and she slipped into the space between them. From their respective positions within the open gates, the three could see one another but nothing more, and it was difficult to hear over the sound of the rushing water in Aravoth. Toba picked the book up from the ground and handed it to Nehama.

The book had already been read and the gate opened, but Nehama read it again, in Aravoth, and a second gate seemed to open atop the first, a second flash of light that seemed to make the gate even brighter than it had been.

Nehama handed the gate to Naftaly, who did the same, laying another gate on top of the one that Toba had built. He handed the book back to Nehama, and together they began to recite the spell left by the sages of Luz, to reaffix the gates to the firmament.

The words began to lift off the pages of the book, ink becoming something else, some glowing magic which swirled and danced and became a light as bright as the gate itself.

There was a flash that blinded all three for a moment. And the sound of rushing water stopped.

No one had so much as sensed Tsifra as she'd slipped through the gate from P'ri Hadar; she'd learned to render herself utterly invisible from the Peregrine, and there could have been no greater teacher when it came to stealth. She'd watched them with their map, and she'd watched them open the new gate from the book. Her orders had been to allow Barsilay to repair the gate before killing him, and she did not know enough to tell whether that was finished or not.

As Tsifra observed, she heard the approach of horses.

Five Maziks rode toward them, and by their size four were Alaunts. The fifth, she guessed correctly, was Tarses himself. Turning to Elena, Barsilay said, "You cannot fight them. Hide."

The woman became a stone in the exact spot she'd been standing.

"Omer," Asmel told his friend—the very friend Tsifra believed she had murdered, "Tarses doesn't know you're alive or off Te'ena. There might still be a way for you to escape this."

Omer said, "I won't leave Nehama in Aravoth while I hide."

Tsifra thought, *These people are all about to die.*

The horses were upon them now, close enough that Tsifra could see the smoke from their nostrils. They loomed over the three men in the grove, circling, and the only sounds were the waves and the horses' hooves shuffling in the sand.

From Barsilay's expression, he expected some conversation from Tarses. A compromise, perhaps, for the lives of his friends. Instead, the men drew swords and attacked without a word, blades slicing the air, while Omer and Asmel defended themselves as best they could. Asmel sent out a brilliant flash that blinded the horses, forcing the men to dismount, where they were taken by surprise by the salt beneath the ground.

They were no match for Alaunts, any of them, but Asmel and Omer seemed prepared for the salt and able to work around it—or else they were just men who had known pain and no longer feared it. They hurled objects and sent up plumes of sand to blind Tarses and his men. And then Asmel had an idea pass visibly through his mind, and he held up a hand and called to the wind.

The sea wind sickened them all, but the Alaunts had lived all their lives in the mountains and were less ready to cope with its effects. The one nearest Asmel, who was looking like he might be about to kill him, suddenly cried out and went down, though no one had actually touched him. Then another shouted as if he'd been stabbed and fell face-first onto the sand.

Tsifra smiled to herself a little. She only knew one Mazik capable of such maneuvers.

Tarses now turned a circle with his sword up. "What devilry is this?" he demanded.

Barsilay said, "The only devilry here is your own."

There was another brilliant flash then, bright as looking directly into the sun, and a figure Tsifra could not make out was thrown from the gate, only to vanish from her sight once she tried to identify it. Elena transformed from a rock to a woman and rushed forward, crying out.

Tarses raged at this. "Where is my Courser?" he railed.

"Your Courser is not here," Barsilay said. "You are outnumbered, Tarses, and now you will lose."

"No," he said. "I have already seen what will happen, what is happening now. You will never be King!"

"Tsifra!" Tarses called—not her full name yet, but a warning, and she could not quite believe he'd risked saying that much in front of all these men. But he believed they'd all be dead in a moment, so confident was he in her.

Half her name had been enough, and she allowed herself to come solid from shadow.

Tarses smiled grimly at her and said, "The gate is secure. Carry out your orders."

"My buchuk is already carrying them out," she said, seeing through the other woman's eyes. "She has the seer in mortal Luz."

Barsilay's muscles all went visibly slack, and he turned to Elena for confirmation. "Where is he?" he asked, and Tsifra realized the person he was asking must be Toba. However she answered, Tsifra could not hear.

One of the remaining Alaunts suddenly seemed to realize that Toba and Elena were there and ran at them. Elena pulled a handful of salt out of her pocket and flung it into his face, and he screamed.

"Why are you not moving?" Tarses raged at Tsifra. "Why are you not killing them?"

She hesitated, looking for some other way out, and Tarses yelled at her, "Tsifra N'Dar, kill everyone here, starting with that salt-wielding mortal!"

Tsifra's face went very white, and she looked at Elena, who had armed herself with another handful of salt. Barsilay began to run, to put himself between Elena and her death.

In her pocket was the feather of the Ziz, as much freedom as Elena had been able to buy her. She must have known the things Tsifra would be ordered to do before Tarses ever thought to order her to take her own life. Already Naftaly was about to die; Toba would follow in a moment, along with the heir of Luz, and the rest of them. She would return to Tarses's side, and he might be content with her for a long time. It might be another age before he became angry with her again. Perhaps he never would. She was no seer. She had no visions to bet her future on.

Elena ought to have killed her when she'd had the chance, and then it never would have come to this horrible, wretched moment, when she stood looking down at the woman who had bought her a speck of freedom at the cost of her own murder.

Tsifra slipped the feather between her lips and felt the magic of the firmament against her tongue, sharp and clear as ice on a hot day, and she turned her face toward Tarses and said, "No."

BARSILAY WANTED TO laugh from the shock of it, and Tarses did not seem to believe in the possibility of what he was hearing. "What did you say?"

"Do you know why I am your Courser?" she asked. "Because she tricked you. The great Tarses b'Shemhazai, Caçador of Rimon, who sees the future and razes cities to ash, was tricked out of his heir by an old mortal, and that is why I am your Courser, and not Toba. Because you were made a fool."

Tarses turned to his last Alaunt and shouted, "Kill her!" and the man made his sword into a bow in one quick movement. He cried out as if he'd been stabbed, but he'd already fired, sending an arrow into the Courser's chest as Elena screamed.

She fell back, blood pooling on the sand beneath her, and cast her eyes toward Elena before closing then.

Tarses howled. And then he set his sights on Barsilay and knocked him to the ground inches from the gate, kneeling on his chest with a blade to his throat, and Barsilay realized, *He means to push me into the edge of the gate.*

His eyes went to the blue sky overhead, and for an instant, he wanted to allow it to happen.

But what Naftaly had said to Barsilay had been this: "Shi'vit Chal'mot, I will give you two orders now. The first is that you must not go through this gate today. No matter what you might see, your place is here. And the second is this: You must preserve your own life, at any cost."

So for that instant when he longed for death, for the void, he was bound to Naftaly's command. Barsilay felt the land beneath him—Luz, the city of almonds, the first trees to bloom and the last to bear fruit. He felt the land, the salt in the ground sharp against his back, and told it, *Hold fast to me, and I shall hold fast to you.*

The magic in him held, and Tarses, in a rage, found the other man could not be moved.

Elena saw Tarses kneeling on Barsilay's chest, and some new anger—which was actually a very old anger—took hold of her. This… This was the creature that had murdered her child, would have murdered Toba, had murdered his own child rather than let her live another moment beyond his control. And here he knelt on top of her friend.

Elena felt herself rise, and run, and she came from behind Tarses and wrapped her arms around his shoulders and threw them both into the gate.

She'd expected to be in mortal Luz, but instead she realized she'd carried them both to Aravoth. Nehama was there, farther away than she ought to have been, sitting on the ground.

Elena was all that was between Tarses and the gate. He'd impaled himself on his own blade as he'd fallen; pulling it slowly from his thigh, he aimed it squarely at her.

She was out of salt and she was no match for him; at most, she could only hope to slow him down. *A moment,* she thought. *I can buy a moment.* And as she put her hand into her empty pocket, he hesitated for the space of a single breath.

It was a moment enough. As she watched, silver magic like bubbles of air in a fountain began to push their way through Tarses's skin, and he collapsed, screaming, as the magic abandoned him. His eyes were on Elena, and she did not look away.

She told him, "Die. And may your memory be erased."

He collapsed and did not rise again.

"Elena?" Nehama called. "Elena, if you are here, you have to leave. You cannot survive here."

"But why are you still here?" she asked.

"Because," Nehama said, waving her hand over her face, "I can't see."

"I'll help you," Elena said, and Nehama said, "No, you have to leave right away. There's no time."

"Don't be absurd," she said, and went to where Nehama was. Oh, but this place was strange—she wondered how she hadn't noticed it immediately. The colors were wrong, and the ground was alternately soft and hard, and then her eyes found a dark place, off at the horizon. "What is that?" she asked, her voice odd in her own ears.

"Elena," Nehama begged. "Don't look at that. You mustn't. Take my hand and we'll go back to the gate."

"But I want to see it," Elena said. "I can almost see it—it's like, there's a form, in the back of my mind, but I can't quite think about it all the way or it slips out."

"Elena," Nehama said. "Please."

"Just a moment longer."

"Grandmother!" Nehama snapped, and Elena suddenly turned back toward her. "If we don't leave here right now, in another moment you shall be mad and then I will be lost here again."

Elena's focus, however, had begun to fade again, and inexplicably, she began to weep. She did not know why then, and could not have said later; she simply felt as if everything was suddenly too much, and she was so hopelessly inadequate that she could not bear it.

"I am sorry," Elena said, and she did not know to whom she was sorry, or why, but she felt it so deeply it was as if her regrets were all bubbling through her skin, as Tarses's magic had done.

Nehama only wrapped her arms around Elena's old shoulders and pressed her face against her hair. In another moment, the gate would be closed, but Elena could not find it in herself to remember it.

"Grandmother! Nehama!" came Toba's voice, through the gate. "Can you hear me?"

"I can't see, and Elena's not well," Nehama called back.

"Come to my voice, then," Toba called. "The gate's not going to hold more than another few moments at best—you need to hurry."

Elena, however, could not move. So Nehama lifted her into her arms as if she were a child, walking toward the sound of Toba's encouraging words, and together they navigated out of Aravoth.

NAFTALY FOUND HIMSELF thrown from the gate into the mortal world. His eyes were momentarily too dazzled still to see properly, and he rubbed the afterimage from his eyelids as he got to his feet. He needed to return to Barsilay, and quickly, but before he could take a step he found the Courser looming before him. Her arm was already a blade, and she told him, "I will make it quick."

A hand clapped down on the Courser's shoulder, belonging to a man who had appeared from no place at all, and she spun to face him, leaving Naftaly to fall backward onto the ground. There was a woman with him, and Naftaly realized then that both had square-pupiled eyes. They were Maziks—no, it was daylight, and not even during the moon. They were two half-Maziks, a man and a woman, dressed as one would expect mortals to be dressed: she in a veil, he in a tunic of deep blue that looked like it was probably very expensive. There was something familiar in their faces. On the man's shoulder was a demon shaped like both a raven and a cat at the same time; it curled around his neck and turned its smoky eye toward Naftaly.

The Courser, too, was so perplexed by their appearance she seemed not to know what to do next. Her blade-arm hung at her side.

"She's a buchuk," the woman said. "And at the end of her lifespan, too."

"What?" the Courser protested, but the woman pulled a dagger from her belt and stabbed her through the heart with it, as easily as one might cut a piece of fruit.

The Courser exploded into a shower of sparks, which then slowly winked out.

"What did you do?" Naftaly whispered, because he had never seen a Mazik die like that.

"That is how buchuks die, did you not know? She was pretty well done, but she looked not to have more than an hour or two left in her at best anyway. Cousin Naftaly, you are as white as paste."

Naftaly startled at his name, and then realized further that these Maziks had been speaking to him in Rimoni the entire time. "How do you know me?" he asked.

"The Queen told us all about you," the man said. "But I think he's handsomer than she said."

"I agree," said the woman. "But that gate is fading fast; I think we had better go, don't you?"

"Wait," Naftaly said, as the pair hoisted him to his feet. "Why did you call me cousin?"

"Did you not know?" the man asked. "Our father is Dawid ben Aron."

Chapter Thirty-Three

Toba dried Elena's tears and, together with Nehama, soothed her 'til she regained a sense of herself. "That place," she said. "I can't…"

"It's all right," Toba told her. "I understand."

"Tarses is dead," she said.

They'd left his body in Aravoth, where the angels could do what they liked with it.

No sooner had she announced that than from behind the dead trees of the grove stepped the Peregrine. She walked forward to meet Barsilay, saying, "I told you I would come back when he was dead."

"You came a little before, if I'm not mistaken. It was you who killed those Alaunts."

"I never liked them," she said, and then, from behind the same trees came a line of darkly dressed women: the survivors, Toba guessed, of Tarses's purge of the Falcons. At the end of all of these came Saba.

Naftaly shouted at the sight of him and he and Barsilay went to embrace the man, whose face and arms were lined with faint scars.

The Peregrine, though, knelt on the ground where Toba knew Tsifra must be lying. She was beginning to make out the edges of the other woman, and she knew there could be only one reason: Tsifra was dying.

"Grandmother," she whispered. And Elena, understanding, whispered back that she should see her sister, now, and then she did, her body lying in the sand, an arrow still impaled in her chest.

The Peregrine looked up to Saba and said, "Can you save her?"

Saba knelt and put his hands over her breast. "The arrow missed her heart but nicked an artery. She hasn't much time left. But are you sure?"

This question was directed to Barsilay, and Toba understood it as him asking if he wanted him to save a person Barsilay himself was about to execute. Barsilay blew out a long stream of air and looked to Nehama. "You had an objection to an execution with no trial involved, as I recall."

Toba wondered what Nehama might say to this, as someone Tsifra had murdered. It would have been very easy to tell Barsilay to let her die. Instead, Toba was somewhat surprised when Nehama said, "Yes, I did say so."

"That is good enough for me, then," Barsilay said.

And Saba put his hand over Tsifra's wound and began the process of putting her back together.

The Peregrine said, "I still want my new name."

Barsilay said, "If I ever figure out how to become King, I shall give you one."

And she said, "Are you not King?"

Much of Tarses's army was killed in the battle for P'ri Hadar. The remaining troops fled north; there was a discussion about pursuing them, but Ayleth's own army was in poor shape by then, too. Still, there had to be some accounting, Barsilay reckoned, or else the men would return to Rimon and cause further troubles there, so he sent the Peregrine and her remaining Falcons after them. When they caught up to the remnants of Tarses's forces, they made them a deal: They could either swear fealty to the rule of Luz, or they could agree never to set foot in a Mazik city again, or else the Peregrine would kill them all.

All of them chose to give their oath to Luz. Most claimed they had never really wanted to serve Tarses at all. Barsilay, of course, knew better, but he allowed it. Rimon had lost enough of its people already.

Toba returned to the palace, half destroyed by Tarses's army, and carefully made her way through the rubble up to the room she had shared with Asmel. There was salt everywhere. The Maziks had sent shades in to try to clear it out, but they kept dispelling, and so it looked like the half-Maziks were going to bear the brunt of the work. This, of course, meant herself, Nehama, and Naftaly, but also Timna and Tiria, Ayleth's own children.

She wondered that she had not understood what Ayleth had said before, that her mother trusted only blood, and that it had been her own children she'd dreamed of all those long years. Children conceived when Dawid had been in the prison of P'ri Hadar and Ayleth had fallen in love with him. Ayleth had been made to forget Dawid, and the children had been sent to the mortal city to bolster Kasfia's rule. It was not so different than how Tarses had hoped to use Toba.

She wondered, too, if all half-Maziks lived so long. There were three who had survived an age or longer, and of them only Nehama's face showed any signs of aging. Toba asked Timna, Ayleth's son, about that, and he told her, "It is mostly a matter of will. If a half-Mazik believes he will age, then he does. And if he doesn't, well, you see us."

"And Naftaly?" she asked. "He is less Mazik than the rest of us."

"We shall have to see," Timna had told her. "He is less Mazik, true, but he has no less will. Or haven't you noticed?"

She had, of course. The five of them had scoured the palace for the worst of the salt, leaving the shades to sweep up the lesser dregs, until all that remained was Toba's own rooms. The door had been pulled from its hinges and the room itself was a shambles... scorch marks on the walls and carpet, the bed cut to shreds. On the table beneath the window, all her work had salt tossed over it.

She could hardly understand it... Why waste their salt on her books and papers? The almond branch, which had been left in a pitcher of water, had been blessedly left alone, or so she thought.

But, no, it hadn't. On second inspection, she realized there was salt on the rim. Someone had poured salt into the water. What a cruelty. If they had burned it, she would have come back to it already dead... Now she was going to watch it wither and die. Only the branch looked as fresh as it had when it was first cut.

Leaning closer, the smell of the blossoms was strong—stronger than it had been in weeks. "What has happened?" she muttered.

Behind her, Asmel's voice called, "Is it safe to come in?"

"I haven't finished clearing these rooms yet," she called back. "You shouldn't be here."

"That's what they told me," he said. "But I didn't think you should be alone here. Ah. It survived. I was worried it might not."

"I'm worried you might not," she told him. "There's salt all over the room."

"I'll keep my boots on," he said. "The others have all finished. I was concerned for you."

"There's no need," she said. "Come look at this."

Asmel came and stood beside her. "The branch looks well, under the circumstances."

"To you, too?" she said. "I thought I might be imagining it. Look." She pointed out the salt around the rim. "They poured salt into the water."

It was spilled across the table, too. "Shouldn't that have killed it?" he asked.

She leaned forward and sniffed the water itself and had a strange notion. Dipping her finger into the pitcher, she tasted it. "It's fresh." She turned to Asmel. "Nehama said it does not rain in Aravoth. I did not think what that might mean. The trees there must survive only on groundwater—the waters of the firmament."

"And the waters of the firmament," Asmel concluded, "are salt."

NATIN, WOKEN FROM his enchanted slumber by Nehama, was giddy at the chance to examine the almond trees in the grove of Luz. He ran his hands over one tree and then another, marveling at how much of their structure had survived beneath the sea.

Nehama was with them, and she said, "The trees in the groves are not ordinary trees."

"Someone of my stature has hardly had the opportunity to

study the grove trees," he said. "I've never even been in a grove before today."

"You've never passed through a gate at all?" Toba asked.

"Why would I? We have enough flowers and trees in the Mazik world. What would I do with the mortal variants?"

"You might be surprised," Toba put forth, and his eyebrows shot up.

"Do you think so?" he asked. "Then maybe I shall go after all."

Toba did not know how to answer that. But she said, "Nehama believes that the grove trees were descended from the trees in Aravoth, and that they adapted to live here."

"Adapted how?" he asked.

"First, there is no sun in Aravoth."

"I don't see how a tree could grow without sun," he said.

"And second, the water there is all salt."

"Salt! What a horrible place it must be, with no sun and salt everywhere." He took Nehama's hands, as if to say, *Thank goodness you were rescued from such a place.* Then he said, "Now, what are the trees like there?"

Nehama smiled a little at his eagerness. "They look like they are made of stone. More even than the branch you saw."

"Stone! What a thing. I should like to see one someday, if it didn't mean going to a world filled with salt and no sun. Could you draw me one, so that I might see what it looks like?"

"I promise I will do so," Nehama said indulgently. "But these trees—"

Natin had walked to another and put his hands on the trunk and closed his eyes. Shaking his head, he then moved on to another.

"What is he doing?" Toba asked.

"Just let him be," Nehama said, and then, on the fourth tree, he said, "The roots on this tree are dormant. But they aren't dead."

"Are you sure?" Toba asked, rushing over, and he put her hand on the trunk under his and said, "Do you feel it?"

She was not sure what she felt, and she leaned into the tree with her magic. She felt something, something that was not just an inanimate object. "It's alive," she marveled. "Are there others?"

Natin made a circuit of the grove, checking this tree and that, until he'd come back to where he'd started. Each time he found one living he cried out in glee, and laughed, and nearly jumped for joy. At the end, there were five still living—the largest of the specimens, and perhaps the oldest among them.

"Five!" he crowed. "Who would have ever guessed, the trees drink salt and live without sun in the depths?" He caught Nehama in his arms and spun her around as she laughed.

"Natin," Toba called to him. "Could the cutting I showed you be grafted to one of these trees?"

He nodded sharply. "I think that might work. Would you like me to do it?"

Toba said, "I think someone else must do it. But could you show us how?"

"Do you mean the heir of Luz?" he asked. "If you want me to show Barsilay how to do a graft, I would be happy to do it." He looked all around at the grove. "Do you think he will want a garden here in Luz, once the salt is all out of the ground?"

"That might take a very long time," Nehama said.

"No, I don't think so," he said. "You've just said this Aravoth tree drinks salt if it's available. If we make a graft and revive this tree, and then use that tree to make graft, I think it will take the salt out of the ground here rather quickly."

Toba had not considered such a thing might be possible, nor did she know what a Mazik might consider "rather quickly." But a few days later they brought Barsilay to the grove, and Natin showed him how to score the side of the largest of the dormant trees, and how to use magic to affix the new branch.

Barsilay gently did as he was shown. Then he set his hand over the place where the branch met the existing tree and closed his eyes.

The scent of almonds was heavy in the air and while Toba watched in wonder, the branch began to grow and bloom, and then other branches began to leaf out all through the crown of the tree—green leaves and blossoms sprouting forth as if a hundred springs had come together in an instant. Barsilay pulled his hand back and looked up to the crown, his face bearing an expression of wonder.

All of them were very quiet, 'til Natin set his own hands on the tree, and then pressed his face into the bark. "It's awake," he said quietly, and then, "Hello."

Barsilay stepped back, and Toba and Nehama went to him. "Barsilay?" Toba asked him, because he was so quiet, and because something about him seemed quite different.

"I think," he said, "that I am King."

THE NEW PALACE at Luz was only half complete, but Elena had moved into it along with the old woman and Naftaly. Toba and Nehama seemed to be splitting their time between the new city and P'ri Hadar, as they were still in the process of helping Ayleth sort out the damage to her own city, which would take time to clear of salt before the people of the city returned from Baobab.

The survivors of Zayit and the Queen of P'ri Hadar had been the first to pledge their allegiance to Luz, followed closely by Habush. Ayleth had something of a scare a few weeks after Tarses's defeat when the southern army had finally shown up at the gates, but then Othnel had come forward and announced that they had only elected to continue their advance so that Barsilay could keep his promise to grant them all new names.

"It isn't really necessary any longer," Barsilay had pointed out. "Tarses is dead."

"We can't be sure he hasn't told anyone else," Othnel said. "Or written them down."

"But if I grant you a new name," Barsilay said, "I must know what it is. It won't be private to you only."

"We are all aware," he said. "And we trust you more than anyone associated with Tarses."

So Barsilay had held court in his newly made palace pulled up from the ground by Toba and Nehama and the children of Ayleth, and he'd changed their names, one by one. It had taken him three days, and at the end, he'd been hoarse for a week. But then he'd had word from the Queen of Katlav and the Kings of Erez and Tamar both, thanking him for sending the lentils, and wanting to know what he intended to do as King. And he'd told them, honestly, that he was still deciding, but that so long as he lived, no city in Mazikdom would ever starve or go to war. And so he'd had the allegiance of those three cities, too.

Anab was a bit tricker because Tarses's garrison troops were still there, and it took the Peregrine and the Falcons to convince them to renounce Tarses and return to Rimon. Their King, of course, was still dead, and there was no obvious person in charge, so Barsilay told them to put together a council and rule that way for now.

Fortunately, the Anabis did recall some basic democratic principles and managed to put together an election of sorts, and based on this they assembled a governing body of some twenty-five Maziks who voted that they would take Barsilay's rule under advisement 'til he came up with some sort of plan.

"It's not unreasonable," he said, when Naftaly had grumbled over their refusal to declare loyalty right away. "I wouldn't accept a king as aimless as I am unless he proved himself to be more useful than he appeared."

"Not aimless," Naftaly had said. "Thoughtful."

"What a nice point of view." Barsilay kissed the top of his head.

Elena had wondered if Barsilay did have a plan. So early in his reign he seemed to have little time but to rebuild the city and change names. Of course, he looked well enough to the Maziks who had just peeked out from beneath Tarses's boot, but once the novelty of Barsilay's charm and kindness had worn away, he had better have something in mind besides collecting taxes from his throne.

This left the outlier cities, which—true to form—had barely any idea they were on the verge of conquest 'til the whole thing was nearly over, and had sent word, like Anab, that they would wait and determine the best course of action once Barsilay had proposed some sort of constitution. This left only Rimon, where Oneca was still Queen, but barely, as it had been her troops that had died all 'round the Dimah Sea carrying out her husband's plans.

If history followed suit, Asmel had told them, there would be a coup in Rimon before the year was out. But Oneca's reign was ended even before that, as Barsilay heard from old acquaintances that Oneca had indeed been dispatched, but not by any seeking power.

She'd been enjoying her garden, as Relam had been wont to do, contemplating—Barsilay remarked, when he'd told the story—the violent end to her marriage, when the Ziz had come for her chicks, imprisoned in the Queen's menagerie.

In Barsilay's version of the tale, she'd also been taunting the chicks, eating legs of pheasant and clucking like a chicken—so the truth of this story was known, perhaps, only to the Ziz herself. In any case, the Ziz had come to the menagerie and found the Queen there with her young, and then, according to Barsilay, she had swallowed Oneca whole.

She had broken the cage that held her children and together they had flown away, no one knew to where. And no one, Barsilay said, closing the book on that final chapter, had seen them since.

No one, it turned out, ever would.

ELENA FOUND HERSELF at odds with her own future. She wished to stay with Toba and Nehama (how much the latter was really her grandchild seemed to depend on the day), but Alasar was still in Pengoa, very much alone, and each night as she dressed for bed she thought of Naftaly's vision, long ago: the Inquisition come to Pengoa, and Jewish children thrown into the sea.

Toba and Nehama were safe and seemed content enough where they were. Toba, she knew, planned to return to Rimon with Asmel to reopen the university. Nehama would stay in Luz, where she and Omer had already begun work on a new observatory, and on alternate days she designed Luz's new garden with Natin. Elena would never be quite at home in either place. She had done all she could for Toba, for both Tobot. But she owed something to Alasar, still, and she did not quite know how she would make herself leave safety and comfort to return to a world that hated her.

She had just taken down her hair and combed it out when Naftaly found her; he was so much a grandson to her now that she cared not that he saw her hair loose, or her nightdress. She seemed to have left modesty behind back in the mountains of Rimon. "It is late for a visit," she said. "Is something amiss?"

"No," he said. "It's just that I had a vision, and I have been unsure whether to tell you about it or not."

"A vision—of what?"

"It was of you," he said carefully. "Only I was not sure if it was fair to tell you, because I don't want to take your freedom from you. You still have a choice—my visions are not always what they seem. But I thought you should know the choice existed, in case it mattered to you."

"Go on," she said. "What did you see?"

"You and Alasar," he said. "Together, but not in Pengoa. Based on the buildings, I think it was a northern city."

Elena nodded. "And you think my choice is to stay here or return to the mortal world?"

Naftaly hesitated so long Elena thought he'd changed his mind about telling her. But then he said, "It's rather who I saw you with that is the issue."

So Elena listened to him a long time, and thought a long time, and she asked, "By any chance, have you shared this vision with anyone else?"

"I went to Toba and Nehama both," he said.

"And what did they say?"

"That the choice is yours alone," he said.

Elena lay awake all that night, staring at the moon, which had again grown full. For the first time in all this age, the gate opened in the grove of Luz under a full moon, and the few Maziks who had come to live there—the refugees of Zayit and Te'ena, mainly, along with Barsilay's own companions, and a smattering of the members of the southern army who had elected to stay—danced in the grove, where the light made the almond blossoms on the revived tree glow like stars.

There would be others soon. Natin had told them to wait at least a few months before grafting some of the newly made tree to one of the other dormant specimens. Eventually, the grove would be a living thing again. Elena wished she could stay long enough to see it, but she was old and she had already stayed past when she should.

In the morning, she dressed and went to see Barsilay, and said, "I have a proposal for you."

ALL THIS TIME, Tsifra sat in the prison of P'ri Hadar alone. No one had been to visit her, not even the Peregrine, and she was relieved. She was, she felt, the freest she had ever been. She did not much care what happened to her next, whether it was the void or prison for the rest of her life. No one would use her name against her. She would never again be tempted to weigh her own life heavier than another person's. She simply ate her lentils, and rested, and wished for nothing else.

More than a month passed like this, and she began to suspect Barsilay had forgotten her, when the door to her cell opened, and there on the other side was Elena.

Tsifra did not know what to say to her, so she said nothing at all, nor did she rise from her seat on the floor in the corner. Elena shut the door behind her, and took a deep breath and said, "You killed my grandchild."

Tsifra flinched from the truth, but she said, "I am sorry for it. If it helps."

"It doesn't," Elena said. "You killed a lot of people. You also tortured my friend and tried to kill Omer and Naftaly and did a lot of other unspeakable things."

"I don't deny anything you say," Tsifra said. "I don't deny being other than I am."

"What, then, do you think we ought to do with you?"

"I don't know," Tsifra said. "I suppose the King will either leave me here or execute me."

"That's a fair assumption," Elena said. "Those were his two choices."

"Were?"

Elena closed her eyes a moment before she continued, "Here is the third choice. My child was taken from me. I have no one to care for me or my husband in our old age, which you see is now upon us. If you agree to pull your magic out, make a safira, and become mortal, you will return with me to the mortal world. You will be as my grandchild, and you will care for us as if you were ours. You will have no husband, you will bear no children, and when the end of your life comes, you will go to whatever afterlife awaits Maziks without magic."

The void, this meant, but Tsifra cared not so much for that. She said. "A safira?"

"You will have no magic," Elena said. "Barsilay will give you a new name that even you will not know, so that none may ever again control you. You won't remember who you are, or anything you have done, or ever having been a Mazik."

Tsifra had begun to weep. She said, "I don't wish to remember. I don't want to remember any of it." She looked up at Elena from the floor. "I will believe I am yours?"

"Yes," Elena said. "If that is what you wish."

Tsifra was weeping so hard she could barely speak, and she could not see Elena at all as she said, "It is all that I wish."

Elena took her hands and pulled her up, saying, "Then come with me. At the next moon, your mind will be wiped clean of Tarses, and we will take a ship to Pengoa so you can meet your grandfather."

Tsifra could barely stand. Elena put her arms around her to steady her, and Tsifra leaned her head down to her shoulder and whispered, "Thank you."

Chapter Thirty-Four

Tsifra, in the dungeon, had made her safira and every day she knew herself a little less.

Toba did not go to see her.

She had given Elena her blessing to take Tsifra back to Alasar, but she did not like to think of her eating at her grandmother's table or studying with her grandfather. "You could have told her no," Nehama reminded her.

"You could have," Toba replied.

"Elena is going back either way," Nehama said.

And that was the crux of it; Elena could not stay. She was part of the mortal world in a way Toba never had been. If taking Tsifra—or whomever she was now—would give her some comfort, it seemed wrong to deny her that. She owed her that much. And she owed something to Tsifra, too, who had killed Toba but also returned her life to her.

So while they waited for the next moon, Toba sat with Elena, recalling as much of her old life as she could while she still had someone with whom she could remember. Once she had no one with whom to share those stories, they would begin to fade, as they already had for Nehama. Mostly they talked about Alasar. Sometimes they talked about Beladen, and occasionally about Penina.

The moon came, and Elena took Tsifra—bearing a new name

that Toba would never know—and left. They departed at the gate of P'ri Hadar, where they would take a ship to Pengoa. "I will see you again," she told her grandmother. "There are twelve gates. One of them will lead to you."

Elena had been too emotional to speak, but she'd kissed Toba, and then she'd gone.

The farewell felt a little like the void.

Toba's arms ached when the wind blew, and sometimes, when she was in the dream-world, she found herself with wings, flying among the dream-world stars. When she woke, she wept, and she took to spending more time indoors, away from the sky.

A storm came through, and Toba had to curl up in a corner of her room to resist it, her hands over her ears because the wind itched to be inside her. "I don't understand," she told Nehama, who had come to stay with her. "You don't long for the sea."

"You were too young for this," she told her. "And the firmament is not the deep. There isn't so much to long for down there. You go deep enough, it starts feeling like the void."

Toba shuddered. "Will I improve with time, do you think?"

"I hope so," Nehama said, but Toba was not sure. The next day, after the storm had cleared, she was well enough to leave her room and venture out to the garden, where Natin was checking on his precious almond trees.

"Are they all right?" she asked him.

"Oh yes," he said. "They seem to be quite durable, these new trees. I was very worried about them, though. I barely slept last night— Ah, it's the King."

In fact, Barsilay had joined them. As he approached, he reached out a hand and stroked the nearest branch, saying, "I heard you were ill."

"I am better now," Toba said.

Natin, who had finished his ministrations, bid his farewells. Toba would have gone, too, but Barsilay stayed her. "I have been thinking," he told her, "about the name I tried to give you. I think I should try again. I think it might help."

Toba said, "Marah's name?"

"No. I realized I cannot give you an ordinary name. What you need is a name that will ground you. You are a creature of the earth, but your name is wrong for that. If you'd never gone into Aravoth, I think it would not have mattered—"

"But I did."

"You did," he said. He took her hands between his, which were very hot. "I will give you this new name, if you want it. But you will be of this earth, for always."

No more dreaming of flying among the stars, no more feathers peeking through her skin. "I will be ordinary," she said, and he laughed.

"No," he said. "You will not. But you won't be turning into a Ziz again, either. And if you go into Aravoth again—"

"I won't," she said. "This is what I want."

"Very well, my friend," he said. And he leaned forward and whispered in her ear, "You shall now be Behema N'Dar." Toba felt the name settle inside her like a very heavy blanket. Her feet gripped the ground in a way they never had before; Barsilay's hands were more solid. She felt herself, but somehow shifted, as she whispered back, "Behema N'Dar." The Splendid Beast.

DAYS LATER, TOBA sat on the sand overlooking the sea at Luz, feet bare, the waves lapping against her soles. She understood why Nehama had been so hard to keep dressed, when she'd first returned from Aravoth. She had a strong need to feel everything, to be aware of her own body, lest she slip away from herself again.

This, even with the new name she'd been given by Barsilay. She'd settled into it well. Food tasted a little better to her, the ground more solid beneath her, Asmel's touch went through her in a way it had not before. She filtered the sand through her fingers, and thought of making sand creatures, as she'd made with mud as a child, then later for the King of Rimon.

It seemed like it might be a mistake now, like tempting her name to draw her away from herself again. So she refrained.

Nehama came and joined her, saying, "Isn't that water horribly cold?"

"Not really," Toba said. "Look at the callouses on my feet."

"Goodness," Nehama said, as Toba wiggled her toes. "I saw an elephant like that, once."

Toba laughed. "None of my shoes fit, and I haven't bothered making them bigger."

Nehama flopped down on the sand beside her. "I want to show you something. I found this among the old woman's things when we were moving her out of P'ri Hadar. Look."

She took out an iridescent box and opened it, revealing a pearl the size of an egg.

"The bezoar," Toba said. "Why did she have it?"

"She got it from Yefet somehow. But look at it." She carefully took the pearl from the box and held it out to Toba. "It's not solid," she said. "I feel… magic? Listen. Put your ear to it."

Toba put her ear against the pearl and said, "It has a heartbeat."

"It is an egg," Nehama said. "The Leviathan's last, not a bezoar at all."

Toba put it carefully back in the box, lest she drop it. "We should return it to the sea."

"Yes," she said. "But not here, I think. It should go into the deep sea, far from any Mazik. Far from the Shamir."

"Will you take it, then?"

"I was just coming to say goodbye," Nehama said, and she pulled off her dress, took the egg, and ran into the sea, turning, once she was past the waves, to call, "Tell Natin I'll be home before the moon!"

IN HER NEW study in the palace of Luz—she had insisted on having her own, rather than sharing with Asmel as had been suggested—Toba was reading through a sheaf of papers. It was a thick stack, and she'd been at it for some time when Naftaly appeared. He bore in his arms a platter of food she surmised had been sent by Barsilay, because the man could not seem to help himself. Seeing her at her work, Naftaly asked, "What is that you have?"

"Some reports from Anab," she said absently, taking a bite of fruit and stuffing it into her mouth, where she chewed it rather openly, a bad habit she had picked up from Nehama. "Barsilay passed them to me. A description of how they've laid out their new government. It's quite interesting. Each household has a vote in the assembly, and then the assembly itself elects a minister who oversees the entire… apparatus. They're still refining it, but so far they've managed to get themselves together enough to repair the infrastructure that was damaged when the Peregrine had to go in there and root La Cacería out."

"Hm," Naftaly said, picking up a pear and sitting down in the chair that normally belonged either to Asmel or Omer, when they came to have a good long argument.

"You disapprove?"

"It's just," he began, "I wonder if that's really better."

"Than kingship?"

"It seems innately risky, doesn't it, to give so much power to what amounts to a mob?"

"If you presume your populous is a mob," she said.

"We've just come from Rimon, need I remind you," he said. "The mob took every chance it got to kill us."

"That's true," she said. "But it was a Queen who cast us from our homes and stole everything we owned."

"I think we have just concluded that it is people who are the problem, always."

"It does seem so. But Barsilay seems inclined to follow a model more like Anab. He was in here just yesterday with Asmel, discussing what a senate might look like, with representatives from all the allied cities."

"That sounds like it would require a lot of legwork, to administer so much land. We'd end up with another Rome, and see how that went."

"It wouldn't be enough on its own," Toba said. "There would still need to be local governments. Asmel is studying mortal civics. He thinks they might have had some better ideas, in the past."

Naftaly said, "But all those governments failed."

Toba laughed at the absurdity of the entire affair: of Barsilay the King, of Asmel trying to find a better government in the history of a dead society. Still, they would keep trying. There was honor, Asmel said, in the struggle.

* * *

SHE RETURNED TO Asmel not long after. He was eager to make his way back to Rimon, but without the convenience of the gate of Luz in a book, who knew when he would be able to see Barsilay again. As a creature of two worlds, she understood exactly how he felt. She'd said her goodbyes to Elena, watching her pass through the gate with tears running down her face. Part of her had wanted to return, to live in the world she'd been born to, but there was so much more she could do where she was, as she was. She loved the world—both worlds—with a fierceness that sometimes took her breath: a gift, perhaps, of her new name.

Asmel had fallen asleep beside the window, the afternoon light catching his hair, and she stood in the doorway and watched him 'til he sensed her and opened his eyes.

"I wasn't asleep," he said.

"Of course not."

"I was reading."

"I could tell."

"Come here," he said, and she climbed into his lap there in the windowsill. Below them was the garden Nehama and Natin had designed, still unfinished (and she suspected it always would be). There was a fountain below, and in it, swimming in lazy circles, were a pair of speckled carp. "Don't you dare fall out this window," he told her, because she had leaned out a little further to look at the fountain.

"I don't intend to," she said. "Asmel, if you want to stay here longer, you've earned that right. Rimon is hardly in a fit state for anything right now."

The city, it was said, had gone through another three kings after Oneca had died, before finally settling on a ten-year-old princess who ruled through a regent clever enough not to be seen in public. Asmel hoped that reopening the university might lead to reforms in his own city, but Toba knew that also posed a risk to both of them.

When she closed her eyes, she saw the rings the angel had shown her in Aravoth, of time. She could not help but think if they pressed against their own ring a little harder, it would tug at the edges of the mortal world, too.

Asmel said, "It will take a long time to undo the work of La Cacería. Who will do it if I will not?"

She leaned into him, and he stroked her hair.

"I don't ask you to go with me," he said. "You could stay here with Barsilay and Nehama."

"No," she said. "I have seen what your university looked like in your memories, and I would like to see it that way again. But we still have a little time. The bridge isn't repaired yet."

"Well, 'til then, I say we enjoy ourselves," he said. "What would you like to do?"

She turned to face him on the windowsill. "Could we go to Katlav?"

"Katlav?" He smiled and said, "You want to see the great library."

"Could we?" she asked. "Before the bridge is done—"

"Toba, I will take you to any city you wish to see. If you want to go to Katlav, let's leave next week."

"Oh!" she cried out, and flung her arms around him, kissing his neck while he laughed.

"Why stop there?" he asked. "There are books in Tamar, too."

"Tamar! I hear they have the most beautiful buildings there."

He said, "Perhaps you'd better make a list."

She got up then and went to find some paper and a pen.

NAFTALY POURED A glass of wine for Barsilay, who was slumped in his chair, poring over letters from Habush requesting he send more people to help them repair the Saharon bridge so they could reopen the trade routes by the summer. A demon shaped like a cat was curled up in the corner, either sleeping or pretending. Barsilay had granted the demons permanent ownership of the Gal'in his first day as King, but this one had stayed behind, at least for now. "The mountains are far," he'd complained. "And we are tired from pretending to burn Habush."

Barsilay set down the letter he'd just finished and told Naftaly, "I should send you to help. I just heard from Tiria last night—

you know there is a statue of you just inside the gate now? It's supposed to be a very good likeness. Naftaly, the Hero of Habush. There are songs about you. They want to give you an adonate."

"For goodness' sake," Naftaly said. "What would I want it for?"

"It probably comes with money," Barsilay said. "An estate, possibly. Better marriage prospects, certainly."

"Oh, shut up." Naftaly laughed. "Everything seems to be going well for us."

"For the moment. It does."

"So you agree?" Naftaly asked.

"I do—what are you getting at?"

"You're unhappy. You don't sleep."

"Well, I'm busy," Barsilay protested.

"It isn't that, Barsilay."

"All right," he said. "I feel… I feel that I am postponing the inevitable."

"How do you mean?"

He said, "I want to leave things better than they have been. I don't want people to point at me, one day, and say, 'That bastard is no different than the rest of them.' I want to make it so we never have another Tarses. Or another Relam. Or even another Kasfia—"

"Or another Yefet."

"Oh," he scoffed. "I forgot about Yefet—you see my point. I am trying like hell to improve things, but the reality is someday even I will die."

"Don't say such things."

"Naftaly, it is the nature of life. I will die, and then, who knows? Everything is in the hands of someone who could be just as bad as Tarses. And I have no idea how to prevent that." He sighed. "I suppose this is why kings have children. It gives them some sense of control over the future."

"Barsilay," Naftaly said. "What is it that you want?"

"I've just said—"

"In simple terms. I am a tailor."

"Try saying that in Habush."

"Barsilay—"

"I would like to make it so that no one can ever be King again," Barsilay said. "But that's impossible. Kings and queens rise and fall out of nowhere all the time. Look at Relam. Or Oneca."

"Yes, but those weren't real monarchs by Mazik law, were they? Aren't you the only real King?"

"For the moment. But again, when I die, that passes to someone else."

"So make it so that it doesn't. Can you not name your own heir? Mortal kings do, sometimes. It isn't always the eldest son who is chosen."

"How does that help, though? I die, my chosen heir takes over, and then at some point in the future everything again returns to how it was. It's the nature of the mandate."

"Ah, the mandate," Naftaly said. He looked at the papers Barsilay had been reading—he couldn't make out a word of any of them. Mazik writing was beyond him, much to his embarrassment. Toba would translate some of it if he asked—she seemed to enjoy doing it, too—but it shamed him. He wished he'd been better educated.

Omer and Nehama would have their university in Luz before long. Perhaps they would accept him as a student. He said, "What if you picked someone who had no heir—who would be guaranteed never to have one? What happens to the mandate if the line is simply cut?"

Barsilay said, "Is such a thing possible? Any one of us might have a child someday. Even I can't discount the possibility."

"Must it be a Mazik?"

A look stretched between them. Naftaly's face bore the very beginnings of a smile, and Barsilay was very perplexed and then suddenly very much not.

Barsilay stood up then. "Ah," he said, "son of a tailor. Son of a tailor, indeed. You see everything."

"I haven't even said—"

"You don't have to," Barsilay said. He took Naftaly's face in his hands and kissed him on both cheeks. "You are the most beautiful creature that has ever existed. And you are a genius."

* * *

WHEN THEY ASKED the old woman if she would become the next heir of Luz, she laughed at them so hard Naftaly thought she might die on the spot. "You've all gone mad," she said. "It's the strain."

"It isn't," Barsilay said. "It is a way to preserve all that we are doing here."

"Because I'm an old bag with no children who is likely to die soon," she said.

Barsilay hemmed and hawed, and then said, "That is the sum of it, yes."

"Aren't you worried I shall be the wickedest queen alive? I do have a certain reputation, you know. I am a witch in P'ri Hadar. Children scatter when they see me coming."

"I am not worried," Barsilay said.

She sighed, rolling her eyes heavenward, and said, "What would I have to do?"

"Very little," he said, patting her wrinkled hand. "But you might start by telling me your name."

ANOTHER YEAR PASSED, then two, then three. Barsilay had his Senate, with representatives from all the allied cities, which by then included Rimon. The Queen of P'ri Hadar had set up her own provisional government and was in the process of transitioning power away from herself, at least in part. She was too popular to retire in any meaningful way.

And in Luz, the Queen was to be a mortal with no children, no brother nor sister, no parent, nor aunt, nor uncle, nor cousin. She was, as Asmel's blood spell had concluded, completely alone.

When he'd done the blood spell, the old woman had wept.

And now that Barsilay was satisfied his work could not be undone, he was set to pass his title to her. He'd worn no crown, but it seemed to all of them that a mortal taking the throne of Luz would need a little more legitimacy than Barsilay himself had required. So Naftaly designed a crown with silver almond blossoms set with pearls. The first time they set it on her head, she'd turned to him and said, "It's pulling out what remains of my hair, you fool."

And one of the other Maziks had taken it out to be tweaked by someone with a better hand at metal work, her silver hair still sticking to the blossoms. Naftaly had laughed that day. He never told anyone why.

It was only a few days later, with a much smoothed and simpler crown, that Barsilay stood in the almond grove—which now bore some twenty living trees—and took the old woman's hands in his, put the crown on her head, and declared her Serah bat Asher, the last Queen of Luz.

She had been wrong, however, in believing her life was nearly at an end. With Saba managing her care and a constant stream of visitors—including Ayleth's grandchildren, who demanded she perform feats of witchcraft (which meant she would point out an animal or object and explain how it used to be a Mazik who had crossed her, all while the children shrieked)—she lived another twenty years.

One day, during one of those waning years when she had grown too frail to walk, Naftaly brought her outside to the garden that Natin and Nehama had built in the center of the city, where she liked to sit with the sun on her face and listen while Naftaly told her whatever news he had heard lately. That day, he told her that Asmel and Toba had succeeded in opening their university in Rimon.

"Were they ever married?" Serah asked. "I can't remember just now."

"Last year," Naftaly told her. "You sent them a gift."

"Did I? What was it?"

"The statue of the Ziz," he reminded her. "It's in the great hall of the university there now. I'm told all who see it stop to stare in wonder."

"The Ziz," she said, remembering. "She was something."

Naftaly told her, "She was a wonder."

"What else?"

"Hmm," he said. "Efra and the others made it to Zayit, Barsilay said. They will start rebuilding in the spring when the ground is warmer."

"But not Saba," she said hurriedly, and he patted her hand.

"No," he reminded her. "Saba will stay with you so long as you need him."

She laughed a little. "Who knows how much longer that will be?"

"A long time, I'm sure," he said. "He's a very good doctor."

She nodded a little. "And your Mazik?"

He would always be so, to her, and Naftaly smiled. He said, "Barsilay is well enough. Busy with Senate business, you know."

"He still loves you," she said.

"He does."

"Good," she said. "He'd better. And what about the mortal world?"

Here, he hesitated. Elena, he knew from his long-ago vision, was safe in the northern country she had moved to, and would be for some time to come. She had been very old in his vision—older, perhaps, than Serah was even now. But he had no way to reach her. She lived too far from a gate, and while Toba sent messages to her through the gate at Rimon, there was no way to know if she ever received them. Naftaly liked to think she did. Toba hoped to travel to Tappuah the following summer and cross over then, to try to find her. But that tale would have to wait until after it happened.

He heard bits and pieces through P'ri Hadar, which had taken to trading with mortals. The city had rebuilt after the crusade. In Rimon, the Inquisition carried on, a thorn in his heart. Whether Toba's understanding of the Mirror was true, and their efforts would leave ripples in the mortal world, he could not say yet. If time really did grow outward like the rings of a tree in Aravoth, then their work had meaning everywhere, pulling at the arc of history.

"I don't hear much," he said, because she always knew when he was lying. She'd begun to nod off, but she raised her head to ask, "I should like to know what happened to Isaach Burgos."

"Isaach Burgos?" he repeated, because it was a name he had not heard in years. "The oil merchant?"

"He was going to Anab," she said.

"I will look into it," he promised. "I'm sure he's doing well."

"And the future?" she asked. "What have you seen lately?"

The truth was that Naftaly had not had a vision in a long time. Saba could not pinpoint the reason. Perhaps, Saba thought, the visions had been a response to stress, and his life was relatively peaceable these days. He did not mind so much, to be honest. He had his own theory: The visions were gone because his future now was unfolding exactly as it should.

He took her hand in his and said, "You will just have to wait around and find out."

"Oh," she said. "Cruel thing."

"Would you like to go inside?" he asked. "Are you tired now?"

"No," she said. "I would like to sit in the sun."

He turned to the Maziks attending them—because the Queen of Luz did not simply go sit in the garden alone—and said, "The Queen wishes to remain in the sun."

She fell asleep on his shoulder and they stayed like that until the sun went down, and the garden was filled with Mazik fireflies that resembled for all the world a cloud of living stars—the stars of the dream-world. When she opened her eyes again, she said, "Oh. You let me stay."

"Of course I let you stay," he said gently. "And look, now."

She smiled at the fireflies in the beautiful garden, at Naftaly's warm hand in her own, at all the wonders they had made. And then he kissed her weathered cheek and brought her back inside the palace for dinner.

Glossary

Note: ç (c-cedilla) is pronounced as in Medieval Spanish: "ts."

Adon/Adona: Lord/Lady. A title among Mazik nobles.
Alcalá: Castle.
Alcázar: Palace.
Amapola: Extract of the opium poppy.
Aravoth: In the Jewish mystical tradition, the circle of heaven in which Hashem resides with the angels. It exists between the mortal and Mazik worlds.
Atalef: Bat.
Behemot: One of the three mythical giant animals mentioned in Jewish scripture and folklore. The behemot is the Queen of the Beasts.
Buchuk: Literally, "twin." Toba is an example. She is notable both for having developed a separate persona from her progenitor, the original Toba, and for having survived after the original Toba's death.
La Cacería: Literally, "the Hunt." The Rimoni Mazik organization charged with protecting the gates, limiting contact with the mortal world, and bolstering the rule of the monarch of Rimon. La Cacería has two main divisions: the Hounds (and their elite force, the Alaunts), led by Tsidon the Lymer and responsible for Rimon and the dream-world; and the Falcons, led by the Peregrine, responsible for espionage and assassinations abroad.
The Caçador: Literally, "the Huntsman." The title for the head of La Cacería, Tarses b'Shemhazai
The Dream-world: The shared dream-space of all Maziks.
The Fall: The great disaster in which the mortal sages of Luz pulled out their gate and hid it in a book. The resulting tear in the firmament led to the inundation of Luz and the formation of the Dimah Sea. Te'ena was also made an island in this event.
Get: A divorce.

Ha-Moh'to: A secret society once based in Luz, led by Marah and devoted to resisting the rule of the Queen. Their watchword was *Monarchy is Abomination*. Most of ha-Moh'to's members were presumed to have died in the Fall; others include Barsilay b'Droer, Rafeq of Katlav, Omer of Te'ena, and Tarses b'Shemhazai.

Leviathan: One of the three mythical giant animals mentioned in Jewish scripture and folklore, the Leviathan is the Queen of the Sea. She is said to be able to generate enormous whirlpools with her magic, which is believed to come from the sea itself.

Safira: A blue gemstone made of magic removed from a Mazik, either voluntarily or as a punishment. After the removal of their magic, the Mazik will quickly lose their memories and sense of self. However, this also makes it possible for a Mazik to survive in the mortal world outside of the full moon.

Savia: Literally, "wise person," in Zayiti. One of the administrators tasked with the oversight of the running of the city. The Savia della Mura ("Wise Woman of the Wall") was in charge of Zayit's defense; she is the only Zayiti official to survive the burning of the city.

The Void: Nonexistence. Maziks may experience two types of death: a dreaming death, in which a Mazik will permanently remain in the dream-world, and an unbroken death, in which a Mazik will cease to exist completely, usually as the result of violence. All Maziks share the void-terror; most are unwilling to put themselves at significant physical risk because of it.

Ziz: One of the three mythical giant animals mentioned in Jewish scripture and folklore. The Ziz is the Queen of Birds and is said to be able to blot out the sun with its enormous wings. Marah hid the Ziz in the realm of Aravoth to conceal her from Tarses, believing the Ziz was necessary for the restoration of the gate of Luz.

Acknowledgments

Many fingerprints have been left on this series over the past seven years, apart from my own. For everyone who has worked on this story from concept to print and beyond, I am grateful. In particular, thanks are due to Hannah Bowman and the team at Liza Dawson Associates, who have supported The Mirror Realm and myself from the beginning.

Enormous thanks also to the two editors who worked on *The Kingdom of Almonds*, Amy Borsuk at Solaris/Rebellion and Viengsamai Fetters at Erewhon. Thanks also to the rest of the team at Solaris/Rebellion: Jess Gofton, Chiara Mestieri, Natalie Charlesworth, Dagna Dlubak, Kate Nascimento, and Micaela Alcaino; and to the team at Erewhon: Diana Pho, Martin Cahill, Kasie Griffitts, Cassandra Farrin, Kelsy Thompson, Rayne Stone, Samira Iravani, Aubrey McConnell and Michelle Addo. And thanks again to Sarah Guan.

I am also grateful to the booksellers who have invited me into your shops over the past years, and, of course, to the readers who have been with the series from the beginning.

And as always, thank you to my family for their love, support, creativity, and friendship.

About the Author

ARIEL KAPLAN GREW up outside Washington, D.C., and spent most of her childhood reading fairy tales and mythology before settling on a deep love for Jewish folklore. She began studying the history of medieval Spain and the Convivencia while working on a Monroe Scholar project at the College of William & Mary, where she graduated with a degree in History and Religious Studies. She is the author of several books for younger readers.

FIND US ONLINE!

www.rebellionpublishing.com

/solarisbooks.bsky.social /solarisbooks /solarisbks

SIGN UP TO OUR NEWSLETTER!

rebellionpublishing.com/newsletter

YOUR REVIEWS MATTER!

Enjoy this book? Got something to say?

Leave a review on Amazon, GoodReads or with your favourite bookseller and let the world know!